SCENES ORIGINATING
THE GARDEN OF EDE

By the same author

Fiction

THE SECRET LIVES OF ELEANOR JENKINSON
MATILDA'S MISTAKE
THE MEN'S ROOM

Non-fiction

ESSAYS ON WOMEN, MEDICINE AND HEALTH
SOCIAL SUPPORT AND MOTHERHOOD
TELLING THE TRUTH ABOUT JERUSALEM
TAKING IT LIKE A WOMAN
THE CAPTURED WOMB
SUBJECT WOMEN
WOMEN CONFINED
FROM HERE TO MATERNITY
HOUSEWIFE
THE SOCIOLOGY OF HOUSEWORK
SEX, GENDER AND SOCIETY

SCENES ORIGINATING IN THE GARDEN OF EDEN

ANN OAKLEY

HarperCollins*Publishers*

HarperCollins*Publishers*
77–85 Fulham Palace Road,
Hammersmith, London W6 8JB

Published by HarperCollins*Publishers* 1993

1 3 5 7 9 8 6 4 2

A catalogue record for this book is
available from the British Library

ISBN 0 00 224303 2

Set in Linotron Galliard by
Rowland Phototypesetting Ltd
Bury St Edmunds, Suffolk

Printed in Great Britain by
HarperCollinsManufacturing Glasgow

For K.C.T. and R.M.T.,
in living memory

And the Lord God planted a garden eastward in Eden; and there he put the man whom he had formed.

And out of the ground made the Lord God to grow every tree that is pleasant to the sight, and good for food; the tree of life also in the midst of the garden, and the tree of knowledge of good and evil.

And a river went out of Eden to water the garden . . .

(Genesis 2: 8–10)

It was commonly presumed that the Garden of Eden was vegetarian . . . Approaching the Fall from this interpretation deflects attention from the role of Eve as temptress, and removes the patriarchal obsession with the feminine as the cause of the evil of the world.

(Carol J. Adams, *The Sexual Politics of Meat*, 1990: 112–13)

Contents

1	The Flasher in the Cathedral	1
2	A Weekend in Town	12
3	A Place in the Country	25
4	Starting a New Life	40
5	Not the Place for Hot Flushes	54
6	Omens	65
7	The Disappearing Gwater	84
8	Little Tricks	100
9	Daughters of Meltshire	113
10	Man's Dominion	125
11	The Curse of Women	146
12	War in the Gulf	163
13	News from the Past	175
14	The Ides of March	197
15	Lambing Time	209
16	Relieving Tensions	226
17	An Unfortunate Episode	236
18	Looking Back	258
19	The Black Dog and the Rainbow	270
20	Cook's Way	281
21	Adam and Eve	300

1

The Flasher in the Cathedral

ON ITS LIMESTONE HILL the cathedral sits, sunning itself and lording it over the city. Its triple towers rise like decorated lemon lollies against a peacock-blue sky. Tufts of ivory clouds layer a countryside golden in the full bloom of summer; fields of oats, and wheat and barley open to the hot ripening sun, scarlet poppies nodding at their edges; white and red-brown butterflies, birds of all kinds, pollinating bees – all of rural life encloses the luminous city, with its cathedral, which Flora Penfold and her friends have come to visit, up there on the hill.

The west front of the cathedral is being renovated; scaffolding and noticeboards cover the great twelfth-century frieze. Jim and Marilyn Hoskins, Flora's visitors from California, are disappointed to have come all this way merely to see scaffolding. Jim, who is a poet, wants to see the whole exterior structure of the building first before going inside, as this is how he writes poetry: by envisioning an empty architecture, and then filling it with words. Flora, who is hot, wants to go inside straight away, because it will be dark and cool and restful. So in she goes, while the Hoskins walk off, carrying their guidebooks, and with their arms round each other's thickening denim waists. Flora imagines the touch of flesh in this heat – ugh!

Inside the cathedral, a smiling woman with a choker of pearls round her lined pink neck hands her a leaflet. It's not dark inside, though it is darker. Flora's eyes adjust slowly to the shaded, vaulted luminosity: a light at once thin, clear and crisp like a mountain stream, and heavy with the debris of history – dust, dead cells and choruses of voices caught in the etiolated atmosphere. The interior is huge; one's eyes go from side to side and then up and up beneath the ribbed Gothic roof, trying to take in the acreage of claimed space – like a child trying to grasp the concept of life that evolves, but is at the same time finite; like Flora herself trapped in an appraisal of her own existence, this creature, Flora Elizabeth Amaryllis Penfold, shifting as though propelled by some neat plan through the closing years of the twentieth century.

But whose plan is it? Who schemed for Flora to be born on St Valentine's Day 1952, to be called Flora, to be living in a so-called garden flat in Thornaugh Road, London N19, with a self-centred, often out-of-work actor, two moody cats and a collection of dying indoor plants? Who ordained that she should be earning £30,000 per annum as Director of the Islington Arts Centre, should work a twelve-hour day taming the capricious temperaments of those who call themselves artists, and should blow her silver flute melodiously in an amateur chamber music group from time to time? And who decided that for these few days in August 1990 she should be chauffeuring her American friends round some of England's best and least acclaimed tourist sights? Flora's mould is that of late-twentieth-century liberated woman – monthly salary deposited in a Midland Bank Meridian account, and coil-sprung diaphragm deposited, though without interest similarly accruing, in her vagina, the two guaranteeing those *sine qua nons* of autonomous female existence, financial and bodily viability. Flora can pay her bills without incurring any that she's not chosen. And not only the diaphragm but all of it fits; the plan works. Except that lately she's had more than a minor sense of chafing at her chains – for chains there are.

Talking of chains, Flora moves the strap of her shoulder bag to a more comfortable place on her shoulder, and looks around her at the other cathedral-gazers: a party of all-male German tourists, with nearly shaven heads, wearing knee-length shorts and talking in hard annunciative voices; a middle-aged English couple from somewhere like Birmingham, her beige bra strap showing beneath a crimson and white paisley sun dress – the strap cuts into the woman's flesh as Flora's own shoulder bag had been doing a few minutes before – the man's feet, decked in new shiny brown sandals, shuffling along the old stones, and his forehead sweated to the same even chestnut glaze; a bevy of green-check-dressed schoolgirls, holding notebooks to their warmly giggling chests. A nun in grey and white sails past, poker-faced, with a gliding motion, as though on divine runners. In turn these other inmates notice Flora: a slight, crisp figure with olive-skinned silver-bangled arms up which the air of the cathedral travels before entering the body of her sleeveless blue linen dress. The dress matches Flora's cornflower eyes. She is pretty, self-contained, not a woman (is there one?) to be tangled with.

She crosses the breadth of the nave and looks at the Norman font, imagining downy babies' squalling heads being dipped in cold water. The marble is ice-cold to the touch, and Flora, who is still hot, would like to rest her head against it. The heat doesn't usually bother her this much, but she's been working very hard, and feels very tense. The cathedral, which should be a place of unusual peace, seems to project her own tension back to her in its highly strung arches and meticulously vaulted ceiling. Both Flora Penfold and Lincoln Cathedral are like wires, humming fully stretched over little portions of God's domain, fragile, capable of breaking into little pieces.

It's a long time since Flora's had a holiday. And these few days driving Jim and Marilyn round England are all she'll get this year. Her live-in partner, actor Barnaby Gunn, wants her to go with him to watch them filming on location in Cornwall, but Flora would rather stay in N19 and revive her indoor plants. Her mind flits to the mass of caramelized spider plants and other desiccated greens hiding in the unvaulted spaces of her North London flat. How nice it would be to have time to carry out a thorough overhaul, and get some new plants going before the end of the growing season! The grinding job routines, the polished social performances that go with the job, the frantic socializing of Barney's acting world, all sit like an Atlas weight on Flora's narrow but capable feminine shoulders. Most of the time she has no time to notice time passing, but it does. She feels herself wanting to know about these choices she's made – were they really choices? Where's it all going? What's it all for?

Flora moves on down the nave towards the carved wooden pulpit in the middle. Outside the cathedral, the sun, bursting the seams of the heat haze for a few moments, scatters the colours of the huge thirteenth-century stained-glass window in a jewel of brilliance on the floor – red, blue, green, yellow, purple, silver. The refracted colours of the Last Judgement swim and slip in a soft blurry pond on the inhospitable stone. Flora half-believes that it'd feel like a thick decorated pile carpet beneath her feet if she walked there; the air would smell of spring flowers decking a Swiss mountainside. Images, perfumes, fancies crowd her head. Looking up at the clear-cut geometric patterns filtering the sun from sky to stone, she recalls the angular uncompromising text of the Chagall windows in Jerusalem, which she'd seen once with her father many years ago. Too many experiences, she thinks, are had in a manner that strips them of their meaning. But what's the message of that – that one should do only what one truly wants? Flora shakes her head to clear it of these silly thoughts. When her eyes refocus themselves, she's looking straight at one of the thick pillars that hold the cathedral erect; she to it and it to the cathedral are, she imagines, like fleas to an elephant leg. But the pillar and the cathedral, unlike elephants, are not on the move. Interrupting the tangle of idle thoughts in Flora's head, a man steps out from behind the pillar, placing, as he does so, one foot in the splattered flower bed of colours. It's a jerky, provoking action. Something about him is odd, and draws Flora's eyes up that leg to . . . Cold with sweat, Flora Penfold finds herself looking at a flasher in the heart of the cathedral. The flasher is wearing a raincoat in this heat – one of those light nylon ones that fold up small and were popular when she was a child; she remembers her mother making her take one on a school trip – a white one, with a white nylon ribbon to fasten the hood. The flasher's raincoat is open, he's holding it open with one hand, while his other hand grasps his erect penis, which is an ungainly polished reddish-purple, not at all like the soft jewel of colours on the floor spread there benignly by the sun. For a long sweaty moment Flora Penfold stares at the flasher – or rather, at his hand and its contents which, rudely nestled, seem to grow even as she looks. It isn't quite what she came in here to look at. Nor what she imagines the other people came for – where *are* all the other people? Taking her eyes off the flasher for a moment, she looks around her – they've all gone. They must all have moved up towards the chapels, the choirs and the cloisters. Only the pearl-hung woman is behind her, but she's facing the other way, watching for what comes in, not for what has come.

When Flora looks back, the flasher's gone. Where he stood displaying his wares is air only, dusty and dissembling the secrets of time. Staring hard doesn't bring him back. What it does bring, by a strange concordance of time and intent, is the staccato burst of the organ above and ahead, trumpeting into Bach's 'Jesu, Joy of Man's Desiring', and diverting Flora's consciousness of Man from this, his fleshly representation. The huge sound is physical as well as aural, the chords shaking the air and the stones and the bodies within. Gargantuan music is trying to cancel the wretched efforts of the flasher – not in size only, but in morality. Flora traces the sound to its source, and can see the organist sitting there, rosy-cheeked, dressed in a green and white tennis shirt. She hurries out of view, wanting to make herself as inconspicuous as possible. Invisible, preferably. It's not as though she's never been flashed at before. She's getting on for forty, it's 1990, and she's lived in a big city all her life. Like most women, she can count on the fingers of one or more hands the episodes in which some man or other thought he had something intimate worth showing to a stranger – a need to impress, to silence, to frighten. Flora herself is shocked, as one always is when something out of place happens. But most of all she is, when the shock waves subside, angry at the flasher's imposition on her of something which is his – *his* flesh, *his* need, *his* view of women as an audience for whatever he cares to show them.

How long has she been in here? How long before she'll greet Jim and Marilyn again, and be soothed by the comforting banalities of their sightseeing companionship? Flora will tell them, of course. While Jim's carrying on with his architectural descriptions, Flora will interrupt and capture both their attentions with, 'Well, I saw something you didn't – something, as it happens, entirely non-architectural . . .'

Her watch says she's been there only five minutes. She resolves to walk quickly round all there is to see – including, perhaps, the flasher himself. She's not afraid to face him, even to report him to the police. Perhaps there's an extra excitement to be had from making an exhibition of oneself in a sacred place; cathedral-flashing's a different sport from, say, underground- or park-flashing. But it's not a sport, is it? Abruptly, Flora turns and walks back to the door, where pearl-choker woman is standing with a bunch of leaflets in her ringed hand. 'Excuse me,' says Flora, 'but I think you should know that a man just exposed himself to me behind that pillar over there.' She points back up the nave. It does sound odd, what she says, both in itself and against the lyrical Bach cadences. Pearl-choker stares at her, as though trying to estimate the likelihood of Flora's speaking the truth. 'How perfectly frightful,' she responds eventually, in a measured voice. 'Are you sure? There can't be any mistake?'

How could there be a mistake about that? Flora, speechless, shakes her head.

'Would you like to sit down for a while in the Minster office? I'm afraid I can't leave just now, but a colleague will be here soon to take over from me. I could fetch you a glass of water, and you could rest for a few minutes. Or the police . . .'

Flora envisages the scenario of going with Pearl-choker to file a complaint, answering police questions ('Are you sure, madam? Perhaps you imagined it?'). A misspent afternoon that would have nothing to do either with catching the flasher or with preventing such incidents happening to herself or anyone else again. 'I don't think it'll do any good, will it?' she answers interrogatively. 'And I've got much better things to do with my time. I expect you have, too.'

The woman looks relieved. She's arranged to meet her daughter for tea; they're going to a bone china sale together. Flora walks away, simmering. Not only at what happened, but because of her powerlessness in the face of it – to do anything but cause herself extra tension and unpleasantness. She marches through the length of the nave and down the southern side of the cathedral, to where the choir is now assembling to practise for a recording intended to raise money for the building's renovation. 'Your Hundred Best Tunes from Lincoln Cathedral.' That's why the organist in the green and white tennis shirt is here. As she hurries down the northern aisle back to the front, the choir breaks into Monteverdi's 'Beatus Vir'. The jewelled pool of colours has gone from the floor, and there on the left are the reassuringly querulous figures of Jim and Marilyn, looking at an exhibition of the Magna Carta. Long before she reaches them, Flora can hear them exclaiming to each other. 'Look, honey,' Marilyn is saying, 'this one went to Fort Knox the year you were born!'

'Not this one, Marilyn,' corrects Jim. 'It's only a facsimile.' He points out to her their manner of making the ink, so that it would last. The homely details travel one way to Flora's ears, the choral sounds the other.

'I think I'd like to get out of here,' Flora says, rather abruptly, when they turn to greet her. Outside, on a patch of grass, she tells them about the flasher. Marilyn considers it's a good title for a short story. 'The Flasher in the Cathedral'. Jim wonders whether it might provide the bare bones of a poem: 'You know, serving as a metaphor for the disjunction between sacred and profane in modern life.'

As Marilyn wants to see the cloisters before they leave, they walk round to the side door. The grassy courtyard holds the golden summer light, threading it carefully through the stone on to the outer walls. The pattern of light and shadow, the sense of guarded enclosure, calm Flora down. 'You all right, honey?' Jim looks at her intently. 'What you need, my friend, is a good bottle of wine and a nice sunset. We'll have a great evening tonight, ladies!' he chants. Jim's hair is grey, and his face wears a lean, patriarchal cowboy look – a look he dresses up to with Levis and checked shirts, golden leather boots, and a belt studded like a horse's saddle.

Flora, Marilyn and Jim walk round the streets leading down and away from the mounded cathedral. They visit a few shops. Jim buys another guidebook, and Marilyn buys some presents for her friends and family back home – a caddy of Earl Grey tea in a grey-green Lincoln Minster tin, a set of lace mats, a patchwork tea cosy. She gives them to Jim to carry. He takes them without saying anything; it's part of the way they operate together. Flora studies other couples quite a lot these days; she finds them a good deal more interesting than her own relationship with Barney.

Flora makes her daily call to her office from a phone box at five. She must call regularly to reassure herself of her indispensability. 'Hallo, Stu, how are things?'

Stuart Blair, Flora's assistant, pulls towards him the pad on which he's been collecting a list of things to raise when she calls. 'No major dramas. But there's a fax from Mizuno about the Japanese print exhibition, it'll be arriving a couple of weeks later than expected.'

'That's strange. The Japanese are usually so efficient. How does that fit in with our schedule?' Flora flips through the timetable in her head. 'We had it down for early May, didn't we?'

'Yes, but we can move it a couple of weeks without trouble. More than that and it clashes with Mrs Grumble's grasses.'

'Don't call her Mrs Grumble, Stu, you might do it in front of her.' Christina Gumble is trying to separate the preservation of flowers, which she regards as a sophisticated art form, from its homey Women's Institute image.

'What else?'

'The tea roses have arrived for the front garden.'

'Come on, Stu, you can handle the domestic details.'

'They're pink. I thought you wanted white.'

'I did. Send them back.'

There is a pause. 'And I've booked the St Jude's wind ensemble for the September slot, but their agent's asking for more than we agreed.'

'How much more?'

'A lot.'

'Tell him we won't pay.'

'But Flora . . .'

'No buts.' Flora is a hard businesswoman, which contributes to her success, but does little for her peace of mind.

Half an hour later the navy Peugeot leaves the city, streaking out of Lincoln in the rush-hour traffic, back to the honeyed, now more temperate, composure of the countryside. Jim offers to drive, but Flora declines the offer. The car is a new one, and she's protective of it. Barney teases her about it. He says the only thing she's maternal towards is her car.

They've booked for the night into a seventeenth-century manor hotel by the edge of Jacob's Water, a landscaped reservoir in the heart of England's smallest county, Meltshire. Flora's never been to Meltshire, but many people have spoken to her of its miniature towns and velvet hills. Meltshire's a place of myths, of fairy tales. One can't be quite sure it really exists. She decided to include it in the Hoskins' tour as much for her own sake as for theirs.

Jim reads the map. In the back of the car, Marilyn dozes off. Jim looks at her affectionately and says confidingly to Flora, 'Maro didn't sleep well last night – she's got the curse, she had the devil's own set of cramps.'

'I thought the devil was supposed to be male.'

Jim laughs. 'That's what I like about you, Flora Penfold, you never miss one, do you! English sarcasm. A very special and cutting kind of humour; the biting comment delivered oh-so-politely out of the corner of the mouth. We Americans are too fond of the sound of words, we miss the significance of the way they're said. And of course we don't hear silences at all.'

Flora drives on silently, thinking about what Jim's said. Perhaps it's not what happens that's so important, but what *doesn't* happen. Not that there was a flasher in the cathedral, but that most of the time those huge sun-shafted spaces are uncontaminated by Man's unholy fleshly desires. It's not what you have done, but what you haven't. Not who you are, but who you feel you might have missed the chance to be.

A rabbit scampers across the road, then another. The sun, low over the cornfield, glances off a combine harvester chugging away in a far corner. There's another on the other side. 'Must be the hot weather,' says Jim. 'They've got to get it all in before the weather breaks.'

'You know about these things, do you?'

'Some. Remember, I was raised on a farm in Virginia.'

'The good life, was it?'

'I s'pose. Farming's the hardest work there is. But it's old Mother Nature who sets the rules. The time of day's not set by the clock – it's the light, the weather, the appetites of animals that count.' He pauses, looks down at the map. 'You gotta take a left at the next junction. A couple of miles and we're there.'

Marilyn snores gently. Jim looks at his watch. 'Let's give ourselves an hour before dinner. To take a shower and freshen up. I'll reserve a table. It's warm enough to eat outside, doncha think? The book said they have a terrace. I hope to hell it's got a view.'

It has. At 8.15, they're sitting on a white-railed protuberance fitted over a rose garden on a level with the tops of the shortest trees fringing the water. The sun is low, not quite about to set. It lays its amber rays on the backs of sheep and cows grazing the water meadows: grey-white, fattening spring lambs, and sleek chestnut cows, the colour of the new sandals in Lincoln Cathedral. The water scarcely ripples except when a flock of white birds lightly skim their feet over it. Otherwise, it simply resides there, collecting the colours of evening sky, green trees and vegetation, collecting them together and holding them for inspection like an artist's palette.

Jim points down into the water. 'There are five farms, two villages, and one and a half churches buried in that.'

'I'm afraid he's been reading his guidebooks again,' sighs Marilyn, refreshed by her noisy nap.

'Don't apologize for me, honey, it's a noble pastime.'

Flora, chewing on an olive, thinks about Americans, the flasher, the countryside, and her distinct, though generalized, unease. 'I don't suppose you've got a cigarette, have you?' she asks suddenly.

Jim and Marilyn look at her as though she's mad.

'No, of course you haven't. I'll just go and get some.' As she picks her way through the tables, she can feel their eyes lancing her back: What's old Flora up to now? Smoking! Whatever next! Actually, she just feels like a cigarette. She used to smoke once, quite heavily, in the days when her youth prevented it interfering with the amateur embouchure of her flute-playing.

Back on the terrace the first course has arrived, and the Hoskins are attacking theirs – 'My, but this is good!' exclaims Marilyn.

'Give us a break, Flo, don't blow smoke all over the salmon, it's had enough of it already,' pleads Jim.

'Okay, okay.' Flora stubs out the cigarette. 'But don't call me Flo.'

She eats her duck pâté with its frilly accompaniment of baby salad leaves. The sun sinks lower over the water, translating it into melted gold. 'Here's to the two of you,' invites Flora, remembering her manners. 'But hang on a minute – why are we drinking champagne? Are we celebrating something?'

'Oh, didn't we tell you?' Marilyn and Jim exchange a horribly cosy look. 'It's our wedding anniversary!'

'Is it? Happy anniversary!' She raises her glass of non-vintage champagne: primrose bubbles dance inside. 'May you have many more!'

'Anniversaries, not weddings,' adds Jim, thumping Flora on the back. 'Thanks, honey.' He looks soulfully at Marilyn, who's changed into a white cotton dress edged with broderie anglaise – a curious mix of virgin and sailor. She twists her wedding ring till it catches the same light as the champagne. Jim slides a little box out of his pocket. 'A little something to add to that,' he offers, and watches while Marilyn's eager face falls first on the box and then on its contents, a flashing circle of diamonds. 'It's an English habit, isn't it, Flo – sorry, Flora?'

'Is it? What is?' she asks, peering at it and wondering what they'll say if she lights another cigarette.

'An eternity ring,' Jim explains. 'Diamonds are for ever, and so forth.'

'Oh Jim!' Marilyn gets up to kiss him. 'You are an old romantic!'

'I've written a poem as well,' he confesses, 'but I'll keep that until later.'

He's flushed with his success, and she's flushed with champagne. Flora both envies and despises them. She'll be ready to make her escape soon. The sun sets in the middle of her trout with almonds. 'I'm going to leave the two of you now,' she announces a few minutes later. 'I'm feeling increasingly out of place here. Don't take it personally. You've made me very welcome. But I have some things to do that I'd like to get on with before I collapse. Oxford tomorrow, remember! More guidebooks, Jim. I'll leave my copy of James Morris's *Oxford* at the desk for you. We shall approach the town from the same vantage point as the photograph between pages 208 and 209. You may like to judge the effect of history on the view.'

Flora takes a bath, then slips on a pair of light cotton trousers and a T-shirt. From the balcony of her room, she can see that Marilyn and Jim have left the terrace. After the enclosures of the day – all that driving, and then the episode of the flasher in the cathedral – she doesn't feel at all ready for bed. She needs to get out into the air – she feels that the warm night full of wild life is calling her. She takes the car out of the car park, and drives a few miles just to be clear of the hotel and its environs. She parks the car in a passing place before a crossroads and gets out. By now it is 10.30. Though the sun has gone, it's in league with the moon, which has taken its place in the sky, not looking all that different. It's a wide-mouthed yellow-gold with a bit lopped off one side – the full moon's not due for a few days. The indentations of the moon's face are obvious. It's like a livid human watching her – an angry father or a menopausal woman, the normal landscape of human emotions lit by an interior orange furnace. Pale-orange signposts point over fields sloping and groaning with cinnamon wheat. There's no wind at all; the air is breathless, trapped in a tight layer between moonshine and hot red-brown earth. Flora walks between the fields, head held high, creating her own slight air currents as she goes. And in her head a plan, also of her own, begins to form. Underneath the golden moon, by the fields of tawny cereals waiting to be cropped, the decision is born in Flora Penfold to change the course of her own life.

Flora's change of mind and heart has something to do with the impressive colours and resonances of nature – the moon, the earth, the fields of grain, and all that lives in and scutters through them, carry part of the responsibility. Her emerging decision also has something to do with the few days carved out of busy everyday routines to show the Hoskins a bit of England – time away is time apart, an occasion for breaking set, if there is even the remotest tendency in that direction. But before that, underlying it, there's a web of myths about the generation of human nature from its roots *in* nature. Flora Penfold lives a fragment of an old fantasy about fertile gardens and frightened people. Something very old, clamping the imagination with a power beyond knowledge. She's a product of her culture even at the point of determining to break its rules; whatever we do, the world that grew us lumbers on in perpetual argument with the one we're trying to create. But Flora, who walks now down a country lane brushing the moonlit meadowsweet with her small capable hand, and smiling with her soft sarcastic lips to see the mechanical harvesters slashing the proud beauty of the corn, remains for the moment innocent of the ramifications of her plan.

2

A Weekend in Town

PABLO AND DOLLY, Flora's two cats, are waiting for her at the top of the metal staircase leading down to the basement front door of the North London flat when she gets back from her tourist trip with the Hoskins. The cats are galvanized into a flurry of mewing when they see her, wrapping themselves round her legs, climbing and scratching the door as she fits the key in. 'Didn't you get fed, then, my lovelies? Of course you did, but it's cupboard love all the same.' They rush inside and lie on the deep-pink carpet, rolling around with sensual feline pleasure. Pablo, an immense tabby eunuch named after Picasso for his unoriginal behaviour towards women, is more outrageous in his pleasure than Dolly, whose size and satiny blackness beside his bulk suggest another species altogether.

Flora checks the mail and the answering machine. Barney's voice is there: 'Sorry, love, I won't be back today after all,' it says. 'We've got to remake a couple of scenes. It should be Sunday night, but latish – don't wait up. Hope you enjoyed your US tour.' A civilized message, for him. Probably recorded early in the morning before the hype of the acting or the booze got to him.

A weekend to herself! She'll make plans. An early bed tonight, cocoa with Pablo and Dolly curled up at her feet and no protesting Barney making Pablo mew in that curious way of his that sounds so like emotional pain. To the office on Saturday to get some work done. She'll call Miranda – maybe they could go to a film Saturday night. She might go and see her mother for lunch on Sunday.

Flora's relations with her mother have improved since her father's death in a car crash three years ago. Irina Penfold, *née* Gachinova, lives in Bloomsbury, in the flat where Flora and her brother Jonathan were brought up. It's emptier now, since Samuel died, but the spaces between the furniture are packed tight with Irina's memories. Not only of her big husband Samuel, who always seemed too large for the flat, except when fitted into his very own specially bought armchair; and of Flora and Jonathan as children in pastel baby clothes and soft daffodil shoes, and then in school uniform with ink on their fingers, and as intemperate adolescents with urges too primitive for their own grasp of language at the time, and certainly for the sober flat with its brown-painted rooms and view over the rooftops to the British Museum, but of her own childhood and youth in Berlin, as her father Boris moved his family round Europe evading revolutions, wars and other disasters, but, as it happened, taking an awful lot of them with him. The Gachinovs were like a nest of house martins at the top of an apple tree – they quarrelled and made such a kerfuffle with their wings all the time that they caused heavy apples to fall all round them. Flora had heard Irina on the fortunes and misfortunes of her family many times. The older she gets, the more time Irina spends quarrelling in apple trees all over Europe, and the less she spends doing anything sensible in Bloomsbury. Though at sixty-six she's hardly old, and well occupied with the biography she's been writing for many years of a little-known, faintly related figure active in the Russian Revolution, one Galia Molokhovina by name.

'Mother, it's me.'

'Hallo, darling, how are you? Could you hold the line a moment, I have some soup warming and I should not like it to spoil.' Every language her mother speaks is precisely spoken, and she speaks five of them – English, French, German, Russian and Japanese, the latter acquired when she was working for the International Labour Organization before her marriage to Flora's father.

'Borshch,' says Irina, returning to the phone. 'I'm working my way through Grandmother Sofka's cookery book. It is difficult to afford the ingredients, but never mind. Did you call about anything in particular, darling?'

'I wondered if you'd like to have lunch with me on Sunday, Mother.'

There is a silence. 'Well, that would be nice, I was going to make Grandma's kharcho. A Georgian speciality, you know. Though what I shall do for pomegranate juice, I'm sure I don't know.'

'I could bring you something. Or we could go out.'

'I don't think so, darling. It's too hot at this time of the year.'

Irina hardly ever goes out, but this is an unspoken secret between them. When Flora invites her, there is always an excuse: it's too hot or too cold, Irina has a sore throat, her leg hurts, she's expecting her sister to ring from Prague. She never says, 'I don't go out', and Flora never says it for her.

'Okay, Mother, I'll come to you. About one?'

Saturday morning is blue-skied and full of urban janglings and bustle. In the street, men wash their cars with radios turned up; front windows are open and children's television programmes fall out into the sunlit air. Flora, leaving the house, steps into a pile of dog turds parked next to a discarded black-and-gold cigarette packet, their pungency intensified by the sun. Scraping her shoes on the kerb, she has to avoid a lorry loaded with a crane approaching a man who grasps and operates a pneumatic drill with his smutty muscular arms. The noise of the drill almost cancels out the other disturbances and irritations. But in the car, driving to the office, she continues to notice the urban detritus and decay. Holes in the road – great egg cups into which the car's tyres can't help but descend – broken paving stones; the marked desecrated fronts of houses lining traffic-filled roads. Empty petrol cans, hamburger boxes and chip cartons. Squashed Coca-Cola cans, and begrimed lemonade straws. In the gutter, a used condom. By the Underground station on a patch of grass with a seat and two telephone boxes, people grapple with broken communication systems, and winos with bleary eyes suck on empty bottles. One sleeps, laid out on the littered grass, his flies undone. Children with unwashed faces and stringy hair shout from pushchairs laden with cheap wares, and drop sweet packets for the wheels to crush. Women struggle with bags, purses, children and life. Men hurry or linger. There are shops advertising closing-down sales, shops and houses and flats and cars waiting to be bought. Market stalls sell damaged fruit, their vendors slipping worthless foreign coins in with the change. All signs of the recession. Not just economic, but of civilization itself, thinks Flora, imagining herself instead back in the fields round Jacob's Water, cropped and studded with bales of hay, with the sun shining low over the water, its warmth unequal as yet to the task of penetrating to the depths where the buried villages lie.

Stuart has left a note on her desk:

> Yes, I thought you might come in today. Don't be cross, Whitmores wouldn't take the roses back.
>
> PS I'll be late in on Monday, I've got a dental appointment for some root work.

Flora shifts the pile of mail around on her desk. An envelope about halfway down is marked 'Personal'. She opens it. It's from Clarissa Barker, the Centre's publicity manager. 'Dear Flora,' the letter runs,

> I'm very sorry to have to write you this letter, but I'm afraid matters have built up to such a point that I have to offer you my resignation. It is quite impossible to work in such an environment. I know you will understand my meaning. I'm sorry if this makes things difficult for you. I wouldn't want you to take it personally, I've always enjoyed working with you.
>
> Yours, Clarissa.
>
> PS I will, of course, work my month's notice as per my contract.

All these PS's. Flora folds the letter up and puts it back in the envelope. She never liked Clarissa much, anyway. Too fussy, too punctilious, too deferential. 'Clitoral,' Barney had once said, meaning it, she thought, as a criticism. Well, I don't know about that, says Flora to herself. The next letter in the pile is from the Max Mountjoy Foundation, which puts up most of the money for the Centre. 'Dear Miss Penfold,' this one begins,

> We are writing to inform you of certain recent changes in the constitution and functioning of the Foundation, which will affect the future status of our grant-receiving bodies. Following the death of Mr Simon Mountjoy – as you know, the last surviving family member to have an interest in the Foundation – the Max Mountjoy Foundation will become a public liability company on the first of September 1990.
>
> While a portion of our investment income will be retained for charitable purposes, most of our work will in future be more commercially orientated, and in addition, there will be a new environmental emphasis, following the terms of Mr Simon Mountjoy's will, which mentioned diversification into environmentally friendly product development. Consequently the monies available for funding enterprises such as the Islington Arts Centre will in future be restricted. The Foundation will, of course, wish to ensure a smooth transition out of this difficult period for all the activities presently funded by it, and to this end the Trustees will be

> arranging a meeting with you in the near future to discuss the implications of these changes.
>
> Yours sincerely
>
> Russell Marcus, MD
>
> PS I wish I didn't have to write this letter, Flora, as you know how highly I think of your work at the Centre. Would you have dinner with me sometime? I'll give you a ring when I'm next in town.

Another PS. Well, that clinches it. Flora sits back in her chair and surveys the tastefully decorated room – the off-white paint, the frieze of plants and flowers hand-painted after a design of William Morris's own, the white shelves displaying sculptures, glass *trompe-l'œil*, even a miniature of Christina Gumble's dried pansies and buttercups. The circular pine table at the north end of the room used for staff meetings carries a blue-and-white vase full of ivory peonies; two fallen petals lie at angles to one another on the smooth surface of the table.

It'll all have to go, thinks Flora, I'll have to live without it. *They'll* have to live without me. I must go to the golden countryside, where the moon sisters the sun, and the cow parsley acts as umbrella to a thousand happy, crawling creatures. I must go where the air is clean and rushes into my lungs without carrying dead things with it. Never mind the flasher, who started this: those are the impulses of the country, too. Flesh and earth; warm, pulsating, humanity: wildlife, life itself. Before she can change her mind, she flips up the lid of her Epsen portable and composes the draft of a resignation letter to Russell Marcus. The Islington Arts Centre is more than just one of the Max Mountjoy Foundation's enterprises; it was started by them. Withdrawal of their support is tantamount to closure of the Centre, and they know it. Flora's letter to Russell Marcus suggests that, in the circumstances, she not be required to work out her notice, but that the Trustees convene an immediate meeting to consider the future of the Centre, including those of the staff remaining in it, though not Clarissa Barker, who's leaving because of some atmosphere of which she, Flora, has – unhappily or happily – not been apprised.

She reads the letter through on the screen, makes a couple of changes, and – not to be outdone – adds a PS. Hers says:

> PS My decision crossed with yours. I've decided to go and live in the country and make an honest woman of myself for a change.

She saves the text to the hard disk, thereby giving it a certain permanence as a record of her thoughts, and goes next door to Stuart's room, where she switches on the big computer and printer, and prints the letter out twice on headed notepaper. She reads it through quickly, then signs it, puts it in an envelope, and stamps it. She waters the pink tea roses, locks the office and goes home, posting the letter on the way.

'The evil deed is done,' she tells Dolly, who's positioned herself on the front wall in the sunshine, and looks questioningly back with misty green eyes that remind Flora of the spilt colours on the floor of Lincoln Cathedral. She shivers slightly, remembering the cold of the floor, the warmth of the day, the burst of the musical organ, the pale mahogany of the other one. She looks down at Dolly. 'How will you get on with the sheep, pussycat? I think your friend'll have to be sedated, otherwise the shock'll be too much for his poor old heart!'

Flora looks at her watch: 3.30. The estate agents will still be open. She goes inside, makes a cup of tea, and phones a couple – the one who sold her the flat seven years ago, and another, whose boards she's seen a great deal of recently. 'I remember the flat,' says the first. 'Nice patio garden, wasn't there? And gold taps on the bath, if I remember right.'

'You do, though the hot tap needs a new washer at the moment. Can you come and measure up now?'

She fixes appointments for the two of them half an hour apart. The first one's just turning the corner when the second arrives. Both go on tediously about the depressed state of the housing market, and ask if she's got her next home lined up.

'Yes,' she says, thinking of the sun on Jacob's Water.

'So you can move at any time?'

'Yes,' she says again, worrying about Pablo and Dolly. Pablo had, indeed, hardly survived the last move, and Dolly's never known anywhere else. She was born next door, at the same time as a baby; the baby's mother, complaining that people came to see the kittens, but not the baby, gave them away. The children never forgave her. But at least Dolly only went next door – the other two were dispatched to somewhere unspeakable near a naval base in Kent.

After the estate agents have been and gone, Flora drives to meet Miranda in Notting Hill Gate. The film is short, something Italian with subtitles. Flora finds it hard to concentrate, except on the landscapes, which are stunning. The burnt-orange sky of the sunsets behind Vesuvius immediately refixes her in the rural paradise she's sketched in her head, which is only partially composed of scenes from the real world of Meltshire. How could it be otherwise, seeing as she hardly knows it yet? After the film, she and Miranda repair to the pizza restaurant next door, where Flora confides her plans to Miranda, who has known her for twenty years. They were at Art School together. But whereas Flora took what Miranda regards as the easy route of going into administration for a living, she, Miranda, has stuck like a leech to painting. Her gaudy characterizations of scenes from contemporary urban life are a cross between the superficially emotionless American primitive and the macabre remonstrations of Lowry; but they are now recognized as constituting a distinctive style, and Miranda's making enough money from them to more than survive. She's cornered a neat market in murals for the new private hospitals and clinics that are cloning themselves everywhere under the impact of Conservative health policies.

Despite her addiction to art at all costs, Miranda is not impractical. This means she is bound to pour cold water on her friend's plans. 'Listen, Flora,' she says, grasping her wineglass firmly between her workwomanlike hands, with their nails cut short, so as not to interfere with the art of brushholding. 'Listen, Flora, what are you going to live off? Even those cats of yours must cost a few quid a week to feed.' Miranda's allergic to everything feline, which is why cats easily spring to her mind, as they do to her body, in any consideration of Flora's lifestyle.

'I knew you'd say that,' replies Flora cheerfully. 'But I've got it all worked out. It goes like this. One, as you know, my father left me some money. It's been hard to find out how much, as his stockbrokers have been very dilatory about tracking down some of the share certificates.' She pauses. 'You know, Miranda, it's a constant surprise to me how capitalist my father was in private, given that his public protestations were all of the other sort.'

'Parents are essentially immoral people,' observes Miranda. 'They drum moral stability into us, but they've got none of it themselves.' Her own father left her mother some years ago to live with his boyfriend in South Africa.

'Anyway,' continues Flora, 'I think it's about £100,000. I've put my flat on the market for £155,000. Out of that I should net £130,000.'

'Assuming you get the price you're asking, of course,' interjects Miranda gloomily.

'Don't be such a spoilsport. It's a nice flat. The patio's very desirable, and so is the leaking gold tap. That makes £230,000, doesn't it?'

'I suppose.' Miranda can see nothing wrong with Flora's arithmetic.

'I'd buy a house for, say, £100,000. Spend say, £20,000 on it. Invest the rest – £140,000. At 10 per cent that gives me a basic income of £14,000 a year. What's wrong with that?'

'£230,000 minus £120,000 is £110,000,' comments Miranda, having spotted a hole in the logic at last. 'But where will you find a house for £100,000? And how can you live off £11,000 a year? And even if you could, what would you do all the time?'

'Meltshire,' says Flora. 'And I can't. But, one, I shall grow all my own food and, two, I'm sure I've got other talents.'

'Such as?'

'Well, I could teach the flute.'

'Would you want to?'

'I might. Ten quid an hour for ten hours a week is . . . another £5000 a year.'

'Five thousand two hundred.'

'Just so. And remember what I was doing when we first met, Miranda?'

Miranda hunts through the cupboards of memory in her head until she finds the one she was looking for: Flora Penfold first glimpsed by her in 1970 in a corner of the cafeteria in Hampstead School of Art, dressed entirely in purple, decorating the college timetable with savage cartoon drawings. 'But have you done any since?'

'Oh yes.' Flora thinks of the drawers crammed with paper back in N19. A thought strikes her. 'That's interesting.'

'What is?'

'The word "drawer". It means, one, a box you slide in and out of a hole, two, someone who draws, three, knickers. I wonder why that is.'

'I wish you'd stop enumerating things.'

'Sorry.' Flora turns to her friend and smiles. 'But I *was* thinking about the cartoons I've collected over the years. It's been my alternative to psychotherapy – whenever anything upsets me, I get the pen and paper out. I certainly wouldn't describe it as a hobby.'

'You were quite good,' reflects Miranda.

'Of course I was. Well, I could do that for a living down in the country. Or up in it, or whichever direction it is. Will you come and see me, Manda? Down or up in my rural retreat?'

'From time to time. But don't expect me to rave about it the way you will. And you'll have to lock those cats of yours up.'

'How do you know I'll rave?'

'You'll have to, won't you?'

'It's not a passing fancy, you know,' says Flora to Miranda – and to herself on the way home. When she tells her mother about it over borshch in the Bloomsbury flat the next day, she's gratified to find a more positive reaction.

'What a delicious idea, my dear!' says Irina Penfold. She rubs her sparrowlike hands together and projects her head, with its dyed black hair, forward in a darting motion emphasizing her rounded shoulders. Her face, its dark foreign beauty accentuated, not decreased, with age, lights up with pleasure. 'You can grow some botva for me. There's a recipe in Grandmother Sofka's book which calls for those – in botvinya, you know, a kind of fishy soup – and I haven't been able to find them *anywhere*. But you should make sure you get the sun, darling. Botva need sun, it says so in the book. Will you be taking your young man with you?'

Irina always refers to Barnaby as 'your young man'. They have a distant, though not unfriendly, relationship.

'I don't think so,' says Flora.

Irina looks at her sharply. 'Because he wouldn't want to, or because you wouldn't want him to?'

'A bit of both.'

Irina nods. And that seems to be the end of it as far as she is concerned. When Flora leaves at five, Irina clutches her at the door with her thin brown arms and says, 'I'm very happy for you, darling. Almost I wish I was young again, to begin on such an adventure.' When Irina Penfold's emotions are engaged with something, her language slips a little, picking up the cadences and habits of the one she learned first; the first lexicon remains the one through which emotional experiences are filtered.

Flora knows Barnaby has arrived when she gets back to Thornaugh Road after having lunch with her mother, because Pablo and Dolly aren't waiting outside for her. Barney's watching television – a programme about the possible US response to the Iraqi invasion of

Kuwait. Petrol-coloured planes take off noisily from the slate-grey decks of aircraft carriers; smoke trails against the blue of sky and sea. A troop of ill-assorted ships is shown occupying the Eastern Mediterranean. 'The man must be mad,' declares Barnaby, pouring himself some more wine, and passing the bottle to Flora, 'don't you think? Hallo, old girl.' He strokes the cat absent-mindedly.

Flora notices for the first time that the same mode of address does for the cat and for herself. She takes a clean glass from the shelf, sits down on the cane chair opposite Barnaby, and pours herself some wine.

'That's right,' he says, watching her. 'If you can't beat 'em, join 'em.'

'Oh, Barney,' she sighs, 'what a mess. And I don't only mean this' – she waves a hand in the direction of the television. Pablo stalks in from the kitchen, sitting tiger-like at Flora's feet. Ensconced on the sofa against the line of Barney's thigh, Dolly purrs and throws a superior look in Flora's direction.

'Yes, indeed. It is, isn't it? And I don't only mean that either.' He plonks the glass down on the table, dislodging Dolly in the process. 'Now, tell me about the "For Sale" sign. Are we? And if so, why?'

'That's not the problem, Barney. The problem is us.'

'I find it easier to start with inanimate objects.'

'Turn the television off.'

'Why should I?'

'You always were desperately childish, weren't you? If you think you're doing what I want, you won't do it. What's wrong with pleasing somebody? I know the answer to that; it's all about your mother, isn't it? *You* have to want something first.'

'True enough. Well, some of it, anyway. Though I don't go for the bit about my lovely Mum, as you know.'

'I think it's a good idea to have the TV off if we're going to have a serious conversation, don't you?' He jumps up and switches it off. 'You see, I've made it my idea. So now it's all right.' He swings his legs on to the sofa, so he's lying full length on it. Dolly, alarmed, springs off and scuttles away, watched by Pablo with a 'Now whose turn is it?' look.

Barnaby flicks a fly off his shirt. 'All right then, fire away, I'm a lying target.'

'I've put the flat up for sale,' begins Flora, as matter-of-factly as she can, 'because I've decided I'm going to give up my job and move to the country. I'm fed up with London, and with my job. I feel I've reached a time in my life when I want to take stock of things. Just because I haven't married and had a family, I don't have to stay on this one-dimensional career-woman track for ever. There are more things to life than going to the office and making money.' She stops, unsure whether she's said enough or too much.

'And where do I fit into this new life plan of yours?' Barnaby's grey-green eyes level at hers. 'What about Our Relationship, Flora?'

If she didn't know him as well as she does, the pathos with which he utters the last sentence might have turned her heart.

'Stop acting.'

'I can't.'

'Do you love me, Barney?'

'What should I say to that? Yes, for ever? As much as I can? Sort of? Do *you* love *me*?'

'I don't know.' Flora looks down at the carpet, streaked with black and tabby cat hairs. 'Sometimes I think it's just a habit. We've been living together seven years. I'm used to you. But we argue about the same things all the time. I wonder if we've got all that much in common.' She looks up again at him, spread out like a feast on the velvet sofa. Barnaby Gunn is a beautiful man, which deceives some people into thinking he's a good actor. 'I know I'm fond of you, Barney. I'd miss you if I didn't see you any more.' She feels tears salting her eyes but, unwilling to let *him* see them, she gets up and moves awkwardly into the kitchen. Pablo follows her, flipping his hot tail against her bare legs. He thinks it's feeding time, and starts his yowling. She reaches for the cupboard, the tin of catfood, the tin opener. A couple of clean plates. It's reassuring to perform automatic actions. She opens the tin, bends down and forks the brown gelatinous lumps on to the plates. Dolly prances up and comes round the side of Flora's legs so she's opposite Pablo, and the two of them are chewing in rhythm. Pablo purrs sonorously at the same time – it's the only time he ever does it. Flora straightens up, puts the fork in the sink.

Barnaby's standing in the doorway, the evening light from the living-room window giving him a softer outline than he normally has. 'You could be right,' he says, surprisingly. 'Maybe it's time to split.'

She starts crying then. 'Come here, old girl.' He puts his arm round her. He feels her firm rounded flesh under her cotton dress, noting, almost as automatically as she fed the cats, that she's left her bra off. Because of the heat, he assumes. Certainly not in order to be more alluring to him. But as he holds her, in a gesture intended originally to comfort, the habits of seven years reassert themselves. Touching her in the vapid kitchen, his body, threatened with its last such meeting, recalls their first, in a friend's country house; they'd gone for a walk in the sloping mock-eighteenth-century garden with its assembly-line statues and carved peacock trees. The moon was full, and there was the definite scent of honeysuckle. He'd kissed her by the wall; her skin smelt faintly of soap. Which it still does now. 'So that's why you want to live in the country,' he says.

'What?' She sniffs against the wine stain on his shirt.

'Remember when we first met?' Holding her at arm's length, he can see from her eyes that she does. Two moonlit figures walk there, between the peacock trees.

She half-smiles. 'No, that's not the reason. Though it was good, wasn't it? Once.'

'Come here, old girl,' he says again, and leads her into the bedroom.

She starts to protest.

'For old times' sake. What harm will it do?'

She thinks of the first kiss, and of the scent of honeysuckle in the moonlight.

He thinks briefly of Judy Nightingale, his co-star in *The Panda Man* – of her honey-coloured legs twisted round his in a hotel set on a Cornish cliff, of her great dark eyes in which waves seem to roll and crash as they do in the sea outside. 'Who is this woman you live with?' Judy had asked.

'She's called Flora. She runs an Arts Centre.'

'Do you love her?'

'What do you think?' Never answer a question directly if you can help it, that's Barnaby Gunn's motto.

He lifts Flora Penfold's dress over her shoulders. No underpants either. 'They're all dirty,' she says, 'I haven't had time to do any . . .'

Mouth to mouth, like the moon on the peacock trees, the bee visiting the honeysuckle. Limbs intertwined like wall and climbing honeysuckle branches, like his and Judy's. Like all lovers everywhere. The one thing that can be depended on, when all else fails. Back to the awful, amazing urge that propagates humankind, spilling fertile seeds that grow into mistakes of their own, whatever their originators might choose to do with them. Barnaby Gunn kisses the crevices of Flora Penfold's arms, licking the soft hair that rises there, moves his head with his own long fringe of golden hair that she likes to run her fingers through, down, down, to the curve of the white breast with the pink upstanding nipple, a cherry, a flower, which he licks with the long tongue of a horse mating in a summer field. And then down some more, across the flat terrain of Flora's stomach, to where hair rises again on another, darker mound, and, parting her legs with a light touch of his forefinger, to where the body divides, not two any more but one, relinquishing its symmetry to a slippery ocean of dark-pink fiords, inlets and pools where one may get lost but also find oneself.

His tongue wraps itself in and around, and Flora, stroking his back, moans, reaching out to hold him like the flasher in the cathedral – to hold his penis strong and soft, smooth and unresisting. 'Put it in,' she says. And he, willing this time to be commanded, enters and sails in her like a prince and she, feeling regal enough herself, settles her fiords round his boat, so that the two of them set off on a journey – the last of many and perhaps – who knows? though they both think it – the last of all such they will go on together.

3

A Place in the Country

'HOW MUCH are we asking for the flat, then?' inquires Barney from underneath the duvet on Monday morning.

When Flora tells him, he whistles through his white teeth (attended to by a Finchley dentist a few years ago to improve his television image). 'That'll come in handy,' he remarks.

'Yes, it will,' says Flora, thinking of her place in the country.

He lays a hand on her thigh. 'How are we going to divide it, then?'

'We aren't,' she says, removing it. 'The flat's mine. I bought it before I met you, if you remember.'

'But I've contributed to the maintenance,' he cuts in quickly, 'haven't I? I've paid half the bills. Well, some of them. What about all the DIY?'

Flora thinks of the bookshelves Barney constructed after a prolonged argument one wet winter; of the kitchen cupboards with the missing door (dropped and chipped and put out for the dustman). 'I really don't think that entitles you to anything.'

Barney throws off the duvet and gets out of bed. 'I'm sure the law gives men like me some protection.' His lean body is caught in the morning sunlight coming round the edge of the curtains. 'After all, I'm like a wife, aren't I? Wives can't be cut off by their husbands without a penny.'

She looks at him: he's scratching his balls with one hand and his head with the other. 'I don't think you're much like a wife.'

'We'll see about that.' He scoops up his clothes and shuts himself in the bathroom.

The agent rings. 'Unexpected interest, Miss Penfold,' he says. 'I've got two clients who'd like to take a look at the property. One wants to come round now – a Mr Findlake.'

'Good,' says Flora. 'How much money has he got?'

Mr Findlake is a schoolteacher, with a new job as the head of the science department at a local comprehensive. He is accompanied by his wife, who is fat, like a Michelin tyre man. 'Angela and I have always wanted to live in this area,' he announces. 'So handy for everything, don't you think? But we don't need a whole house. Angela's infertile. Blocked tubes. So it'd be a waste of money, really.' The two of them prowl through the flat like dogs trained to detect bad smells. Withdrawing his head from the built-in cupboards in the bedroom, Mr Findlake asks, 'Why are you moving, then?'

'I'm going to live in the country,' Flora informs him.

He laughs. 'Very nice. I hope you enjoy it there. I had a spell in Lincolnshire. At what they call a community college. You know what they say about the fens?' He doesn't wait for her answer. 'Enormously high incest rate. Shows in the kids. Dumb as hell. Still, I suppose that won't bother you. When are you going?'

'As soon as I can sell this place.'

He peers at the agent's hastily put together details in his hand. '£155,000 – you don't think that's a bit steep?'

'It's a very nice flat,' she says. 'The patio's very well designed. In fact, it was a very high-standard conversion altogether. The architect's quite well known. And then there are the gold-plated taps. Take it or leave it. I'd take it, if I were you. What do you think, Ang – Mrs Findlake?'

'We'll take it,' says Mr Findlake. 'Won't we, Angela?'

Angela nods. It's hard to tell if she means yes or no. 'I think it's just right, Curtis.'

'But at what price?' demands Flora. 'I know you're supposed to tell the agent, but it would speed things up if we talked about it ourselves now.'

Curtis Findlake wipes his brow with the back of his hand and squints at the sky through the window. '£148,000?'

'£153,000,' says Flora promptly.

Angela Findlake bends down to stroke Pablo, who has ambled in from the garden. He hisses at her, fur uprising. She withdraws.

'He's a bit fierce till he gets to know you.'

'£149,000. It's a falling market.'

'£150,000.'

'Okay, okay,' says Curtis Findlake wearily, conscious that he's not nearly manful enough for this.

Having sold the flat, Flora is at the office by ten. Stuart is waiting for her, holding his jaw with a handkerchief. 'It's just coming round.

Very difficult job, the dentist said. I've got an impacted wisdom tooth as well.' He looks almost proud of this biological defect. 'I'm going to have that out next Tuesday. I'm sorry about the roses. Did you know Clarissa's resigned?'

'There was a letter on my desk.'

'Has she talked to you?' Stuart looks worried.

'No, but I'm sure she will.'

'Can I have a word first?'

'Go ahead.'

He shuts the door and sits down at the pine table, picking up the fallen white peony petals and crushing them between his fingers. 'I didn't do anything,' he says. 'Whatever Clarissa says, I'm not guilty.'

'Look,' says Flora decisively, 'you can tell me your side of whatever story it is, and Clarissa can tell me hers. I've no doubt it's my role to listen. But I have to tell you that events have overtaken whatever silly squabbles are going on here. In the first place, the Foundation is withdrawing its financial support. Not all of it, and how much isn't yet clear, but the future of the Centre really is very much up in the air at the moment. And in the second place, I myself have decided to leave. I'm going to give up this ridiculous high-stress existence before it's too late, and move to the country. So you see, Stu,' she finishes, 'whatever Clarissa says about you, or you about her, it's the end of an era. And in the light of all this, I shouldn't bother about the colour of the tea roses. I may even decide to take them to the country with me.'

There's a knock at the door. Maureen holds out a piece of curled paper. 'Fax from Russell Marcus, Flora. I thought you'd want to see it straight away.'

'Dear Miss Penfold,' the limp paper reads,

> Regarding your letter of August 21, the Foundation is of course sorry to receive notice of your resignation. This is to confirm acceptance of the same, and to thank you for your commitment and hard work as Director of the Islington Arts Centre over the past eight years. I know the other Trustees would wish to join with me in conveying our thanks and wishing you the very best for the future.
>
> In the circumstances, it would seem appropriate that your contractual obligation to work out one month's notice be waived. Meanwhile, we will be in touch with you to arrange

an emergency meeting to discuss the future of the Centre.
Best regards, Russell Marcus

PS [handwritten] Dinner on Tuesday? Will phone you when you've received this to confirm. Russell.

Flora's eyes move from the curly fax to the anxious waiting faces of Stuart, still crushing peony petals at one end of the room, and Maureen in the doorway at the other. 'You've read this, I suppose, Maureen?'

Maureen nods.

'Have you said anything to the others?'

Maureen pauses. 'Not really.'

'That means yes. We'd better have a meeting. Please can you organize some sandwiches at one?'

'What about Mizuno?' wails Simon. 'And the St Jude's fee? God, my mouth hurts.'

Flora opens the drawer of her desk and breaks off a couple of paracetamol from a foil packet. 'Take these. Go and make a list of all the outstanding problems. And see if you can find Clarissa; I want to see her next.'

Clarissa is full of self-righteous something. 'It's sexual harassment,' she insists. 'He pinned me against the noticeboard. Not to mention the offensive remarks he was always making about my behind.'

'What's wrong with your behind?' Flora tries to remember what it looks like.

'Like a couple of ripe young plums, he said.' Clarissa's face reddens slightly, but she clasps her hands together firmly. 'I told him his attentions were unwelcome – I'm celibate, you see. It's the only solution these days. But he would keep on. I've had enough of it.'

'Yes, I quite understand,' says Flora unsympathetically.

'I'm going to Singapore. Daddy's got a business out there, silk stuffed animals and other oriental trophies. He's already sent me a ticket.'

By 4.30 Flora's exhausted. The staff, nervous about their own futures, whether at the Islington Arts Centre or not, are tetchy with her – almost, she feels, blaming her for everything. However reasonably she points out that events at the Foundation were nothing to do with her own decision, they see her as the instigator of all their problems.

On Tuesday, at dinner with Russell Marcus in a newly opened Greek taverna in Crouch End, he confesses to her that he was not the instigator either, and he has his own problems. 'It surprised us all, did young Simon's will. We always called him young Simon, though he was a good deal riper than all of us. Riper and battier. Frankly, my dear, he was quite batty. Had a thing about hygiene. Always scrubbing things. Very keen on soap. Hence the cleaning powders that are kind to trees, not hands. Dreadful business. Most sorry about the Centre, as I said.'

Later in the dinner Russell Marcus admits to Flora his own fantasies of flight. 'A man of my age', he says – in much the same tone as Flora herself has been beginning sentences with 'At my age, women . . .' – 'has to take stock of things. After Simon's death, I went for a BUPA check-up. My cholesterol's 8.2. I've had to keep it from Rosemary, she couldn't handle the anxiety – her nerves are in a dreadful state since her mother's death in a swimming pool in Majorca last year. It certainly makes you think. I take these pills now' – he produces a pill box from his jacket pocket – 'before every meal. And of course I've had to adjust my diet. It's been hard explaining that to Rosemary, especially in view of her own fondness for things with cream in them, you know.' He swallows his pills and tinkers with a fish kebab. 'No red meat, you see. Now, Flora, what about your own plans?'

The fish is chewy, and Russell Marcus has to ask the over-zealous Marios, working hard to attract customers, to turn the music down; between it, and his chewing, he can hardly hear Flora speak. But he does hear the word Meltshire.

'Ah, Meltshire,' he says, pulling a fish bone from his mouth. 'Now, there's a truly magical place.'

'You know it, do you?'

'I went to school there, my dear, in Oakingham. Ghastly school – well, perhaps all schools are – but the town and the countryside were wonderful. We used to sneak out and buy our barley sugar from Baylis's in Seaton Lane. There was a most delectable cake shop too,' he recalls, his eyes misting at the mounds of cholesterol heaped like prizes on the other side of the slightly rippled glass. 'As a matter of fact, maybe I could help you with some contacts.'

Russell Marcus would like to do something useful for Flora. He's always fancied her in a paternal kind of way – her economical figure, the dancing blue of her eyes, remind him generally of his youth and specifically of the opportunities missed by having only sons. He takes a silver ballpoint pen from his top pocket, and with the other hand the menu. 'Bream Oliphant (Lord),' he writes. 'Stuck-up wife,' he says.

'Overton Hall, Great Glaston. And Henry Gosling, solicitor, Oakingham. Though I hope you never need one,' he adds. 'Now, what else?' he mutters, sucking the end of the silver pen. 'Ah, I know, a most unlikely one! Chap I went to school with, Andrew Mattock, runs a garden centre. Specializes in climbers. I expect you'll need those. Martinsthorpe, or is it Thistleton? Next to a BP garage. Rosemary and I went to see them last year. Lives with a woman called Romita. Funny name, funny woman. One leg shorter than the other.'

'I'm all set up now, aren't I?' Flora smiles like a little girl who's just unwrapped a particularly welcome present. 'You must come and see me, Russell, in my country abode. When I've found it.'

On Friday, Flora drives up the A1 listening to a repeat of 'Gardeners' Question Time' (a long item about tea roses). Now to plunge into another set of estate agents and find that stone-built eighteenth-century cottage with roses (not tea) round the door, and a view over open fields to a river, perhaps, with lush water meadows supporting golden cows, marsh buttercups and an abundance of all forms of non-human life. Apart from the fact that she shouldn't spend more than £100,000 on her country abode, the house must, of course, be genuinely old, with character. It must have a garden, big enough for the things she wants to grow – runner beans, potatoes, blackcurrants, strawberries, gooseberries, roses (white and pink), campanula, snapdragons, fuchsia, plenty of aubretia and lobelia packing the borders or trailing down from dry-stone walls and sunlit baskets. A few geese, or chickens; a goat maybe? Wired off from lawns where Pablo and Dolly can roam. A greenhouse would be nice, a garage not necessary. And the house itself should have a big stone-flagged kitchen – a Mrs Beeton kitchen, cool in the summer, warm from the old kitchen range/new Aga in the winter. A small sitting-room, cosy, with a woodburning stove. A couple of bedrooms, and a room for her work. A bathroom without leaking gold taps. And all this must be in a village with a Post Office and a village store. Within sight of others, but not too close. A church clock should chime the hour, but again from a reasonable distance, so it doesn't disturb the peaceful blackness of the rural night.

'Four rooms, k and b,' she says to Lionel Tupper of Tupper, Tindale & Co. in Melton. 'Not more than 100 k. With a view and half an acre in a village. And now.'

Lionel Tupper hasn't sold anything for three months. He's beginning to resent showing people around – it uses petrol (the price of which is now escalating horribly due to the Gulf crisis), and none of them ever does anything as a result. He sees them all as voyeurs with macabre hidden intentions that have nothing to do with house purchasing. Moreover, he's just eaten an enormous lunch: the Exeter Arms' best steak and kidney, with three vegetables, and apple pie and custard washed down with a couple of pints of beer. He feels dazed, depressed, overweight and above all hot, when Flora walks in, cool as a cornflower, with her bright-blue eyes and jaunty, beginning-a-new-life step. Moreover, he finds it awfully hard to work out in which client category she belongs. Slightly landed aristocracy? Wife of videoman or shoe corporation manager? Schoolteacher? She doesn't seem to know a lot about the area. He has to show her the various desirable locations on the map.

'You're lucky,' he says, trying to belch silently, 'there's a lot of choice at the moment. Now here's a village I'd particularly recommend: West Panton – very good beer and a dinky geese farm.' He tucks his tie into his shirt to hide the gravy stain. 'Though decimated by a nasty virus this year, I hear. Nice two up and two down there, only ninety thou.' He pushes the leaflet into her hand:

> Charming Cottage in sought-after village location. Comprising Breakfast Kitchen, Lounge/Dining Room, Cloaks lobby, bathroom, Two Good Bedrooms. Delightful gardens. Early inspection recommended.

'Okay,' she says. 'I'll have a look at it. But perhaps we should make a collection of these first. Then you can take me on a tour. You can, can't you, this afternoon?'

Lionel sighs. He'd been planning to go home early and have a kip before supper. Then he and Gupta are going to a jazz barbecue in the Fox and Hounds. 'I don't mean to be rude,' he ventures, 'Mrs . . .'

'Miss Penfold.'

'Miss Penfold, but are you serious about this?'

'Why, don't I look serious?' She straightens her backbone and flashes her laser eyes at him.

'It's not that,' he laments unmanfully, like Curtis Findlake. 'It's just that I'm . . . well . . . not feeling very well, and business has been kind of slack recently.'

'Well, here's your chance to change all that. If you don't want to believe I'm serious, that's your problem. There are, of course, plenty of other agents . . .'

Lionel Tupper knows when he's beaten. 'We'll go to West Panton first,' he says, and a few minutes later he's crashing the gears of the firm's scratched white Montego. 'Would you mind opening the sun roof, Mrs Penfold?'

'Miss.'

'Oh yes.' He glances down at her. 'What do you want a place in the country for, then?'

'To start a new life.'

'What was wrong with the old one?'

'Isn't that my business?'

'Yes, I suppose so.'

'Here we are.' He screeches round the village green; a faded manila cat just makes it with an inch to spare from the Montego's dented hubcaps. They draw up in front of a small, squat building with one window at the front, a brown varnished door, and a modern concrete garage.

'No,' says Flora.

'But you haven't seen it yet!'

'Yes I have, I can see it now, it's horrible. There's no point in wasting both our times. Let's go.' She folds her hands in her lap and looks straight ahead.

At this rate, they'll be through the properties in time for him to have a nap before the barbecue. He lifts the pile of leaflets from the dashboard and shuffles through them. 'What about this one?'

> Berry's cottage, Barley. The property is pleasantly situated in the heart of this popular Meltshire village conveniently located for the village centre (Post Office, general stores and butchers) yet within easy walking distance of the delightful countryside around. The Property benefits from *Full Oil Fired Central Heating*, this being complemented with the *Roof Space Being Insulated to Regulation Thickness.*

'It's one of the empty ones,' says Lionel Tupper. 'Owner did the renovations, then had to move. Very sad story.'

Flora says nothing.

'Wife went bananas. Claimed he had another woman hidden behind the wallpaper. Tore it all off one night, taken to hospital with bleeding fingernails.'

After a short drive and more jerky parking, he lets her into a tiny entrance hall leading on the right into an equally tiny sitting-room, and on the left into a very pleasant south-facing kitchen. Cobwebs dangle from an exposed beam. Sunshine glistens on a new red Aga.

He sees her looking at it. 'Nice, isn't it? Did you want inglenooks? I should have asked.'

Flora's through the kitchen by this time and out the other side. Behind the house is an overgrown vegetable garden, with runner beans going to seed, and wild mint having a field day. To the side is another sizeable plot of land, mostly grass, with a few desultory flower beds. She can see it heaped with sweet-smelling honeysuckle and lavender, with clouds of gypsophilia and scarlet heuchera, with orange marigolds and blue campanulas. It'll need a trellis and some climbers at the back. If she got going on it quickly, she could have a Russian vine in and a Virginia creeper more or less established before the autumn.

She goes back into the kitchen and up the steep stairs, Lionel Tupper trailing behind. 'Three good-sized bedrooms,' he intones, 'all with dimmer switches.' She's already standing in the first. 'The master bedroom,' he says, throwing open yellow louvred cupboards. 'It's been repapered since.'

Still without saying anything, she marches into the two smaller rooms, and then into the bathroom. 'Pampas suite,' he proceeds, 'panelled bath with Victorian-style brass taps incorporating shower fitting. Glazed tile surround. Pedestal wash-hand basin with glazed tile splashback, and matching brass bib taps. Close-coupled WC suite. Twin inset spotlight.'

Inset in what? Flora peers out of the window. Sheep sit in a meadow between dancing silver birch trees, and a church spire rises in the distance.

He can't tell if she likes it or not. She goes downstairs, out into the garden again. 'How long has it been on the market?'

'A longish time.'

'So the owner's desperate to sell?'

'Well, fairly.'

'And what's the price?'

'£95,000.'

'That's a bit high, isn't it?'

'Well . . .'

'I like it,' she says.

'Good.'

'Can we have a look round the village?'

He starts to open the car.

'No, walking.'

She advances at a spanking pace and he ambles behind, conscious that there's one piece of information about Berry's Cottage he needs to give her. 'Miss Penfold . . .' he lumbers after her. 'There's something I ought to mention.'

'What is it?'

She's ploughing back through the kitchen again.

'The plot at the side.'

'The flower garden, you mean?'

'That bit,' he waves, not having access to her mind, which, as we know, has already stocked it with delicious variegated blooms.

'What about it, Mr Tupper?'

'Well, you see, it's not exactly for sale with the house. The owner's got planning permission for a rendered bungalow.'

'Why couldn't you have said that to begin with? You are a fool. I don't want a bungalow in my flower garden. No wonder you can't sell anything. I think I should find another agent.'

Lionel Tupper mops his brow and pleads with Flora. They sit in the car. 'I'm really disappointed,' she says. 'I like this place. The view's good, especially from the bathroom. I can imagine my cats sitting by the Aga. The village green's very scenic. You do realize it's a rural dream I'm after, Mr Tupper? You're playing with fire leading me on and then telling me the hitches.'

Lionel Tupper apologizes and sweats some more. 'At least let me show you the other four. Please, Miss Penfold.'

'Only if you promise to tell me the truth.'

What is this, a marriage? She sounds like a wife or a school prefect. Lionel Tupper thinks fondly of Gupta's easy desire to please. 'I promise.'

Number three is the one whose owner wasn't in. It's down a bramble-ridden lane, and stuck on to the side of another house. 'Apple Tree Cottage' says a curly cast-iron sign on the peeling whitewashed wall. Lionel Tupper opens the garden gate and knocks at the front door. When there's no answer, he pushes the door open and bellows 'Hallo!'

This time Flora follows him. 'Are you sure it's all right?'

'Owner's a friend of mine.' They step into the kitchen. 'By Kitchen Creations of Oakingham, if I remember correctly,' says Lionel Tupper expansively. 'Oak-edged worktops, bowl-and-a-half cream single drainer sink, inset four-burner Neff Propane Gas Hob.'

'Yes, all right,' says Flora crossly. 'I'm not really interested in kitchens.'

A woman not interested in kitchens? Lionel Tupper stares at her, stopped in midflood. But he soon recovers. 'And there's your inglenook fireplace,' he says, pointing at the opposite wall, 'with concealed lighting incorporated into a range of base unit cupboards with glazed doors.'

'It's not *my* inglenook; I can't bear the beastly things.' Flora's gone again.

'The rest of it's not up to much, I'm afraid,' calls Lionel. 'He spent all he had on the kitchen.'

'I can see that,' comments Flora, poking around behind a dingy orange curtain which hides a mound of damp newspapers, and then exiting to survey the garden. A non-musical composition called 'Big', by New Fast Automatic Daffodils, is flooding the countryside from the open windows of a modern house painted pale cerise which overlooks Apple Tree Cottage. 'Let's go, Mr Tupper.'

'It's not fair, Miss Penfold,' complains Lionel Tupper, forced ultimately to defend himself. 'I'm not responsible for the neighbours' music. You could get that anywhere. You don't think you're a bit . . . well . . . fussy?'

'That's my business.'

'Quite so.' He's beginning to get the measure of her now. In fact, he's quite rising to the challenge. Perhaps that's one reason he's been feeling depressed recently – there's not enough challenge in his life.

'I think we'll skip the next one,' he tells her, gripping the wheel decisively. He's just remembered it backs on to a farm tool shop. 'And proceed straight to the third. We made an appointment with the owner, a Miss Greetham. Another Miss,' he adds inconsequentially. 'The village is called Little Tickencote. It's not in the guidebooks, which is just as well.'

Three or four miles along a humping Roman road they turn right and climb a long hill edged with handsome century-old horse chestnut trees. The branches bend and billow, forming verdant shady domes. 'Little Tickencote,' says the sign. 'Please drive carefully through our village.' Past the sign and up the main street, there's a little green with a spreading cedar tree (Flora imagines its roots dappled with crocuses and daffodils in the spring). Opposite there's a duck pond, enclosed with white rails and home to a bevy of glistening green ducks. Lionel Tupper's car shrieks past a hobbling mallard.

The cottage is plain, square, sensible-looking. Four windows and a door, like a child's painting. With a path up to the front gate set in a dry-stone wall. Two front lawns with pansies, white geraniums, and great bushes of dark purple lavender. Miss Greetham, a picture-book little old lady, white-haired and wearing a pink check dress with a pink-and-white smiling face to match, is waiting for them. She holds out one of her bony hands to Flora. 'Do come in; I hope you think my little cottage is worth a visit. Of course, it's all a bit much for me now, but I've tidied up as best I can. Could you manage a cup of tea and some scones?'

'I think this just might be it,' pronounces Lionel Tupper, striding up the stairs. It's cooler now, and the steak and kidney pie's gone down at last. He's just recollected the remarkable view from Miss Greetham's bedroom. 'Come here,' he says, and beckons Flora with a pasty finger, 'and look at that!'

The cottage, on a street behind but parallel to Little Tickencote's main street, has a view from its upper storey as quintessentially rural as anyone, including Flora Penfold, could want. First the eye skims the creeper-covered dry-stone wall enclosing the garden, and skirts between the fruit trees – the apple on the left, the cherry on the right – to a broad curved white-gold field in which a few sleepy cows stand, nuzzling the earth. After dropping into a copse of trees, the view rises again to a matched field of sheep who even now, as Flora stares with the feeling of enchantment she'd been waiting for, let out a few appropriately sheep-like cries. On the horizon to the left is a pale-grey spire with a clock which will, in a few minutes, chime the hour, thus fulfilling another of Flora's requirements.

The second bedroom's difficult to get into, it's so full of packing cases and bags and mounds of things. 'The old lady's been here a lifetime,' explains Lionel Tupper. 'In fact, this is undoubtedly her life you see before you.' The third room is built on over the kitchen extension right out, it seems, into the old apple tree. Green apples hang in bunches of three or four, knocking at the window glass. 'Needs pruning,' comments Lionel. 'There's an attic, too – could be converted to another room if need be. The facilities are downstairs.'

'Facilities?'

'Bath and wc. They often are in these old cottages.'

Miss Greetham has a pot of tea and scones and cream and jam on a table by the tree. 'We won't sit under it,' she says. 'Things tend to hit you.' She pours the tea. 'Well, do you like it, my dear?'

'I do, Miss Greetham, I do.'

'I hoped you would.' An apple starts its movement through the thickly leaved centre of the tree and crashes to the ground, followed by another. 'The old tree's finding it all a bit much now,' she observes with a thin smile, 'rather like me. I'll be sad to leave here, very sad. I'm going to live with my sister in Norwich. It's a housing estate, but she's younger than I am. I was born here, you know – Mr Tupper does; I expect I've told him often enough – on the summer solstice, the very year and the day Rimsky-Korsakov died.' She pauses, for effect. 'I used to teach the piano, Miss Penfold. I've got a little one still, a rosewood Yamaha, in the parlour. I expect the conjunction of the two words surprises you. It dates from the 1920s. Yamaha only started making motor bicycles because they knew from making brass instruments how to silence things. Not many people realize that. We got it from Boag's in Melton. The old one had woodworm. Oh yes, this house has been full of music in its time!' Her face saddens, and her eyes wander past the falling apples and the grazing cows and sheep to the far-off blue horizon of locked-up memories.

Lionel Tupper helps himself to another scone. It's amazing how much space the steak and kidney pie has left. His actions bring Miss Greetham back to the present. 'Oh, I'm sorry, how awfully remiss of me! Would you like another scone, Miss Penfold?'

Flora accepts, and while she's spreading it with cream and jam – rhubarb and quince, from the garden – Miss Greetham watches her. 'May I be so bold as to ask you what you want with a place in the country, Miss Penfold? You look like a town person, if I may say so. You see, I wouldn't like to think of my little cottage going to a week-ender. One of those brash what do they call them – yuppies – with a fast car and a head full of nonsense about the charms of rural life. You haven't got a head full of nonsense, have you, Miss Penfold?'

Lionel Tupper looks sideways at Flora. He has doubts about this himself. A passing ringdove delivers a splash of white on to the bald back of his head.

Flora explains.

'Well, I hope you'll be very happy here.' Miss Greetham, relieved, gets up as another apple hits the earth, and Lionel Tupper mops his head. 'You do have to mind the sky in the country. But that's marvellous news, that is! I'll just go and top up the pot.'

Flora realizes she's not said she wants to buy the cottage. Still, she does, and what's wrong with Miss Greetham saying it for her? She leaves Miss Greetham and Lionel Tupper chatting in the kitchen – completely unmodernized, no Neff hobs and fortunately no inglenooks with concealed lighting, either – while she has a quiet prowl around by herself. The squarish garden, bounded on three sides by old walls, is south-facing; the roughly paved area outside the kitchen must get the sun most of the day. She sees Pablo and Dolly stretched out on it, while they learn to ignore the calls of birds cutting clearly through the sky above them. A couple of partially disintegrated outhouses lean against the wall of the neighbour's house, their irregular creamy stones glowing in the afternoon sun.

The other downstairs rooms are small and rather dark, with Miss Greetham's Victorian furniture crammed into them, but again Flora's imagination has no trouble dressing them into aesthetic, airy places. There's even a pantry with a marble-topped slab in it, and an old mesh screen to keep the flies out.

'Does the place have a name?'

'Only The Cottage, I'm afraid, dear,' says Miss Greetham. 'It's always been called that, as far back as I can remember. You might find an older name if you look through the county archives. The Cottage in Cabbage Lane, that's where we are.'

'And the name of the village?' persists Flora. 'What does it mean?'

'"Tickencote" – "cote" means shelter, "ticken" for kids. Goats, that is. There may have been a Greater Tickencote. There was a Tickencote-by-Water once.'

'Where's the water?'

Lionel Tupper knows the answer to this one. 'There is a small stream, a tributary of the Gwater. But once there was a lake. It dried up around 1850. No one knows why.'

'Magic,' observes Miss Greetham. 'Witches' magic.'

'Probably worldwide climatic change,' rejoins Lionel Tupper. 'I don't believe in magic myself. In any case, they've made up for it now, haven't they, Miss Greetham, with Jacob's Water.'

'Ah yes.' Flora recalls the harvest moon that started all this. 'Is that far from here?'

'Five miles or so.'

'Why is it called Jacob's Water?'

'"All ye who come to drink, rest not your thoughts below, remember Jacob's Well, and think whence living waters flow,"' recites Agatha Greetham unexpectedly. 'It was a sign on the old school of Bisbrooke village. One of the drowned villages, you know. It comes from the

Bible. Genesis 29: "Then Jacob went on his journey, and came into the land of the people of the east."

'"And he looked, and behold a well in the field, and, lo, there were three flocks of sheep lying by it; for out of that well they watered the flocks: and a great stone was upon the well's mouth."'

Unease grips Flora for some reason; she wants to change the subject. 'Are you going to take your piano with you, Miss Greetham?'

'Oh yes. Why, did you want it? Do you play, Miss Penfold?'

'A little. The flute is my instrument.'

'Oh really!' Her eyes shine. 'How nice! To think that there will be music in my little cottage again.'

Flora rereads the leaflet about the house. 'It hasn't got central heating,' she points out, 'and I noticed the roof's got a few slates missing. All of it needs painting, of course. I'll have to have a survey done.'

Miss Greetham looks a little hurt.

'But it *is* what I want. How about £90,000?'

'That's all right, dear,' responds Miss Greetham immediately. 'I told Mr Tupper we were asking far too much. It only cost my grandparents £200. I've got my pension, and you're the right person for it.'

Lionel Tupper, who'd been about to interpose some businesslike remarks about the prices of comparable property in the area, shrugs his shoulders and gives up at this point. At least he's made a sale. Though who would have thought it, when Flora Penfold walked into the office this afternoon! There flits into his usually unimaginative mind a portrait of Flora Penfold thirty years on, beginning to look remarkably like Miss Greetham does now, and having reduced the place to a similar state of comfortable rack and ruin, though in between times no doubt all sorts of renovatory episodes will occur.

Before going back to London, Flora drives back along the Roman road to Little Tickencote. The domed avenue of horse chestnut trees is undercut by beams of slanted light. Just before the village green she parks and walks territorially past The Cottage, which is bathed in magical light – whatever Lionel Tupper says. A couple of chickens peck in the hedges, and a dove calls from Miss Greetham's chimney: coo-*coo*-coo, coo-*coo*-coo. Flora fancies that a crabby hand at the window flicks up a corner of the cream lace curtain, but she's not sure.

4

Starting a New Life

IN THE weeks following the discovery of The Cottage, Flora Penfold ties up the various ends of her old life so that she can start her new one.

The Max Mountjoy Foundation Trustees have their meeting, and relieve Flora of her responsibilities. Angela Findlake comes round to Thornaugh Road to measure up. Flora uses Russell Marcus's solicitor friend rather sooner than expected, as she needs a survey of The Cottage. Henry Gosling is happy to oblige – he has fond, though idiosyncratic, memories of Russell at school, caught committing fellatio with an Indian boy, the son of an MP, by a homosexual history master who turned the proverbial blind eye, or rather realized he could do the same himself.

'Where are you buying, Miss Penfold?'

Flora tells him.

'I know it well. My mother used to drag me there for piano lessons. Miss Greetham was a hopeless teacher – never remembered what she'd done the last time. But she loved music. I didn't. I suggest you use Clayton and Noyes for your survey. Alan Pridmore's the name.'

A week later Alan Pridmore's report on The Cottage emerges from the Islington Arts Centre fax machine:

> Detached house with date plaque on the main building of 1788, but with more recent extensions. Old brick-built chimneys in satisfactory condition for age with lead flashings . . . PVC gutters and downpipes satisfactory as far as we could tell in light rain prevailing at time of inspection . . . Internal joinery very mixed and of various ages . . .

and so forth. There is a complex paragraph about flues and damp penetration, and mention of the old apple tree and its unstable leanings.

'All I want to know', says Flora on the phone to Alan Pridmore, 'is whether the apple tree is dangerous.'

'To sit under, yes,' comments Pridmore, 'indubitably. To the house, only eventually. How old are you, Miss Penfold?'

'Why?'

'I wasn't being impertinent. I was only guessing that the apple tree and the house will continue to coexist peaceably for the rest of your natural lifetime.'

So that's all right.

Less all right are the mood and present disposition of Barnaby Gunn. He comes home every few days, inebriated, and passes out on the sofa. Flora passes him on her way to work in the mornings. She's gone before he stirs. Then one day he turns up in her office. 'Can't you think about my position, Flora?' he appeals, conscious of Judy Nightingale's words in his ear. Judy doesn't want Barney penniless and homeless on her doorstep. She's in two minds about the relationship anyway – Barney's not as well known as she is. 'I shall have to find somewhere to live,' continues Barney, in a pathetic voice. 'I've got £750 in the bank. I won't even have a bed. Or a washing machine. And what about the gramophone records?'

'You can have them,' she says generously.

'Really? Are you sure?'

'I'll miss them,' she says, 'but remember I'll have the sounds of the countryside as my music. Birdsong, and the lambs calling to their mothers in the fields, the wind in the trees . . .'

'I don't believe you're serious, Flora. I suppose I could move into Cal's spare room. For a while, at least.'

'We've got two options, haven't we, Barney? Either we can turn this whole thing over to the solicitors, who'll have a whale of a time at our expense. Yours can represent and misrepresent your position, and mine can do the same for me. Or we can come to some agreement between ourselves which cuts out all of that.'

She's right. But isn't that effectively what he was saying? 'I'll give you £15,000,' says Flora. 'That's 10 per cent of the sale. You've paid half the bills about one-fifth of the time – I worked it out the other night.'

'What about the washing machine?'

'No, Barney. You'll have to get one of your own. The country's a dirty place. Think about the sheep droppings, the horse manure, the fields flooded in the winter, floating cowpats . . .'

Moving day's set for 29 September. A party is held for Flora at the Islington Arts Centre on 15 September. Maureen cries, and Clarissa stands stiffly against the wall sipping lemonade, her ticket for Singapore in her handbag. Stuart gives Flora a large parcel wrapped in William Morris paper. Inside are *The Reader's Digest Encyclopaedia of Garden Plants and Flowers*, an eighteenth-century oak barometer, and a hot-water bottle in a powder-blue nylon cover with the face of a rabbit on the front.

'That was my idea,' admits Clarissa uncertainly. 'I know how cold it can get in the country. That's *one* reason I'm going to Singapore.'

'I'm very grateful to all of you,' says Flora, 'and I'm sure the presents will come in very useful. At least the barometer will tell me when to fill my hot-water bottle, and then I can get into bed and read my *Reader's Digest Encyclopaedia*. And I have enjoyed working with you all, really. By the way, Russell Marcus telephoned me this afternoon; they've appointed my successor. It's a man called Jerome Flagstaff. A Californian. He used to run an advertising agency. Russell described him as a hard-hitting businessman with an interest in modern painting.'

The rush of sadness that comes over her as she closes the door of the Centre for the last time as its Director is for pre-Thatcher England as well as for her relinquished status, power, salary, work and friends. Her sense of fleeing from political and material corruption to a purer, cleaner, nobler world will carry her through the tide of manoeuvres that have to be accomplished before she can sit near – though not under – the unstable leanings of The Cottage's apple tree.

Amongst these manoeuvres is the coaxing of her future part-time career into being. Flora makes phone calls and gets specimens of her work out from her overcrowded drawers. One journalist thinks a man from the *Daily Record* may be interested in Flora doing a weekly slot on rural life. The clientele for the flute lessons will have to wait until she's moved in and can establish local contacts.

'It's not going to be easy,' she complains to Miranda.

'Well, perhaps you should think about some other options, then. What about a restaurant? Or a telecottage?'

'What's a telecottage?'

'A place full of computers and printers and faxes and things. A sort of local resource. I was reading about them in *Homes and Gardens*.'

Flora thinks of Miss Greetham's parlour. 'Not enough room. And not organic enough.'

'Suit yourself.'

Then there's all the organizing of possessions to do. Hers and Barney's to be separated, hers to be packed and moved. While Barney's in Amsterdam filming a scene on a bridge near the Leidseplein which requires him to stand still with Judy Nightingale for three hours while the light changes, Flora packs his clothes and their joint record collection and takes them round to the house of Cal Dreifus, a producer friend of Barney's.

Flora's father, Samuel Penfold, left her some papers which she's never even looked at, but she intends to look at them now, so their removal to the country must be organized as well. The papers were identified in his will: 'Six boxes of papers marked with her name for my daughter, Flora.' The papers sit, waiting, in the office of Professor Julian Peacock, Samuel's literary executor, in Queen's College. Flora hears Samuel's voice in her head, urging her on: 'Go for it, my girl. Rural life's an up-and-coming subject of study again. But of course, you're not a sociologist, are you? Well, not formally, but you see the world with my eyes. My daughter, Flora, my one and only.'

Samuel had done all the things that fathers are renowned for – danced her on his lap, bathed her, and dusted her with talcum powder; read her stories, and admired her homework; told her to respect her mother, marched her round St James's Park, tried her out on the theatre; launched into debate with her about The Meaning of Life, seen her through the religious crises of adolescence, waited for her key in the lock at night. Samuel had, above all, worried about her. 'But have you *talked* to her, Irina? The girl needs guidance, you're her mother, it's your job.'

Irina, reading with a magnifying glass some new find concerning Galia Molokhovina, had been only slightly interested. 'Flora can take care of herself,' she'd admonished firmly, knowing perfectly well that Flora had embarked on the shedding of her virginity some months before with a friend's brother in the gardens of Mecklenburgh Square one hot July night.

Samuel had been the more maternal parent – showing care, affection and sensitivity to the growing Flora. He'd played the same role in brother Jonathan's life, overseeing Flora's own wrath at Jonathan's entry into the Bloomsbury household when she, aged five, was firmly of the opinion that she didn't want a baby anything. Irina had produced the child with as much vagueness as she did everything else. When she went into labour she walked straight to the hospital, quite forgetting her suitcase of front-opening nighties and baby clothes, or to tell anyone at home. The labour ward Sister telephoned Samuel a couple of hours later to tell him a son had been born.

Flora had taken one look at her brother and dropped portions of her doll's tea service on his head. She was surprised by her mother's interest in the baby. They all were. For a time, anyway, it seemed as though this real person had supplanted Galia Molokhovina in her attentions. Samuel was surprised by Flora's jealousy of the baby, and consulted a psychiatric social worker about what he should do about it.

'She's entering the Oedipal phase,' counselled Miss Marchmont, 'and she fears the infant, especially because he's got something she hasn't.'

'What would that be?' inquired Samuel, whose imagination was welded to literal themes.

'A penis.'

Though he couldn't do a lot about this, he did do as Miss Marchmont advised and give Flora extra attention. The phase passed. But Flora's memory of her father remained one of his great solicitude towards her, his quick sensitivity to her wants, needs and moods, his affectionate cherishing of her, all wrapped up in the most unlikely persona of a dark, big-framed, heavy-set man, more Russian-looking than his wife, really, though raised in Jewish Whitechapel, amidst poverty but also riches – the riches of what he would later learn, when he became a sociologist, to call a close-knit extended family.

Samuel Penfold had become a household name in sociological circles by the time he died. His death accentuated this, and several of his books had been reissued, including *The Theory and Practice of Sociology* (a classic undergraduate textbook), *The Social Cohesion of Immigrant Communities, with particular reference to Jewish immigrants in the East End of London* (his doctoral thesis), and *Acting it Out: social roles and postwar European drama*, the book that had taken Samuel's name outside narrowly academic circles and reflected his lifelong passion for the theatre. Two posthumous collections of essays, carefully harvested by Professor Julian Peacock, whom Samuel had trained and then worked with, had also been published. *Marginal Man* traced Samuel's professional concerns with social groups at the margins of mainstream culture – immigrants, actors – to his own childhood in the East End. The other was his annual collection of undergraduate lectures, delivered year after year, in Samuel's amusing and incisive style, to the students of Queen's College.

Samuel himself was a man with charisma. When he spoke, people believed what he said; when he closed his mouth, they wanted him to open it again. When he said goodbye, they wanted to hear hallo instead. He was a man who, simply by being there, increased people's feeling that there was some point in being alive after all. As a father, he gave Flora optimism, ambition and an unerring sense of herself as the centre of her own life. This was sufficiently unusual at the time to make Flora an unusual woman, whatever the specifics of her chosen career. And to Samuel, Flora remained an exception – a woman who was everything, who could do everything, who was as smart and as strong as any man. She was the exception that proved the rule, so that the boat of Samuel's sexism (no more and no less than was rife in academic communities of the period) didn't have to be rocked.

He died in November 1987, driving back from Oxford after giving a lecture on sociology and revolution. This was a subject in which he'd recently become interested through rereading the work of Pitrim Sorokim, a Russian sociologist exiled from his native land in 1922. It was a black wet night. A car had crossed the central reservation on the A40, just south of the Headington roundabout, and driven directly into Samuel's old Renault 16, breaking his neck.

His friend and colleague, Julian Peacock, had sorted the papers into some sort of order. Julian had them put in boxes and printed out a catalogue of them: Correspondence 1950–2, ESJ Editorial Board meetings, Examination Board meetings 1960–70, and so forth. Julian did wonder why Samuel hadn't left any of his papers to his son, Jonathan, but when he met him at the funeral he understood why. At thirty-three Jonathan Penfold was a merchant banker, with clipped nails, short back and sides, an exercise bicycle in his bedroom, and very little interest in anything except making money. Even his wife Janet was a form of investment – a good cook, handy with the ego-stroking. Their son, Oliver, was hyperactive according to Janet, and according to most of the people who met him. Janet sometimes wondered if God had sent her Oliver on purpose so that she'd never have a chance to do anything else.

On 29 September, a Pickfords van lumbers up the A1 with Flora's navy Peugeot following. Pablo and Dolly are quiet on the back seat next to the cleaning equipment. 'Bringing Gas to Your Village' say the black and yellow signs parked outside the villages of Meltshire. The roads are, indeed, up, and giant-sized furrows cut across the fields. It begins to rain as they turn right up the avenue of horse chestnuts leading to the village. Through the open car window, Flora smells the air – the fresh scent of the earth, releasing other scents under the impact of rain. She breathes deeply, thinking with excitement of how everything in her life will be different from now on. She'll be close to the vapours of the earth, in touch with life. There'll be so much to find out about – not only her new neighbours in the village, but the naming of plants and birds and trees, the beginnings and ends of seasons, the way things fit together – the angle of meadowsweet and the flight of the dove, the striding of the farmers across their land, the routines of the hedgecutters cropping growth from the sides of lanes. How wonderful it will all be!

Lionel Tupper's standing in the doorway to The Cottage, looking wet. 'I've got the key,' he says to Flora. 'It was quite a struggle. The poor old dear was very upset; she left you a note.'

Flora finds the note, enclosed in an ivory envelope on the mantelpiece in the sitting-room. 'Dear Miss Penfold,' it reads:

> I hope you will find everything satisfactory. I'm afraid we had a little trouble with the floorboards when we moved the Yamaha. You may need to set the mousetrap in the kitchen (Derby is best). The climbing rose has blackfly. I've asked Eddie (milkman) to leave you a pint of gold top. Dustmen come on Thursdays. Don't forget to check the gas (Ketton's in Oakingham). I do hope you will enjoy living in The Cottage. I have, as you know, many happy memories of it.
>
> Yours sincerely
>
> Agatha Greetham

'What does she mean, a little trouble with the floorboards?'

Lionel Tupper points – in the corner of the room a couple of boards have crumbled into dust about two feet from the side wall. 'Your surveyor's report probably didn't spot it, she'd never have allowed him to move the piano. Well, I'll leave you to it,' he says as the doors of the van swing open and loud humping noises begin.

The rain intensifies. Flora plugs in the kettle and peers at the garden. It doesn't look quite as she remembered it. The brilliant flowers and butterflies of August have declined; the climbing rose with blackfly droops; and there are weeds between the crevices of the stones outside the kitchen door.

After she's handed round the tea, she fetches Pablo and Dolly's baskets from the car. She carries the baskets into the bathroom and releases the catches. Dolly crouches frightened at the back of her basket. Pablo yowls and strolls out, sniffing. 'Here we are, then, my lovelies,' says Flora encouragingly. 'This is our new home. Don't be put off by the' – she glances around at the uniformly peeling green paint and scabby wallpaper – 'decor, we'll soon get rid of that.' She pauses on the 'we', understanding – perhaps for the first time – that there isn't any we, it'll all be up to her from now on.

'Hallo! Hallo! Is anyone there?' A tinny voice wafts through from the front hall. Flora goes out. A woman with yellow hair, wearing a T-shirt and jeans, and a little girl, also with yellow hair, are standing there. 'I hope you don't mind us barging in like this, but we thought we should come and introduce ourselves and see if you needed anything. Annabel Lancing' – the woman holds out her hand – 'and this is Gwendolyn. We live next door – that side.' She waves her other hand, 'Wisteria Cottage. Our garden backs on to the side of yours. Oh dear,' – she breaks off abruptly – 'is that one of ours?'

In the bathroom, Pablo's roaring like a hyena. 'No, it's mine. He's rather cross at being shut up. I'm Flora Penfold, by the way.'

The little girl looks at her from underneath a heavy fringe of hair. 'Have you got any little boys? I hate little boys.'

'Now, Gwenny . . .'

'No, it's just me and the cats.'

'Excuse us.' Two of the removal men edge their way past with the bottom of Flora's bed.

There's a crash from the kitchen, and then something streaks past her. 'I think that's one of your pussies,' says the child Gwendolyn, sucking her thumb.

Flora, in pursuit, is just in time to see Pablo hurl himself over the garden wall. 'Oh my God! Listen, Gwenny . . .'

'Gwendolyn.' She takes her thumb out.

'Gwendolyn. Do you think you could go and find the other one for me and shut it in the bathroom? It's a little black one. I asked the removal men not to open the door.'

'Aren't they awful!' commiserates Annabel Lancing. 'I remember the day we moved in here, they let the rabbit out and Bronwen found it hours later in the fridge.'

Gwendolyn comes back. 'There's a man doing a wee wee in there,' she announces matter-of-factly. 'I can't see the little black one *anywhere*.'

'Sorry, love,' says the man in question, pushing past them in the hall, 'got to answer the calls of nature. No, I haven't seen your other pussy either.'

'I know what!' says Annabel brightly to Flora. 'Why don't you come and have supper with us this evening? I'm sure you haven't had a chance to think about food, have you? And by then you'll need to get away from all this' – she gesticulates as two men carry a packing case into the wrong room – 'I should think.'

Flora accepts, her mind on Pablo discharging his bulk into the open, unknown countryside, and on Dolly, presumably cowering somewhere while the insensitive removal men urinate and crash around her. She finds her eventually in the airing cupboard, which is no longer warm, as of course Miss Greetham turned the immersion heater off before she left, but at least it's dark and relatively quiet. She takes food and milk in there, and some sheets of newspaper, strokes Dolly's frightened head, and shuts the door on her, thinking nature sometimes finds its own solutions which are better than those man or woman dreams up.

By 5.30 the van is empty and the men, inadequately tipped, are complaining about Flora Penfold as they start their ascent back to the A1. 'Probably a lessie,' says one of them. 'Did you notice her tits?' 'No,' says the second, 'she hasn't got any, that's why. Nice bum, though.' He strokes his bristly chin thoughtfully, wondering what it is that turns some women to other women and away from men.

Flora keeps going out into the garden of The Cottage to call Pablo, and every time she does, a nearby dog – she supposes it's the Lancings' – barks at her. The rain's stopped; she takes a kitchen chair and a cup of tea into the garden. But drops of water fall on her from somewhere, and she retreats inside again.

Where it isn't exactly a picture of domestic comfort. Packing cases huddle in the centre of each of the six rooms, and her furniture, stacked at odd angles to the walls, looks back at her, wondering what she's let it in for. She's tired – she got at up six – but won't allow herself to feel dispirited. Come on, Flora, you've got the rest of your life in this place, you don't have to do everything now. It goes against the grain, though. She scrubs the floor in her bedroom and cleans the windows and fireplace, makes up her bed and pins two old sheets over the windows. Then she puts the immersion heater on, and bathes in Miss Greetham's enamelled, black-holed bath – one of the many fixtures that will need to be renewed. Dolly's still in the airing cupboard. She lodges food for Pablo under the apple tree and calls him again, but only the Lancings' dog answers, as usual. It's dark now, a strange thick blackness, unrelieved by the constant flashing lights of the city, or by any moon on this cloud-filled night. Indeed, she has to watch her step quite carefully, walking up the crazy-paved path to the door of Wisteria Cottage. Which is opened by a tall, fresh-faced man in an open-necked white shirt and grey trousers: 'Jasper Lancing – welcome to Little Tickencote!' His handshake is particularly gripping. Flora follows him into a prototypical modern farmhouse kitchen – huge pine table, jars of glowing preserves on the shelves, big dresser with casually though cleverly arranged boldly flowered plates, dog, cat, children, cooking smells, woman in apron mistressminding it all. 'Do have a drink,' invites Jasper. 'I expect you can use one. Sherry, Scotch, G and T? Or there's some wine open. Do you remember when we moved in here, Annabel? Absolute chaos for weeks. Same time of year, wasn't it? Rained cats and dogs.' The dog, an untidy caramel spaniel, barks at this. 'Sorry, Big Ears. Can't say the word D-O-G without him hearing it. Anyway, as I was saying, it was extremely wet and everything that could have gone wrong did. Previous people weren't even out when we got here. Electricity Board cut the power by mistake, Annabel was pregnant with Gwenny, weren't you, Annabel? And the rabbit got out. Bronwen found it later . . .'

'I've already told Miss Penfold that story, Jasper,' reprimands Annabel, turning away from the stove, where something is boiling very fast, creating a lot of steam.

'Put the fan on, darling,' says Jasper, 'we didn't have it fitted for nothing.' Annabel presses a switch, looking at him crossly.

Against the whirring, Flora says, 'Not Miss Penfold, please, Flora. And I'll have a Scotch.'

'Very sensible, so will I. What about you, Annabel?'

The Lancings have three children – Gwendolyn, now asleep, a boy, Alun, aged ten, and a fourteen-year-old girl, Bronwen. Bronwen looks like her father, and is going to be tall, like him. She's already taller than her mother, and evidently looks down on her in other ways too. 'Bronny's doing her GCSEs this year, a year early,' Annabel tells Flora. 'She's going in for science, aren't you, Bronny? She's got a mind like Jasper's, haven't you, Bronny?'

'I've got my own mind, thank you very much,' says Bronwen, accurately. 'And actually, you may as well know I went to the careers office today. I thought I might train for midwifery.'

Her mother laughs nervously. They eat pork and apples, carrots and roast potatoes. 'Do you grow your own vegetables?' asks Flora.

'Good God, no. I get them from the Co-op in Oakingham. Though the apple sauce is windfall apples, we're simply swimming in them here. I do make gallons of that and put it in the freezer, don't I, Jasper?'

'What do you do, Jasper – for a living, I mean?' Flora's eager to learn about her new neighbours, to place them in her new social universe.

'I'm a software engineer. I run a firm in Melton. We relocated from London. Most of the staff live in Melton, in the new estates the other side of the town, but Annabel and I decided living in the real country was better for the kids.'

Tickencote, mutters Flora. Shelter for the kids.

'Well, I'd rather live in Melton. Or Birmingham, come to that,' says Bronwen at the same time. 'That's where most of my friends live. But you didn't consult us, did you?'

Jasper ignores her.

'You were only ten at the time, Bronny,' says Annabel defensively. 'And you thought it was a very good idea to come here. Remember the pony . . .'

'You can stuff the bloody pony,' says Bronwen, scraping her chair on the polished red-quarry tiles and running long-legged out of the kitchen.

'Oh dear,' says Annabel, who seems to say oh dear rather often. 'I'm sorry about Bronny, Miss – Flora. She's at an awkward age, you know.'

'It's just a phase, isn't it?' comments Alun cheerfully, passing his plate to his mother. 'Can I have some more, Mum?'

The conversation's rather disjointed, what with the children's interruptions, and the dog, and Jasper has to make some phone calls, and Flora feels increasingly like creeping next door and sinking into a dark renewing sleep. The Lancings do, of course, ask about her own motives for moving to Little Tickencote, about her own survival plans. She takes the opportunity to ask them if any of their children would like to have flute lessons.

'You'd never get Bronny to stand still for long enough,' observes her father. 'Waste of money, it'd be. Like everything else with her. Now Gwendolyn . . .' He rather likes the picture of yellow-haired Gwenny, in a nice flowered white-collared dress, getting silvery noises out of a slim silver flute.

'Sexist, aren't you, darling?' comments Annabel, surprisingly. 'Think of Alun. He's the obvious choice.' She turns to Alun. 'He's very musical, aren't you, Alun? Do you know, Miss – Flora – when he was only two I caught him singing the "EastEnders" theme perfectly in tune!'

Flora notices that the Lancings don't comment when she talks about the attractions of living in the country, but they do warm to their descriptions of the environment she's chosen, particularly in contrast to the one she's left. 'We lived in King's Cross before,' recalls Annabel. 'It was simply *terrible*. You could never park your car, and I couldn't let the children out of my sight. Bronny was accosted once, she was seven. No, it was the year I – she must have been eight. Eight and a half or thereabouts. She came home in tears and said this man invited me into his car. He had three My Little Ponies on the front seat.' Annabel shudders at the memory. 'And the school, of course, and the *health* service . . .'

'It's a national sickness service, isn't it?' suggests Jasper unoriginally, stretching his long legs out across the marbled carpet in the inglenooked sitting-room. 'Fortunately, the firm pays for private health care now.'

Flora never goes to the doctor, and certainly hasn't thought about how medicine functions in the country.

'There's a very nice NHS one in the village,' offers Annabel, seeming to read her thoughts. 'Dr Simpson. I've heard very good reports of him. He's done wonders for Shirley's bronchitis. Shirley's my "help". Are you going to have a help, Miss – Flora? That's another thing about the country – it's much cheaper. I can get away with £2.50 an hour here; it was £4.50 in King's Cross.'

'It's an odd sort of village,' Jasper goes on – the Lancings appear to take very little notice of what the other one says, conducting conversations in parallel like railway lines. 'When you get to know it, you'll understand what I mean. There are people like us – and you' – he glances doubtfully at Flora, wondering if she really falls into the same category as his own happy family – 'and then there are the long-time residents, people like Miss Greetham, who were born here and probably have never been further than Melton in their life. Can you imagine that?' He muses for a minute on the improbability of limited horizons. 'There are three working farms in the village. The Wates's is the biggest. You can see their silos from our bedroom window. Beyond the meadows. South-west of the church. Then there are the Pringles, but they haven't been here as long. And the Fanshawes. Finding it hard to break even, I think. Of course, Frank Wates is moving over to organic farming now, under the influence of his son, Pete. Daft idea, if you ask me. All farming's organic, and what's the point of ignoring the benefits of modern science and technology? They don't call it *fertilizing* the soil, you know, they call it soil *amendment*.' Jasper's laugh is like the bark of the spaniel, now closeted in the kitchen.

'Problem with Pete Wates is his visions. I'm always wary of people with visions. Speaking of which, the vicar's a nice bloke, very trendy. Uses the new Bible and talks about AIDS. Of course we only go to church when we want something.'

'Jasper, really!'

Flora can see that Annabel's not sure whether she, Flora, might be offended by this. 'It's all right,' she says, 'I don't go in for religion myself.'

But Jasper hasn't heard anyway. 'We had to go when we first came here to get Gwenny christened. Since then we've only been to ask for the vicar's help in stopping this wretched plan of the Neveres to put a dormer window in overlooking our garden.'

'The Neveres?'

'Armand and Petula. Mind you, I don't think they're married and I'm sure as hell those aren't their real names. They live in the house whose front you can see from your upstairs windows. Tiptree Cottage. Named after the jam. Armand says he works in the cinema industry, he's got a flashy card with a Wardour Street address. Petula – well, I don't know what Petula does. You'll see her watering the garden in her stiletto heels. She fell in the asters once, but she was out again the next day, tottering around as usual.'

'I expect Flora's tired,' says Annabel after a while. 'It's a momentous day, isn't it, moving house. Did you find your pussy?'

'One, but not the other.' Flora gets up, thanks the Lancings for their hospitality, and goes back to her garden to see if there's any sign of Pablo. The food is gone, but that doesn't mean anything. There must be dozens of cats in the village. She calls softly in the darkness. The Lancings' dog inside doesn't respond, but some screeching bird answers her from the top of the apple tree. The garden folds its damp dark undergrowth around her. A light wind passes through the uncut grass, shepherding scattered clouds on their way. No Pablo materializes, and there's nothing more Flora can do.

She goes inside, locking the door firmly. The cold tap in the kitchen leaks, like the one in the bathroom at home – not at home, but in the Thornaugh Road flat, now owned by Curtis and Angela Findlake. Flora imagines the folds of Angela Findlake's flesh in the bath, and Angela Findlake's mouth going on about the missing bathroom cabinet (a fixture, but Flora took it with her). A *frisson* of regret passes through her, like the wind through the grass, for the familiarity of her old life – knowing where everything is, knowing what to do each day, the neat pile of faxes in the pottery tray, the waiting faces of her colleagues, Barney on the sofa, Barney in bed, his hand on her thigh at midnight as the orange urban light sneaks through the slats in the blinds. Has she done the right thing? She can't be sure, of course she can't.

Flora gets into bed and lies there wakefully, watching unfamiliar shapes of light and dark on the walls of Miss Greetham's bedroom. Though she imagined it would be silent, it isn't. Something moves in the trees, perhaps only the wind. The Lancings' dog, out in the garden again, barks briefly. And another some distance away. Somebody's gates creak on their hinges. Water pipes expand and contract. The elder by the front door, tall and naked in its winter guise, knocks against the window. But these are the identifiable noises. Below her, in the garden, the undergrowth appears to move. Above her something crashes in the attic. An owl, which Flora had imagined piercing the blackness with its trumpeting call, would not, after all, be so welcome, as now she realizes how ominous sounds can become when one is alone in a house in the country. The house itself settles around her, its frame disturbed by the day's removals and reinstatements. The junctions of walls and floors, untouched for decades, find their alignments altered, and windows parted from familiar clothing adopt a different stance, letting in altered and mysterious shapes of the night. In the kitchen the tap still drips, and what was that Miss Greetham said in her letter about Derby being best? Flora gets up and fetches Dolly from the airing cupboard. Woman and cat shelter in the darkness, consoling each other.

5

Not the Place for Hot Flushes

FLORA'S WOKEN BY the doorbell. 'Good morning. I'm Eddie, your milkman. Miss Greetham asked me to leave you a pint of gold top, but how many pints of what do you want normal-like?' Seeing Flora standing there, ruffled and rosy from sleep in her short cotton nightie with black cat's hairs streaking the white, he realizes he must be too early for her. 'I'm sorry Mrs, did I wake you up?' He peers round her for signs of someone else.

'It's okay. I had to get up. I'd like one pint of skimmed a day, please.'

'Skimmed? Completely skimmed?'

'Yes, please.'

Eddie makes a note in his book. There's too many skimmed in this village; he doesn't approve of it at all.

Flora makes herself a cup of tea, and has some muesli with the remains of yesterday's gold top. There's a yowling in the garden; Dolly, excited, is dancing around in the kitchen making her bell tinkle. Flora opens the door and Pablo ambles in as though he'd been there all the time. She makes a fuss of him, ruffling his fur and burying her face in it in a way that he hates. But the two animals are the living residue of her old life, and have therefore become momentarily more important to her.

She throws on jeans and a jersey and gets going on the kitchen. Miss Greetham's old green cupboards'll have to do for now. She lines them with her own plates and glasses and casseroles and bowls and saucepans and tins and packets. She plugs the fridge in, but there's nothing to put in it. Flora must go shopping. She's brought a basket with her, the sort she envisaged people going shopping with in the country, and she takes that and the front-door key and strides out as confidently as Pablo into the morning.

It's raining still, though today's version is a light drizzle and there's a sizeable patch of blue sky ahead. Flora walks towards the centre of the village, where the Post Office/shop is up a slight hill, perched next to a bank of flowers. 'Post Office Mon 2–4, Tues 2–4, Thurs 2–4, Fri 2–4 and Sat 9.30–12.30,' says a notice on the door. Next to it, a sign says 'SUPPORT YOUR LOCAL POST OFFICE WE ARE UNDER THREAT OF CLOSURE', and underneath it are two more: 'Little Tickencote Council meeting Thursday 4 October, Village Hall 7.30'; and 'Women's Institute Coffee morning, Lady Oliphant, Overton Hall, Great Glaston, Friday 5 October, 10.30. All welcome.' Great Glaston is the next village. Isn't Oliphant the name of Russell Marcus's friend?

Flora goes in. There's no one behind the counter. She looks around; sweets, canned food, and a freezer cabinet full of ice cream; wire trays with a few withered potatoes, apples and onions and tomatoes. Opposite there are some more trays with sliced white bread. There's a rack of birthday cards, and some cardboard boxes full of pens and pencils. From the doorway at the back comes a balding man with a tuft of hair sticking up like a duck. He's singing 'I'm Going to Wash That Man Right Out of My Hair', and doesn't notice Flora at first. Flora can hear a woman's voice on the phone in the back: 'What was that, the DHSS? Well, it's all right for them, they're sitting in government offices on blinking government money, isn't they?'

'Excuse me,' says Flora.

'Oh, sorry, love, thought I was on me own.'

'Have you got any . . . well . . . food?' inquires Flora.

'Only what you see before you.'

'Oh.'

'You new?' He's giving her his full attention now.

'I moved in yesterday to The Cottage on Cabbage Lane. Miss Greetham used to live there.'

'Ah yes.' He bends forward, puts his hands on the counter. 'Well, for food most folks go to Melton or Oakingham. If it's an emergency we can usually help you out. Joan keeps a good kitchen. We supply aspirin, branded, Elastoplast, cigarettes, women's necessaries – excuse me mentioning the item, but we do live in advanced times, don't we – Lucozade, baked beans, got some sausages out the back I think, TV and dog licences – not car, they won't let us do those – stamps, National Savings Certificates, family allowances and old age pensions, as they used to be called in the good old days. Childless, are you?' He narrows his eyes at her. 'And not exactly an OAP either?' He laughs, not unkindly.

'Where's the nearest place I can buy fresh fruit and vegetables?' Flora asks.

He scratches his head. 'Tesco's, I should think. Or the Co-op. Oh, there is a farm shop Tuesday and Thursday in Great Glaston. By Overton Hall.'

'Well, I'll take some bread and some butter and those – those tomatoes.'

'You can have those half-price,' he says expansively. 'They've been there since last Tuesday. My name's Jack, by the way. Been here twenty-five years.' He looks hard at her.

'I'm Flora Penfold.'

'As in the margarine?'

'Yes.'

'And as in pinfold, you could say.'

'I beg your pardon?'

'Pinfold. An enclosure for animals. Old English word.'

'Is it?'

'It is indeed. Unfortunate, is it, having a name people comment on?'

Flora says nothing. He can see she's not amused. He wouldn't like to cross her, that one.

'And I'll have ten first-class stamps, Jack, please.'

'Not until two o'clock, you won't,' says Jack, indicating the sign on the door. 'Come back then, you can have as many as you like.'

'Newspapers?' She's beginning to get the hang of things now.

'Not any more. You can try Rawles in Great Glaston. If it's a big enough order they'll deliver.'

'Eggs?'

'Ah, there I can help. Pat Titmarsh, second house on the right past the church.'

After Flora's put her purchases in her basket, Jack Roebuck goes into the back room and tells his wife, Joan, about the newcomer. 'Well, at least she's not a weekender,' says Joan confidently, 'or she wouldn't be here on a Tuesday. Miss, did you say?'

'No wedding ring.' Jack prides himself on his powers of observation. When Annabel comes in with Gwendolyn for a packet of Smarties after lunch, he says, 'Nice new neighbour you've got there, Mrs Lancing. Permanent is she? Single woman? Got her own means?'

'Miss Penfold's an artist,' enunciates Annabel clearly. It's much better, in her view, for the locals to be given small definite pieces of information than to be allowed to speculate. Jack will do his damnedest to elaborate on what she's just told him, anyway. By tea time Flora will be a ballet dancer, or a circus artiste. She'll probably also be an escapee from a battering husband, or a semi-recovered alcoholic.

'That'll be 10p. Your Bronwen been giving you trouble lately?'

'Why?'

Jack has seen Bronwen Lancing out late recently, doing a little more than just taking the night air. 'Just wondered. Can I interest you in some stamps, Mrs Lancing? The Post Office counter's open now.'

Pete Wates, from the farm, comes in next for some cigarettes. 'Yes, I've seen the navy Peugeot,' says Pete. 'You need something new to gossip about, don't you, Jack?'

'You know me, Pete, always take a keen interest in village affairs.' Jack looks after Pete thoughtfully as he climbs into his old Austin and chugs off down the lane. Peter Wates is a bit of an oddball. Farms with his dad, Frank, but lives in a tied cottage across the field from the farmhouse, and has odd ideas about organic husbandry and homeopathic veterinary care. Goes away for long periods from time to time. Gregarious, but not noted for the ladies. Maybe he and Flora Penfold . . .

'I think a spot of wallpaper-stripping is called for,' says Flora to the cats back in The Cottage. 'Something physical and therapeutic. And obviously I shall have to find Tesco's.' This time she sets off in the car for supplies.

And so Flora settles into her new life. She finds a way of shopping, a way of eating, a way of wallpaper-stripping. She buys a spade and digs up a corner of the garden, preparatory to vegetable-growing, purchasing a book about the same from Woolworth's in Melton. And she begins to find a way of being alone. On the afternoon of the sixth day (feeling a bit like the Book of Genesis herself), she returns to the Post Office at the right time to buy some stamps from Jack, and captures, to boot, two empty glass sweet jars for thirty pence each. The weather's brightened recently, the sun gleams hard from behind a thin screen of silver-white clouds. Tall grasses left by the sheep pop up here and there, dried sheep droppings rolling amongst them. As Flora crosses Sheepdyke Field with the two glass jars under her arms, three malted brown horses stand elegantly in a farmyard, and the church clock chimes four. A woman comes out of the gate dividing the field from Cabbage Lane as Flora approaches it – a stout grey-haired woman with glasses on a chain round her neck, wearing a scarlet cloak, which billows out at the sides, like bloody bats' wings. She appears to be deep in conversation with herself – so much so that she and Flora practically collide just in front of the gate.

'Oh, I'm so sorry!' The woman peers at Flora. 'Ah – yes. I meant to come and see you, didn't I? How rude of me. I'm Olga. Olga Tuchensky-Kahn, Number 8 Church Lane. I took down the name. Woodbine Cottage, I didn't like it. You're Flora Penfold, aren't you? Jack Roebuck told me about you. I'm very pleased to meet you.' She holds out her hand, but both Flora's hands are occupied with the glass jars. 'Well, hallo anyway. Let me help you through the gate. Perhaps you'd care to come and have a glass of sherry with me later? Say six? I should be finished by then.'

Olga Kahn's house actually has roses round the door. 'Deep Secret,' she says, when she comes to answer it, and sees Flora looking at them. 'Hybrid musk. They were here when I came, otherwise I would have put in something like Peaudouce or Tequila Suns, much hardier and more resilient to disease. Are you a gardener, Miss Penfold?'

'No, but I'd like to be.'

'Good, good.' Olga Kahn claps her hands together like a schoolgirl. 'We can have fun teaching you, then, can't we?' She uncorks a bottle of Bristol Cream sherry, and goes into the kitchen muttering, 'Peanuts, I thought I saw a packet the other day. But no,' she reappears, 'either they've gone or I've forgotten what I'm looking for.' She smiles knowledgeably at Flora, displaying teeth capped with bright gold crowns.

Olga Kahn pours two glasses of sherry, and invites Flora to sit down on one of the two paisley-decked armchairs by a fireplace in which a gentle log fire is burning. The room is extremely booklined. A leather desk in the corner groans under a pile of papers. A Corona typewriter stands at the ready. Seeing this, Flora asks: 'Are you a writer, then, Mrs Kahn?'

'Good Lord, no!' Olga Kahn knocks back her sherry in one, and laughs a surprisingly throaty laugh. 'I have the most tremendous difficulty with words. Concepts are my forte. Mental structures, not verbal ones. No, I'm not a writer, Miss Penfold, I'm a psychoanalyst.' The log fire splutters and kicks a flurry of lighted splinters into the room. 'That surprised you, didn't it?'

'Well, yes,' admits Flora.

'You're thinking: what's a shrink doing holed up in Meltshire with a Corona typewriter?'

'Something like that.'

'I've had an interesting life, I'll tell you about it some day. I trained with Karen Horney, you know. I take it you've heard of Karen Horney, Miss Penfold?'

Flora shakes her head.

'No? It's remarkable how few people have. Karen Horney developed a most modern view of feminine psychology before the fables of Freud took hold. Her 1924 paper postulating the castration complex in girls as a defensive reaction predated Freud's own arguments in that direction. But of course Karen Horney believed in the vagina, and Freud didn't. Freud thought the penis was everything. Very unimaginative, Freud was, especially for one so hooked on the imagination. He was very rude about Horney. She was a most fascinating woman, and a very skilful teacher. After sitting at her feet, I practised for twenty years, in Hampstead. Being half-German helped – it gave me what I believe they call these days street cred. There's a lot of work in Hampstead, as you may know. Some of it's genuine distress, but I have to say I couldn't drum up a lot of sympathy with some of it. Nervous intellectuals and bored housewives. A good dose of manual labour would do wonders for the first, and the second would benefit from the tonic of a job. I expect that sounds quite outrageous to you, doesn't it?' She laughs again. Flora sees her as a youthful iconoclast upsetting all the psychoanalytic patriarchs with her naughty, sensible ideas.

Olga Kahn fetches the Bristol Cream and pours herself another glass and then, as an afterthought, Flora too. 'Must get myself some peanuts,' she mutters again, 'this stuff's very acid on the stomach.'

She knocks the second glass back with the same speed as she disposed of the first. 'I was married to a scientist, when I lived in Hampstead. Raphael was obsessed with genetics – he did some brilliant work on the factors promoting gene translation responsible for making haemoglobin. He wanted to cure blood disorders. He didn't, of course, it was all much too difficult. He died a disappointed man. I wasn't too bereft, he was quite difficult to live with.' Olga Kahn leans nearer the fire, parting her legs to let the warmth up, and revealing the tops of thick brown stockings. 'Speaking of blood, the village could do with some of the new sort. How old did you say you are?'

'I didn't, but I'm thirty-eight.'

'Er-hum. Not menopausal yet, good. This isn't the place for hot flushes. You're better off in London with those. Oh, it's not a bad place, once you understand its little ways, not to mention its mental structures. I chose it because I wanted to retire somewhere where I wouldn't keep meeting my ex-patients. We call them patients, you know,' she reflects, nursing a hairy mole on her chin, 'but I've never really thought that was right. Some of them are, and the rest we turn *into* patients, but it's not the right mind set really. Are you mentally healthy, Miss Penfold?'

'How would I know?'

'Of course, Karen Horney distinguished between normal neurosis and the other sort. "I call normal that which is usual in a given culture," she said. Strange sentiment, isn't it? But correct. In true neuroses the need for love is abnormal. Most women come in that category at some stage in their lives. "The tyranny of the should," she called it. Love as the ticket to paradise. Love as morbid feminine dependency. Are you running from love, Miss Penfold? As well as from the city? You've got two themes there, haven't you? The paradise of love and the paradise of Eden. Man and woman and nature. Union, that's what it's all about. But with what? And for what? But I'm droning on, aren't I? You've no idea how much of a relief it is to be able to talk freely after having to be quiet for fifty minutes at a time for all those years!' She grins naughtily at Flora, showing her teeth. 'You don't have to answer my question, my dear. I've forgotten what it was, anyway.'

'You asked me about my mental health, and I said I don't know. I've never felt unhealthy. My father, who was a sociologist, was rather rude about psychoanalysis, Mrs Kahn. He always used to say Shakespeare understood more about the human condition than anyone who called themselves a psychoanalyst.'

'Er-hum,' says Olga Kahn again. 'But could Shakespeare cure? Did he have the capacity to transfer that understanding in a healing way? Were you close to your father, Miss Penfold? Don't answer if you don't want to.' She sounds like Magnus Magnusson on 'Mastermind'. 'But since we're going to be neighbours for what I imagine might be a sizeable chunk of time, until either I peg out or you move on, you might as well tell me about yourself. I'm not overinterested in the superficial stuff – dates of schools, degrees, property owned – but I should like to place you *relationally*, if you understand my meaning. Do you smoke?'

'Sometimes.'

'Well, this can be one of them. Mine's a pipe, and no, I'm not emulating Freud, I started later, after Raphael died, he was a frightfully fastidious man. I use a different tobacco in any case.' Mrs Kahn offers Flora a packet of Kent. She then goes through an elaborate routine, transferring a cloud of yellow stuff from a dingy piece of kitchen paper to the bowl of a mahogany-coloured pipe. Bits of yellow float around, joining what Flora now recognizes as others embedded in the carpet. Eventually Mrs Kahn is safely embarked on her puffing.

In the growingly caustic atmosphere, with its now three sources of smoke – one fire and two women – Flora tries to talk about herself relationally for Olga Kahn's benefit – or her own.

'Were we close? Yes, I suppose so. He made me feel I was the most important person in the world. He was a very large man, but with a most extraordinary gentleness.' Now Flora pauses, feeling her eyes begin to water – is it the loss of her father's love, or is it the smoke? Other figures dart in and out of the smoke in the room and in Flora's head: Barnaby Gunn, the actor, acting up in N19, and in the country garden where Flora first walked with him in the moonlight; Lars in Denmark, golden, scheming, and more knowledgeable about Flora's body than she herself, but by no means an expert in mental structures; Bruce, the young man in Mecklenburgh Square Gardens, with red hair and a body the texture and colour of candyfloss; the man behind the pillar in Lincoln Cathedral, with the raincoat Mrs Kahn's batwinged cloak had reminded her of earlier today. Under the influence of the sherry and the oxygen-deprived air, all these figures appear momentarily to coalesce, acquiring the same elemental form. She shakes her head. 'Perhaps we could open a window a little, Mrs Kahn?' she ventures. 'The atmosphere's getting a bit thick, don't you think?'

Olga Kahn gets up, scattering more yellow filaments. She pushes one of the small front windows into an opening position. 'Well, perhaps this isn't the time to go into all this in depth, but do tell me, Miss Penfold, about your mother. I'm most interested in mothers. Now, in Karen Horney's case . . . She had three daughters, you know. But you mustn't let me interrupt myself, it's a most appalling habit. We weren't talking about Karen Horney's mother, a most beautiful Dutch woman, married a much older man, a Norwegian sea captain, away a lot, oh Lord, there I go again!'

'I am fond of my mother,' states Flora, going on to explain how Irina's lifelong obsession with Galia Molokhovina had made her less than convincingly maternal at least some of the time.

'Er-hum. So your mother was Russian, and you're half-something else too?'

'I am,' admits Flora. 'Though I don't particularly feel it.'

'It affects you, though; we're all émigrés of The Other. You'll feel it more as you grow older, and forgive your mother, and understand that rejection is only another form of identification. You felt your mother lived in a world of her own, yes? With this woman from her own cultural past she was writing about?'

'I suppose so.'

'Er-hum. Obsessions are incompatible with having children. That's what Raphael was like. And Karen Horney. Though her daughters, being sensible, well-trained young women, recovered. But the transposition of gender, of course, alters the entire psychodynamic effect.'

Flora is saved the necessity of commenting on this, as the opened window, creating a cross-draught, suddenly has the opposite effect to the desired one, and enormous clouds of smoke from the fireplace are drawn into, instead of out of, the room. Both women cough convulsively. Olga Kahn gets up to close the window, pointing to a black-and-white-framed photograph on her wall on the way back. 'Gustav Mahler, my other obsession; you might as well know about all my little foibles! In a patriarchal culture, the study of male genius provides a short cut to women's understanding. Of themselves, that is. I listen most often these days to his *Das Lied von der Erde*, and to his *Kindertotenlieder*, incorrectly described in the *Penguin Music Masters* series as "Dirges for Children". Do you know his music, Miss Penfold?'

Flora shakes her head. 'Not well.'

'Mahler was a great nature-lover. I take it you have come to Little Tickencote for the nature? For the rural idyll? For the holistic sense of union between humankind and planet earth, carpeted in flowers and all forms of untamed life? Yes, I thought so. I hope – I do so hope – you won't be disappointed.' She pauses, looking into the red heart of the dying fire, drawing in upon itself. 'Mahler was psychoanalysed by Freud, you know. Well, no, you probably don't, and you probably don't want to, either. Mahler's wife was going to leave him. Par for the course, especially since he put the lid on her musical career when he married her. Can you imagine that?' Olga Kahn's tone of voice reminds Flora of Jasper Lancing's incredulity at the restrained geographical wanderings of some Meltshirians. 'So he sought out Freud. Cancelled his first two or three appointments, but then they met in the Dutch town of Leiden. I've been there – it's a most bland place, not at all the kind of atmosphere you'd imagine for such a momentous encounter. It didn't do Mahler any good, of course. Not musically speaking. But the habit he wanted to stop, of the interruption of serious passages of music by quirky jokes and references . . . am I boring you, Miss Penfold?'

Again Flora shakes her head. 'No, I'm just tired.'

'Er-hum. We'll talk again when you're more rested. Perhaps. I'll open the window again now.'

'That reminds me,' Flora takes the opportunity to say, as Olga Kahn slides open the window on to Church Lane, 'I need a builder. Can you give me the name of one? Somebody local and not too dear.'

'I'm surprised you haven't asked the Lancings. You had dinner with them on your first night here, didn't you? Oh, I know, because Jack-at-the-Post-Office told me; he tells everyone everything. Jasper Lancing's bound to try and take you under his wing, if he hasn't yet. Well, I used Percy Grisewood when I came here. Lives up the hill, towards Great Glaston. Slow but solid. Watch out for his plumber, though – I don't mean his plumbing, that's all right. But he has a way of conducting himself – well, you'll see what I mean.'

Olga Kahn gives Flora Percy Grisewood's telephone number and then, shifted by the smoke problem from historical psychological matters to a consideration of present-day ones, runs through some of the other characters Flora will encounter in the village. 'Brian Redfern – opposite the duck pond. Rather smart house with a yellow door and nasty neo-Georgian touches. Brian's some sort of property developer. A widower, pretends to be very sorry for himself. Wife died of breast cancer – both breasts at the same time. And the Crowhursts – she lives one end of the village, he lives the other. They seem ordinary enough to me. Er-hum. By the way, I say that a lot, as we shrinks are taught to. It suggests we're listening, though we're only hearing what we want to. You'll get used to it in time. Think of it as a kind of nervous tic. Oh, and you're bound to be called on by the vicar – he needs watching. I'll talk to you about religion another time. The Oliphants of Overton Hall at Great Glaston, they're our nearest landed aristocracy. They've got a remarkably fat daughter, Cornelia. Marrying a guardsman sometime soon, I think. Then there's Abraham Varley, he lives in the cottage up on the hill by the Wates's silos. Always looks the other way when you meet him. Abraham minds the fish in Jacob's Water. You know about Jacob's Water, do you? The fish were a kind of sop for the drowning of his farm. Abraham'll never get over it – if you go down there around sunset most evenings, you'll see him, just staring into the water. And you know you asked me if I was a writer? Well, we do have one of those. Jane Rivers, last house in the village going towards Great Glaston. Very overgrown garden – lots of fruit bushes, but she never prunes them. Every time I see her I tell her she ought to. Of course it's probably not her real name, but it'll do, like most of ours! Jane writes classy detective stories. They remind me a bit of Patricia Highsmith. You know, Ripley. Well, Jane Rivers's hero is called Georgia Kelly. I've some of her books; perhaps you'd like to borrow one? The latest has a most intriguing title: *Problems in Paradise*.'

6

Omens

A FEW DAYS after the smoky evening with Olga Kahn, Flora opens the back door to let the cats out and finds a dead bird waiting for her. Pablo and Dolly crowd round it, and Pablo puts out a mauling paw. She shuts them both in the kitchen. Something draws her to look at the dead bird more closely: it's small with brown plumage, full-chested – Flora thinks incongruously of Cornelia Oliphant and her guardsman. The bird is lying on its side, apparently undamaged, with its eyes shut, and one stick-like leg arranged stiffly above the other. It's very windy this morning – it could have been the wind that was responsible for the bird's death. The pale grey-brown down on the bird's chest moves gently in the air as Flora watches. Its outline on the yellowish paving stone is traced by a border of dampness; there are two bird shapes on the stone, one larger than the other; one material, soon to be attacked by the ravages of fleshly decay – maggots and the like – the other nothing more than the pattern of water, caused by the bird's soaked feathers transferring their liquid to the ground. In her ignorance, Flora wonders what kind of bird it is. She goes inside to fetch her Collins Gem *Guide to British Birds*, and is standing there reading it when the Lancings' middle child, Alun, bounces up the garden path.

'*Anthus pratensis*,' he says, bending down to examine the corpse. 'It's a meadow pipit. Very common in Britain. Can you see its long hind claws, Miss Penfold? This one's not very old, I'd guess. Struck down in its prime, you could say.'

'How come you know so much about birds, Alun?'

'I like them,' he says simply. 'I'll show you my Desmond Morris video, if you like. It's called "The Winged World". You know that noise the hummingbird makes, it does that by flapping its wings more than four thousand times a minute! Or I could take you to the fens over by Cedarton, where you can hear a bittern. It's rare, you know.

You can't see them but you can hear them sometimes, if you're ever so still. Oh, I nearly forgot, Mum sent me to say your cat's been in our house. He likes cheese, doesn't he? Gouda, with caraway. Dad brought some back from his last trip. She thought you'd lost him.'

'I've never given him cheese. He has come back though, thank you, Alun.'

She's going to have to move the dead bird, or Pablo'll have its innards all over the garden. But what with? She's got no spade, and she can't go out – the builder, Percy Grisewood, is due in a few minutes.

He's forty minutes late, a small round man in clean blue overalls with a cap in his hand. 'I've got a list of things I want done,' says Flora, 'beginning with repairing the floorboards underneath Miss Greetham's Yamaha.'

Percy nods.

'The big job is moving the bathroom upstairs.' The 'facilities', as Lionel Tupper had called them.

'That's structural, that is,' says Percy Grisewood, pinging the braces of his overalls. 'That means redoing your entire system. That means a tank in the loft. That means . . .'

'Well, I'd like a quote for that, please, Mr Grisewood. And then perhaps we could go round the house and I'll show you the other things?'

All the time Percy Grisewood mutters and demurs, and thinks of objections. But this is only his style, as at the end he's saying '£12,000 or thereabouts. I can't start till Tuesday.'

'That's fine.' They step outside into the back garden so that Percy can appraise the state of the external pipes and gutters. He stares at the dead bird. 'That's not very nice, is it, Miss Penfold? Someone put it there for a joke, did they? Someone trying to tell you something?'

'Oh no, I don't think so. Why should they?' The thought hadn't occurred to Flora until Percy mentioned it.

'Better move that,' he says, still staring.

'I suppose so.'

Percy looks at Flora with his tiny deep-set brown eyes, and she realizes this is the first time he's actually looked at her face. 'I'll do it for you, Miss Penfold,' he says carefully, 'seeing as I'm going to be working for you. If you like, that is.'

Percy Grisewood gets his spade from the van and digs a hole in Flora Penfold's garden between two peonies and carries the little meadow pipit caught short by death to its last resting place. Flora sees him from the kitchen, where she's making a cup of coffee. When's he's loaded the earth on top of the little brown body, Percy stands upright for a minute, tilting his cap to the back of his head and keeping his hands still on the spade. At the same moment the wind drops; the trees don't rustle, and the calls of other birds cease. Flora shivers.

When he goes home, Percy Grisewood will tell his wife about this young woman called Flora, a ballet dancer, Jack says, who's moved into Agatha Greetham's cottage, and doesn't know how to bury anything.

'Is she pretty, then, Percy?' Olive works in a charity shop in Melton, and is often to be found in the evening knitting things for it; this evening it's a Union Jack tea cosy. Olive's a cautious, quiet woman, somewhat frightened of the world after being knocked unconscious by an Alsatian at the age of six. The world enters Olive's imagination through her charity shop customers and Percy's stories. It's amazing how much builders learn about their customers – almost as much as psychoanalysts do about their patients.

'Yes and no,' says Percy, after considering Olive's question for a while.

'Oh, come on, Percy!'

'She's not like one of them magazine ladies.' He points at the pile of women's magazines Olive uses as a resource for knitting patterns.

'She doesn't wear make-up, you mean?'

'I do. She's got a little face, like a Conference pear. Pale skin, blue eyes. Nice girl, in fact,' he says reflectively, remembering the one time so far he's looked at her face. 'Or woman. Maybe.'

'And what colour hair?' Olive needs the details. Her needles click rapidly.

'Brown. Light brown. Short, hadn't been combed recently, I'd say.'

'What about her figure?'

'Nice figure.' He doesn't need to say more.

'Oh Percy, you are a one!'

In the extremely slow but otherwise capable hands of Percy Grisewood, The Cottage begins to be remoulded, and in Flora Penfold's rather than Agatha Greetham's image. Removal of the facilities from the ground floor to the first will mean losing one of the bedrooms, but it'll provide a laundry room downstairs. Percy will also carve a space out of the attic for her workroom. 'I want floor-to-ceiling windows,' Flora demanded at first, until Percy reminded her that Little Tickencote is a conservation area, and Flora remembered the saga of the Neveres' attempts to get planning permission for their dormer window.

One evening she's up in the attic after Percy and his men have left. She has to tread carefully, as many of the beams need replacing before new boards can be put down. A hole is where the curtailed window will be – not floor-to-ceiling, but sufficient to allow a good view of the countryside: the edge of Little Tickencote falling to the meadows, where the cows graze, and up again to the hill and beyond. It's a beautiful late-October evening. Mild, but now rapidly chilling, as the sun has set on a cloudless sky. Through the plastic draping the hole, chiffon scarves of pink trail the trees on the horizon, and on the trees both near and far the leaves are beginning to turn; the pink light picks out the reds and yellows of autumn colours. Flora can see through the hole that will be the window into the Neveres' garden. They're both there – he's just driven home in his Alfa Romeo, parking it smartly in front of the cedar-fronted double garage. She's in the garden spraying something. He walks over to her in his suit, his pink tie matching the sunset.

Flora can see the high heels even from here. What was it Jack-at-the-Post-Office had said about her? 'She's his Pet all right, but before that she was somebody else's. It was all over the papers four or five years ago. One of them lascivious Tory MPs' – Jack's choice of words often surprises – 'left his wife for a lady of vice, there was a nasty divorce, he was chucked out of the Cabinet. Don't you remember, Miss Penfold? Morrison was the name. Never hear about him these days. Drowned in the ignominy of it all. You can take it from me, Mrs Petula Nevere's got hidden talents.'

Flora's beginning to get a queer feeling about the village. There are the throwaway remarks people make – Olga Kahn's comment about Little Tickencote not being a good spot for menopausal women, Jasper Lancing's 'It's an odd sort of village'. True to Olga Kahn's prediction, Jasper has knocked on her door and offered himself as a repository of knowledge about DIY. 'These old places can be full of snags, don't want you to think you've always got to get the professionals in. Remember you can call on me any time.' He peered into the kitchen, but she felt reluctant to ask him in. The other day the vicar, Trevor Tilley, cycled down the lane. He's an albino, with a head as polished as the brass pulpit holding the Holy Bible in All Saints' Church, and little eyes as pink as the berries on the evergreen pernettya in the corner of Miss Greetham's garden.

Flora still thinks of the garden as belonging to someone else, though she's beginning to make it hers. There are a few rows of carrots in now, and some perpetual spinach, though Olga Kahn says she doubts it'll take root before winter. The vicar showed an interest in the garden, too. 'God lives in people's gardens, you know, Miss Penfold,' he observed, looking quietly around him. She felt obliged to make him a cup of coffee. 'Yes, I remember Miss Greetham's apple tree well, Miss Penfold – or rather, my head does.'

When she gave him his Nescafé, she said, 'You should know that I don't believe in God, Vicar.' She paused slightly before the word 'Vicar'.

'Of course you do, Miss Penfold,' replied Trevor Tilley jovially. 'You believe in the wonders of nature, don't you? Well, that's only God in disguise.' And then he added his remark about the Lord loitering in people's vegetable gardens. 'You've some thriving St John's wort, I see.' He pointed to an untidy bush. 'It's not common round here. That's a good Garden of Eden plant, that is. There's a play about the Garden of Eden MADS – the Meltshire Amateur Dramatic Society, you know – did a few years ago – helped to raise some money for the church roof – in which the serpent lies on a St John's wort. You'd better be careful, Miss Penfold!'

Inspired by the vicar's cycling – though not by his other habits – Flora buys herself a bicycle. She's not been on one for years. Cautiously at first, then more confidently, she launches herself on the various roads out of the village. It's an amazingly exhilarating feeling, spinning down hills with the wind in her hair, though less so in first gear hauling herself up them. But the countryside is different from the vantage point of a bicycle. You can smell it, for a start. Your nose picks up the changing scents of different fields and hedgerows – the briar rose, the overgrown mint, cidery, decaying apples like the ones that litter The Cottage's garden. To feel the air on one's skin is a different aspect, also. And the sense of cycling along, one's mind in harmony with the regular click of the wheels – well, there is a sense of – dare she call it – organic wholeness with Planet Earth. Mediated by man's manufacturing habits, naturally. But one *is* part of the earth as one cycles along, even at this time of year, when the cold sharpens one's nose to a dripping red and one's gloved hands to a quick numbness. Flora experiences the motion of cycling as liberation in the same way, she imagines, as Victorian women did, fighting for their right to ride on wheels down country lanes as much as to vote. What is freedom, after all?

And what is the freedom of the city and citizenship compared to these lush, scantily peopled pastures?

Flora wonders if she's spending too much time on her own, and invites Miranda to stay. She arrives on a fine Saturday morning with a bag of goodies. 'Marinated bean curd, I'm sure you can't get that here, Sarah Lee fudge brownies, I expect you can, but I need to make sure of my supply. Camomile soap with jojoba oil to get rid of the smell of cowpats, and *Time Out* so you can see what you're missing. Oh, and I picked this up in a second-hand bookshop.' She hands Flora a paperback with a cartoon of a tractor and some daisies on the front. '*Green and Pleasant Land* question mark, by one Howard Newby. I thought it might dissuade you from the worst of your rural fancies. How are you, Flora? You *look* well.'

She does. Flora's face is either tanned or unwashed. Her eyes sparkle and she's let her hair grow; it's behaving like a hedgerow of unmown mixed grasses. She's tied it up with an old Indian scarf, and is wearing an equally old pink grandad T-shirt under denim dungarees.

Miranda prowls round the house. In the third bedroom, the new bath and lavatory sit waiting, dressed in cardboard. The speed with which Percy had these delivered may have lulled Flora into a false sense of timing regarding the completion of the building work; Percy got them cheap from a builder who'd gone bust, and had to move them quickly. In Flora's bedroom, Miranda plonks herself on the bed, whence she has the aforementioned unparalleled view of church and rolling, sunblessed hills. 'Hm,' she says. Flora leads her upstairs to the converting attic with its expansive window-hole, through which the sun is now streaming on to the boards and the spaces between the boards waiting to be filled.

'Hm,' says Miranda again.

Flora shows Miranda the Picasso print of a woman with green eyelashes and a distorted, overnostriled face she intends to hang on the attic wall. 'Dreadful,' Miranda judges. 'I'll give you one of mine, if you like. Something more positive and less misogynist that will suit the view. A room with a view, eh?' She gets up and walks round, smiling to herself.

They eat lunch at the table Flora's put in the garden in the sheltered spot outside the kitchen door. 'I hope you made the cheese yourself,' says Miranda, 'and the chutney. What about the bread?'

As they sit there, chatting about their friends in London, and the cosmopolitan world of arts and artists from which Flora has removed herself, the Saturday noises of Little Tickencote float round them: the Neveres' lawnmower (a vehicle type driven by Armand in the manner of a sports car); the Lancings' dog, and their children – Gwenny crying, Alun shouting, Bronwen's 'Iron Maiden' seeping through the holes between the bricks; a tractor in a field, sheep, of course, and birds in Owlston Wood; the distant ring of Dr Simpson's outdoor phone hooked under the clematis, the jangle of an ice-cream van, and then an aeroplane from the army base over the other side of Jacob's Water. 'God, Flora, what a racket! Is it always like this?'

The church clock chimes.

'I suppose that's on a timer. What are we going to do with the rest of the day?'

'There's a bring-and-buy sale in the village hall.'

'Thrilling!'

'Or we could go for a bicycle ride round Jacob's Water.'

'Too energetic. What about a stately home?'

'You mean this isn't?'

They go to the bring-and-buy sale because Flora wants to take every opportunity to immerse herself in village life. Annabel Lancing is there, just inside the door, with a chutney stall. Green apple, green tomato, plain onion, rhubarb, and elderberry. 'I'll have some of the elderberry, please,' says Flora.

Miranda peers negatively at it. 'I'll teach you how to make this, if you like,' offers Annabel. 'You've got an elder in your front garden. These came from all over the place, but Alun did strip the Neveres' tree for me one day when they were out.'

'Crime in Meltshire,' mutters Miranda behind her. Flora introduces them. 'Ah,' says Annabel, 'talking of crime, there's someone you haven't met yet – Jane Rivers. She's over there. Jane!'

A stooped bespectacled figure, dressed entirely in black, comes towards them. Her hair's black, too. Jane Rivers frowns as she listens to Annabel Lancing's introduction, as though she's pulping the maximum meaning from whatever's being said. 'I'm going to read your *Problems in Paradise*,' Flora tells her. 'Mrs Kahn lent me her copy. Is the village Little Tickencote? I suppose everyone asks you that.'

'Yes, everyone does.' There is a silence. Jane clearly doesn't intend to say any more than that. 'I see you bought some elderberry chutney. A very wise choice. I always think the black berries look so surprising on the end of those red stalks, don't you? You must come and see my garden sometime, I've got one border that's completely black.'

'Weird woman,' comments Miranda, when Jane has passed on to the organic wine stall.

'No, interesting.' Flora can see Olga Kahn sorting through a huge pile of second-hand clothes. She goes over and says hallo. 'Buy all my clothes at these things,' heaves Olga Kahn. 'Saves a lot of trouble driving to places.' She smells strongly of tobacco. 'Auctions are good, too. For plates and fireguards and so forth. I got a photocopier once for £1. I thought it was too good to be true, and it was. Have you been to an auction yet, Miss Penfold? I suppose I'd better start calling you Flora. I'm Olga,' she announces, stretching an odoriferous hand out to Miranda, 'and you must be Flora's friend Miranda, from London. Oh, don't look so surprised, Jack-at-the-Post-Office told me. You must have said something to him,' she reprimands Flora.

'I only said I had a friend coming down.'

'There you are, then.' Olga Kahn pulls a nasty yellow-and-red jumper triumphantly out from the bottom of the pile. 'That'll do, won't it? Ten pence, did you say?'

'Let's go to an auction, Miranda. Is there one today, Mrs Kahn?'

'Every Saturday. Stark's Auction Centre by the station.'

In a large room, the size of a station, the auction of general household effects has been in progress for several hours. There are twenty or thirty people there, a very mixed crew – some local, some not so, some there to bid for something special, some to buy as much as they can provided the price is low enough. An electric convector heater, *circa* 1950, is currently on offer for £5. 'No? £1. Going to Mr Blake for £1. £2? No. Going to Mr Blake.' The auctioneer's hammer hits the table, and his moon-like face looks down, then up again. A woman, next to him, wearing a tight grey dress, is writing in a shorthand notebook. 'Onwards!'

'That could be useful,' remarks Miranda.

Flora's studying the catalogue. 'Tell me another one.'

'I thought you said you hadn't been gasified yet,' says Miranda.

'Number three hundred and fifty. Statue of the Three Graces. Hold it up, Dick!' A man in a white overall lifts a greenish statue into the air.

'There you are, charming piece. Very innocent. Better than a gnome. Start at £20? Who'll bid £20?' The Three Graces go for £85. 'Onwards! Number three hundred and fifty-one. Another statue, not so innocent.' Dick holds up a two-foot-high Adam, his hand between the statue's legs. People titter. 'Come on, Dick, remember the ladies!'

Flora can see the statue in her garden, at the back where the clematis has stopped flowering. It is, in fact, exactly what the garden needs. It'll be a kind of memento to her former life. Every time she looks at it, it'll remind her of Barnaby, or of Lars, or of . . . She wonders what Olga Kahn will make of it. Flora's aware that she hasn't made a great success of her relationships with men. Olga Kahn's remarks about morbid dependency and love echo in her head. Flora was actually engaged once – or thought she was – to Lars the Dane. That was before she found out he was already married. He gave her a silver ring set with sapphires – 'the colour of your eyes at night' – and trichomoniasis.

But if Flora has turned her back on marriage, has she said no to children? Biology will do that for her in time, as it has a habit of doing. But there are, as she confirmed to Olga Kahn, no hot flushes as yet; Flora feels as oestrogenized as she ever has. This is apparent to others – indeed, didn't Miranda comment this very morning on how well she is looking?

In the auction room, a number of people are observing the two women. It's not that usual for two women to be bidding together. Apart from that, several of them have seen Flora around the streets and fields of Meltshire – including Pete Wates, there to pick up a few bits of furniture for his stripping business, and Abraham Varley, who regularly visits the auction centre, though he never buys anything.

Pete Wates is attracted to Flora Penfold, and will soon be doing something about it. Just now, he's leaving her to settle in. But Bonfire Night is coming up, and he's got his eye on that: the warmth of the big communal fire, the rural conviviality, the sparklers, the big bangs. Pete can wait – he's not in a hurry. Take life as it comes, that's his motto.

Across the other side of the room, from his usual vantage point by the old cracked sink, Abraham Varley watches everything, including Pete Wates's eyes on Flora Penfold. The auction's by way of being a sport to him, like fishing. He gets some satisfaction out of seeing how the value of objects and fish is set only by the pursuer's keenness to possess them, not by the intrinsic value of the things themselves. Abraham knows as much about Flora as anyone in Little Tickencote. Well, not perhaps quite as much as Olga Kahn, though Jack-at-the-Post-Office has bled her for a bowdlerized version of some of that. Abraham watches Flora. She's a woman, isn't she?

'Who'll give me £20?' The auctioneer's voice cuts into the unvoiced human complexities of the scene. Flora looks at Adam, and raises her hand.

'Are you mad, Flora?' hisses Miranda.

'My garden needs decorating.'

The bidding rises rapidly to £60. 'Going to Mr Whitwell for £60.' The auctioneer looks hard at Flora. 'But I think he'd rather go to a lady. £65?' Flora nods.

'Going for £65. Going, going, gone. To?'

'Penfold.' She shouts her name across the room.

'Mrs Penfold.' The woman in the tight grey dress writes Flora's name in her notebook with tidy satisfaction.

'I can't afford it,' groans Flora to Miranda. 'What have I done?' Pete Wates, hearing this, smiles. Abraham Varley, who also hears it, makes a little tut-tutting noise. If she couldn't afford it, why did she buy it? Women are all the same, profligate irrational creatures.

'You'll have to buy Eve now, we can't have Adam pining away on his own, can we?' says Miranda. 'Okay, Flora, I'll buy Eve for you.'

They stagger out with Adam and Eve and Miranda's car vacuum cleaner (a bargain at £2).

While Miranda makes the tea, Flora settles Adam and Eve into their new home. She positions Eve so that she appears to be looking sideways at Adam. But Adam stares resolutely at the ground, taking no notice. Pablo comes to sniff – not only at Adam, but round the dead meadow pipit's grave. Flora imagines a rotting aroma settling between the winter-flowering pansies. Their dense purple blooms, at once ingenuous and concealing, fold open under the chalky late-autumn sky. She looks over the wall beyond the slope of the Neveres' garden to the trees ranged in their layered darkening colours against the grey-white background, and to the chimneys of Little Tickencote. Woodsmoke spirals up, overlaying the scent, the sense, of rottenness.

Miranda calls from the house to say that the Earl Grey is made, and the Sarah Lee fudge brownies are waiting on the table. Their teeth full of the chocolate stickiness, the two women begin to notice a change in the interior climate of the house. 'Oh my God,' says Flora suddenly, 'I know what it is – the gas has run out!' She hurries out to where the orange canisters are lined up like toy soldiers against the long wall of the kitchen extension: the dial is, indeed, on red. 'What's the time?'

'Five-thirty.'

'Oh my God!' she says again. 'They'll be closed.'

Miranda sips her tea, trying to look implacable.

'I hate being cold,' announces Flora.

'I'm not too fond of it myself.'

Flora dials Percy Grisewood's number. Olive answers. 'Is that Mrs Grisewood? This is Flora Penfold here. From The Cottage in Little Tickencote.'

'Oh yes,' says Olive laconically, remembering Percy's opinion of Miss Penfold's body.

'Is Mr Grisewood there?'

'Oh no,' says Olive. There's a silence.

'Oh,' says Flora. 'Do you expect him back later, then?'

'It's hard to tell,' says Olive uninformatively. Percy's on the toilet with the *Meltshire Echo*. He'll be there for a good half-hour yet. 'Did you want him for anything in particular, Miss Penfold?' inquires Olive primly, allowing the accent to fall on the 'Miss'.

'My gas has run out,' explains Flora.

'Should have thought of that before, shouldn't you, Miss Penfold!' replies Olive tartly. 'My Percy' – here the stress is definitely on the 'My' – 'isn't on this earth to solve other people's problems, you know.'

'Who was that on the telephone?' asks Percy, emerging later, leaving the newspaper spread out on the toilet floor.

'I expect you've left the paper for me to tidy up, haven't you?' says Olive happily. 'Oh Percy, you are a one! It was only a wrong number. We seem to be getting a lot of them nowadays. I wonder if it's them pylons across Windy Bottom?'

'We'll have to go out,' says Flora to Miranda. 'To get warm. Then we can make a fire in the sitting-room, and we can both sleep there.'

They walk down to the Old Sun Inn. The village is a pool of textured blackness with diamond stars. It's very cold, the first night of winter frost. Flora hugs her old red coat round her; Miranda complains about her freezing hands. But in the pub it's warm, there's a real fire, and an assemblage of real rural figures are propping up the bar.

'Hallo, Flora!' says Jasper Lancing gustily. 'Welcome to the local hostelry! Come and join the crowd. Have you met the Neveres?'

Petula's ash-blonde hair sparkles with something glittery. Between the high-heeled patent leather shoes and the conclusion of her close-fitting black velvet trousers is a gold chain with a black cat studded in it. 'Pleased to meet you,' say Petula's strawberry-and-cream lips.

Armand Nevere, in a suede jacket, leans past her to shake Flora's and Miranda's hands. A thickset man with crinkly gingery hair, his face is as unmarked as a baby's. It's impossible to imagine a razor being dragged over it, or gingery stubble poking up like spring corn. 'And how are you finding life in Little Tickencote, Flora?' he invites familiarly. 'A change from London, isn't it, eh?'

Petula's laugh tinkles like the glasses behind the bar. 'This is Ted-behind-the-bar,' confirms Jasper. 'And Bridget Crowhurst, from Main Street, and her husband – beg your pardon, *ex*-husband, isn't it? – Martin, from Manor Farm Lane.'

Bridget sits at one end of the bar in jeans and a white Aran sweater, Martin at the other end in a navy one. This is the couple Olga Kahn told her about. They both smile in Flora's direction. Bridget is drinking beer, Martin a glass of wine. Flora's eyes go back to Martin; there is something faintly familiar about him, but she can't work out what. Bridget and Armand turn to each other, and are soon deep in discussion.

'I expect you're finding the garden's in need of some attention, aren't you?' begins Petula chattily. 'Miss Greetham rather let it go recently. Our gardener remembers it from the old days, doesn't he, darling?'

She pokes Armand in the back. He jumps. 'Don't interrupt, Pet, Bridget and I are talking about something important.'

'Which is?'

'The future of education in Meltshire,' says Bridget quietly.

'Well, I don't know why you should be interested in that, Armand,' says Petula crossly. 'You're not going back to school, are you?'

'Shut up, Pet.'

'Bridget's a teacher,' says Jasper helpfully to Flora.

'Oh, where do you teach?'

'Melton Comprehensive.'

Flora's about to ask another question, when Miranda hands her one of the two vodka and oranges she's ordered, and Pete Wates opens the door. 'No, I don't want my usual, Ted,' says Pete to Ted-behind-the-bar, whose sofa-like moustache drapes lips of such thinness that it's hard to see them at all. 'Don't let it get to you, Ted, but have you by any chance a bottle of Blue Nun to hand? It's my mother's birthday, you see. Dad was going to take her out, but he's had one of his turns. It's my mission to cheer her up.'

'Take her to the George,' instructs Petula. 'We went there on Armand's birthday. I've never seen such a sweet trolley. Piled high, it was. Your mum likes puddings, doesn't she, Pete?'

Flora's mouth drinks her vodka and her eyes drink in Pete: his casual farmer's clothes of patched tweed jacket and corduroy trousers, the Dirk Bogarde eyes, the newspaper – most surprisingly *Marxism Today* – then under his arm, now laid on the bar as he counts his change for the Blue Nun Ted has found for him.

'You must be Flora Penfold,' says Pete, across all the other conversations. 'I was a friend of Agatha Greetham's. We used to belong to a little reading group. It helped to pass the long cold evenings.'

Culture in Meltshire? 'What did you read?'

'Thomas Mann. Engels, *The Condition of the Working Classes in England in 1846*. *Little Women*. The world was our oyster.'

'Don't believe him,' says Petula Nevere, tinkling. 'He's making it all up.' Pete Wates smiles at Petula and then at Flora, but Flora can't tell what kind of smile either of them is. He strolls out enigmatically, wrapping *Marxism Today* round the bottle of Blue Nun. Out in the blackness, he whistles 'Drink to Me Only with Thine Eyes' to himself as he gets back into the old Austin and chugs back to the farmhouse, where his father, Frank, is having a turn, and his mother, Doris, is having her sixty-sixth birthday.

'Do people in Meltshire normally read *Marxism Today*?' inquires Flora of Ted with the sofa moustache, as the exhaust of Pete Wates's Austin fires into the blackness.

Ted folds his arms and stands back against the shelves of upturned bottles. Jasper, who's heard Flora's question, laughs. 'Hardly. But Pete's not normal, is he Ted?'

'Hardly.'

They laugh together, with Petula Nevere's tinkle providing the descant. 'I wouldn't know, of course, would I?' she says, and all three of them shake even more conspiratorially.

'This is all a bit too much for me, you know,' says Flora, suddenly and honestly.

They turn to look at her: Bridget Crowhurst at the end of the row in her white Aran, Armand Nevere with his baby face, tinkling Petula, Ted-behind-the-bar, Miranda, Jasper Lancing from the Melton software firm, and Martin Crowhurst with his polite glass of wine. It's Martin who speaks. 'Don't let it worry you,' he advises. 'They're just trying to wind you up. Pete Wates may be a farmer's son, but he hasn't lived in the village all his life, and he doesn't only do farming. Country villages don't tolerate departures from convention well, do they, Bridget? So that makes him abnormal to folks round here.'

'Thanks for explaining. I didn't mean to be rude.'

'I like a plain-speaking woman,' pronounces Ted-behind-the-bar suddenly. 'Don't I, Jasper?'

'That's why she left you, isn't it, Ted?'

'That's right.'

'Here we go again,' mutters Flora to Miranda. 'Let's go and sit by the fire.'

'Have another drink first, ladies,' says Armand, overhearing. 'Fill them up, Ted.'

'Pleasure,' says Ted.

'You like filling up ladies, don't you?'

'Don't we all?'

'Well, some of us.'

'Cool it, chaps.'

'It's too hot in here,' complains Miranda.

'Maybe that's why Mrs Kahn said it's not the place for hot flushes.'

'What?'

'Never mind. Why don't we have something to eat?'

'If she left him, who does the cooking?'

Fanny Watkins does the cooking. At seventeen, she's more capable than most people of her age. Six months out of school, she was taken in by Ted and his wife to help in the pub. Fanny was in retreat from parental control – in fact thrown out by her parents for being beyond control. It was Ted who urged Patsy to give it a go. 'It'd be one thing to have a lass of our own to tangle with,' Patsy said, 'but this could be something else.' Which it was. Ted cajoled and persuaded, and Patsy gave in. It was her undoing. Fanny thirsted for experience – and not only of pub kitchens. Two months later she'd taken Patsy's place, and Patsy had taken herself to live with her sister in Streatham.

'The duck's off,' says Fanny, mentally checking the contents of the freezer. 'But we've got a very nice Poolay oh Rees with mandarins.' Its best-by date was a week ago; she needs to get rid of it. 'Or you could have an egg omelette, I suppose.'

'Is that all?'

Fanny stares back at Miranda. 'Or sprats.'

'Sprats?'

'Little fishes with lots of bones,' fills in Fanny.

'I know what sprats are,' protests Miranda.

'That's all right, then.'

'What about vegetables?'

'Garlic mushrooms, cauliflower florets, corn on the cob or Mrs

Titmarsh's bolted Webbs,' recites Fanny, who has the advantage of a reasonably good memory.

'One Poolay,' orders Miranda, 'and my friend here will have another one, I expect.'

'We've only got one.'

'In that case, it'll have to be an egg omelette. And we'd both like a salad of Mrs Titmarsh's bolted Webbs. Oh, and a bottle of house wine. White.'

'We don't have no house wine. You want some Blue Nun?'

'Haven't you got anything else?'

'I'll ask.' Fanny comes back a minute later. 'Mr Rippington says we've got a bottle of Between Two Mothers.'

Behind the bar Ted brushes his silky moustache across Fanny's kitchen-flushed face. 'I heard you over there, my little one,' he says. 'What else do you make omelettes with but eggs?'

'Leave off, Ted, I've got to get the Poolay out of the freezer.' Fanny pushes him away sharply, watched by Jasper Lancing who, sweating slightly, loosens the top button of his shirt.

The food's not bad, though the less known about its origins the better. Later on, when the table is cleared, Bridget Crowhurst comes over with her third half-pint of non-alcoholic lager. 'Mind if I join you?'

'Go ahead.'

'You must be quite confused by all this.'

'It's as clear as mud,' says Flora.

'My friend's had too much to drink,' explains Miranda.

'So have that lot.' Bridget nods in the direction of the bar. 'But it's the same everywhere in the country. Nothing to do, you see. I don't usually go to the pub, but I felt like getting out of the house tonight.' She thinks about her little cottage stuck on at the end of the last row in the village, with its upper windows like a permanently open eyelid perusing the lowest part of the valley of the Gwater. She sees its tidy, lit interior – the yellow kitchen with the brass-bottomed pans hung on the wall; the sitting-room with its full log basket and fluffy hoovered carpet, overlaid with the Persian-style rug; the pile of marked essays resting on the oiled teak table; and upstairs the bed with its white candlewick cover, and the peach winceyette nightie folded under the pillow. Its order is like the warm glow of a radiator. Much better now that Martin has left. She can hardly bear to think of his abode, high on the hill towards Oakingham, a shack inside a half-converted barn piled high with books and dirty cups and cigarette ends. But Martin himself is another story.

'I wonder sometimes why new people come here,' says Bridget Crowhurst, speaking her thoughts out loud. 'It's a dreadful place, the country.'

'You mean, why do people come to this village?'

'Yes, that as well.'

'Well, why are you here?'

'I came when I married Martin. His family live in Melton. He wanted to be near them. He said it's where we should bring up our children, in the country.'

Miranda asks politely how old the children are.

'We didn't have any.'

'Well, I expect there's plenty of time,' says Miranda consolingly.

'Do you? I'm not so sure. You'll note a general absence of children round here. Just in this village and the next one, and from here to Jacob's Water. The village school was closed ten years ago because there weren't enough children. Up in Melton, they're all right.' Flora and Miranda exchange looks, which Bridget sees. How am I going to make a living teaching the flute if there aren't any children to teach it to? thinks Flora despairingly. 'I expect you think I'm off my head. Well, I'm not. You didn't come to the country to have children, I take it?' She addresses Flora.

'Good God, no.'

Bridget stares at her. Flora notices that the roots of her hair are darker than the ends, which flash with henna. 'Oh, I stopped using that, I thought it might be the cause of the problem. I gave up meat and alcohol. I even drink the vegetable water. But none of it makes any difference. My gynaecologist said it must be psychosomatic. That's why Martin left.'

'How does that help?'

Bridget looks at Flora absently, as though something has just struck her for the first time. 'You're right, it doesn't.'

'Maybe you meet in the woods like Lady Chatterley and her lover? Do you crush the flowers with the weight of your bodies and flatten the lichen with your passion?'

'Really, Flora!'

'I don't mind,' says Bridget. 'I've just marked thirty-five essays on *Lady Chatterley's Lover*. Mostly I teach biology, but sometimes I stand in for the English teacher. Her dog's just died. How did you know?'

'Same way as you knew I'd noticed the henna.'

'Lady Chatterley's husband couldn't get it up,' says Bridget non-committally. 'There's nothing particularly psychosomatic about that, is there?'

'Not really.'

Bridget and Flora giggle. 'Perhaps Ted gave me cider instead,' remarks Bridget. 'I feel quite happy for a change. I think I'd better go home before it hits me.'

'Before what hits her?' says Flora to Miranda as they struggle arm in arm down the frosty road back to Cabbage Lane. Miranda's about to answer when Flora grabs her and says, 'Shush, can you hear that, Manda?'

Miranda listens, but the church clock chimes, hiding whatever it was she was supposed to hear.

'It's a sheep peeing.'

'Don't be daft.'

'They're an awfully odd lot,' says Miranda back in the cold cottage. 'Have you heard from Barney recently?'

'No. Why should I?'

'Well, I just thought that . . .'

'It's over,' says Flora firmly. 'Men are behind me. This is another era of my life.'

'That Marxist farmer is possibly fancyable,' observes Miranda dangerously.

'Oh, do you think so? I don't.'

'Have it your way, then. You will, anyway!'

They stack up the fire with logs and drag a mattress and a heap of duvets and blankets down in front of it. Miranda undresses and gets into bed shivering. 'Do me a favour – check the gas next time I come, Flora!'

'I'm really sorry, Manda,' admits Flora. 'Truly I am. But it'll be nice and cosy here, you'll see.'

Pablo and Dolly scratch at the door. 'Oh no! Not the animals!'

'They're used to sleeping with me,' defends Flora.

'But I'm not used to sleeping with *them*!'

Pablo and Dolly don't understand, and are quickly curled up at the end of the mattress. 'What about my allergy?'

'I expect it's psychosomatic,' says Flora sleepily.

Miranda sneezes defensively, but only twice. She lies down and shuts her eyes. 'If I sneeze once more you'll have to throw them out.'

'Done.'

Flora watches the fire; flames curl and dance energetically for a while, and then there's a great subsidence; a half-burnt log shakes and settles itself into a new position. Grey ashes seep across and over the tiled surround, a field of repeating yellow lilies. Cinders crackle noisily. 'What was that?' Miranda starts, and opens her eyes.

'Only the fire, go to sleep.' Miranda turns, pulls the duvet up to her shoulders. Her long dark hair is glossy in the firelight, the blush of her sleeping cheek apricot in the glow. Beside her Flora snuggles and burrows down, like a rabbit or a mole in the pink darkness. Her nose is cold, but she presses it into the pillow and thinks of the warmth in the pub, of the characters lined up against the bar: of the Crowhursts, pale in their separated look-alike outfits, Bridget musing the secret doom of their joint infertility; Jasper Lancing straight and tall as a silver birch, coated with airs as obvious as the leaves on trees; Petula Nevere with her leopard-skin cleavage, metallic laughter and clotted-cream curls; husband Armand with a skin as clear as Miranda's apricot sheen; and Pete Wates with his Blue Nun wrapped in *Marxism Today*, and the polished walnut of his brooding film-star eyes. Their voices jostle for her attention, and she is the target of multiple meaningful looks. The firelight in the Old Sun Inn and the firelight of The Cottage run together and become one; a great orange fire burns, consuming everything in its path. But Flora is not afraid, nor are the others who wait there in its avaricious light, naked and white like the statues in her garden. Standing still, they look sideways or at the ground, and then they start to dance. Armand is humming, as his gingery crepe hair takes on the appearance of a flame itself, and fastidiously he passes Bridget's hand from one of his hands to the other in an old-fashioned quadrille. Bridget's body is square and white like schoolteacher's chalk; her breasts, instead of bouncing with the rhythm of the dance, are solid stone. Armand's body is pink and completely hairless; between his legs hangs one unripe fig, but nothing else. He's absurdly proud of this, and leaps around to show off its hard little curves in the firelight. Petula is dancing with Jasper, a tight formal waltz, round and round and off into the trees, passing Martin Crowhurst and Pete Wates as they go. The two men are laughing at something, some private joke. And then Flora, in the dream, sees what it is that is causing such merriment: Martin Crowhurst and Pete Wates each has, instead of a penis, a bottle of Blue Nun.

She wakes in the night, feverish with images. The fire is out and the room is cold. But the fire is in Flora – not only from the odd hot dream but from her own body, whose needs she has been ignoring these past few months. It wants another, but not glass bottles, or warnings of misadventure. Next to her Miranda sleeps peacefully, at her feet the two cats, their breathing the only sound in the room. Resisting an impulse to draw nearer to Miranda, Flora passes her hands over her own body, feeling it as someone else would: the slope of the inner thigh, the sticky living hair, the flat terrain of the stomach, the dip of the waist, the satin globe of the hard-tipped breast. It isn't easy to be lover and loved; it isn't what she wanted, though it might be what she's chosen. Firing old connections in her mind, touching takes her back five, ten years to the company of her Danish man one summer when they toured the coast of Jutland. Between phone calls to his wife when he picked old phone boxes to mimic the disturbances of a transatlantic line, and back up his story of travelling in Washington DC, they walked together over silver sands and into frothy water, and lay coupling in the tufted sand dunes while people walked nearby, as over their graves. There was almost no sun that summer. Tepid silvery clouds lay over everything. As Lars entered her one afternoon her period came, and a long trickle of scarlet blood zigzagged across the white sand. He dipped his finger in it, traced the words 'I love you' across her breasts, kissed her and said, 'When we are old, this is what we'll remember, wherever we are – this moment of joining bodies and fluids under the flat Danish sky.'

In front of the cold grate in Little Tickencote, Flora Penfold's mood saddens for what has passed as well as for what may be yet to come. Dreams, memories and fancies eventually drive her into sleep again, and in the morning she remembers none of it until she goes into the garden to check on Adam and Eve, and notices that in the night Eve has acquired the decor of two second-class postage stamps on her little stone nipples.

7

The Disappearing Gwater

'WELL, I don't understand it,' says Annabel Lancing to husband Jasper one Sunday morning a few weeks later. 'She's quite an attractive woman, really. Though she could make more of her appearance. How old do you think she is, Jasper? Thirty-five? Forty?'

'Why don't you ask her?' says Jasper, irritated. He's trying to mend a weak connection in his hi-fi.

'You can't ask someone that unless you know them really well.'

'Well, get to know her really well, then.'

Annabel sticks her tongue out at his back. 'And I don't understand why she's on her own. Perhaps she's a widow. Maybe she doesn't like men.'

Jasper pretends not to hear. 'I saw Petula Nevere in the Post Office yesterday.' His voice is muffled against the wall. 'She says they're putting in another planning application.'

Annabel sighs and wipes her hands on her apron. Behind her in the kitchen her white bean soup bubbles animatedly, and the countryside, golden and sheep-dotted, regards her through the crisscrossed window. 'You'd think they'd give up, wouldn't you?'

'*You* wouldn't,' points out Jasper.

'We've never found out much about Petula, come to that,' Annabel meanders. 'Perhaps I should have one of my coffee mornings.'

'You do that!' says Jasper, emerging satisfied from his fiddling inside the speaker.

And so Annabel Lancing invites Petula Nevere, Flora Penfold, Olga Tuchenksy-Kahn, Bridget Crowhurst and Jane Rivers not to coffee but to tea one Thursday, a day when young Alun will be fetched from his Oakingham school by the mother of one of his friends to go home with them until supper time. Gwendolyn will eat crumpets with five-year-old Susannah Tennison at the other end of the village, and

Bronwen will be visiting her young man, whom no one but she knows about, in a hamlet the other side of the oxbow of the Gwater.

Annabel cleans and shines and orders Shirley-who-does-for-her to do more than she usually does. She crops Michaelmas daisies and the dark-pink heads of sedum from the garden and sits them in the blue Staffordshire vase she bought in an antique shop in Melton. All this activity is entirely wasted on psychoanalyst Olga Kahn, crime writer Jane Rivers and career-changing Flora Penfold, though Petula Nevere, houseproud village non-wife, and Bridget Crowhurst, obsessional arranger of children's minds and objects, would notice if there were a hair out of place. Annabel Lancing, her yellow hair, clumped in a neat ponytail, lying like a thresh of corn down the back of her light-brown cashmere jersey, stands impeccably there offering them a choice of types of tea to accompany the cucumber sandwiches, the light jam sponge, and the home-made shortbread lightly dusted with sugar and lurking in the kitchen. 'Typhoo, my dear,' booms Olga Kahn, and 'Do you mind if I smoke?'

Olga Kahn's tobacco, the colour of Annabel's hair, is not welcome in Wisteria Cottage, but Annabel hasn't the nous to say so. Jane Rivers watches with interest. 'Oh, I don't mind what I drink,' she says. 'Or what I eat. You can fill me up with anything you choose.'

'Have you herbal tea, Annabel?' inquires Bridget keenly. 'I've given up caffeine; you've no idea what a difference it makes.'

'What difference does it make?' asks Petula Nevere, whose tastes favour stimulants of various kinds. Bridget Crowhurst explains how she experienced several episodes of disturbed vision earlier in the year before omitting caffeine from her diet. 'And that's apart from any other effects it has,' she hints, darkly.

'How fascinating,' murmurs Olga Kahn, layering the carpet with tobacco and not believing a word of it.

A motley crowd. In the middle of the conversation, caught in its ebbs and flows – more ebbs than flows – Annabel asks Flora not how old she is but whether she's ever been married, this seeming the more polite question. Flora mentions Barnaby Gunn – the general incompatibility of their lifestyles and the rakishness of actors. Annabel finds it all rather exciting. Flora asks Annabel if she's thought about Alun's flute lessons. She needs to get going on the flute-teaching and her other projects. She's just produced her first set of cartoon sketches. The central character, Rosey, otherwise known as Rural Rosey, is a self-sufficient, warm-hearted, hyperallergic animal-loving organic market gardener with wild curls and an equally untamed Afghan coat (ideological contradiction there, but then Rosey's charm doesn't lie in consistency). Flora has sent the sketches off to Jeff, her man on the *Daily Record*, and is waiting to hear. Even in the uncertain limbo of waiting for Jeff to respond, Flora's drawn repeatedly back to the character of Rosey as some kind of alter ego whose own fate, once captured and revealed on paper, may contain a clue or two to her own. She begins to talk to Rosey around the house: Rosey listens, even answers back from time to time, though with remarks which echo her own problems with the rural scene rather than Flora's.

Annabel doesn't believe a word of it either – or rather, she doesn't believe that cartoon-drawing will keep Flora in the country. Music-teaching sounds more like it, though she herself intends to pay Flora as little as she can get away with for Alun's tuition. Jane Rivers of the black garb asks: 'What else do you do with your time?' Flora explains about the building work, and about her father's papers. In both of these domains she is grappling, not altogether happily, with men. Samuel Penfold presents different versions of himself, but is slippery. Percy Grisewood arrives for work when he feels like it, which isn't often. The new facilities, still boxed, await their instatement in the unconverted third bedroom. The attic room, half-boarded, also awaits Percy's unpredictable attentions, and Flora, who cannot really tolerate any of this, writes about Rosey in bed, which is where she is whenever Percy comes, thus confirming all Olive's worst and most uncharitable thoughts, and making it even less likely that Percy will come the next time.

In all these various ways, Little Tickencote is having some difficulty coming to grips with Flora Penfold, and she with it. 'Give it time,' admonishes Olga Kahn as they leave Annabel Lancing's sitting-room that day. 'Put your roots down first. It's like planting trees; you must dig a big hole and manure it first. We've got to teach you about gardening, haven't we? Though I hear you've acquired some colleagues for the garden.'

'How do you know about Adam and Eve?'

'Jack-at-the-Post-Office.'

'How does he know?'

'Er-hum. I expect it's the Ketton's van. You do have Ketton's for the gas, don't you? Yes, I thought so.'

'Mrs Kahn . . .'

'Olga, please.'

'Olga, a really strange thing happened the day after I bought Adam and Eve. Someone stuck some stamps on Eve.'

Bedding rooks swoop and call over the trees in Sheepdyke Field. Olga's thick brown shoes stop in their tracks.

'I'd like to think I dreamt it, but I didn't. What does it mean, do you think?'

'I'm only a psychoanalyst,' complains Olga briskly. 'I can't be expected to explain real life, that's quite a different matter. "I am inclined to be satisfied with the theoretical understanding." Karen Horney to Karl Abraham, who analysed her. After she'd had her first child, she tried to terminate the analysis. Too tired for it, I expect.'

'Perhaps someone's got it in for me.'

'Er-hum. Why on earth should they, my child?'

'I don't know. I'm a newcomer. Perhaps they don't want me here.'

'Give it time,' says Olga again, trudging on. 'The young are so *impatient*. I could say you're trying to dig your roots into a long-established rural community, but most of us, as you've noticed, are only newcomers like you. No, just give it time.'

Back in The Cottage, Flora opens a tin of baked beans and studies the oak barometer the people at the Islington Arts Centre gave her as a leaving present. The needle points to stormy weather. How long am I supposed to wait for this bloody builder? rants Flora to Rural Rosey. What would you do in my place?

Phone Percy again, advises Rosey.

I've phoned Percy sixteen times at least. He's never there. I doubt whether that woman who answers has passed on a single message.

Go round there, then.

Maybe. Flora is spurred on by the recent behaviour of the downstairs facility in The Cottage. It's developed a trick of returning to its owner material deposited in it; the bend in the U pipe at the back is cracked. Sometimes it doesn't happen; mostly it does. But even when it doesn't, smells linger.

Flora eats her baked beans and puts on her duffel coat and red woolly hat. It's late October, and she remembers the barometer's needle. Percy Grisewood lives up the hill towards Great Glaston. It ought to be Great Tickencote, reflects Flora, climbing the hill in the darkness, or this should be Little Glaston. You should have taken the car, reprimands Rosey. Where's your rape alarm? Shut up, Rosey. This is the country. A place of safety, not like the town.

Halfway up the hill there's a terrible skirmish in the field to Flora's right. Terrified, she shrinks into the hedge. A car comes past, a white Citroën with big headlamps, and in their light she sees three or four rabbits scuttling across. She remembers this is where the rabbits live; Alun Lancing told her not long after the meadow pipit incident, when he was filling her in on the wildlife of the neighbourhood. 'Dead Bunny Lane', he called it.

Just outside the first cottage in Great Glaston, Flora steps on something soft and squashy – one result of the Citroën's journey, a mangled, dying rabbit. She hurries on, wiping the sides of her shoes on the grass verge and trying not to look. Slippery slimy guts of rabbit: the baked beans rise in her stomach. This is disgusting, Rosey, quite disgusting. You haven't seen half of it yet, replies Rosey sweetly.

Olive Grisewood is knitting a baby's blanket in front of 'The Price is Right'. They've had their dinner, a nice dish of rabbit stew and Olive's special dumplings. Percy's out the back banging around in his workroom. He'll be in later, they'll have a cup of tea and a plate of biscuits. If Flora hadn't come, the blanket might have been finished by then.

'Yes?' says Olive at the front door. Her blank face and thick neck remind Flora of a Japanese wrestler.

'I'm Flora Penfold.'

'Ah, yes.'

'I've come to talk to Percy.'

'Is he expecting you?' asks Olive, knowing perfectly well he isn't.

'Not exactly.'

'Ah well, he's not likely to be here then, is he?'

The logic seems faulty. 'I'd like to speak to him, please,' says Flora firmly, thinking of the brown floods in the downstairs facility, not to mention her unfinished floor and the cardboard-clad new bathroom suite.

'Is it about your gas again?' asks Olive suspiciously.

'No, of course not.'

'Well, how am I to know?'

Flora peers past Olive into the narrow hall, with its flocked wallpaper and embossed cinnamon carpet. There's a nauseous dank stench of something emanating from it. Her foot recalls the squashy feel of the murdered rabbit. She coughs.

'It's no good looking for him, he's not here,' says Olive pertly.

'Mrs Grisewood,' begins Flora again, in a different tone, 'please understand: I'm not trying to be a nuisance. But I've a floor missing in my house, and the bathroom's waiting to be built, and the downstairs facility leaks – in fact what it does is so indescribable I wouldn't want to upset you with the details.'

'Return flow.' Olive nods wisely. 'Not nice, is it?'

'And your husband agreed to do the work. Every time I do succeed in speaking to him he says he'll come, and then he doesn't. What can I do about it? I need him, Mrs Grisewood. I wish I didn't, but I do!'

Has she got through to Olive? Olive is silent. Something is ticking in her brain. The word 'need' set it off. 'Wait there,' she commands.

Flora hangs around on the doorstep. Why doesn't the bloody woman ask her in? Doesn't want to, says Rosey. No manners, these country people. Flora's train of thought is cut off mid-flow as she recognizes, still peering into the Grisewoods' hall despite being told not to, a replica of her statue of Adam, only bigger, and wearing a pair of black satin boxer shorts tied with string. It isn't the only object in the hall, admittedly; in fact the hall is stacked high with stuff – boxes, cans, bathroom suites, creosote, nails, rolled-up bits of carpet – but it does rather stand out. She's only started to speculate on the meaning of this sight when Olive comes back with a satisfied look on her face. 'I've spoken to him,' she says, without saying how, 'and he'll be there Monday morning at eight with Ron.'

'Who's Ron?'

'The plumber.'

Someone warned her about the plumber, but Flora can't remember who or what they said. 'How do I know he'll come?' she asks, thinking of Percy's many broken assignations.

'He'll come,' says Olive definitively, shutting the door in Flora's face.

I've got to walk home again now, complains Flora to Rosey.

So you have. Or perhaps not.

Pete Wates's Austin is chugging through Great Glaston on its way back from Melton. Pete sees Flora and stops. He winds down the window with a scratching noise, and smiles at her. 'Flora Penfold,' he says, pronouncing it clearly and carefully, as though unwrapping a diamond. 'Is this your nightly constitutional, or would you by any chance like a lift home?'

'Thanks, I would.' Flora gets in. They drive off; this time it's the exhaust that produces a jerky sound. 'Do you eat rabbit?' she asks suddenly.

'Not me. I'm a vegetarian,' he says.

'Oh. Is rabbit a popular dish round here?'

'Could be, I suppose. I don't really know.'

'Do the butchers sell it?'

'I don't think I've ever been in one.'

'Isn't that rather unusual for a farmer?'

'Yes.' He turns his dark eyes on her and smiles. 'But I'm not a normal farmer. I believe in the life of the soil, and not disturbing it. And in using nature to treat nature.' Something about Pete's presence next to her in the ropy old car reminds Flora of her wakefulness the other night, when the gas had run out and the cottage was cold, but her body and mental images were not. 'Here we are.' Pete draws up outside The Cottage.

'Thanks,' she says again. Briefly she wonders if she ought to ask him in, but she doesn't. He probably wouldn't accept anyway. Before she's closed the front door behind her, he's driving off singing 'We Plough the Fields and Scatter'.

On Monday morning, Flora's practising a tricky A minor Hoefflin exercise on the flute when Percy and Ron ring the doorbell. In order to teach children to play the flute she has to polish her own technique, and has thus resolved to play for at least an hour a day. She doesn't hear the doorbell – not because of the flute, but because the battery's fading, but she hasn't noticed this latter fact, as nothing has drawn it to her attention, and doesn't now, until she looks up to find Percy and a very large man whom she assumes is Ron staring at her from the sitting-room doorway.

'Bell doesn't work,' remarks Percy. 'Came in through the back.'

Flora groans. 'Nothing works around here.'

'Would that be a closed G sharp or an open one, Miss Penfold?' asks Ron elliptically, gesturing at the flute.

Flora lays the flute down. 'Closed. Boehm system.' Ron doesn't look like a flautist, even in disguise. He's over six feet tall, about twice Percy's size both length- and widthways. His hair stands on end like dune grass, and his face reminds Flora of the Frankenstein father in 'The Munsters', the vampire soap opera, except that it wears an expression of incongruous gentleness. The top of Ron's head is flat, like a moor. Both men are clothed in identical blue overalls and carry tool bags. In his other hand, Percy holds a white plastic lunch box.

'No piano?' continues Ron.

'No. I've got to get one.'

'Might help you there. Know a nice little Bosendorfer,' he offers. 'Cost you £300 or so. Burn on the lid.'

'I thought you were a plumber?'

'There's plumbing and plumbing.'

'Come on, Ron. Return flow, Olive said. That right, Miss Penfold?'

'It is.' The two men disappear to the kitchen. Flora follows them. 'And there's the floor in the attic, and . . .'

'I know, I know,' says Percy equably. 'Put the kettle on, will you? Ron likes Bovril. I'll have tea. Two bags unless it's Liptons, and three sugars.'

'Two spoons,' says Ron. 'Of Bovril. Big ones.'

When Flora takes them their tray of thickly sugared and salted substances, Ron's lying on the floor doing something to the pipe at the back of the toilet, and Percy's fiddling with the cistern.

'Needs borming, this does, I 'spect,' announces Ron in muffled tones.

'Possible,' agrees Percy.

'Borming?' asks Flora.

Percy takes his tea and looks at her with his little piggy eyes. 'Not a native, are you, Miss Penfold? I forget. Local dialect. Means greasing.'

Ron stands up. 'Has you been putting stuff in here, Miss Penfold?' he asks suspiciously.

'Stuff? Well, only the usual . . .'

'I meant *women's* stuff,' interrupts Ron accusingly.

'Well, I . . . well, yes.'

'Don't,' says Ron. 'It's killing.'

'There you are, then,' says Percy, shaking his head and standing there pinging his braces at her.

'How was I to know?'

'Things don't work the same way in the country as they does in the town, does they, Ron?'

'That they don't. You'll need a new bit o' pipe consequently, you will.'

Flora leaves them to it. Jeff from the *Daily Record* has sent her sketches back. 'Not savage enough,' he's commented. Flora takes them out to the garden with her cup of coffee. 'Why should I be savage?' she wonders out loud, surveying the sunlit terrain of crisp autumn leaves and still-flowering roses, of silky emerald grass and ancient stone walls embossed like Percy Grisewood's hall carpet, but here by moss and lichen and tiny ivies licking their way happily from stone to stone. Behind her in the house, Ron and Percy bang and mumble. Along the garden path stalks Pablo, newly majestic in his enlarged hunting-grounds. He pauses, waving his tail in great sunlit arcs and mewing loudly a couple of times in greeting to Flora, before passing out of sight under the quince tree. Perhaps I should abandon Rosey? reflects Flora. Can I make enough from music-teaching? Don't be daft, says Rosey in her ear. How are you going to pay Ron and Percy? You've got to sharpen your tongue and wit with me, that's all. Flora sighs and picks up her pen.

Twenty minutes later, Olga Kahn, in her batwinged cloak, rings the doorbell but, hearing no answering chime, tries the back gate instead. 'Don't mean to disturb,' she booms. Pablo, startled, rustles the quince tree coming out to see what's going on. 'I thought perhaps you'd like to come to Mattocks with us? Silly me, of course I mean to disturb, that's not what I meant – oh dear, there I go again.'

Flora leans forward on the table, her elbows pressing into Rosey's face. The slanting sun caps her head with gold, drawing Olga Kahn's attention, spuriously, to Flora's relative youth and beauty. 'Mattocks? Us?'

'The Garden Centre. Jane Rivers and I are going. She's going to advise me about a fruit tree. A damson, I thought. You know Jane's passion for black? Black damsons – the fruits of evil, she calls them.'

'Well, I certainly need some help with the garden.'

They go in Jane Rivers's car, which is just as well in view of Olga Kahn's appalling driving habits. Mozart plays on the car radio, and the blueness of the sky deepens as they cut across the multicoloured Meltshire countryside. 'Bonfire Night next Monday,' announces Jane. 'It'll be cold if the weather goes on like this. The village has a great bonfire in Sheepdyke Field – if there's anything you want to burn, just take it there – boxes, bedsprings, old clothes. There's food as well, and the fireworks are usually very good. Thanks to Olga.'

'Got a new type of Catherine wheel this year. From Japan. Supposed to be brilliant. I don't do them on my own, Ron helps.' Flora can't help laughing. 'Yes, I know it seems a very unlikely combination: the plumber and the psychoanalyst. But you're probably not laughing at that, you're laughing at the whole concept of a shrink setting off fireworks, aren't you, my dear?'

'Psychic release,' declares Jane Rivers from behind the steering wheel. 'I understand it perfectly well.'

In the Garden Centre Jane and Olga go off to the fruit-tree section, while Flora walks up and down the aisles of seedlings. She doesn't know what any of them are called, and she certainly doesn't know what she ought to buy for her garden. She peers at a few labels: *Lonicera Japonica*; *Rudbeckia fulgida*; *Parthenocissus inserta*; *Passiflora mollissima*. It's all Latin to me, but it sounds wonderful. Perhaps I should change my name. To Passiflora? Or – she bends and turns a label over – or Salpiglossis? No, what about this one – Salvia. *Salvia borminum*. 'A true annual with erect branched stems carrying ovate mid-green leaves. Pale purple flowers, insignificant compared with the terminal tufts of coloured bracts.' Borminum would at least fit in with the plumbing scare.

After a while Jane appears behind her. 'Olga's gone to talk to the man about the new hybrid perpetual she ordered,' she explains. 'Can I help you? Are you looking for something in particular?'

'Well, no.'

'You could do worse than put some more bulbs in, and add to the evergreen stock,' says Jane busily. 'Agatha Greetham wasn't fond of bulbs; I never understood why. And much of the garden was seasonal, if I remember correctly. How about a nice dwarf conifer? Or some evergreen Hebes? Now over here . . .'

Flora wheels the barrow. Behind the counter a Mediterranean-looking woman comes out, limping, to price the contents. 'You must be Romita Mattock,' says Flora. 'I'm Flora Penfold. I'm a friend of Russell Marcus, who was at school with your husband.'

The two women shake hands. 'Andrew eez not 'ere today,' says Romita, 'he 'as gone to Melton to buy zome organic compost. We are zwamped by ze demand for zat. You 'ave no idea 'ow demanding people are.' She looks vanquished.

Olga emerges from the shrubs, rubbing her hands. 'I could spend a fortune every time I come here. Did you see the *Euonymus latifolius*, Jane? Too colourful for you, but I could do with a slash of red on my side wall.'

'Your deveel's feegs, ze are still on order, Miss Rivers,' says Romita. 'I zeeenk they may 'ave to breed zem specially.'

'Don't worry, I can wait. Especially for those!'

On the way back on the B1961, Jane remembers she wants to buy a book about dams for Alun Lancing in the museum shop in Eglethorpe Church. The church, which sits on a stone-dashed promontory on the reservoir's eastern shore, was deconsecrated when the valley was flooded. It's a showpiece now, golden and gleaming like an egg-rich sponge, and with the unusual transparency afforded by the replacement of the original stained glass with plain, set off against a watery background. While Jane goes inside, Olga and Flora stand looking down to the edge of the water, which laps on the pseudo-sandy shore in little waves from the disturbances of boats. Ahead of them, about ten feet into the water, the dead stem of a tree pokes up, a mysteriously rhetorical outline against the blue of the sky. Flora edges closer and peers into the water, remembering what Olga Kahn – and, before her, Jim Hoskins – said about the buried farms and villages.

'It gives you a queer feeling, doesn't it?' says Olga behind her. 'There are people round here whose entire histories are buried there. Their mothers, their fathers, the spaces they slept in as children, the views of fields and foxes they woke up to in the mornings and saw spread out by the light of the moon. The paths they trod to the schools they didn't learn in. I wonder what it does to you, having all that drowned?' Olga's speculations may be professional, but Flora shares them. It gives her a distinctly macabre feeling. It's the same feeling she has when she remembers the flasher that day in Lincoln Cathedral. Life's underside. The world inverted, like in those glass globes that snow when you hold them upside down.

A speedboat passes, gaily throwing up foam, altering the atmosphere. 'Water is symbolically very significant, of course,' offers Olga, as Jane comes out with the book in a paper bag under her arm. 'Freud had a field day with it.' She coughs at her own unintended joke. 'Many people dream of water. Well, why not? It's a pleasant thing to dream about. Of course, for Freud it all had to do with fantasies of prenatal life. One perfectly ordinary dream about a perfectly ordinary landscape such as this one' – she gestures at the fields of Meltshire around them – 'was diagnosed by him as taking advantage of an intrauterine opportunity to watch one's parents copulate. Very far-fetched, if you ask me.'

'There was a lake once that dried up, wasn't there?' Flora recalls the conversation with Lionel Tupper and Agatha Greetham in the garden of The Cottage the day she first found it.

'That's right,' confirms Olga. 'The history of water is linked with the mythology of witchcraft, which is also endemic round here. The witches were blamed for the lake's disappearance – or rather, one witch in particular: Amelia Woodcock. The local wise-woman. A river disappeared as well. There's a book about it in Oakingham library: *The Disappearing Gwater*. Some local people say Amelia Woodcock cast a spell on the whole of Bisbrooke – that's one of the villages they drowned to make the reservoir – and it's because of that that the lake and the river went. To make the reservoir necessary, you understand.'

'What an odd story.' Flora's eyes search the water for the distant shapes of ruins.

'But you can hear the Gwater River still in a most unlikely place: by the altar in All Saints', Little Tickencote. If you stand there on a quiet day, not in the dry season, you can hear the sound of rushing water very clearly. I'm surprised the vicar hasn't been to tell you. He's very proud of it, though of course he's got his own interpretation of what it means, like Freud.'

'Isn't there a piece of music . . . ?' begins Jane suddenly.

'Debussy, "The Submerged Cathedral". We had a young French pianist at the Centre – the Arts Centre in London where I used to work – a couple of years ago who played Debussy exceptionally well. I remember that piece particularly. Spellbinding, it was.'

Olga leaps on the word. 'Spellbinding! There you are! Exactly!'

Back in The Cottage, the three women prowl around the garden identifying plants. 'I know there's a lot of weeding to be done,' acknowledges Flora, 'but how do you tell a weed from a plant?' Her desperation is born of many hours trying to work out the difference.

'You don't, really,' says Olga unhelpfully. 'It's civilization again. Some things are *defined* as weeds. Myself, I let them grow if I like the look of them. To hell with the definition. This here' – she plants a stout foot in the red earth – 'would be called a weed by some. But I like it. It's up to you, my dear; it's your garden.'

'What about that?' Flora points.

'Wild mint. Eat it.'

'And that?'

Jane laughs. 'Yes, I knew there was some in this garden. That's hemlock, that is. *Conium maculatum*. It flowers, to put you off. But this one's better. Look, Olga, do you recognize this?'

'Lungwort, isn't it? You're lucky, dear. A companion for your friends down the end. Adam and Eve, it's called, or Joseph and Mary in some districts. Pink and blue flowers together, you see!'

But although Flora's knowledge of flowers and plants has improved, the state of her downstairs facility has not. Inside The Cottage there's no sign of Ron or Percy, though their tools lie around the bathroom, along with a distinct smell of shit. Flora feels oddly guilty about the women's stuff, but it was a natural mistake, only one of many more she's bound to make. Since she left London (and Barney, though she wouldn't like to acknowledge this), her periods have been unusually heavy. She doesn't want to think about what Ron may discover in his excavations.

And thinking of Barney, here he is on her doorstep the very same evening. Flora is writing out some cards for village post offices to advertise her flute-teaching abilities. So far young Alun Lancing and a friend of his, Donovan Prince, are her only pupils. At £7.50 for forty-five minutes each, that will scarcely keep her in logs and cat food.

Barney taps on the window, seeing a light in there, and Flora bent over her cards in its rosy spreading pool. Flora thinks it's a ghost, but apart from that she doesn't know what to think.

'Well, aren't you pleased to see me?' he demands. 'I couldn't resist it, Flora.'

'Don't tell me *The Panda Man*'s on location in Meltshire!'

'Not exactly. We're shooting a scene at Birmingham Airport tomorrow.'

'That's nowhere near here.'

'Well, no, it isn't terribly close.' He sidles up to her, Barney-like. 'It's nice to see you, old girl. It must be nice to see me – isn't it?'

'I'm not giving you supper,' says Flora quickly. 'I don't do that sort of thing any more.'

'No baked beans? No eggs?'

'Absolutely none,' she says firmly.

'Whisky?'

Grudgingly she pours him some, and puts a smallish log on the fire.

He sits, drinking. 'The water of life,' he murmurs.

Flora thinks of the tree in Jacob's Water. Barney seems paler and somehow less substantial than she remembers. It's two and a half months since she last saw him asleep on the sofa. 'Where are you living now, Barney?'

'Cal's still.'

'Why don't you get your own place?'

'You know me, Flora. I don't like responsibility.'

'What's happened to Judy?'

'How do you know about Judy?'

'I didn't till now.'

'She's got chickenpox. It's thrown the whole filming schedule out. Her face is covered with the most gigantic pustules. Yuk!' He downs the whisky. 'We could go out and eat,' he says, changing the subject. 'Where's the local hostelry? Yes, that's what we'll do. Go and change, Flora. Let's go out and paint Little Ticklewhatsit red.'

Flora looks down at her clothes: aged tracksuit bottoms and a thick black jersey. 'That's another thing,' she says, realizing it for the first time. 'I don't wear posh clothes any more.'

'No suits? No silk blouses?'

'And it's not a town and I don't paint things red any more. If I ever did. The world has changed, Barney.'

'For old times' sake,' he pleads, as he's done before. As she's done before, she responds, though more half-heartedly now. She puts on some earrings and a pair of black trousers and a little make-up, so that the Flora Penfold the Old Sun Inn sees that evening is a slightly different one, and not only dressed up, but accompanied by a very good-looking man with rumpled golden hair, a cheeky grin, and a voluminous capacity for the water of life.

'That trapeze artist is here again,' says Fanny to Ted-behind-the-bar, who's finishing up some out-of-date lasagne in the kitchen with the *Meltshire Echo* propped up against a brown-sauce bottle. Thursday night is always quiet, and Fanny's been serving the few drinks that have been asked for, including Barney's whiskies. 'She's got a man with her this time.'

Fanny's put her hair up tonight, pinned with a velvet bow. She looks like a queen, Ted thinks. He belches. Fanny goes back to the bar and chews a few peanuts, keeping an eye on Flora and Barney and trying to catch a few words of their conversation.

Flora has forgotten how much Barney drinks, and how much nonsense he talks. He goes on endlessly about the filming, about the wet night shoots on Waterloo Bridge, the residents complaining about the bright arc lights they had to have in Hornsey to film a street fight, and about the clapper-loader's affair with the wardrobe woman. He does ask her how she's getting on, but every time she starts to answer him, off he goes again. 'I miss you, Flora,' he says, thinking of the pustules on Judy Nightingale's body. 'Why did you leave me?' It seems he really doesn't understand. That she might have been bored by his ranting, his irresponsibility, is simply beyond the scope of his comprehension. And when he says he misses her, what he misses, she thinks, isn't her, her intelligence, her perspective on life, but her presence as a sounding board, a mirror reflecting back to him his own image. 'My God, I miss you,' he says again, noticing the protuberance of her breasts in the black jersey.

Living in the country has made her throw her bras away. She did it one day after coming back from a walk through the fields and seeing the udders of sheep and cows hanging free. It had seemed unfair to tie her own up after that. By the same token she's given up eating meat now – how could she consume the cows in the fields, the sheep, the pigs? 'I want you, Flora,' says Barney predictably, taking Flora's hand and putting it over his trousers, where his flesh proves both the fullness and ultimate emptiness of words.

'You're drunk.' Flora withdraws her hand. From behind the bar Fanny Watkins watches keenly, ripping a packet of cheese and onion crisps with unusual savagery – the sort Flora Penfold needs to import more of into her media characterizations of rural life.

Flora stands up. 'I'm going home. Don't come here again, Barney, please. I don't want to see you any more.' As she walks past the bar on her way out, she says to Fanny, 'Do me a favour – when he passes out, don't bring him home to me. He's nothing to do with me.' But on the way home, in the darkness of Church Lane, tears mist her eyes. Barney's flesh under her hand was like the softness of the dead rabbit under her foot, like the dreams she had the night when the gas ran out and Miranda was here. Barney still carries parts of her physical existence, its sensuality, like Adam in his boxer shorts in Percy Grisewood's hall, like the erect tree in Jacob's Water keeping watch over the ruins of former lives. It seems as though in the countryside, where it ought to be most alive, sexuality is buried, secret, dark – drowned like the valley under Jacob's Water, dried like the river that disappeared, brooded on at night but not open to the free full air of day.

While Flora goes to bed on her own, in the Old Sun Inn Barney Gunn drinks. Ted throws up the out-of-date lasagne and also goes to bed alone. 'I expect you've got gastric flu,' says Fanny comfortingly, congratulating herself on having eaten an uncontaminated Lean Cuisine. At 10.45 she locks the farmers from the corner table out, turns down the lights a little, puts a James Last tape on, and sits down with Barney, a rum and Coke and a plate of bread and cheese. 'I don't think you should have any more to drink,' she says. 'Have some of this to soak it up. I'm Fanny, by the way. Who are you?'

He stares at her. 'If you don't know who I am, why are you talking to me?'

'Miss Penfold walked out on you, didn't she? I saw it all.' She slips her hand under the table on to his knee. 'Are you a trapeze artist as well, then?'

Fanny's delicate young neck swims towards him in the soft light. Barney blinks. 'I'm an actor.' Her eyes are blue, dark blue, like the colour of Flora's car. She has wonderful dark lashes, like fir trees. He extends a hand and strokes her cheek. 'Nice skin,' he says quietly. 'Baby skin. Oh my baby.' He starts to cry.

Fanny hates men crying. She likes men to be strong. She takes the bread and cheese back to the bar. 'It's time to go,' she says abruptly. 'Come on, out you go.'

Turfed out of the pub, Barney sits for a while on the grass verge before hailing a passing car and just making it to Melton before the last train to Birmingham. Fanny takes herself upstairs to the nauseated Ted, and looks critically at his pasty rounded body in the moonlight before waking him up to satisfy the needs the sight of Flora and Barney has set off in her. 'You must!' she cries. 'I want you to!' Not for the first time, Ted thinks Fanny is Little Tickencote's Lolita – she'll be the death of him and, no doubt, of many others too, if not herself, before she's done.

8

Little Tricks

ON THE SUNDAY before Bonfire Night, Flora decides to support her local church. The vicar's visit could be interpreted as politeness, after all, and she wants to see the place where the disappeared River Gwater may still, on a quiet day, be heard.

All Saints', Little Tickencote, has an elegant Norman arch and hand-carved pews emblazoned with the arms of the ubiquitous Oliphant family (two rams and an owl). Flora counts a dozen people besides herself, including Olga Kahn ('ritual,' she whispers to Flora, 'psychologically relieving, like fireworks') and Olive and Percy Grisewood – the former in a loud knitted crimson hat. The air inside the church is nearly as cold as it is outside, though a small electric fire in the nave warms the stem of the brass eagle, whose outstretched wings hold the Bible, from which Trevor Tilley reads today's lesson, which comes – aptly – from Revelation Chapter 22:

> And he shewed me a pure river of water of life, clear as crystal, proceeding out of the throne of God and of the Lamb.
>
> In the midst of the street of it, and on either side of the river, was there the tree of life, which bare twelve manner of fruits, and yielded her fruit every month: and the leaves of the tree were for the healing of the nations . . .
>
> I am Alpha and Omega, the beginning and the end, the first and the last.
>
> Blessed are they that do his commandments, that they may have right to the tree of life, and may enter in through the gates into the city.
>
> For without are dogs, and sorcerers, and whoremongers, and murderers, and idolaters, and whosoever loveth and maketh a lie.

Flora thinks of the mysteries of Meltshire, of the return flow in her downstairs facility, and of the symbolism of the postage stamps on Eve's nipples, stemming two of life's potential rivers. Trevor Tilley's bald head gleams in consort with the polished golden eagle from which he reads. Percy Grisewood is asleep, slumped against Olive, who is thinking about the apple pie she has made for lunch (association with the tree of life). An old man stands at the back of the church, watching. Flora has a feeling she's seen him before. She asks Olga afterwards. 'That's Abraham Varley.'

Flora spends the afternoon in the garden. Jane Rivers comes by to give her lesson number two in sorting out the weeds from the plants. Flora pulls and cuts and rakes and sorts. Her mother phones: 'How are my botva, darling?'

Later on, Flora goes for a walk. She's beginning to have favourite walks, to know the lanes and footpaths and how one may circumnavigate the village in lots of different ways. It's dark, so she walks only down lighted Cabbage Lane and left on to Barleythorpe Road, which swings round eventually to cross the B1961. At the junction with Wheel Lane by the postbox set in a brambled hedge, she sees Abraham Varley on the other side of the road collecting wood. He tips his cap at her, but says nothing, turning into his cottage and closing the gate. The front garden is a pile of weeds, and the red leaves of the ivy creeping over the front of the house make Flora think of specks of blood.

The next day Abraham's there again, at the village bonfire. A corner of Sheepdyke Field is cordoned off, and Olga Kahn, in brown corduroy trousers and an old tweed jacket, is pinning the Catherine wheels to a special trellis, while Ron, his builder's van backed into the field, holds a torch to a box of fireworks, methodically sorting. 'The red ones are the wheels,' calls Olga. On the other side of the field, the bonfire is already hot. It is, indeed, enormous, and contains all manner of detritus, with skeletons of springs and chairs ink-black in the hot orange furnace. The fire burns one's cheeks; children are restrained by parents from its eager thrusting flames, and the intimacy engendered by its spectre draws couples, neighbours, enemies, friends, momentarily near to one another.

To the left of the fire from where Flora stands facing the fields across Church Lane is a hot dog and jacket potato stall. Smells of food and fire conjoin. The flames crackle, people talk. And then the first of the fireworks – huge rockets – splatter the sky with red and green and the air with bangs. A man she doesn't recognize, in green wellingtons, approaches Flora with a bucket. 'Contribution to the fireworks?' he asks. She drops in a couple of pound coins. He peers at her in the darkness. 'I don't think we've been introduced,' he says. 'I'm Brian Redfern. I live in Pudding Bag Lane. The house with the yellow door. If you need anything in the way of building extensions, tasteful patio doors, that sort of thing . . .' Sensing the expression on Flora's face, he backs off. 'Well, see you around, I expect.'

The man whose wife died of breast cancer. Not a sympathetic character, Flora thinks. She turns to the fire, hands in pockets. It reminds her of the bonfires on Highbury Fields Samuel had taken her to as a child. Irina, locked up in the flat, had issued all sorts of warnings: 'Stand a long way away, put your fingers in your ears. Don't let go of her hand, Samuel.' Irina said the noise of fireworks reminded her of the Revolution, but she'd been confusing her own biography with that of Galia Molokhovina.

'Have some soup,' says a voice behind Flora. Pete Wates. 'It's not very good, I'm afraid, but it'll warm you. Little Tickencote soup reaches parts other village soups can't,' he jokes. 'We're missing the fireworks over here. Ron and Olga are just getting going. Let's move.' He takes her arm and guides her over. She notices his touching her, but for some reason it doesn't seem out of place.

Flat-headed six-foot Ron and stout round Olga are manning the fireworks; he fixes them on the ground or on the wall, and she lights them. Her face, watching as they ignite and send their chemical colours into the sky, is that of a child, amazed, wondering. But Ron doesn't even watch – he's back in the van, sorting out the next lot.

Pete looks at his watch.

'Do you have to go?' Flora didn't mean it to come out like that: do you have to go, because I don't want you to.

'I've got to check on the sheep,' he tells her.

Flora, who knows nothing about farming, supposes that sheep must normally need checking at this hour, so she doesn't inquire why. 'I'll come with you,' she offers, surprising herself, but not him. 'That is, if you don't mind. I need to find out about farming, you see,' she quickly goes on to explain, telling him about Rural Rosey and her escapades.

Pete Wates is an enigma. Flora knows he's a farmer's son, a farmer himself, and that he lives not with his mother, who has recently had a birthday accompanied by a bottle of Blue Nun, or his father, who is subject to unspecified 'turns', but in a little cottage on his own at the edge of the farm. In itself not so odd, perhaps; except that Pete Wates's living arrangement is not to be explained by something as ordinary as a wife and children. No, the reason for it must lie in Pete Wates's own disposition; it must signify some underlying psychic detachment. As well as this, there is the interest in *Marxism Today*. And Flora knows he has a furniture-stripping business in an old engine shed by Oakingham Station. A man of many talents, Pete Wates, as well as of unknown character. She glances at him now in the firelight, standing next to her, hands in pockets, old muffler fronting the flames, dark hair half-tamed, dark chestnut eyes overlaid with amber in the light. Eyes you want – she wants – to look into, as though looking will cause their velvety depths to throw up answers.

Abraham Varley, back to the hot dog stall, and Olga, helping Ron to clip a Japanese Catherine wheel to the wall, see Flora Penfold and Pete Wates leave the field together. 'Women's stuff,' reiterates Ron thoughtfully. Abraham tuts, grinds a cigarette stub into the mushy ground, and turns away to take the footpath home across Windy Bottom. Olga smiles to herself.

The Wates farm, Ladywood Farm, is a mile outside the village. The main farm buildings lie just off the road, a mixture of stone and wartime-assembled corrugated iron. The farmhouse is a plain low eighteenth-century building. A light's on in the back kitchen as Pete and Flora walk down the side path to the sheep in the field beyond. Adjusting her eyes to the unlit darkness, Flora can't at first see the sheep at all; but she's looking for standing, chewing, busy animals, forgetting that sheep, as well as humans, mark the difference between night and day. And then she sees them lying in a clustered woolly contusion round the roots of a big cedar tree. She's noticed the tree before; jutting up from a low hill, it's a local landmark, with its inky branches flowing, stretching out against the ever-changing sky. But she's not seen it nurturing piles of woolly sheep before. Pete Wates walks over to them gently and stands some feet away, observing. He motions Flora to stay still. Then he takes her hand and guides her in a swooping arc past the recumbent sheep to the top of the hill beyond. 'There are a couple missing,' he says.

She's amazed that he can separate the woolly heap into different individuals. 'Does that matter?'

'I'd like to know where they are.' She imagines him counting the sheep like this every night, and suppresses a laugh.

'What is it?' He turns to her sternly.

'You don't suffer from insomnia, do you?'

'No. Why?'

'I just thought, counting the sheep . . .'

'They were served today,' he announces. But this doesn't help her, as she doesn't understand.

'How nice for them!' The star-filled coldness of the air is having the same effect as alcohol on her brain; she feels light-headed, happy.

'I mean we let the rams out to them. One hundred and forty-six days – they'll start to lamb on April Fools' Day. Helps us to remember, you see – from Guy Fawkes to April Fools.'

Aware of the capriciousness of conception in humans, and having hitherto supposed that sheep, like (some) humans, dwell in a permanent state of sexual cohabitation, conceiving and delivering randomly throughout the year, Flora tries to take this in. 'It doesn't seem very fair,' she comments.

Pete laughs. 'Well, it doesn't always work. Though there *are* little tricks we use to increase the chances.'

'Such as?'

'Well, number one, we let old Randy out on them first. He's vasectomized, but they don't know that. He gets them nicely switched on, ready for the real stuff.'

'Are you serious?'

'Perfectly. Ask any farmer. After old Randy's done his work, 80 per cent of the ewes get knocked up at the first go. We get the rest served again a week later. And so on. And of course we raddle the rams, which helps. But then no doubt you don't know what "raddle" means, do you?'

'It's probably another bit of your revolting agricultural detail, isn't it?'

'Correct. The rams wear a harness which is fitted with a coloured crayon. So each one leaves its mark.'

'Very practical. Could be useful in humans, too.'

'Indeed.' He laughs again, then points: 'There they are.' Two sheep lie in the shelter of the fence, a moonlit distance from the rest of the flock. 'That's all right, then. Sometimes they get a bit overexcited and wander off. Last year one fell into the stream. It landed up in Lyndon Lake. Abe Varley found it.'

Flora thinks of the poor sheep exposed to the trauma of their annual fucking. 'Well, perhaps it's not surprising. It must be quite a shock to the system.'

'You're over-identifying,' Pete observes. 'Animals aren't like us.'

'How do you know?'

'I don't. As a matter of fact, I'm inclined to do the same myself. That's the reason I won't eat them. I wouldn't like this lot to eat me.' He gesticulates to the woolly backlit shapes. 'Therefore why should I eat them?' He pauses. 'Have you read *The Sexual Politics of Meat*, by any chance?'

'Good God no, I don't read any books with *Sexual Politics* in the title.'

'Why ever not?'

'You think I should read them just because I'm a woman? Why do *you* read them?'

'Because they're interesting,' he says. 'And because the nights are long in the country. And because we must treat all living things with respect, including women and sheep.'

'And we have to read books about sexual politics in order to do that?'

'Civilization advances by a process of dialectical enlightenment. Unless someone does the enlightening, and we participate in the process by allowing new ideas to take hold, cultures stagnate and decay. I don't want to live in a cesspool, do you, Flora?'

Pete engages Flora in this argument by the carefully placed use of her forename. But she isn't sure if he is being serious or not. On the one hand, it *is* all said with perfect, believable gravity; on the other, the setting is so incongruous she finds it difficult to believe what she hears. Pete isn't some university professor speaking to an audience of literati in a gilded hall; he's a farmer in a patched jacket and holey muffler, casting his philosophy out into the cold night air layered over a field of sheep.

'I'm not sure I understand why you live in the country,' says Flora moderately. 'There are more books in towns. Civilization is urban; it could be argued that this is a backwater.'

Beside her in the darkness Pete Wates tightens his muffler against the night air. 'Oh, but you see, Flora,' (her name again), 'my political vision *is* about the country. The country *is* my utopia, but not because I want to go backwards in time. I believe in the capacity of human beings to live without towns and without the alienation and damage of capitalism. Nature – the experience of nature – can heal social relations. Man is a natural being, Flora. He is that first and last. Cultures come and go, and shape man's natural faculties in different ways – even sometimes so that we lose sight of the original groundplan. It's important to believe we *can* change the world. That we can get back some of the good bits of the old order without its hazards – without the power relations of squire and peasant, without high rates of disease and death, and *with* the benefits of modern science. That's what it's all about.' He smiles at her above his muffler. 'There you are, then – I'm sorry about the lecture.'

'I can't make you out,' she says, seeing him spilling his grand words over the field with the sheep in it – sheep, moreover, who have just been . . . 'What do we do now?' she asks suddenly.

Pete looks at his watch again.

'Do you have to check on something else?'

'I have to make a phone call.' Flora's face must have registered something, for Pete adds quickly: 'It's not a phone call about sexual politics. I edit a European newspaper. The phone call's to Amsterdam. Why don't you come back with me – we could have a drink afterwards.'

Pete likes Flora Penfold. He feels comfortable with her, as though he's known her for a long time. Her naive passion for the countryside pleases and excites him; he wants both to educate and be educated by her. Their easy companionship in the dark field of just-fucked sheep is leading him on – he doesn't want to be without her.

His cottage is at the end of a terrace of three, pink-washed and peeping over the valley in which Little Tickencote lives. Though the air in Sheepdyke Field, and in the fields guarded by the cedar tree, was still, up here it's gusty, and the door slams behind them in the wind before Pete can get hold of it. The cottage is tiny – only one long room and a kitchen at the back downstairs. The decor of naked light bulbs and piled-up books takes Flora back to her student days. The glow of a woodburning stove promises captured warmth, and the only other bright place in the room is the coloured monitor of a computer screen on a table at the far end. Flora doesn't know which focus of light to move towards, but she picks the stove, rubbing her hands in front of it and making up for this choice by facing the computer and saying, 'What a surprising man you are, Pete Wates!'

He comes up behind her and opens the stove's closed doors without comment. On his way back to the kitchen, he switches the computer off. 'I'll just make the phone call and the cocoa. Cocoa is all right, isn't it?'

'Fine.' She hears him talking in the kitchen, and sounds of milk being poured, saucepans, matches, more flames. These days she can't hear the hiss of gas without worrying about the orange soldiers of canisters lined up outside The Cottage in the interregnum before rural gasification. On both of Pete Wates's sunken armchairs by the stove are piles of books and papers and computer printouts with their serrated holey edges; she moves one and sits down, taking off her boots as well, and resting her feet on the grate.

After a while he comes in with two mugs of cocoa. 'Do you want something to eat? I've got some crumpets in the fridge. We could toast them. Like your feet.' He looks down at her, smiling.

The wind blows outside, and through the cracks in the stones, and the gaps between the window panes and under the front door where Pete Wates has forgotten to reposition the draught excluder. For underneath his air of calm detachment, a *mélange* of feelings are whirling around like a steaming, boiling mudpool; the glutinous liquids seize and swirl, and globules of trapped steam rise and fall, adding insistent plop-plopping noises to the atmosphere.

'You'd better tell me if there's a man in your life,' he says simply, in order to release some of this, and while the first crumpet is toasting at the end of the long brass fork with the gargoyle for a handle. He turns the fork over, and looks at the gargoyle's teeth bared in the palm of his hand. Waiting for her to answer his question (and knowing what Jack-at-the-Post-Office had told him about the pale, straw-haired man who swallowed whisky in the Old Sun Inn the other night), Pete's aware of not wanting to look into Flora's eyes at this particular juncture. And Flora, seeing the flames dance behind her cocoa, imagines she can see the face of Barney in them; and behind him other faces, other times, even back to Samuel Penfold, her father, sternly guiding her in the ways of patriarchy. It's time for me to get down to his papers, she thinks, and then – 'No, not at the moment,' she says suitably guardedly, in order not to give Pete Wates the wrong idea (and despite the fact that she'd be hard-pressed to say what that is). 'I don't want the rest of my life to be dominated by sexual politics,' continues Flora. 'There are more important things in life, don't you think so, Pete? Like nature. And peace.'

If she was expecting him to comment on this, she's wrong. 'Here's your crumpet,' he says, and hands it to her, thick and steaming. 'There's butter on the tray.'

She takes it and butters it carefully, still waiting for him to respond.

When she bites into the crumpet, melted butter seeps down over her chin. 'I thought of that,' he says, watching her, 'there's some kitchen paper on the floor behind you.' He watches while she bends and tears a strip off the green-striped paper and wipes her chin with it, and screws it up and tosses it on to the fire. Saturated with the butter, the paper detonates instantly into a red fireball, radiating intense heat and energy for a minute as they both watch it, his eyes now turned from her to what she has caused to happen, and then after this burst of life the paper's cinders fall into the fire, and it relapses back into its comfortably smouldering mode.

'November the fifth,' she says gently. 'The day of insemination.'

'I put purple crayons on the raddles for a change,' he adds thoughtfully.

Flora thinks of all those woolly bottoms, smeared with purple. And what does the farmer himself do? 'Tell me about your newspaper,' she says, not quite daring to voice the question she's just asked herself in the way she framed it.

'Some other time. I can give you some back numbers to read, if you like.' His manner is offhand. Isn't the newspaper important to him? What is? Why doesn't he say or do anything? She wishes she could work him out. He finishes his cocoa with a great gulp, and sets the mug down.

'I'd better be going,' she announces. 'Thanks for the cocoa.'

She gets up, puts on her coat, walks to the door. He follows. 'Flora . . .'

Her back is turned to him: she smiles into the space between herself and the front door. Then she turns to face him, looking at him directly with her night-blue eyes. 'Flora,' he repeats.

'Well, I could stay a little, if you like.'

Pete Wates kisses Flora Penfold in the narrow hall under the naked light bulb. It's a strong kiss, but his eyes are closed because he wants to feel her, not see her. The smell and touch of him are as she imagined – firm, rich, earthy. He feels both that he's always known what it's like to kiss her, and that there's nothing better than the fierce magic of the first time. He leads her back into the sitting-room. 'We don't *have* to make love,' he says, 'just because it's the day of insemination. Or just because we're a man and a woman. There are more things on heaven and earth than human beings, in their ignorance, can conceive. On the other hand, we don't have *not* to, just because of convention. I won't respect you any the less if we do, nor you me, I hope. The best lives are the ones governed by their own rules.'

'You like speaking in riddles, don't you, Pete Wates? But I should like to make love. We need to be practical, though. I take it that you're no vasectomized ram.'

Grinning, he shakes his head. 'I'm afraid not.'

'There's nothing to be afraid of. But I don't want to anticipate lambing time, and though I don't read books with sexual politics in the title, I am sufficiently eco-conscious not to take the Pill.'

'Leave it to me. At least my knowledge of biology is superior to that of the next man.'

She feels confident in this, but not in everything. 'What about AIDS?'

'"The threat of AIDS withdraws sex from the present, which is where it should be, and makes it a victim of the past and future." I'm quoting,' he says. 'But it's true. I'm not a victim of AIDS so far as I know, but I can't guarantee anything. I'm willing to trust *you*, though. I want us to be in the present. Nowhere else.'

It is hard to say whether sexual encounters with unusual farmers *are* part of the life Flora has planned for herself in the country. She herself would say no, but might be aware of slight contrary protestations from her unconscious. The bizarre eroticism of the dream she had after first meeting Pete Wates in the Old Sun Inn still lingers; undercurrents of nakedness and troubles with human flesh decorate her excursions through frosty fields of sheep and fireworks, and the manufactured warmth of farmers' cottages. Whatever it is that is happening to her now is linked with the quirky neighbourhood in which her dream figures danced; is part of the spell of water, earth and fire which she has apparently chosen to enter by coming to live in Little Tickencote.

Pete carries an eiderdown from the bedroom, and lays it in front of the fire with cushions and a rug. The light is turned off, and a beeswax candle lit. He puts some more wood on the stove, and his clothes – all of them – on a chair. In a few minutes he stands before her, naked as the light bulb. His body is firm and flat, and dark hair rises like the hides of sheep in little woolly curls from groin almost to neck. Flora finds it strange, the experience of being fully clothed and looking at a man naked for the first time in front of you. It's another way in which he surprises her. In her experience, men have always been reticent, removing one garment for each of hers, in a conventional game of parallel revelation – one which usually, moreover, now she comes to think about it, starts with them unclothing her, releasing a button on a blouse, reaching, all thumbs, for a zip. But here stands Pete Wates without a stitch on, letting her look at him, all of him, apparently without any shame or embarrassment at all – like Adam in the Garden of Eden before the naughty serpent came along – and looking at her, but only some of her, not being able to see beyond the jumpers and trousers and socks and undergarments she layered herself with for the thermal exigencies of the Little Tickencote Bonfire Party. She ought to feel like a voyeur, but she doesn't. He isn't a sex object to her, though she wonders if he is to himself. 'What a funny man you are!' she says again, leaning forward in the firelight and gently stroking the outer parts of his white dark-curled thighs; her hand traces the shape of his waist, round and up the furry bear front, and sideways to each of the little nipples, which make her think of the fate of Eve's stone ones, stuck down with the blue head of HM the Queen.

And all the time he watches her with his Dirk Bogarde eyes. A scene flashes through her head from a movie with Charlotte Rampling; Dirk and Charlotte coupling on the floor, she riding him like a stallion, him talking about it in an interview later: 'And I thought, what the hell am I doing behaving like this!' After that he got out of making such films, and wrote volumes of autobiography from his house in Provence instead.

Morality, thy name is not Pete Wates. Flora's forefinger drops down his midline, where embryos are joined, seamlessly for most of the way. Round his navel her finger flickers, describing circles, one after another; as it does so, the line of his penis changes and starts to rise, though she hasn't, and will not, touch it yet. He closes his eyes and puts his head back a little, as though to counterbalance the shifting of blood below. Flora feels herself flushing with the fire, her clothes, this maleness displayed like a Statue of Liberty with increasingly uplifted torch before her.

'It's getting hot in here,' says Pete Wates, eyes still closed.

'Lie down,' she advises, 'while I take my clothes off.'

From a horizontal position now, he watches her again. Off with her boots and her thick socks. Off with her coat and her scarf. Her trousers in a pool on the floor. 'That's enough,' he pronounces, 'for the time being.' In her white cotton pants and black sweater she kneels next to him; the candlelight and the firelight counterpoint a song of light and shadow, and the beeswax and the burning wood join honey to birch tree in a vapour of euphonious aromas. Flora's hands, passing over Pete Wates's body, bring messages to her brain which frighten her.

'Don't expect anything,' she says, 'I'm not in love with you. I'm not looking for a man to live with.'

'Don't worry,' he says, 'neither am I!'

They laugh, and she lies down next to him, propped up on one elbow. 'Feel free to admire my body,' he says. 'I won't even touch yours unless you want me to.'

'More and more peculiar,' she thinks – and says. Her hand exerts more pressure now in its downward motion, and parts his legs as it touches his inner thighs. His penis, which had become flaccid, rises again. Curious, as though seeing this sight for the first time, she watches it standing to attention, and with the wrinkled foreskin pulled back so that the pink glans glistens like the bald head of the albino vicar in All Saints' Church. 'That's nice,' he murmurs. 'Go on.' Her fingers move round the little figs of his balls – each one just like Armand Nevere's in the odd dream she'd had; round and touching the bumpy seam and then, at last, to the stem of his penis, stroking, stroking, and taking it in her hand so that a rush of fluid appears, milky, like the vulva of sheep in a misty field waiting to be served. 'I want you,' he urges, guiding his hands out to feel her, too, for the first time. But she has this completely unsolicited impulse to take him in her mouth and lick and swallow the fluid, the most intimate of acts. 'Careful!' he warns. 'Not too fast!' and pushes her head away and his hands under her sweater, gasping with pleasure to find her breasts, hot and heavy and waiting for him. She lies down and he takes one in his mouth, sucking and licking, and then the other. Then he lies on top of her like a flame curling and licking her and lying there lightly, tense, erect, against her, moving up and down, and kissing her face, her ears, till she smells of him, and then with a motion like that of a fox or a squirrel or a rabbit darting in its warren, he slips himself into her and she cries and he holds himself absolutely still, still as the heavy honeyed air, still as the frost that's beginning to coat the landscape outside, and for a moment everything is motionless, frozen; he looks at her, his black eyes and her wide dark-blue ones; 'Flora,' he says, 'Flora', saying it carefully the way he did before, in the field with the sheep, and she puts her hands on his white buttocks and presses him into her and feels him filling her up like the rams did the ewes in Cedar Field this morning, and her cunt aches with waves of pleasure and longing for his seed to come into her as theirs had shot into the waiting spaces of the sheep, but the mixed promise and danger are part of the present moment, the joining of bodies into one, the forgetting of time and identity, and then, after a while, he moves a little inside her, as the candle flickers in a cross-draught ribboning from window to door, and their humped shadow against the wall enlarges and then shrinks again, larger than life and then less than it was, each time he moves the waves start inside her and then as he stops they stop. 'I can't bear this,' she protests; saying nothing, he bends and takes her breast in his mouth again and draws the nipple out, pulling on it slightly in a teasing, regular gesture, and then, releasing her breast, he raises himself above her on his hands and throws his head back like an animal, and pulls and thrusts, thinking, it seems, for a few moments only of himself, and then, returning to her, looking at her, he says, 'You must come first,' and she feels it happening; 'Not yet, not yet!' she says, wanting to make it last, and then 'Now,' she asks, 'now, let it happen now!' and he gives her a careful, thoughtful measuring look, and moves once, twice, three times more, and she explodes under him in what feels like a rush of fluid, losing herself, falling over the edge of time, until she pulls herself back, is pulled back by him because, though she has forgotten, he has promised to protect her from the lambing season, and, after two or three further movements he slips out of her with as much facility as he used going in, and with a taut spent cry floods her stomach with an enormous pool of semen, though when she dips her hand in it she realizes it'd scarcely be enough to mark a sheep's bottom.

9

Daughters of Meltshire

ON A FROSTY MONDAY MORNING six weeks later, in mid-December, Annabel Lancing taps the glass of Flora Penfold's sitting-room window, knowing that Flora is very likely to be in there working, as Percy and colleagues' progress on the attic is proceeding at a pace which is normal for such affairs – they are up there now, playing a duet on the floorboards, Olive's lunchbox, filled with white-bread ox tongue and horseradish sandwiches, resting precariously on one of the cut joists.

Annabel looks pale, alarmed. One wing of her blue-and-white-checked shirt collar sits above her dark-blue sweater, the other beneath, in an uncharacteristic untidiness. 'You haven't by any chance seen Bronny, have you?' she asks. 'There's no reason why you should have done, but she didn't come home last night. We've rung all her friends, and she isn't anywhere. Jasper's just gone to the police station.'

Flora is uncharitably irritated by this neighbourly interruption. Rosey Mark 2 was coming along well. She's become a country housewife instead of a market gardener (not much difference, some would say). With a bunch of runny-nosed wellingtoned kids to occupy her, Rosey can now be much more scathing about the delights of country living. Flora likes her less now – her dual role as alter ego has faded. Don't you believe it, admonishes Rural Rosey, reproduction is only one of the structures of women's oppression; we're all sisters under the skin. I'm just like you really, and you'll certainly be just like me one day.

'No, I haven't seen Bronwen,' says Flora crossly to the anxious Annabel, 'but I was in all last night and I got up late.' Pete had stayed with her; he'd left at six, but she'd gone back to sleep in the comfortable hollow of warmth left by his body. 'I don't think I'm likely to have noticed anything.' Annabel's face falls. 'I could make you a cup of coffee, if you like.'

'No, no, I must get back in case there's any news. I can't stay,' protests Annabel, and then does. She pulls and twists at her yellow ponytail, and her sleepless eyes dart like agitated moths in her pale moon of a face. 'We've been having a difficult time recently with Bronny, you know; she's often out late, she won't do what we say, her school work's deteriorated, Jasper says we should send her to boarding-school. Bronny says she wants to go to Melton Comprehensive and be a garage mechanic. Imagine!'

'I thought she wanted to be a midwife.'

'The truth is she doesn't know what she wants. And one moment she wants us to treat her as a grown-up, the next she's a little child again. I watched her the other day on the back of Mort's motor-bike – she's got a boyfriend, you know, Mortimer Fanshawe, the son of Roger and Clarice Fanshawe, who have the farm over by the disused quarry. She tried to keep it secret. We don't like him at all. But there was Bronny on the back of his Honda sucking her thumb!'

'I expect it's quite normal,' is all Flora can think of offering.

'You should be thankful you don't have children,' says Annabel sharply. 'At times like this one simply feels one can't cope.' Her face crumples and large tears are manufactured on it. Flora hands her a tissue. Where are you now, Rural Rosey? she asks in her head. You see what I mean, says Rural Rosey back. But I'm not like her/you, protests Flora. She finds Annabel silly, superficial. Everything is 'we', as though Annabel has no existence of her own. But Flora must try to overcome her dislike. Be nice to her, you silly woman, says non-alter-ego Rosey in her ear. The sooner you calm her down and get her packed off home, the sooner you can get back to me. The twins are awfully near the duck pond, and I'm even missing a left hand at the moment.

Flora thinks back to her own adolescence. Irina at the narrow dark wooden table in the Bloomsbury kitchen, crouched over Russian chronicles while something boils over on the stove behind her. Samuel booming, blocking out the light. Coming home with worn bulging briefcase, smiling at her, dissolving tension: 'And how was school, my little one?' Brother Jonathan, noisy, dirty, interrupting. The summer nights in Mecklenburgh Square. The feeling of being trapped in the centre of London, in the centre between her parents, of not being able to breathe free. By comparison, she can't imagine what Bronwen Lancing has to complain about.

'That's Jasper back!' Annabel hears a car outside and jumps up to meet him.

Flora follows to find out, in a neighbourly way, whether Bronwen Lancing has turned up. Jasper shakes his head at the two women. 'Nothing, I'm afraid.'

Annabel cries again. 'Is there anything I can do?' Flora asks.

'No thanks, we'll let you know if there is,' says Jasper.

While the Lancings withdraw to Wisteria Cottage to remonstrate with one another about their relative failings as parents, Flora finishes Rosey and puts her in an envelope ready to be sent to Jeff, the *Daily Record* man. The rest of her day is mapped out. Bills to pay, shopping in Oakingham. From 3.45, three flute lessons. Donovan Prince, eleven-year-old Mary Pickworth from Barnsdale, five miles east, and Alun Lancing, if he's not too upset and/or his mother lets him come on a day of such tribulations. As Flora's name spreads round the villages, the music lessons are beginning to flourish. She's careful to be clear about her qualifications: music to A level, the piano to Grade 8 and the flute to Grade 10; amateur chamber music experience. But an experienced flautist willing to tame the musical urges of the Meltshire youth for a reasonable fee is a rare find indeed.

This evening Flora's going to have dinner with Olga Kahn. She's not sure what kind of culinary experience it'll be, but at least the conversation will be interesting. Before she goes out, she goes up to find Percy in the attic. 'I need to talk to Ron about the piano,' she says. 'Where is he, do you know?'

'Ah well, I'm not sure I does.' Percy inserts his hands secretively into the bib of his dungarees. 'Mebbe he's down at Overton Hall. Lady Oliphant's taken delivery of a new washing machine. A Zanussi; Olive says they's got thirty-six different washing programmes. Olive says they . . .'

'Yes, yes.' Flora's impatient. 'And if he's not at Overton Hall, where might he be?'

'Hum,' says Percy, looking out of the window. 'Mr Crowhurst's having trouble with his radiator. Bleeder doesn't work. Most likely an airlock, Olive says.'

'Thanks.'

As she flies through the house collecting her bag, shopping list and map (she thinks she might call at Overton Hall in pursuit of Ron, but has only the vaguest idea where it is), the phone rings. 'Flora, it's Janet. How are you?' The schoolmistressy voice of her sister-in-law is, like Annabel Lancing's, not terribly welcome. It soon becomes clear what Janet wants: she's ringing to invite Flora to Christmas lunch with them in Guildford. Janet pities Flora, a woman on her own.

'That's very kind of you, Janet, but I've already accepted an invitation in the village,' Flora tells her. 'I won't be going anywhere over Christmas. It's my first Christmas here, you see, and I'd rather not be away.' Most of it's true, apart from the invitation. But who in their right mind would pass up the opportunity for a rural Christmas? Snow-kissed fields, and an abundance of holly berries, carol singers and home-made mince pies, etc., etc.

Janet Penfold is very taken back. 'But Jonathan wants to see you!' she tries again.

'In that case, tell Jonathan he can come and see me here. You too, if you want. You're both most welcome.'

'But Oliver's looking forward to seeing his aunt,' tries Janet again.

'I'm sure that's not true,' responds Flora with new-found honesty, and remembering ten-year-old Oliver's habit of buzzing around like an epileptic bee (so unlike quiet, serious Alun Lancing next door).

'Oh Flora, how can you say that?'

Easily, remarks Rosey, taking Flora's side for a change. Go on, Flora, what are you going to say next? 'Don't take it personally, Janet. Women who live on their own in the country do get rather eccentric, or so I've heard.'

Strapped in the car going gently down the long avenue of horse chestnut trees that leads out of Little Tickencote, and by means of which Flora first approached it, she realizes she does have plans for Christmas. Her plans centre on Pete Wates. She really would like to spend it with him. Their relationship, deeply animalistic, has not yet reached much of an articulation on the emotional plane. Its pagan sensuality thrives on – necessitates – an absence of emotional commitment, responsibility, arrangements. He drops in to see her without warning, and without much consistency. Sometimes he stays the night, sometimes he doesn't. Sometimes she goes to sleep with him beside her, but at two or three or four, when the moon's bright, Pete Wates is up and dressed and out on his travels. The day after Jack-at-the-Post-Office said to her, with a sinful gleam in his eye, 'Pete had trouble with his car the other morning, did he?' Flora resolved to try visiting Pete instead. His little cottage can't be seen from the Post Office. But then, no doubt, someone would tell Jack about Flora Penfold's car parked outside, and she certainly isn't going to walk everywhere or drag herself up an impossible hill just in order to conceal her affairs from Jack. Rural Rosey has tried to talk her out of this old-fashioned prudence. You're a free woman, says Rosey; no ties – you can grow gently into middle age like a fine salmon-pink tea rose, unlike me, trapped with my troupe of little wellingtons. You can flower when you want to, and grow your thorns – it's nobody else's business, whatever that man at the Post Office says. As a matter of fact, he and that wife of his deserve watching – there's something funny going on there.

Flora stops and consults the map. Overton Hall is marked on the other side of the main road skirting Jacob's Water, a little to the north. She read the description in Pevsner last night: 'Overton Hall, built in the sixteenth century, with pretty seventeenth-century arch to the garden. Some interesting high chimneys and buttresses. A fine hall, with a wooden ceiling.' She drives slowly up the toffee-coloured drive, looking for Ron's blue van. The house watches her, immense, like a piece of giant fudge. Round the side a long conservatory juts out into the garden, and next to it is the van, with Ron poking around in the back of it, though not, this time, for fireworks.

''Allo, Miss Penfold. Is it the return flow again?'

'No, it's the piano, Ron. You said you knew of one, didn't you? Where is it? What is it? Can I have it? I need to buy one urgently.'

'You *is* in a hurry.' He beams down at her. 'All of a tether, isn't you!'

The conservatory door opens and a majestic-looking woman in tweed trousers, a silk polo neck and a loosely knitted Liberty scarf sails out on to the gravel. 'I told you, Ron,' she alleges crossly, 'I want the hot feed as well as the cold feed connected.'

'Yes, Ma'am!' He pretends to touch his cap. 'I's jest looking for the female connection.'

'Oh, I'm sorry, I didn't see you there!' Lady Oliphant stares at Flora.

'This 'ere is Miss Penfold,' says Ron. 'And this 'ere is . . .'

Lady Oliphant stretches out a well-groomed hand. 'Pleasance Oliphant. You must be Flora Penfold. Jack Roebuck told me you'd moved into Agatha Greetham's cottage. Agatha taught Corney the piano,' she explains. 'Corney – Cornelia – is our daughter. She was very musical as a child.'

Flora's eyes take in Pleasance Oliphant against the bulk of Overton Hall – or as much as she can see from where she stands; the rest can only be imagined. Next to The Cottage, this is a palace. 'Do come in for a moment, Miss Penfold,' invites Pleasance Oliphant. 'And Ron, don't forget what I said!'

Flora follows Pleasance Oliphant through the conservatory, which is beautifully stacked with plants and flowers, rattan sofas and flower-print cushions. With the conservatory door carefully shut behind them, Pleasance Oliphant confides to Flora: 'The poor man's illiterate, you know. There *are* still some illiterates in these villages. Meltshire's a very backward county in many ways.'

Ron's illiteracy must be why Olga was colour-identifying the fireworks in Sheepdyke Field on Bonfire Night. 'But isn't it difficult for him, reading the instructions for things like washing machines?'

'Impossible, you'd think. But he's got a wonderful mechanical sense. To make up for it, I suppose. My husband always fetches him if he can't get something to work. "This one's for Ron" – it's quite a joke in our family. We had a lame peacock jammed in the sauna the other day. "This one's for Ron," he said. And so it was: five minutes and the dear bird was free!'

An Afghan hound sleeps by the Aga in the kitchen of Overton Hall. Copper pans on yellow-tiled walls radiate domestic light, and a trail of old *Daily Telegraphs* on the quarry-tiled floor mark Ron's walkway to the laundry room and the gleamingly new Zanussi, with its male and female connections.

Pleasance Oliphant takes Flora into the sitting-room. 'Do sit down. I wonder – would you like a glass of sherry before lunch? I always have one. Could you forgive me a minute – I must just find Cook. We're having a party tonight, and Ruby Cartwright-Jones has just cancelled; her husband's in with his prostate. Makes up for all the female troubles we ladies have earlier in life, that's what I say!' Pleasance Oliphant's laugh follows her out of the room, like a tonsillitic horse.

On the coral leather sofa Flora waits till the laugh has gone, then gets up to look at the photographs on the mantelpiece. A sepia family group shows three boys with flattened blond hair in stiff little suits posed round a straight-backed Victorian mother with an unsmiling face above a large cameo brooch, and a standing paterfamilias with moustache and walking stick. There's a gilt-framed picture of a girl on a horse, and another of a man holding a baby in a frilled organdie dress; the baby has a bubble of spittle in its mouth. The largest photo is of a wedding couple: Pleasance Oliphant many years younger than she is now, in a high-necked ivory dress, wearing flowers in her hair.

Spectacle frames levelled off at the top date the photograph. 'Aren't they simply dreadful!' says Pleasance, re-entering the room. 'Of course I've got contacts now. And Bream – Lord Oliphant – had a hangover; you can see it in his eyes, can't you?'

She hands Flora a crystal glass of sherry. 'And what led you to Meltshire, Miss Penfold, may I ask?'

Flora tells her. Lady Oliphant hears the answer with a bored expression on her face; her interest was in asking the question, not in having it answered. 'Ah, there's Corney!' Through the window Flora can see a white Volvo drawing up outside, and a young woman getting out with difficulty, laden with parcels and with a considerable amount of excess body fat. 'Corney's getting married next week. To a guardsman,' announces Lady Oliphant. 'It's quite the wrong time of year, of course, but the young will have it their way, won't they? I said to Corney: Why don't you wait? If it's in the summer, or even the spring, we could put a marquee up on the back lawn. But as it is, the house'll have to do. We'll open up the library . . . would you care to see over the house, Miss Penfold? Most of it is seventeenth-century. It's in Pevsner, you know. Corney can show you. Ah, here she is!'

Lady Oliphant's face positively beams as Cornelia, plump and breathless, comes into the room and lowers herself on to the second coral sofa. 'This is Miss Penfold, darling. She's taken over Agatha Greetham's cottage. You know, where you went to learn the piano.'

Cornelia, a plain young woman, smiles briefly at Flora in greeting. 'Oh yes. How do you do, Miss Penfold? I've had a perfectly *ghastly* time, Mummy! The man in Brentham's was absolutely *useless*, and I can't get lemon silk gloves to match *anywhere*! But I did buy this, Mummy – it's Miss Rivers's latest. Did you know, Miss Penfold, we have a real live Agatha Christie living here!'

Pleasance Oliphant looks disapprovingly, and with strangely pursed lips, at the gaudy paperback Cornelia fishes out of her bag. 'She's not a very *good* writer, Corney.'

Cornelia puts the book down and struggles out of her coat, revealing a waistless cream dress. 'I'm simply *ravenous*! What's for lunch, Mummy?'

'Seafood ragout. Cook bought some crevettes from Manny's. And tarte au tatin.'

Cornelia's eyes swim with happiness. 'Yummy!'

'I must go, Lady Oliphant,' says Flora, feeling slightly sick. 'Perhaps Cornelia could show me the house another time. Could I have a word with Ron on the way out, perhaps?' She's just remembered why she came here in the first place.

In the laundry room, Ron's holding the Zanussi instructions upside down. 'Can I help, Ron?'

'It's this,' he says, holding a piece of pipe in his other hand. 'Not male or female, it isn't. Can't work out where it goes.'

Flora studies the diagram, but the text is in Italian. 'This is in Italian,' she says.

'Well, I'm buggered!' Ron scratches the table top of his head.

'Listen, Ron, about this piano . . .'

'Bring it up tonight,' he says.

'You mean you've got it already?'

'Out the back, yes.'

'But how do I know it's any good?'

'It's good,' he says. 'Concert pitch. Double strung. Burn on the lid the only problem. As I said. Trust Ron.'

As Flora walks through the kitchen on her way out of Overton Hall, she sees Cornelia Oliphant at the table, piling seafood ragout into her mouth. The Afghan hound is eating a plate of macaroons, and 'The Archers' emanates from a ghetto-blaster on the window, while white-aproned Cook, even vaster than Cornelia, rolls out puff pastry for the Oliphants' dinner party.

Having completed her purchases in Oakingham, Flora calls on the Lancings. 'Any news yet?'

Jasper shakes his head again. 'Annabel's in bed with Valium.'

'Are you sure I can't do anything? What about Gwendolyn? Who's fetching her from school?'

'She's going home with Suzy.'

'Alun's got a flute lesson later – do you think he'll want to come?'

'Dr Simpson said we should stick to the routine as far as possible. Alun will come.' Behind Jasper, the telephone rings. 'Excuse me, I'd better answer that.'

In The Cottage, Flora puts her purchases away and goes out into the garden. She turns Eve a little further to the left, so that she can see the blooming cotoneaster. Pete Wates strolls in through the garden gate. 'Close your eyes, Flora, I've brought you a present!'

Something trundles up towards her, and the most awful smell hits the sharp clean air. 'Horse manure!' proclaims Pete proudly. 'Wonderful stuff. Costs a fortune at garden centres. Yours for nothing. Gratis. Free. Aren't you going to thank me? You can thank me in kind, if you like.' He grabs her round the waist, slides his hands up her sweater. 'Got our thermals on, have we? Come upstairs, my lady. Time for a quick one.'

'No there isn't,' she says. 'It's 3.15. I've got a pupil at a quarter to four.'

'Okay, have it your way. We'll do it downstairs to save time.'

Ten minutes later Jasper Lancing, on his way to tell Flora the news about Bronny, is alarmed to see Flora's music stand, with the carefully arranged Kohler exercises Book I, topple and fall diagonally across Pete Wates's naked bottom. Because of this, it's serious little Alun Lancing who tells Flora that his sister appears to have bunked off up North with Mortimer Fanshawe. 'Mrs Fanshawe phoned the bank. Someone's taken one hundred and eighty pounds out of her maintenance account. Mortimer doesn't belong to Mr Fanshawe, you see, he came with Mrs Fanshawe before she became Mrs Fanshawe.' Alun pauses, not sure he's got it right. Flora, entering into the spirit of the thing, says, 'But Alun, if Mortimer Fanshawe doesn't belong to Mr Fanshawe, then why is he called Fanshawe?'

'Adopted, I 'spect.' The child looks at her with grave green eyes. 'I found out what they're called yesterday, Miss Penfold. There was a piece in the newspaper. Reconstituted families. Like soup.'

'So where's Bronny now, Alun?'

'We don't know. The money was taken out of the bank in Oakingham. Mortimer's clothes are missing, and his CD player. Bronny's taken her rabbit. Mummy says Thank God she's safe, except that she isn't, is she? I mean we don't know, do we?' He looks confused. 'I want Bronny to come home. Even if she and Mummy do shout at each other all the time.'

'Shush, Alun, don't worry. Let's play some music and take your mind off it.' The child picks up the silver flute Annabel bought in Peterborough, and plays a D major scale. 'Very good, Alun. But the C sharp is flat. Do you remember what I told you last week about your embouchure?'

When Alun's finished his lesson, Flora helps him pack up his flute, and goes with him back to Wisteria Cottage. This time it's Annabel who answers the door. 'Jasper's gone to work,' she says. 'He's complaining Bronny's wasted enough of his time. Did Alun tell you what happened?' Flora nods. 'Of course, we don't know for certain. It's odd, isn't it – it feels like a relief, though God knows what the two of them are up to. I'm so *cross* with Bronny . . .'

Flora makes her excuses and leaves. She has to do something about the horse manure Pete brought round, and she must get ready for dinner with Olga Kahn. She's also just remembered Ron's promise to deliver the piano.

While Flora digs the manure round the tired roots of everything she can identify as a plant, in the builder's yard up the hill Ron is playing Rachmaninov's 'Variations on a Theme of Paganini'. He's got a worn old record at home of Rachmaninov himself playing it, but Ron needs to hear something only a couple of times to be able to get it more or less right. If it takes his fancy, that is. It has to be something with a broad, sweeping tune, and a lot of noise in it somewhere. Something that makes him think of queer things – foreign countries, beaches, casinos, deserts, camels, diamonds. Hunger for them, almost; though it's a pleasant sort of pain – a kind of awareness of life beyond Little Tickencote, the valley of the Gwater, the fertile oxbow of land lying between Windy Bottom and Sheepdyke Field, and containing the corrugated-iron shack on the border of Woodcock Spinney, where Ron himself lives when he's not out studying upside-down Italian instructions for washing machines, or having a go at Rachmaninov in a builder's yard. 'Da da da *da*,' sings Ron, his big hands thumping away. If Percy were there, which he isn't – he has to be home by six, when Olive puts the dinner on the table – he'd turn a deaf ear to it. Ron's a good man with a good head for connections; he's never ill, never off attending to family matters, never late, always polite, and permanently underpaid. Ron'll never join a union; he takes Percy Grisewood's money at the end of the week and stuffs it in his back pocket without counting it or even spending half of it.

Eventually Ron remembers he's got to get the Bosendorfer shifted. He backs the van up into the yard, and coaxes and shoves the piano on to rollers and a home-made ramp. The combination of Ron's size and mechanical ingenuity makes this sort of thing quite effortless for him. He drives off, still singing 'Da da da *da*', and, coming through Great Glaston, hardly notices Cornelia Oliphant backing the white Volvo jerkily out of the drive of Overton Hall. He stops just in time, but the piano is jolted loose from its moorings, snapping the thin rope Ron used to tie its legs to the bolts either side of the van, and it comes crashing down on to the back of Ron's head with a great jangling of strings. Ron falls forward on to the wheel, and the van moves forward more than it was meant to. Cornelia Oliphant, peering mistily into the right-hand wing mirror of the Volvo, sees through a curtain of tears that something awful is about to happen, and cries even more loudly than she was crying already. Lady Oliphant in the dining-room, on the phone explaining to the vicar that the wedding is off, looks up as Ron's brakes screech, and the van and the Volvo collide, and Lord Oliphant, returning from a saunter with the hound, is just in time to sort out the whole nasty mess.

Ron comes round on the four-poster bed in one of the Oliphants' guest rooms. A large seventeenth-century oil painting opposite the bed, of Lady Dorothy Oliphant and her daughters, fixes three pairs of genteel grey-blue eyes on Ron's, but that doesn't help, as all Ron is able to remember is the Rachmaninov. He feels perhaps he's still playing it. He tries singing again, but his head hurts.

Downstairs, Dr Simpson has administered tranquillizers to Lady Oliphant, sympathy to her daughter Cornelia, and is now engaging in some man-to-man straight talking to Lord Oliphant who is, as it happens, fairly philosophical about it all. 'From what you say, Ron'll be round soon. There must be some advantage in having a head like that. The insurance'll cover the car – God knows what the man was doing with a piano in a builder's van – and I'll get someone to phone Grisewood about the van. As to the other sorry business, I've been telling Pleasance for months about Corney's weight. The girl's far too fat for anyone to marry her. It's got a lot worse since the engagement. No wonder young Robert's ardour wilted. Wouldn't yours? Mine would. Mind you, I love the girl, of course I do. You'll have to crack it, Mervyn. Whisky?'

Olive Grisewood telephones Flora. 'There's been an accident,' she says, with a certain edge of salacious enjoyment to her voice. 'I'm afraid your piano may have sustained internal injuries. Percy will keep you informed.'

It isn't until Flora's seated in Olga Kahn's sitting-room amidst the coltsfoot tobacco and her second glass of sherry that day that she has the details filled in for her. Olga Kahn has invited Jane Rivers to supper as well, and Jane arrives with the news, transmitted via Jack-at-the-Post-Office, that Cornelia Oliphant's guardsman changed his mind at the last minute. Apparently he telephoned Cornelia that afternoon to say that he thinks he isn't ready for marriage. The news upset Cornelia greatly. She took the Volvo out to drown her misery and backed into Ron, who was consequently hit by a piano '*My* piano!' groans Flora.

Jane takes off her dark glasses. She's wearing black again: black sweater and skirt, black leather jacket. 'I don't know who I feel most sorry for,' she says. 'That young guardsman must feel atrociously guilty. Lady Oliphant's probably tearing her hair out. The engagement of one's only daughter isn't a thing to have broken in *those* circles. Cornelia, on the other hand . . .'

'. . . is tremendously fat,' finishes Olga Kahn. 'She's much fatter than me, for instance. Though God knows, I'm no sylph. But everyone knows women are supposed to get fatter as they get older.' She looks down at her firm bulk with pride. 'It helps to ward off osteoporosis, anyway.'

'The question is', continues Jane, '*why* is poor Cornelia fat?'

Flora thinks of her stuffing her face with seafood ragout. 'Because she eats too much.'

'Electra complex,' advises Olga. 'Though I regret to say that if you look up "Electra complex" in the index of my edition of Horney's *Feminine Psychology*, it says "see under Oedipus". Cornelia Oliphant eats to avoid being like her mother, and to please her. Both at the same time. Pleasance isn't an easy mother to have, I imagine. Very rigid. Now the role of the cook they have in that great place, the cook's function as a role-model . . .' Olga's voice disappears into her own cogitations.

Jane listens. 'I admire the complexity of your explanation, Olga. But there is, as always, a far simpler way to understand what's happened.'

Flora and Olga look at her. 'Go on, then,' urges Flora. 'Spill the beans.'

Jane smiles enigmatically. 'Not on your life. Work it out for yourselves, my friends.'

Around nine o'clock, when the sherry's all gone, Olga produces a dish of stewed chicory, another of carrots and a third of falafel balls made from a packet, reconstituted like Alun Lancing's families. They drink tea with the meal. 'Next time I think we should go out to eat,' says Jane. 'You're a rotten cook, Olga.'

'I know. But there's a very simple explanation for that. I shan't tell you what it is, though; you'll have to fathom it for yourselves.'

'It's strange, isn't it,' Flora ruminates later over a pile of After Eights Olga finds behind *Civilization and its Discontents*. 'Both Cornelia Oliphant and Bronwen Lancing on the same day.'

'Both Cornelia Oliphant and Bronwen Lancing *what*?' demands Olga.

'I don't know. Escaped, I suppose,' says Flora. 'Or had a hard time.'

'Same thing, really,' says Jane, putting her dark glasses back on.

10

Man's Dominion

JUST BEFORE DAWN on the first day of the year after Flora Penfold moved to Meltshire, Abraham Varley is down at Jacob's Water. It's still dark when he gets there; the undergrowth and the trees and the water and all the hidden, living things wait in the dusky misty zone of disappearing moon- and starlight for the new light to break at the eastern edge of the sky. Until then the only light there is for the earth is the greeny-blue shimmer of glow-worms calling for their mates. Behind Abraham, as he stands there, a badger scampers back to its home and a community of squirrels quarrel. In front of him, the water gives gentle signs of movement, lapping in clean little crescents on to the pebbled shore. Abraham's eyes trace the dark silvered surface of the water: taut like aluminium foil, it stretches over the bowl of land beneath. From shore to shore, from one side, which used to be Bluebell Wood, where lacy infant trees now sentinel the difference between earth and water, to the other, where the cows Sally and Rainbow and Curly once grazed in Buttercup Field, chewing and ruminating and being called to milking twice a day. The cold air would make others shiver, but not Abraham, who is impervious to meteorological change, wearing the same clothes summer and winter: a poorly cut pair of grey flannels, a hand-knitted grey jumper with shirt underneath, a brown zipped windcheater, a checked brown cap. He walks up and down the shore looking to the west, where the blond spire of the half-buried Eglethorpe Church presents its timeless profile against the sky, and to the east, where fingers of pink light are now beginning to paint the horizon. Another year gone; another to come – Abraham counts the years since he has had to stand here: sixteen in all now. In a few minutes, when the sky has more light to offer, he'll take the small boat moored in front of the squirrels' home out to the middle of the water to above the very spot where, had Jacob's Water not been created, he would now have been lying in bed in his house hearing the world wake up around him, the beautiful living world of Bisbrooke Hundred, and of Eglethorpe, with its Main Street and its Saxon pinfold and its Norman church, with its stiles and its nicely rotting compost heaps, cidering under the weight of many pounds of windfall apples; of Spring Farm, where his family, the Varleys, had been for hundreds of years, with its fields of sown wheat and golden barley edged with poppies as translucently orange and red as the crepe paper sold in stationers' shops, with its cows and goats and horses and chickens and geese, with Abraham's vegetable garden, now at this time of year hosting rows of healthy dark-green kale and Brussels sprouts and straight white onions protected from frost by the wall of the farmhouse and by the fires within, which warmed not only the vegetable garden but Abraham Varley's own heart: *his* fire, *his* house, *his* garden, *his* farm, *his* land. Abraham's eyes are dry – he's never cried in all his life, nor did he then, nor will he now. There's enough water here for anyone, besides: water flowing, replenishing; water drowning, destroying. Abraham hates water. He'd avoid it like the plague if he could: it *is* the plague to him. But they put him in charge of the fish as punishment, though they saw it as recompense. And so Abraham farms fish where once he farmed the land. What he hates is the only link that remains with what he loved.

The silver is striped with pink now; pink and grey and slats of orange light. The warming light finds the odd white streak at the front of Abraham's hair and burnishes it coral – a jewel among the dark, greasy rest. In the advancing sun's path, clumps of oat grass and weed, and the strange curt lines of the dead trees you get above the surface of Jacob's Water because of what's beneath, throw their own black shadows down, back into the water, as though trying to deny the submerged reality. Each shape exists three times: once above the water, once beneath, and once inverted in its own semi-reflection.

Abraham unties the boat, gets in, pushes an oar against the bank. He and the sun now make different etchings across the water's surface; while the sun alters the appearance of the water, he disturbs its material reality. As he rows out to the middle of the water, birds begin to call: coots and redshanks and tufted ducks and herring gulls. Abraham hears the birds, but, like Pleasance Oliphant, does not listen, for he knows the calling will only set up resonances in his ears of other times, times when he could walk out of his house in the living, breathing morning, and see the birds in flight and singing there before him.

Up over the edge of Jacob's Water comes the ginger globe of the sun. With it, the new year; another, just like the old. Abraham stops his rowing, and after a bit the boat stops too. His eyes are not on the sunrise, which he does not wish to see in its present manifestation, but on the water; down, down, he looks to where the earth stops twenty metres or so below the surface. In his mind's eye it is all there still. The house as he left it that morning with the bulldozers waiting like monsters at the farm's gate; the fields harvested and ready for their winter sowing; the cowshed where the cows had been milked for the last time; the chicken run where he'd gathered twenty warm brown eggs only that morning. His ancestors too – their memories; their ghosts drowned in Bisbrooke churchyard. 'Here lieth the body of Abraham Varley 1609–1650', and all the others, and Abraham's mother, Martha, who died holding her newborn son in her arms. It's all waiting for him still, under the water, if only he could get to it.

The child, Abraham, had been born on Armistice Day at the end of the 1914–18 War; Martha Varley had laboured for two days and a night to give him life, and she lived to marvel at the glow of his sweet pink limbs and blue staring eyes, and to feel the weight of him against her, so comforting after the loss of the weight inside. But the infection that killed her was raging then, and the drugs that would later remove this scourge of motherhood hadn't yet been invented. So Martha Varley gave up her ghost to the fields and hedgerows of Bisbrooke Hundred and died as the soldiers celebrated the winning of the war; and Big Abraham Varley took the baby and nursed it as best he could with the help of sister Norah a mile away; and then, twenty-eight years later, Big Abraham himself caught scarlet fever and died the day before the NHS arrived to prevent things like that from ever happening again. On the anniversaries of her birth, marriage and death, on Christmas, New Year's and Easter days, and on the winter and summer solstices, Big Abraham took little Abraham to Martha's grave, and they put poppies there, or red dahlias, or holly berries, or any red flower in season to remember Martha's blood nourishing and shed for her son. When Big Abraham got into the grave next to hers, their son went every day in the evening, in the interval between the evening milking and his own supper, until the intervals lengthened to once a week or more, but were never forgotten. By then Abraham was a loner – not unhappy; indeed, far from it: he was a man content with the limited life of the farm and his curtailed familial inheritance. As it had happened that way, so that was the way God had meant it to be; but hadn't Abraham been given that most wonderful gift – a portion of God's England, with all its living creatures and flowers and plants and growing herbs, just for him to guard and nourish, and protect from the ravages of man and time?

Big Abraham's voice from his deathbed: the bed where he and his son and all the other Varleys had been born, where the hymens of Martha and her predecessors had all been supposed to be torn, staining the ancestral sheet, where life had been made and given and then extinguished, including Martha's own – Big Abraham's voice: 'Look after the farm, son. And find a good woman to help you. It's a good life at the best and worst of times, but it's not a burden to shoulder on your own.' Abraham had failed his father on both counts. He hadn't protected the farm, and a good woman had proved impossible to find. There was a story behind each failure, the details of which Abraham finds it increasingly hard to remember now. It's the bitterness that sticks in his throat. Being left by women, leaving the farm. As though their sin in abandoning him had caused his own feat of abandonment. An eye for an eye, a tooth for a tooth. Abraham reads the Bible, Abraham goes to church – not Bisbrooke or Eglethorpe any more, of course, but Little Tickencote, where he bought his cottage with some of the government's compensation money. He chose it because from its upper windows he can see Jacob's Water. This very spot where his boat's now poised motionless, not causing much, really, in the way of an indentation on the mirrored surface, is visible to him every hour that God hangs a light of any kind up there in his heaven.

As Abraham moors the boat at breakfast time, Lord Bream Oliphant's Land Rover passes on the road the other side of the trees. His Lordship is speeding into Oakingham to buy a New Year's Day gift for his tranquillized wife, Pleasance, and his fat daughter, Cornelia. Unable to have much impact on their emotional trauma, he thinks he will try a physical ruse instead. It's now ten days since Cornelia should have become Mrs Robert Belton in Great Glaston Church, wearing cream satin as thick as her own flesh. The wedding presents have been sent back; the library table where they lay displayed is bare. Stamfords' in Melton, who were to do the wedding food, have redirected the pâté de foie gras and some of the other goodies to the marriage of an industrialist's anorexic daughter in Birmingham. The only money that's been lost is the wedding guests' expenditure on the wedding list; and the Oliphants' own – kitting Cornelia out in the cream satin, and the going-away outfit of lemon velvet, whose matching gloves Cornelia had been unable to find the day of Flora Penfold's visit to Overton

Hall. In the face of such ignominy, Pleasance Oliphant, popping little blue Valium pills diluted with a fair amount of alcohol, staggers on – not exactly pretending that nothing has happened, but trying to use the rest of life to make up for it. Cornelia's taken to her bed, where she hides her rejected obesity under a duvet of flying ducks and marsh lily flowers, and feeds it with anything she can find. She plays her Sony stereo loudly – songs entitled 'I don't want to love you', 'Three times a lady', 'They'll be sad songs', and 'If you don't know me by now', by Harold Melvin and the Bluenotes – and watches videos of horror movies on the 24-inch remote-control colour set at the end of her bed. Plumped up against the pillows with her array of remote-control devices, she scarcely has to move at all, except to void the waste products of her inexecrable bingeing, and she'd do that by remote control too, if she could.

Lord Oliphant chooses the menu carefully with Cornelia in mind. Smoked salmon and baby tomatoes, he thinks, as the rising sun glances off the road ahead, not cream cheese, definitely not. A pot or two of caviar with Scandinavian crispbreads. A thin wine with more bubbles than sugary substances. Chestnut purée, but not a chocolate in sight.

Like the Varleys of Bisbrooke, the Oliphant family has lived at Overton Hall for hundreds of years. And like Abraham Varley, Bream Oliphant was born in the ancestral bed where deflowerings and conceptions had also happened, last breaths had been taken and dying instructions given. In the removal of birth and death from the home to the hospital, distinctions between the classes have grown up where there were none before; the Englishman's home, hovel or castle, has traditionally marked the borders of existence. Home, the haven, is also the place of transubstantiation: as the bird flies across a room and then out of sight, so we are all only passing through.

Bream Oliphant is sixty-eight, a lion-like man with a proud face and a jawline like a crag. He's never needed to do much with his life, though he does drop in on the House of Lords from time to time. Marlborough, Eton, Cambridge and the Army: the usual record. His Lordship is interested in architecture. Prince Charles is a chum of his (he says). More than once he's wished that his little Cornelia could become substantially littler. He might have fancied some little Princes as grandchildren too. Indeed, he would have liked a son or two himself; but his union with Pleasance Ruddle has been blessed only by the pudgy Cornelia, five pounds at birth but making up for it ever since.

The reason for Pleasance's subsequent barrenness has never been found. Bream has never bothered to research the rumour that the women of the valley in which Little Tickencote and Great Glaston lie are less than normally fertile. The women, not the men.

Bream Oliphant married late, in his forties, and was a reluctant marrier, though once his mind was made up, duty would be fully honoured. Before Pleasance, before 'settling down', Bream had had a good time. At Cambridge there had been some goings-on with various chaps subsequently proved to have a Russian connection. No one was quite sure what Bream's role had been in this, but it was all a long time ago now. Cook, who has a better memory than most people, especially Bream, remembers more recently a scared rabbit of a man called Profumo visiting in the 1960s. After Cambridge, Bream had lived in London, in India, in parts of Africa. Life doesn't tax him a great deal – only the Inland Revenue does that. His life now is the same day after day. The sun rises; he takes Pleasance a cup of Earl Grey tea. He traverses the estate, phones his stockbrokers. Deals with any problems his estate manager can't handle, involving the dozen or so tenant farmers and many others in whose custodial underpaid care it is. In the right seasons, Bream arranges a little shooting, and attends the hunt. Once a month he goes to London and stays in the Oliphants' little Westminster flat which, like Overton Hall, has been in the family for ages. When he's in London he also goes to his club, where he eats steak and kidney pudding, overcooked greens and a spotted dick and custard reminiscent of his schooldays.

The only remotely interesting thing that's happening to Bream Oliphant these days is that he's in the process of having his portrait painted by Mary Widdowson, Fellow of the Royal Academy. It was Pleasance's idea. Bream wears full military uniform, and Mary will provide a background of peacocks and blue Atlas cedar trees. The sittings take place in Mary Widdowson's Chelsea studio. As Mary examines the lines on Bream Oliphant's face and gauntly masculine figure, so Bream examines the lines of Mary Widdowson and her studio, which was designed by William Morris.

In the Oakingham delicatessen, Bream Oliphant selects his purchases, which are charged, without anyone saying a word, to the Overton Hall account. He slips in a bunch of sweet white grapes for Pleasance, and stops to buy her a bouquet of white roses at the florist in Market Square. Then, putting them in the Land Rover, he realizes the error of his ways – Pleasance will take one look at their uxorial whiteness and start crying again – so he takes them back and changes them for yellow ones.

Bream is fond of Pleasance. She's been a good wife to him, and it's for her that he feels the most sympathy now. Cornelia deserved it; she shouldn't have eaten so much. In the same way, *he* would have deserved it if he had been found playing around with little boys at Eton, or hanging a couple of milking pails on the college spire on Founder's Day, or talking to the Russians. But he wasn't, so he hadn't. Cornelia's mother, on the other hand, had done nothing to deserve being cheated of her daughter's wedding. Come to that, she'd done nothing, so far as he knew, to deserve the stigma of her post-Cornelia barrenness. Mervyn Simpson had called it idiopathic infertility. It sounded rude, but it wasn't – idiopathic only meant individual; Mervyn had explained it to him.

Bream Oliphant had grown up knowing the Ruddle sisters of Barrow Grange, Bisbrooke, in that way upper-middle-class rural families have of stringing their families together with the artificial social relations of parties and meets and nannying and schools. Pleasance was the younger of the two, Odile the elder. Odile, who was around Bream's age, had a passion for him in the war when both of them were young, and Barrow Grange and Overton Hall were full of lice-ridden evacuees. Odile would use one of the Barrow Grange evacuees – Charlie from Camden, the runt of the litter she unkindly dubbed him – to take messages to Bream inviting him to meet her in Bluebell Wood at dusk, or at the crossroads in Eglethorpe as the church clock chimed two. Bream always went, because he'd been taught you should respect women's ordinances, until one day in the spring of 1946 when the cowslips in Bluebell Wood were flattened by Odile's body inviting him to have his way with it; and he realized that, much as his own would like to, he'd never again be able to feel towards Odile Ruddle what he'd been brought up to believe one should feel towards women. While others of his class and ilk were insinuating and inserting themselves into any girl who'd give an inch, Bream Oliphant dutifully practised shooting his semen into a carefully folded linen handkerchief with the initials B.O. hand-embroidered in the corner by his old nanny.

Bream's rejection of Odile Ruddle caused a stir in the neighbourhood not unlike young Robert's rejection of his daughter Cornelia forty-six years on. But it died down, as such things always do. A decade later, the Ruddle parents were killed in an air crash. An Iberia jet taking them to their house in Ibiza (before Ibiza became popular) developed metal fatigue in its tail fin. Thus were the Ruddle sisters left in sole charge of Barrow Grange. Odile at thirty and Pleasance at twenty had been elsewhere when the accident happened – Odile in Greece, Pleasance in Florence – but after that they came home to roost, relieved of the necessity to talk to their parents, whom neither of them had liked very much. Bream remembers hearing the news in India in a letter from his mother: 'The unfortunate Ruddles,' she wrote – she always called them 'unfortunate' because she didn't like them, but then the accident did, after all, prove the felicity of the choice of the word 'unfortunate' –

> the unfortunate Ruddles have met their end on a Spanish mountain top. Poor Pleasance was called home from Florence, where she was taking an art course, and Odile from Athens (Mycenaean history). Of course it *is* time they settled down. I hope the Ruddles left a proper will. It's very important, Bream, to make proper provision for one's descendants.

The then Lady Oliphant used every occasion she could to instruct Bream and his two brothers in their respective duties. Bream, the eldest, had learnt his principal lessons by that time, but Liam and Emile needed moral prodding still. Particularly Emile, who at twenty-four had vacated three university places, and was currently to be found dusting the waxworks in Madame Tussaud's.

When Bream came home that summer, he called on the Ruddle sisters in Barrow Grange. It was 1956. The house, a Georgian folly with many queer-shaped turrets and windows, was almost as unfortunate as the unfortunate Ruddles themselves. But it stood in the most splendid garden, and in the midst of highly fertile farmland. The river only trickled, depleted at its source by the demands of the neighbouring Midland towns for water, but everything grew in its wide, damp bed. In the garden around Barrow Grange on this particular day, Bream found himself walking through a nursery crowd of butterflies between lilacs and magnificently flowering roses edging the drive. The door was opened by Smiley, the Ruddles' ill-named and double-chinned housekeeper, whom their family solicitor had wisely advised the girls to keep on, along with her husband, who managed the garden and the car. 'Miss Odile is out,' said Smiley sternly, 'and it tain't no bad thing neither. Miss Pleasance is in the parlour.'

But not counting out her money. It was in that moment when

Bream walked into the bay-fronted sitting-room and saw Pleasance bent over some papers at the round mahogany table that he first entertained the idea of having her for his bride. He didn't do anything about it for years – he didn't need to, not being driven by great passion, or anything silly like that. He also had to wait until the spectre of Odile was off the horizon. For although the story of his spurning of her had long disappeared from the gossip of the area, Odile herself still smouldered with fury, and with what *she* thought of as a passion for the leonine Bream, now seen only on his routinely respectful annual calls to Barrow Grange, or glimpsed in a variety of low-slung cars with a variety of high-strung girls, driving round the area, or heard singing in his rather fancy baritone voice in St Mary's, Great Glaston, on Sundays. Odile would have killed Bream if she could. She was a woman entirely without charity or a sense of humour, those two qualities often being linked through an overweak sense of self. The older Odile grew, the odder she became. Before she got much older, there was the sad episode of the pregnancy – disposed of by a stay in a discreet nursing home, and an equally discreetly arranged adoption. Then, having dabbled in archaeology and caught both hepatitis and dysentery twice, Odile had moved on to photography, and spent a not insignificant portion of her parents' bequest on expensive equipment. Next she had a car crash, and lost most of it and the car in the Thames at Pangbourne, and a year of her life in Stoke Mandeville Hospital with back injuries. Pleasance journeyed to see her regularly, taking fruit, novels and common sense, but nothing could alter Odile's disposition, which was to be angry that life had treated her unfairly – for none of these misfortunes could possibly have been her own fault. When she emerged from the hospital, she announced her intention of going to live abroad and becoming a novelist. 'Provence,' she told Pleasance, 'in an olive grove. I'll see you in a year or two, when my first novel is published.'

Pleasance, despairing, had consulted the family solicitor, a tediously avuncular diabetic who regularly misjudged his blood-sugar levels. 'What can I do?' wailed Pleasance. 'Odile is using all her inheritance; soon there'll be nothing left.'

'Each of us must make our own mistakes,' counselled David Necker, forgetting his insulin again. 'There's absolutely nothing you can do, my dear. Except wait.' While Odile got rid of her inheritance, Pleasance put hers in an offshore account, ran Barrow Grange and the estate with quiet efficiency, and took a part-time job in a local private school teaching art history. The estate at the time comprised a riding stables, and two farms rented out on long leases. By the time Bream had started courting Pleasance in earnest, Odile had reached the point David Necker had told Pleasance to wait for. The house in Provence had not, of course, proved a spur for novel-writing, and Odile had found a chesty young poet admiring her olive grove one day; he bore her off to a lake for the sake of his health. When that foundered, she'd had a go with Bream's younger brother, Emile. The two of them had taken to living expensively in Montreux, where there was, unfortunately, a casino. Odile came back to England when she couldn't get any more money out of Emile, the bank or her sister. She had massive debts, advanced alcoholism, and something which was diagnosed as mental illness. In 1968, when the students stormed the streets of Paris, Odile's current man, a rather sweet crippled otolaryngologist, put her on a plane and sent her back to England, first wiring Pleasance in Barrow Grange to warn her of the approaching package of trouble.

Bream wanted to marry Pleasance before Odile landed at Heathrow. It was the first time Pleasance had seen him even faintly agitated. 'But it's all history now, Bream,' she argued. 'It has been for a long time. Why are you *so* bothered?' Lady Oliphant senior objected on the much more persuasive grounds that there wouldn't be time to organize the wedding properly, and that if Bream and Pleasance got married in a hurry, everyone would think they'd had to. 'Besides which, my young man,' she told the forty-two-year-old Bream firmly, 'you've waited long enough – you can just wait another few weeks. Stand your ground, like a man. Remember the Oliphant family motto: "Patience rewards".'

Bream and Pleasance's wedding, in the very church in which their daughter Cornelia was supposed to be married, had been fitted into the *Sturm und Drang* of Odile's return to England, her discovery of Bream's betrayal, and a series of escalatingly damaging episodes culminating in her admission to a private mental institution in Yorkshire. Everyone except Bream remembers the wedding day as golden; as his wife had confessed to Flora Penfold, seeing Flora examining the wedding photographs on the mantelpiece of Overton Hall, Bream had got married under the influence of an overwhelming hangover. 'Go out and get as pissed as a handcart,' Lady Oliphant had chortled naughtily. 'Go on, my lad, out with the boys – a man must do what a man must do, but don't forget to come back in the morning.'

The sun had shone, the church's golden stone had glowed, Pleasance had looked almost pretty in her own long cream silk dress with the old lace train, and Bream's lion-like mane had caught every beam and atom of light. There'd been yellow roses that day, dozens and dozens of them. So when, on New Year's Day 1991, Lord Oliphant strides in with the carefully chosen non-fattening festive breakfast spread and the bundle of yellow roses, Pleasance Oliphant takes one look and cries – not at the food, but at the flowers, which, although they aren't white, none the less remind her of how the mighty are fallen. Oh, how they are fallen!

Driving up the hill through Great Glaston, past the low wall and white arrow-tipped railings of Overton Hall, farmer Pete Wates, with a truck of discarded pig troughs, sees out of the corner of his eye the flash of gold as Bream Oliphant carries the roses from the Land Rover. Pete raises a hand in greeting: 'Happy New Year!' he shouts. But Bream Oliphant, wrapped in his own thoughts, doesn't hear him.

The truck follows the swooping bend of the road out into open fields beyond the village and there, on Pete's left, lies the glassy plain of Jacob's Water. There are a few cars in the car parks, but it's early. There was a frost last night, and the grasses at the water's edge are like thin iced jade candles. From this particular vantage point, coming out of Great Glaston, it is possible to see almost the whole of Jacob's Water: the large oval and then the small one sitting side by side, linked at the northerly end with the thin peninsula of land in between. It is even possible to see the hotel where Flora Penfold and her American friends had stayed the day the flasher in the cathedral had shocked her into changing her life.

Pete well remembers the furore and the outcry that greeted the original plans to site a reservoir here. It was hailed as desecration of an area of great natural beauty, as nesting the commercialism of the tourist industry in with badgers' setts and the homes of moles and squirrels, not to mention the many humans who would have to live on its fringes and experience the disturbances of ice-cream vans and car parks. Beside such arguments, the possible unquenched thirst of neighbouring industrial areas for water in ten or twenty years' time didn't seem such a pressing need. The arguments raged; the plans were altered, many times. People forgot where the idea had come from in the first place. In the end, it boiled down to the views of those who lived in the valley it was proposed to drown: some three hundred residents of Eglethorpe, another hundred and fifty or so in the hamlet of Bisbrooke; the farmer Abraham Varley and the Ruddles who owned Barrow Grange and the surrounding acres of land, some of which was let out to tenant farmers. Not all these people were implacably opposed to being drowned, particularly as the financial compensation proposed was more than many of them would see collected in one place in their lifetime. But one set of voices had carried more weight than the others in the ultimate bargaining process: those of Pleasance Ruddle and her sister Odile. Though, as Pete seems to remember, Odile was not quite *au fait* with events in the Gwater Valley by then.

Pete himself had been ambivalent about the plan. It would have no effect on the Wates farm, which lay well beyond the limits of the proposed reservoir. On the other hand, the elimination of five farms – Abraham Varley's and the Ruddles' four tenant farms – would reduce local competition. Pete was only twenty-five at the time, and didn't particularly mind what happened. His father, Frank, wanted the reservoir, as he didn't like Varley and wished him no particular good; his mother, Doris, was considerably fussed by the whole thing. It was as though she didn't believe that the reservoir would be contained within its limits; once it was flooded, the waters might get out of hand and spread everywhere. Doris had started to make plans, hoarding food – tins and bottles and containers of all kinds – and was even to be seen raiding the local shops for waterproof clothing, and setting out to survey boatyards with a look of hostile determination on her face. In the end Pete took her to Melton District Council to see the plans and talk to the surveyor who had drawn them up, who could – and did – reassure her that there was absolutely no danger of the reservoir enlarging and swallowing up any more of Meltshire than could be helped. 'I blame it on her age,' Frank had said. 'She thinks she's Mrs Noah, Doris does. The empty-nest syndrome they call it. I read it in the papers. Women shoplift because of that, they do.'

'But Mum's nest's not empty, I'm still here,' Pete had pleaded.

'You're a good boy, Pete, I've always said that. But you do go off from time to time.'

Throughout his adolescence and early adulthood, Pete Wates had struggled with two images of himself: one as a farmer like his father; and one as a political radical, tangling not with local politics but with those of the more universal variety. In the local grammar school to which he went at eleven, bright as a button and to Doris and Frank's great pride, he had the good fortune to be taught history by someone who made it sound interesting. Emmanuel Pringsheim was a Jewish

Marxist, so he also took a particular view of history, which was indeed one of the main reasons he was able to make it sound like a good story – a story with a main theme and various subplots, a story with a beginning, a number of middles, but reassuringly only one proper end. Pete Wates's imagination was fired. After a history degree at East Anglia, he spent two years in Europe. Then he came home to be a farmer. He'd been bred with a closeness to the land and a facility with animals and crops he couldn't deny. At the same time, his education had superimposed on this an intellectual framework within which his and others' particular manual labours took on a special historical meaning. When Pete Wates got up in the night to attend a lambing ewe or a coughing cow; when he tacked nails into farmyard fences in the rain, or drove the big orange combines with strange European names – Deutz-Fahr, Krone-Conqueror, Same-Lamborghini – over fields bringing in the barley and the wheat; when he sowed the oilseed rape and watched it colour the fields with a painter's acrylic yellow – through all these labours Pete knew he was contributing to the great dialectical advance of history.

The modest paper he edits, the *European Labour Monthly*, is an attempt to capture some of the details of this process in print for those who, like him, see the world from a pre-capitalist, anti-capitalist standpoint. Apart from its own merit, the paper has the advantage of keeping him in touch with his friends abroad: funny dependable Horst in Berlin, neat mountain-climbing Constantine in Basel, scatty Florentine Luigi, quick-tempered Costas from Athens, skinny red-haired Michelle in Bordeaux – Pete considers himself lucky to have a dozen or so friends spread round Europe with whom he can always share an easy camaraderie, an identity of political interests, and a bottle or two of wine whenever he chooses. Of all of these, though, he has the most in common with Michelle Lapin. Michelle works the oyster beds in the Bassin d'Arcachon – like him, she's a farmer; like him, she could never bear to be parted from the surface of the earth, though for her it's where the oysters slither and grow, not where the pigs and cows do. The other function of Pete Wates's European network is to co-ordinate the movement towards organic farming. It's gaining ground now – even in Meltshire the vet has heard of homeopathic vaccine against foot rot in sheep, and the use of the male fern's root crushed with garlic for worming cattle.

Coming through Great Glaston now, Pete makes a mental note to call Michelle soon. After delivering the pig troughs to a second-hand farm equipment shop, he decides to drop in on Flora before going back to the farm to help Frank with the winter fencing.

Flora is sitting on the floor in front of the fire with Pablo and Dolly and a manuscript of her father's spread out in front of her. 'Unidentified, probably 1968,' Julian Peacock had written in a note clipped to the front. 'Based on empirical observations carried out by Gareth Hewittson (SSRC student 1959–1963).' The manuscript has no title, but begins straight with Chapter 1. It's typed on foolscap paper, and each letter has that dark blurred look which identifies it as a carbon copy. The first sentence of the chapter is: 'The increasing industrialization of life in Western countries over the last two hundred years has instituted the image of the rural community as the founding myth of a natural past; man's roots are said to extend beyond the complex technological present back into an unproblematic past of harmony with nature.' Flora had no idea her father had ever been interested in such things. She reads on. The first two chapters continue the theme of the opening paragraph, and are by way of abstract speculations on the theme of the rural community and its symbolic significance in people's search for individual and collective identity today. Chapter 3 moves on to recount some observations of a particular place, called in the manuscript 'Woodcock-by-Water' and described as 'a fictional village in the Lincolnshire fen district of England'. There's a map, referred to as Figure 1, attached to the chapter. It shows a pen-and-ink drawing of a village with labelled streets, little square-roofed Monopoly houses, and caricatured perpendicular sketches of ducks and sheep and horses. A church sits grey-eyed (lots of little crosses); a Post Office and village store are marked. The stemmed cloud of a tree stands on a triangular area of ground at the centre of the village. North, South, East and West are marked, with arrows to neighbouring villages and towns. The paper has yellowed, giving it the appearance of a historical document. Flora sets it down, suddenly remembering Samuel presenting her with the fake parchment scroll of the United States Declaration of the Rights of Independence from the English Colonies. Samuel had purchased it in a museum shop on one of his journeys to America, but at first Flora had thought it was real – that her father had brought her the only copy. Then, realizing her mistake, she'd gone scarlet with shame, though Samuel, holding her baby brother high in the air and declaring how much he'd missed him, hadn't noticed.

Lost in the past, Flora doesn't hear the kitchen door open as Pete Wates comes in. 'Happy New Year!' he calls. 'Where are you, Flora?'

On the threshold of the sitting-room, he pauses for a moment before bringing out from behind his back a huge bunch of yellow roses, the same as he'd seen Bream Oliphant bearing to Overton Hall. It's the first time Pete's ever given anyone flowers, so it's quite an occasion; though since Flora doesn't know that, it will go uncelebrated.

'What you doing then, lass?' he asks with the pretend rough accent of a born-and-bred Meltshire man. Kneeling back on her heels towards the fire, she smiles up at him. 'It's truly nicely settled in here, in't it?' The room is warm, and Flora, with her papers and boxes around her, is happy in her little domain. Dolly sleeps in a neat black crescent on one pile of chapters, the tissued sheets of carbon copies making a cornfield bed.

Christmas has passed without misadventure, and with – fortunately – no sight of Flora's brother and his wife, and the hyperactive Oliver. Flora drove to London to see her mother on Christmas Eve and back again the same night. Jonathan, Janet and Oliver spent Christmas Day in the Bloomsbury flat – Janet cross because of the displacement from her Guildford house, but resolved to do her duty; Jonathan, deprived of his exercise bicycle, going off to jog up to the British Museum and back while the turkey protested in the oven; Oliver's chemistry reacting adversely to something in the Christmas pudding, so his shrieking was a few decibels louder than usual; Irina pretending to fall asleep after lunch to avoid having to take part in the conversation. 'I don't know why Flora couldn't be here,' complained Janet. 'What is she doing in the country, anyway?'

'Leave my daughter alone!' The words snapped out of Irina's supposedly sleeping mouth before she'd had a chance to pull them back. 'At least Flora's living her own life, which is more than you're doing!'

'Well I never!' Janet flounced out to the kitchen and banged the plates around, resolving never to do her duty by the old lady again.

In Little Tickencote, Flora went to midnight Mass in the church, which Trevor, the albino vicar, did very nicely indeed, and little Alun Lancing sang 'Once in Royal David's City' just as well as any King's College choirboy; and his mother, Annabel, choked with pride and with gratitude that God had sent her Bronny back in time for Christmas, though in fact it was as a result of Bronny having become disenamoured of Mortimer Fanshawe. The Fanshawes and the Lancings aren't on speaking terms at the moment, but that doesn't matter, and will pass. Bronwen's self-esteem is injured, but she's resting temporarily before gathering some more with which to launch her next attack on convention. Jasper Lancing's invented some new software, which is making him happy, so things are relatively harmonious in Wisteria Cottage.

Flora and Pete spent most of Christmas Day in bed. They had a chestnut roast with Brussels sprouts and parsnips and *pommes frites* and rich cheese sauce. After lunch Flora put Mahler's number six, borrowed from Olga Kahn, in her pink bedside radio-cassette player, Pete read a stern-looking text entitled *Marx and Animal Liberation: A productive dialectic?* and she dipped lightly in and out of the *Oxford Book of Nursery Rhymes* they'd given each other as a present. It was quite the most perfect Christmas Day Flora could remember since the early ones of childhood, when Samuel had dressed as Father Christmas and filled her stocking at midnight, even as she watched him with eyes shut in sleep as feigned as Irina's in the company of her irritating daughter-in-law.

So Pete Wates, Little Tickencote, and rural life are all conspiring to make Flora Penfold happy. This is the first of many New Year's Days she plans to spend here. But she's only as yet at the beginning of her voyage of discovery into rural life, has only begun to feel she may be setting down roots. The quality of the soil – foreign, and dank with mysteries – continues to occupy her. But she is working hard at establishing new social relations, discovering what it is that makes the village and the countryside tick.

'Look at this!' says Flora to Pete Wates, showing him the plan of the village attached to Samuel Penfold's untitled manuscript. 'Where do you think that is?'

Pete takes it and studies it. 'Well, it's not Little Tickencote. Nor Great Glaston. Doesn't look to me like any village I know. Where d'you get it?' She tells him. 'That's strange. Did your father spend any time in the country?'

'Not that I know of. He was away quite a lot, but that was mostly abroad, I think. I could ask Mother.'

'Perhaps your old man led a double life. Perhaps he had a mistress stashed away somewhere in the country.'

'Don't be silly, Pete!'

He sees that she's upset. Flora gets upset at the oddest things. 'Don't fret yourself, lass. I'm only a daft old farmer.' He ruffles her hair. 'What d'you say we go on a jaunt this evening? There's a New Year's Day party at the Old Sun Inn – fancy dress. I don't hold with that sort of thing myself, but Mum won two tickets in the WI raffle. Food and unlimited cowslip wine.'

'I didn't know your mum knew about us.'

'Jack-at-the-Post-Office again. She handed me the tickets with a sly look on her face. "Here you are, Pete," she said. "Frank and I are too old for gallivanting. Why don't you take your new lady?"'

'That sounds as though you had an old one,' objects Flora.

'I did, I did. Eighty she were, if she were a day.'

Flora can't get Pete to be serious about his past. 'How can I go in fancy dress, with half a day's notice?'

'Oh shucks, lass, it's no big deal, you're fine as you are. Now me, myself, I'm going as a vegetable, which shouldn't be too hard. A black radish with a curly green head. Mum's dying a broomhead green. Then it's on with the black tights . . .'

'Very sexy. Perhaps I should be a carrot? Or a swede?'

'We don't have to go as a couple.'

'No, of course not.'

She turns away and tidies up the papers but he, like Samuel Penfold before him, doesn't notice that she's upset. 'You'll think of something. I'll call for you at seven.'

Flora rustles through her sketchy wardrobe. Apart from jeans and sweaters and similar leisure wear, her Islington Arts Centre suits swing primly on their hangers. There are four or five print dresses, and two black ones. A long black skirt and a blue velvet evening dress with a tightly fitting bodice and little straps, which Flora had bought in Copenhagen for a party with Lars Lyngby many years ago. Idly, she wonders if it still fits her, and tries it on with the frosty air of Little Tickencote peeking at her through the window. The zip's tight, but it does still close. She turns this way and that looking at herself in the mirror, putting the bedside lamp on to see better, as it begins to darken outside. The crushed blue of the dress matches and accentuates her eyes. The upper curves of her breasts are as smooth as eggshell, her white neck and small waist set off the colour and texture of the dress like fireworks against a night sky. Impulsively, she takes her light-brown hair, which has grown since she moved to the country, in one hand and piles it on top of her head, finding a few pins in the drawer with which to fix it there. Then, scrabbling in another drawer, she brings out a diamond paste necklace Samuel had brought back from one of his trips – Milan or Hamburg, she can't remember where.

In front of the mirror the vision is completed: Flora Penfold as elegant evening-dress lady, all blue and silver and white, with none of the rough edges of the country showing.

'Look over there!' says Petula Nevere to Armand in the master bedroom of Tiptree Cottage over Pudding Bag Lane. 'At our neighbour preening herself! Who does she think she is?'

Petula turns smartly on her stiletto heels and goes downstairs to watch 'Holiday 91' on ITV. She fancies Jamaica this year. Left to his own devices, Armand swings himself out of bed, where he's recuperating from the flu, and looks at Flora Penfold in the cosily lit window. He is impressed. She reminds him of a Dutch painting. He regrets that because of his illness he will not be joining her in the Old Sun Inn tonight.

Or I could go as a witch, contemplates Flora. There's a perfectly good broom downstairs. What do you think, Dolly? The cat's yellow-green eyes blink. I know – you could come as well! As if understanding what Flora has said, the cat turns and exits, waving her tail with the slow, slightly jerky rhythm of feline displeasure.

Perhaps not. I know – I'll go as a flower! A blue flower. A delphinium, a . . . where's my flower book?

Pete Wates isn't surprised when Flora emerges triumphantly flushed from her afternoon's exertions as a forget-me-not. Blue paper flowers circle her head; a green slash – a chiffon scarf – is shining across her blue velvet hips, and she's found some white evening gloves, which she's dyed with a bottle of green ink to match the sash. 'What do you think?'

'Very rural. Quite fetching, actually.'

'How are we going to get there?'

'We walk, of course.'

'But it's cold!'

'Put your coat on.'

'I'll look pretty silly with all this blue paper sticking out of it.'

'Never fear, the streets of Little T will be running with odd creatures tonight.'

'Proceeds to Cancer Research,' says Brian Redfern, standing with a bucket as he did on Bonfire Night, though this time in the warmth of the Old Sun Inn, which is just as well, as Brian is dressed rather skimpily as Peter Rabbit. His white tights match Pete's black ones. Ted-behind-the-bar isn't wearing tights – he's come as a sheep – but the front of his woolly helmet is up, as he's currently coating his moustache with frothy Guinness to complete the disguise. Fanny is a sunflower in a tight gold lamé costume with bands of yellow tinsel from the Christmas tree circling her head. You can see she's wearing no underwear beneath the stretched nylon lamé. Martin Crowhurst is a jacket potato with a blob of Plasticine butter on his side; schoolteacher Bridget wears a board back and front saying 'Country Calendar'. Pete, looking at this, says to Flora, 'I forgot to warn you the theme is the countryside.'

Petula Nevere is a rose. Two sisters from the cottages the other side of Sheepdyke Field have come as lettuces. Jasper Lancing has difficulty walking as an electricity pylon ('That's stretching the theme a bit, isn't it?' complains Flora. 'It had to be something mechanical,' points out Jasper); and Annabel says she's a water snake, though in a green woolly swimsuit and rubber flippers and a home-made paper hat, she looks like somebody in a green woolly swimsuit and rubber flippers and a home-made paper hat. Jack and Joan Roebuck trundle in as the back and front end of a cow (costume courtesy of the Meltshire Yellow Pages). Flora's glad she chose to be a forget-me-not when Olga Kahn and Jane Rivers make their entrance as two witches. Jane wears black, as usual, and Olga a white version of the same costume: robe, cloak and tall hat. Both carry brooms with paper cats sitting on them – Jane's black, Olga's white. 'Olga's a white witch,' explains Jane. 'You know, the good sort – and I'm the bad sort.'

'Good, isn't it, for a psychoanalyst!' says Olga, smiling, next to Flora. 'May I say hallo to the black radish who is, I take it, your young man that I've been hearing so much about?' Then Percy Grisewood and Olive make a delayed and surprisingly imaginative entrance as a rural plumber and his wife, though the other way round. Olive wears Percy's dungarees with a few chrysanthemums poking out from the metal clips to emphasize the rural note, and Percy staggers in crammed into a pair of Olive's medium-heeled shoes, stockings and a pleated skirt held together with safety pins. His transformation is completed with a padded jumper, a wig and a bag of charity shop knitting. 'Where's Ron?' someone asks.

'Ah,' says Percy, 'he's in the van.'

Ron's not been quite the same since he was knocked on the head by the Bosendorfer. Though he's willing to enter into the spirit of things and dress up as instructed by the Grisewoods, he lost his nerve at the last minute and is sitting moodily in the back of the van on a three-litre tin of caramel emulsion. Martin Crowhurst, the jacket potato, Fanny and Pete go out to retrieve him. When they drag him through the door, everyone shrieks with laughter, as not only is Ron's enormous bulk dressed as the tiniest creature Percy could think of – a little red-breasted robin – but Ron's holding the can of emulsion up as a figleaf to cover the crotch of his brown nylon tights.

'Men in tights,' says Flora again, this time out loud.

'Jesus, Ron!' exclaims Ted, tears falling into his sheepish eyes. 'Come and stand behind the bar, where no one'll see you!' Fanny the sunflower leads him by the hand and sits him on a stool with a pint and some crisps.

'That's better,' says Ron, downing his Guinness. 'That's much better. I feel much happier now.'

'Is this a Little Tickencote tradition?' Flora asks.

'Well, they had one last year and the year before, so I suppose so.' Martin Crowhurst's carrotty head keeps colliding with Flora's blue paper flowers. 'Silly, isn't it?'

'Oh, I don't know, I think it's quite fun. If you think it's silly, what are you doing here?'

'I suppose I just drifted along. Like I drift into lots of things. I sometimes think life's like that, don't you? We never actually *choose* anything, do we? It all just happens.' Martin shrugs his shoulders despairingly. Flora looks at him curiously. 'Oh don't mind me. It's all words really. I don't mean a word of it. I've got insomnia again. Haven't slept for a week. Boring, isn't it?'

Brian Redfern, as Peter Rabbit, is standing the other side of Flora. She feels him watching her carefully. 'Miss Penfold,' he says eventually, in a measured way, 'I hope you don't think everyone who lives in Little Tickencote is crazy. Some of us are ordinary. Take my good self, for instance – I lead a very ordinary life. I'm in property, you know. Nothing on too major a scale, but enough to keep the wolf from the door. I participate in these events out of a sense of civic duty. And because my wife, May – she died last year of cancer – believed strongly one should make a contribution to village life. No, we're not all weirdos!'

At eleven o'clock the door opens and Bream Oliphant walks in, followed by Abraham Varley. Neither of them is wearing fancy-dress costume. 'Good evening, everyone,' says Bream, 'I've come as a landlord' – he turns and sees Abraham – 'and I suppose this is the peasant behind me.'

'I'm no peasant,' snarls Abraham.

Fanny, the gold lamé peacemaker, gets up. 'Come on, Mr Varley,' she says, taking Abraham by the arm. 'There's no need to get nasty. Let's get a drink inside you, shall we?'

Ted watches her aplomb with approval: his little Fanny is beginning to use her managerial talents beyond the bedroom quite effectively now, isn't she! Abraham looks at Fanny's gold lamé nipples and leaps away from her touch. 'Don't you get near me, you . . . you whore!'

'This is impossible!' whispers Pete to Flora, as do various of the fancy dressers to their partners. But only two people, apart from Fanny, get up to do something about it. One is Ron, who can't bear people being unpleasant to one another. 'I should get out of here if I were you,' he advises uncompromisingly. 'Fast.' Drawing himself up to his full height in front of Abraham, which is difficult in his robin redbreast gear, Ron takes the bird's head off and tucks it under his right arm. His left he places on Abraham's shoulder, but it has the same effect as Fanny's much lighter gold lamé touch, and Abraham jumps away from it.

'The touch of flesh,' murmurs Pete to Flora, knowingly.

Bream Oliphant stands to one side. 'I'll take him. I'm sorry, I didn't anticipate this.'

'I want a pint!' says Abraham, standing his ground. 'I'm entitled to a drink. You ain't the only folks to have a good time.' His lined eyes watch them all dully. The assembly of vegetables and fruits and wildlife and electricity pylons watch him back. A nasty hush falls over the Old Sun Inn. Then the black witch, Jane Rivers, steps forward, and walks towards Abraham. She speaks straight into his face without touching him. 'Listen, Dad,' she says, gently but firmly, 'these people don't want you here. Think of it as their fault, not yours. It'd be better if you went home now.' Looking at her for a long moment, Abraham turns and leaves without a word.

11

The Curse of Women

THE NIGHT of the fancy-dress party, Flora can't sleep. She and Pete go back to The Cottage at midnight, hurrying across Main Street and down Pudding Bag and into Cabbage Lane in the icy darkness with Jasper Lancing, the electricity pylon, and his wife, the poorly imitated water snake. 'For God's sake take those flippers off, Annabel,' shouts Jasper. But Annabel, pissed as a handcart in the local phrase, is incapable of steering anything, with or without flippers. Ahead of them Olga Kahn rolls down Spring Lane like a solid sparkling snowball in the crisp air by the duck pond, which is iced over like a thick lemon lolly.

Now, at 2 A.M., Flora lies beside Pete in the big warm bed in a room lit by moonlight splintering the folds of linen curtains, picking its way over chest and chair, showing up the fluorescent crinkles of the blue velvet evening dress cast in a crescent heap across the foot of the bed, seeing its own image in mirrors bought for a song at Stark's Auction Centre. The room is still, but the absence of motion is not tranquillity – rather, waiting: an expectant pause, a prelude, gentle and considerate, a forewarning. By the blue dress sleeps Dolly, and on the opposite corner of the bed, Pablo. Next to Flora, Pete Wates lies on his back dreaming of the lambing time of farms and newspapers. The white duvet rises and falls with the rhythm of Pete's breathing, and his body warms Flora in her strangely wide-awake state – uncommon for her: a product, perhaps, of the unusual evening, or of events earlier in the day – her discovery of father Samuel's rural explorations; Pete Wates's remark, 'We don't have to go as a couple'. Men insinuating themselves into her life, making themselves necessary to her, at the same time as doing queerly independent things, and staking out for themselves terrain she thought was hers. Is that it? Perhaps. And then there are the odd events. The dead bird, the stamped statue of Eve, the unfortunate piano. Is it random bad luck or sinister conspiracy? What has she brought on herself by coming here? Flora turns, closes her eyes: she ought to sleep – tomorrow there are three hours of flute lessons, and Rosey's rural New Year's resolutions to be accomplished (an end to reproduction), and Percy Grisewood to be chased, and Ron to see about the piano, which has gone to Mr Prior in Cedarton to be delivered of the damage caused to its insides by the collision with Ron's head. Eyes closed: the white-blue moonlight's gone, the material shapes of the room fade, but bunnies and witches and birds with heads under human arms appear instead, mocking, laughing, conspiring. A sheep holding a pint of ale, a sparrow with a furry man's crotch, a cow with a gossipy back end: 'Stamps? No. But I can let you have a rumour or two for nothing along with those black radishes what have been lingering there for days, their green feathery tops falling limply through the wire tray; I can tell you of the woman who's new to the village and the man who visits her, of the child that's no longer a child, though she'd rather suck her thumb than anything else, of the publican's wife who scarpered off, seeing what gold lamé nipples do to her inconstant husband's virility; I know where baby-faced Armand Nevere came from, not to mention the brassy Petula, and I've a notion that they'll win their fight for the dormer window, it doesn't matter what Mr Lancing says; will the sheep or the cows mind, in Sheepdyke Field – will they mind Petula Nevere in her negligée looking at them? Or the shrunken Gwater trickling its way through thistles and cowpats ending up as nothing because of what witches do? Oh, I know they say it's the reservoir, but the Gwater was a gonner long before that, and Lyndon Lake's a shadow of its former self, and then, by Bidlington Manor in the old days there was another where lilies floated, where the ducks on Little Tickencote pond came from, in Barratt's Coppice, next to the Neveres' house, backing on to the graveyard, now there's a name for you . . .' 'Shush,' says Joan at the front end, 'I'm on the phone to the DSS and I can't hear a word the poor man is saying.'

'Poor man? I'm a poor man,' complains Brian Redfern, holding out his bucket for coins, white fluffy bobtail sticking to one side like a powder puff on a parsnip. 'Pity me all alone in my house with a yellow door.' 'Not only you,' says Bridget Crowhurst, sporting her Country Calendar. 'Think of me, barren, bereft.' 'Par for the course,' replies husband Martin, butter trying to melt on the side of his brown skin, 'you shouldn't be so houseproud – what's a bit of dust beside the light in the eyes of a baby?' Baby, baby face. Flora's eyes open again. This is an odd village. Something is going on here. Something to do with men and women and water and fertility – 'Adam and Eve and Pinch Me went down to the river to bathe; Adam and Eve were drowned, so who do you think was saved?' The childish chant presents itself suddenly in Flora's head. Adam and Eve in the Garden of Eden; the tree of the knowledge of good and evil. The serpent, beguiling. God's complaint: 'Who told thee that thou wast naked? Hast thou eaten of the tree, whereof I commanded thee that thou shouldest not eat?' 'Not my fault,' says Adam: 'blame the lady. She may be a spare rib, but my God, she's wicked with it.' 'Not so,' protests Spare Rib: 'blame the snake.' Snakes don't answer back. Snakes crawl on their bellies in the dust by holy command. Snakes have voices only in the Garden of Eden. Problems in Paradise – the title of Jane Rivers's book. Flora can see it lying on the bedside table. She's read only the first five pages; she must read more.

It's no good, she's not going to sleep. Quietly, Flora gets up in her long white nightdress and lifts a corner of the curtain. The moon behind the apple tree winks at her. A scudding cloud looks remarkably like a sheep. As she stares out, beguiled, the bell of All Saints' chimes thrice. Across the dark garden and the fields the low thin sound is strung, echoing, like a taut piano string. It bounces off the tops of trees in Owlston Wood and up the hill beyond, where cows graze in all but the coldest season, and weasels jump and swim in the still-running River Lyndon, in their devilish chase for rats and voles near the reedy outlet from Lyndon Lake. It's no good, says Flora to herself again, the countryside is calling me. I'm a country woman now, how can I resist any of the calls of nature? She gets quickly into a tracksuit and a thick jumper and socks. Opens the bedroom door quietly, goes down the stairs, finds her boots and anorak. Turns the big key in the back door, and there she is in her garden in the moonlight. Instead of taking the side gate out on to Pudding Bag Lane, she climbs over the stone wall into the field that slopes down to Owlston Wood. Her boots crunch against the frost crystals forming on the rough grass. Something black circles the air ahead of her, but she's not afraid, even when she thinks she feels it brushing her face lightly with its webbed wing. The tunnel of horrors at Battersea Fun Fair thirty years ago was much more frightening: mechanical, artificial, unreal. A product of civilization which could go wrong. As things had and did in human beings' attempts to wring out of the Garden of Eden an earthly paradise.

There's not much light in Owlston Wood, but sound compensates: owls, of course, hooting from the frost-tipped branches of ash and silver birch trees; foxes rustling their tails through the undergrowth. Flora stands still and breathes the dark living air of the wood deeply into her lungs. She might even be a tree herself, rooted there to the spot, dressed darkly, upright with arms as branches, only white human face giving her away. After a bit, she moves on to keep warm, turning right and taking the footpath across to the Wates's farm. There aren't any lights there, either, though the goat comes out to have a look at her, his beard swinging pale in the moonlight and his chain clanking like an echo of the church bell. It's all right, go back to sleep, Flora whispers. I'm only a madwoman out for a night walk. Treat me as a nocturnal animal. I'm just part of the scenery really. The goat seems to frown at her, then he disappears back into his bed of hay.

Flora goes further now, crossing Barleythorpe Road by Abraham Varley's house to the fields the other side. The road lies like a glow-worm ribbon across the winter-coloured fields. The windows of Abraham Varley's house are dark, though no curtains hang in them. Flora passes on, making for Windy Bottom, where four willows line a brook long since gone, and a spinney grounded in nettles protects a moated site said to date from Saxon times. Standing on the remains of this wall, people can see Jacob's Water, though in the daytime traffic along Weston Way going from Melton to Oakingham and further obscures the view. In the middle of the night nothing does, and Flora, on tiptoe, can indeed see Jacob's Water like a mirror laid flat under the bright moving sky. To her right is the illuminated spire of Eglethorpe Church floating in the water on the promontory of land saved from the reservoir's flooding. The church looks unearthly, an antediluvian structure poised like a ship at its mooring; here today and gone tomorrow. Stripped of its consecration, of its tombs; perhaps even – Flora doesn't know – of the decaying bodies laid under its rich red soil. Not even such thoughts of death and ghosts frighten Flora standing there, though this is much to her amazement, as she would never have considered herself a person unfrightened by tales of the unknown. But she can't stand still for long because of the cold. As she steps down from the Saxon wall, something catches her eye – something between Windy Bottom and the church in the undergrowth the other side of Weston Way. She gets back on the wall to take a second look. It's a human figure, a man, crouching low over something white. Something white that moves – a sheep; Flora can now hear definite plaintive *baa-baa*ing noises. The man seems to be trying to catch it, to restrain it in some way. But the sheep runs on its sticklike legs, its flanks fat with growing lambs, its fleece thick against the winter cold. 'Come here, you bitch!' Abraham Varley's voice shoots like a flinty Saxon arrow through the night. A few seconds later, which seem like hours to Flora's horrified, fascinated eyes, he catches up with it and holds it by the neck; the sheep's lamentations rend the air. Flora doesn't believe what she sees next. Lassoing a piece of rope round the sheep's neck to hold it still, Abraham takes his trousers down and buggers the sheep. It takes only a moment. The sheep's cries are like those of a woman being raped. When he's done, he pulls his trousers up and tightens the rope round the sheep's neck, pulling it so that the sheep falls over in a horrible contused heap. He kicks it several times with his old leather boots and then walks off, leaving it there. He cuts diagonally across the road in front of Flora and then across the fields to his own dark house at an angle which fortunately isolates her in the nettled spinney.

Flora feels sick and cold and panicky, and is more awed by this spectre of man punishing beast than by anything in nature. Indeed, she is literally unable to make sense of Abraham Varley and the sheep. Trapped by her incomprehension, she wants to go back to The Cottage in Cabbage Lane and wake Pete Wates and tell him what she's seen. The poor damaged sheep must belong to the Wates's farm. Flora wants to be comforted.

It takes fifteen minutes to recross the fields and climb back over the wall, let herself in by the back door, remove her clothes and get, chattering with cold and fear, back into bed next to Pete Wates. Pete is in a pine forest with Helga in southern Sweden when Flora wakes him up by putting the icicle of her body next to the nicely simmering furnace of his. 'Bloody hell!' He wakes with a start and sits up.

'Sorry, Pete.'

'What's the matter with you? Are you ill?'

'No, I've been for a walk.'

'At this time of the night? What time *is* it? Are you mad?'

'No. Not me.'

'Come here, let me warm you up.'

He runs his hands over her body, but Flora can't help thinking of Abraham Varley's hands and the sheep. 'I've got something to tell you.'

'Well, make it quick, I was having a nice dream and I want to get back to it.' Flora tells him what she's seen. 'I don't believe it.'

'Neither did I. And don't ask me if I'm sure I *did* see it.'

He takes his hands off her, and lies there thinking. 'Well, there have been some odd incidents over the years,' he says after a while, remembering the crop of premature dead lambs in Long Rotton Field last year, and the weird vulval discharge in the Alpine goats that puzzled the vet last autumn. 'Filthy old man!' declares Pete eventually. 'I hope he catches something back. Bit cold, isn't it, for that sort of thing just now?'

Flora huddles up to him. 'It was horrible, Pete. Men are disgusting!'

'My poor little town girl. You see how strange our country ways are.'

'Not strange. Revolting.'

'It's not unknown, bestiality. There was a man in Great Glaston a few years ago', reminisces Pete, 'who was found with his cock stuck up a donkey. Vaginismus, you know.'

'What?'

'Spasm of the vaginal muscles. Crippled him. No way out.'

'Served him right.'

'Hm.'

'Why do they do it, Pete?'

'Search me.' Pete sighs. 'I suppose I'll have to go and get the sheep tomorrow. You didn't by any chance notice the colour of the crayon mark on its behind, did you?'

'I did not.'

Pete is silent, still thinking.

'What are you going to do about it? It's against the law.'

'I'll talk to my father. Go back to sleep.'

'I don't see how talking to your father is going to help. And how can I go back to sleep after that? Anyway, I haven't been to sleep at all tonight, so I can hardly go back to it.'

'Shush.' He turns towards her and takes her in his arms, placing her head on his chest and stroking her hair. 'Do you want some hot milk, lovey? Will that help?'

In the kitchen heating up the milk, Pete does feel pretty disgusted with the male sex. He wonders if feminism has increased the incidence of bestiality in England. There's a subject for the *European Labour Monthly*: bestiality and the sexual politics of farming. By the time he gets upstairs with the milk, Flora's asleep, so he drinks it himself.

When Flora wakes, it's noon and a pale sun is probing the curtains. With a sick thud she remembers last night's scene. Pete, not surprisingly, is long gone. She wonders if he's found the sheep yet. She'll ring him later, but meanwhile she decides that, to help her make sense of what the New Year has so far brought her, she'll need to seek out the help of Olga Kahn.

Olga's sitting at her typewriter grappling with Chapter 4 of her memoirs. A stray strand of tobacco has jammed the 'R', so every time she tries to type her husband's name, it begins with a splodge. Olga peers through her thick glasses at the badly typed, smudged page. 'During the 1960s, splodge-aphael and I lived in Flask Walk, Hampstead. Splodge-aphael was busy with his study of the multiplication of white blood cells, and I was testing out my theo-splodge-ies on mothe-splodge fixation with some of the Hampstead intellectuals who sought my se-splodge-vices!'

'Have you got a minute, Olga?' Flora's face is pale and drawn.

'Of course. I hope you don't want any sherry, though, I've run out.'

'I don't want anything except your expert opinion.'

'Er-hum, I hate it when people say that.'

'What is the psychology underlying bestiality, Olga?'

Olga frowns at her. 'Ye Gods, girl, where d'you get that one? Not my area, I'm glad to say. From whose viewpoint, the animal's or the man's?'

'It *is* men only, then, is it?'

'Never heard of women messing with animals. Except in those awful feminist sexual fantasy books.'

'Why *do* men do it, Olga?'

'I had a young man once,' Olga reflects, pulling at the hair in the mole of her chin, 'did it on his teddy, or rather *in* his teddy. Cut a hole in it. Had a bow tie, I seem to remember.'

'Is that why he came to see you?'

'Yes and no. He did feel he ought to be able to make it with women. Very messy too, of course. Childhood fixation; fear of the unknown. No *vagina dentata* myth with teddies. Men are like that, you know – one event can cause them to be stuck in a time warp. No natural evolution possible. Even without dental myths. Did I ever tell you about Dr Baumeyer of Dresden and her experiment? She was playing ball with children at a treatment centre one day. The ball had a slit in it. Dr Baumeyer showed the children, by putting her finger in it, then she asked the children to do the same. Only six out of twenty-eight boys did it at all readily. The girls had no trouble. Silly experiment, really,' reflects Olga, 'but then Karen Horney tells it better than I do.'

'I hope you cured him. The young man with the teddy.'

'He cured himself. Became a bishop, actually. Quite a TV personality these days. But I can never see him without remembering his teddy.'

'Olga, I saw someone last night screwing a sheep.'

'Er-hum. Did you now! I won't ask which sheep.' Olga laughs. 'Can't say I didn't warn you about this village. Very unusual collective unconscious. Was it over by Windy Bottom?'

Flora nods. 'How did you know?'

'Stories. I think you'll find a lot of people already know.'

'But if they know, why don't they do anything?'

'What is there to do?' Olga shrugs her shoulders. 'Lock him up? Tell him not to do it? Take him back to his childhood? For some men, the process has gone on too long, there's no way back. Take my advice, child, forget what you saw. Stay in at night from now on. Stick to your young man.'

When Flora's gone, Olga sits for a while staring out of the window, tugging at her hairy mole and thinking. She thinks back to the young man with the teddy. Thirty years ago in Hampstead. He wasn't so young – twenty-nine or thirty. She knew as soon as she first saw him what would happen – he'd find himself a repressed English girl who didn't really care for sex, and they'd get by on the understanding of himself he'd picked up from his sessions with her in Flask Walk; but he'd never forget his teddy, any more than she would. Olga pokes the fire, puts another log on it, and fetches her pipe. As she packs the long golden strands of tobacco into it she thinks, as she often does, that each one is a strand of her life, separate, finite, willing to be intermingled with the others, and to await the final collective conflagration. At sixty-five, Olga doesn't expect to live more than a couple of years at the most. She's got a slow-growing tumour in her stomach. A doctor in Harley Street diagnosed it, a doctor she went to especially because she knew he'd tell her the truth. For Olga decided as soon as she noticed the symptoms that if it was cancer she wouldn't bother with any treatment. She'd rather let it pursue its own course and come to its own resolution. A time to live and a time to die: to everything its own season. It seemed to Olga that twentieth-century culture had lost an appreciation of the seasons, not only of nature but of life. Central heating enabled you to forget the winter, air conditioning the summer;

women, given hormones, might evince eternal youth; teenagers lopped years off childhood by apeing the habits of adulthood: drinking, smoking, conjugating like puppets. No, Olga Kahn did not intend to delay the hour of her own death.

Unlike most other people in Little Tickencote, but like Flora Penfold, there was no particular reason why Olga Kahn should live there. Any reasonably landscaped village with inexpensive housing would have done. When Raphael died, and her disillusion with the ills of Hampstead intellectuals had reached a point where she felt she could no longer go on, Olga had asked her nephew, Raphael's sister's son, to drive her somewhere in the country where she could find a small, reasonably cheap and quick house to buy. Daniel, a polite young civil engineer, had scanned the map and noticed Meltshire and looked it up in the guidebooks and read descriptions of Jacob's Water, and driven his aunt there one wet afternoon. Olga had liked the countryside, even in the rain. Speedily she found her Lionel Tupper and two months later she moved in with her books, her Corona and her pension. Apart from the fact that the bus service was poor, forcing her to keep an old Beetle and drive from time to time, it suited her perfectly. It was quiet, she could write. But not so quiet that the writing and thinking stagnated, becoming a dark, dank pool in which nothing could flourish. The village was built on the steam of living legends, it had an organic connection to the life of the soul. Even its newcomers had a queerness about them, an oddity of image, sense, smell or history. Never a dull moment, says Olga Kahn to herself before the fire, warming the flesh beyond the tops of her cream lisle stockings. It's not unlike peering into people's psyches and reassembling what you see there to make a decent explanation. Except that no one's paying her for the exercise this time, and she doesn't have to sit and listen to them moaning on about their teddies and suchlike, thank God! The two main problems about being a psychoanalyst, Olga had decided long ago, were having to listen to other people's boring moans and pretend they engaged you deeply – that was the first problem; the second was having to put together your explanation from an assortment of old dogmas invented by a pompous sexist shit. Olga laughs into the fire: how she'd believed it all once! Mind you, she's not sorry she did. The progressive disillusionment has made her both humble and wise. The only thing she regrets is that her passion for psychoanalysis, combined with Raphael's selfishness, had deprived them of parenthood. Strangely, she'd never minded much until now, when the arrival of

Flora Penfold in Little Tickencote suggested to her the daughter and the maternal experiences she might have had, and when, as though that weren't enough, she faced more than intimations of her own mortality. Never mind! Olga sighs, adjusting her legs. Never regret anything, that's your motto. You'd be a different person now if you'd done it differently, and you wouldn't like that, would you?

Coming out of her reverie, she notices the light beginning to fade from the sky. Come on, old girl, you must go for your constitutional now, or you won't go at all today. But not alone, I think, she adds. Reaching out for the green push-button-memory last-number-redial phone Daniel had given her as a moving-in present – new at the time, now yesterday's technology – she dials Jane Rivers's number up the hill in Stonecrop Cottage. 'Meet you at Pooh Sticks Bridge, Jane,' she says, 'in five minutes.'

It's an odd sight in Little Tickencote, the spectre of two solidly dressed and respectable single women of uncertain age, one in black, one in her red-lined batwinged cloak, hanging over the little wooden bridge in the lower corner of Sheepdyke Field above the paltry stream, rushing from one side of the bridge to the other, dropping twigs in the water. 'Mine's won!' 'Don't be daft, that one's mine!' 'Come on, let's try again!'

Olga's there first today, standing watching a bunch of sheep grazing, with a thoughtful look on her face.

'A penny for them, then.' Jane Rivers's black Balaclava, worn against the weather, has added a touch of melodrama to her customary melancholy look.

'You a bank robber or something?' demands Olga aggressively.

'I've got earache,' Jane answers. 'I went to see Dr Simpson and he told me to keep them warm.'

'Er-hum. Why have you come out for a walk, then?'

'Because you asked me to, you old bat.'

'Oh that's right, I did. I swear my memory gets worse by the day. D'you think it looks like snow?'

Jane looks up at a heavy silver sky. 'Maybe. But it's not snowed in Little Tickencote for two years.'

'I remember the snow in Vienna,' begins Olga Kahn, 'or was it Philadelphia? No, I think it was Switzerland. Raphael skied, you know. Phallic habit, don't you think? Especially the wooden ones. What's the attraction? I'm sure I don't know. Penguins move in the snow, and polar bears and reindeer, but human beings weren't meant to go out in the stuff – if we were we'd have skis for feet.'

'You know Mortimer Fanshawe?' says Jane. 'I saw his father the other day. Mortimer takes size 15 shoes. Those practically *are* skis. Roger has to get them specially made.'

'What happened to his escapade with Bronwen Lancing?'

'Bronwen complained about the lack of home comforts, apparently. It was a hard life on the back of a motorbike. Mrs Lancing couldn't understand why the police wouldn't go and find them. There's nothing illegal about going for a jaunt, even if you are underage.'

'Er-hum. Of course Karen Horney described it well in her paper on "Personality Changes in Female Adolescents".'

'I dare say. Anyway, Bronwen won't have anything to do with Mortimer now. The boy sits in his room all the time. Roger and Clarice are quite worried about him.'

Olga throws another stick into the stream. 'All love is a bereavement. And all bereavement is an expression of self-love.'

'It's odd you should say that – it's how my new novel begins.'

'This is the sequel to *Problems in Paradise*?'

'In a way.'

The two women walk companionably on, crossing the bridge and taking the footpath over to Bidlington. These walks of theirs happen once or twice a week, or whenever one of them feels a need. Though twenty-three years separate their ages, the projects on which each is engaged unite them. They both pursue with solitary single-mindedness the capturing in words of plots and characters: Olga Kahn of her life, and the life and times of psychoanalysis; Jane Rivers of her novels. They use each other as sounding boards and sources of information and advice. Jane finds Olga helpful, as would be expected, with the psychological underpinnings of her characters; sometimes when Jane can't identify a motive, or describe an orientation, Olga Kahn will do it for her. Olga, for her part, being no born writer or even one trained, as most are, by experience, needs Jane's guidance on how to tell her story. Should the case histories be placed within the main chronology, or separated from it? Does the deep appreciation Olga feels for Karen Horney's work belong with an account of her own, or should it, too, stand alone? How may one best reconcile the intellectual project of describing the evolution and dead ends of psychoanalytic thought with the personal project of chronicling a life? Jane Rivers listens, always thoughtful, always applying a clear pragmatism to the dilemmas Olga raises. She has a mind unusual for both clarity and complexity, being rarely in doubt about what she thinks, though her thoughts are like a kaleidoscope of aligned shapes and colours – each distinct, touching but not overlapping. This is how she sees the reality on which she herself draws in her writing. Nothing is ever simple. Everything is a maze of complexity and contradiction. Wonderful, insane contradiction. Before she devoted herself full-time to writing, Jane Rivers worked in local government; she had a post in a probate office, and spent her days dealing with the winding-up of dead people's financial affairs. It was a strange business to be in: a mixture of computational punctiliousness – getting the figures right – and exposure to profound emotional vulnerability – seeing people through the painful aftermath of death. Bereavement as a form of self-love, as Olga Kahn had put it. The work appealed to Jane's love of complexity and talent at seeing the wood rather than the trees. There couldn't have been a better apprenticeship for a detective-story writer.

Theoretically, Jane could have looked for a job anywhere in the world, but she'd felt an obligation to be near her parents in Dorset, which was just as well for them as, shortly after Jane had started working in the probate office, her father had died and she'd had to look after her mother. Jane had gone back to live at home. Every time she suggested selling the house and making other arrangements, her mother would have none of it. 'I couldn't, dear,' she said. 'I couldn't live anywhere else. All my life is bound up in this house.' She'd touched its frame, the walls, the fireplace, as she spoke. 'All the memories of your father are here.' As to Jane leaving: 'But I'm all alone in the world!' To which Jane's mental reply – so am I – would, she knew, have been interpreted as an indelicate rejection of her mother's superior experience.

Mrs Rivers had developed severe arthritis. She was in pain much of the time, walked with a stick, and became increasingly bent into an old woman's shape. Physical dependency bred the psychological kind. The more Jane permitted her mother to feel dependent on her, the less she was willing to do for herself. But Jane herself felt powerless to stop the process of her mother's escalating reliance on her. 'But where have you been?' she'd demand querulously as Jane came in from the probate office each day. 'I was cold, I wanted my shawl, I've finished my library book, can we have fish for supper, I fancy a nice bit of sole, or a herring, or perhaps some grilled cod roes would be nice. Don't you think, Jane? Your father always wanted cod roes on Saturdays when he came back from the club. With grilled tomatoes, and the football results on the television, you know. Put the television on, Jane, and come and watch it with me, it's "Coronation Street" tonight.'

Wearily, and eventually, Jane did what her mother wanted her to do and gave up her job. She spent her last pay cheque on a remote-control colour television for her mother, a microwave oven for both of them, and an Amstrad word processor and printer for herself. Two years later her first novel, *Paper Murders*, was published. Using her experience of the probate office, Jane had constructed a Kafkaesque account of the workings of small-town bureaucracy, which, as the novel unfolded itself in the livid green text of her word-processor screen, turned out to hide the manoeuvrings of a homicidal maniac bent on exploiting official information for his own satanic ends. Three people had died – one falling over a cliff, one under a bus and one while actually waiting in the probate office – and a fourth was well on his way when Georgia Kelly, an eager, ambitious red-haired journalist from the local paper, cracked the whole sorry business.

Paper Murders had received a good deal of attention in the local paper, not least because the persona of Georgia Kelly bore some resemblance to the woman who ran the paper's agony column. Nationally, it was also well received; reviewers compared Jane Rivers to Patricia Highsmith and P.D. James and Ruth Rendell, arguing that she possessed the quirky imagination of Highsmith along with the literary skill of writers such as A.S. Byatt, and her own peculiar brand of cynical wisdom and sardonic caricature. Reviewers also warmed to Georgia Kelly, who returned the period's focus on feminist antiheroes to the more stridently conventional and ordinarily lustful figurines of paperback soap operas. By the time the next two Rivers novels were published, enough of the world was hooked on Georgia Kelly for Jane Rivers to give up worrying about the size of the Invalid Care Allowance.

When Mrs Rivers died in 1982, her bequest to Jane included the Dorset house, £2014.55 in the bank, and a sheaf of papers to which was clipped a note in her mother's uneven handwriting and dated 1975, the year her memory had really started to go. 'Darling Jane, I'm afraid I never had the courage to tell you this. Please understand and forgive me. All my love, Mum.' The papers proved that Jane had been adopted. She had never had the slightest idea that this might be the case; her birth certificate showed her birth to have been registered in Melton, Meltshire, but this was consistent with what her mother had said about her father – a doctor – being in practice there at the time.

There'd even been an entire account of her birth, with her mother describing how the progress of labour had been long and slow, due, she supposed, to her age – and how Jane's father, being a doctor, had had to be kept out of the labour room because he was too knowledgeable and therefore worried about all the awful obstetric possibilities. Looking back on it, of course, there *were* a few things that didn't quite fit: her father's watchful silence during her mother's references to Jane's birth; the fact that she had only ever been given the shortened form of her birth certificate.

At thirty-four, Jane Rivers had therefore been dispossessed of her entire history through a by-product of her mother's death. She had felt betrayed; the meaning of her life had not been what she'd been led to think. Moreover, as she continued to dwell on the new knowledge, she came to understand that her mother's cowardice in the face of the truth, though dressed as love, had been intended to protect her mother, not her, from the consequences of facing it. Lies breed lies. Her mother's infirmity had prevented any unravelling of the ensnaring spider's web of deception, as Mrs Rivers must have feared precisely the reaction Jane had had: if I'm not your daughter, why should I devote my life to looking after you? Because I devoted *mine* to looking after *you*, Mrs Rivers would have replied.

Today, eight years on, Jane Rivers isn't sure what she feels. On the whole, she doesn't feel a lot, having passed this trait on to her characters – a form of advance literary probate. She's made a life for herself. Georgia Kelly progresses in ambition and cleverness though not, as yet, markedly in age. 'Do you think I should marry her off, Olga?' Jane asks suddenly. The two women are coming into Lyndon now; the church spire rises in front of them against the deepening sky. 'I keep getting letters from readers asking why she isn't married.'

'Er-hum. As though she's really alive. Fascinating, isn't it, how fictional people become more real than non-fictional ones? Perhaps people want to know about the destinies of unreal people because their own real ones are unthinkable.'

'They've got a point there, haven't they, these readers, Olga?'

'Indubitably.'

'What do you think, then? About Georgia?'

'May as well. But what's the bereavement, then, at the beginning of the book, if it isn't something to do with Georgia?'

'The death of a sparrow.'

'We'll have to go back by the road, you know,' observes Olga, 'it'll be dark soon.'

They take a short cut through the churchyard out on to Lyndon Road, which joins Barleythorpe Road and will take them back into Little Tickencote. Jane stumbles and nearly falls on a bramble which has knotted itself comfortably over a crooked row of seventeenth-century headstones. Olga puts out a hand to steady her. 'Do be careful, dear,' she says, thinking of her own demise.

Jane pulls herself up straight, and flexes her ankle. 'I don't think it's broken.'

'Of course it isn't,' says Olga brusquely, maternally. 'Come, we must get on, there's a godawful cloud up there, it's going to rain or snow or something.'

Just before six, the skies open and snow falls gently at first, and then fiercely, splattering the Meltshire landscape – Olga Kahn and Jane Rivers on the road back to Little Tickencote, farmers in their farmyards, men and women in their cars coming back from work, ducks on icy ponds, rabbits in their burrows, sheep and goats and cows and horses in the fields, and Flora Penfold in her cottage, teaching young Alun Lancing his A minor scale and accompanying exercises. 'Look!' says Alun, with a child's joy. 'It's snowing!' Woman and child stand watching as the big soft flakes fall through the sapphire air, catching on the branches of trees, resting on hedges, decorating grey stone walls, flattening themselves against the windowpanes. 'Isn't it lovely!' exclaims Alun, putting his flute down. 'Don't you long to go out in it, Flora? Will you come and play snowballs with me when the lesson's finished?'

'When the lesson's finished,' Flora repeats. 'Come on, Alun, I'd like you to do this passage again. From B.' Gently she coaxes from him a surprisingly melodious sound which rises and soars like an ascending snowflake.

Flora does put on her coat and boots and hat and gloves, and she does go out to join Alun Lancing and little Gwenny in the Lancings' garden, where she's glad to be able to regress a few decades and behave like a child again. Alun's snowballs are tightly packed and well targeted by comparison with Flora's pathetic affairs. 'I'll show you, Flora!' cries little Gwenny, cheeks as red as the holly berries. 'Watch me, how I do it, like this!'

They behave like puppies, pelting each other with snow, falling and laughing. 'I really must go home,' says Flora, breathless. 'It's time for your supper and mine.'

Delivering Alun and Gwenny to the Lancings' back door, Flora refuses Annabel's offer of a drink and plods snowily home back through her own garden, where Pablo and Dolly are wandering around mystified, making paw marks across the white sea of the grass. 'You don't remember, do you, my lovelies? It has snowed before in your lifetimes, but you've no cause to remember, I suppose.'

'There are more things in heaven and earth than human beings can conceive of.' Olga Kahn's words float out of the dancing air with the snowflakes. 'Curiouser and curiouser,' says Flora, going inside. She holds the door open. 'All right then, chaps, are you coming in? Or are you going to wander around out there all night?' The cats pick their way, snowfooted, in, and she closes the door. She feels strangely light-headed, exhilarated – it's the snow, she decides, lighting the gas under the kettle and warming her hands in the flame. The phone on the kitchen wall rings: she unhooks it, presses it to her ear casually, and cradles it there while returning her hands to the flame. 'Hallo,' she says, cheerfully, full of the joys of winter. But she speaks to a void: nobody answers. Instead there's a high-pitched whistling sound that cuts into, and nearly splits, her eardrum. She hangs up. The gas burns an ordinary steady blue-orange in front of her. She shivers. Forget it, Flora, she tells herself, remembering her good, snow-induced mood. Don't you believe it, warns Rural Rosey, it's just more of the same.

The sheep that Abraham Varley screwed lies in a corner of the sheep house as cold as Flora Penfold's hands before she raised them to the blue-orange flame of the gas on her second-hand Tricity cooker. 'Probably exposure,' decrees Mike Ramsay, the vet, a sanguine graduate of Birmingham Veterinary College and life. 'Windy Bottom, did you say? Not the best place for a pregnant ewe in this weather. Or it could have been one of those damn badger setts. They may be pretty creatures, but they're a right menace to farmers. I don't know how we're going to get on with the new Badgers' Act, it'll mean you'll have to have a licence to get rid of the damn things. But I don't know about the contusion round the neck. I suppose she could have got herself hooked on some wire netting. Is there any between here and Windy Bottom? Could be the onset of pregnancy toxaemia, I suppose. Bit early, though. Keep her in for a few days. I'll give her some glucose injections, just in case.'

Of the other matter, not a murmur; for what concern would it be of Mike Ramsay's? Or any other vet's? Frank Wates had been remarkably unforthcoming when Pete had suggested that something untoward between man and beast might have occurred. And all the while the collective unconscious of Little Tickencote is drawing itself together again, hastily repairing all the breaches in its defence, like the flood waters on which Noah launched his ark, while the damaged ewe huddles in the corner of the Wates's sheep house shivering with shock, despite the woolly coat it wears and the little hearts that beat inside warming themselves, though not her, with the promise of lambing time in the spring.

12

War in the Gulf

ALMOST AS SUDDENLY and beneficently as it had first fallen, the snow picks its purifying mantle off the Meltshire landscape and goes elsewhere. 'It'll come again,' says Frank Wates the farmer to his son, Pete.

'Remember 1976,' says Doris. 'It was Pringle's undoing, that second fall of snow.' She closes her lips with satisfaction.

'Always be prepared, that's the farmer's motto,' echoes Frank.

'Like the Girl Guides, Dad!' Pete slaps his father on the back. 'Well, I'm off. Thanks for the dinner, Mum.'

Scraping the plates in the kitchen, Doris Wates says to her husband Frank: 'It's time he settled down.'

'I dare say you're right.' Frank knows better than to disagree with Doris.

'He's thirty-five, Frank.'

'So he is.'

'It's not as though he hasn't had girlfriends. Though what else he does when he goes off on these trips of his, I'm sure I don't know.'

'What the eye doesn't see, the heart doesn't grieve over.' Frank likes platitudes.

'Yours mayn't, but mine does. And that Miss Penfold isn't right for him.'

'Why ever not?' Frank's glimpses of Flora – down the lane from Jack Roebuck's Post Office, and across the field on Bonfire Night – have recommended her slip of a body to him.

'Too arty,' pronounces Doris. 'Not a settler. Why, what's she doing coming to live in a village like this at her age?'

'She's not the only single lady in Little Tickencote,' says Frank defensively, stomping out of the kitchen. 'Maybe it's something in the air.'

Doris puts the washing-up brush and the mashed-potato saucepan down and looks after him crossly. Frank Wates drives round his land inspecting the fencing, a routine winter job. Down in the valley between Little Tickencote and Great Glaston someone's crashed into the fence enclosing Marigold Field. 'Snow skid,' mutters Frank. It happens every year in just this place. As he inspects the nature of the damage this time, Bill Pringle drives up.

'Afternoon, Frank,' he calls. 'I saw the blighter, meant to tell you. Renault van, the florist's in Melton. You know, Jayne-with-a-"y".'

'Not worth claiming,' decrees Frank. 'Hammer and nails job.'

'Had any problems with sheep recently, have you, Frank?'

'Why, have you?'

The two farmers squint suspiciously at each other in the chilly air. Bill Pringle pauses, unwilling to admit to a problem Frank Wates won't. 'Well, now you mention it . . .'

'I didn't – you did.'

Bill Pringle grins. 'Fair enough. Yes, there was one. Death by misadventure, you could say. Rope round the neck, in fact. What d'you make of that, Frank?'

'Who'd want to throttle a sheep? Don't look at me – I didn't do it.'

'Ramsay said he'd seen another case rather like it.'

'Did he now!'

'Your Pete handled it.'

'So he did. You've jogged my memory now, Jim.'

'We can't afford to lose good sheep, can we, Frank?'

'What do you suggest, then? You won't get the police interested in a few dead sheep. They've got enough to handle just with car thefts in Melton.'

'I know.' Bill Pringle sighs. Inside his car the phone rings. 'Mobile phone. Got to keep up with the times, Frank. Well, I'll be on my way.'

Flora's Peugeot, coming back from Melton, passes the farmers by the side of the road. She's been in to fax Rural Rosey to Jeff at the *Daily Record*. All hell has broken loose, as Rosey has mentioned the word 'vasectomy' to the father of the little wellingtons, who doesn't conceive of this as the right kind of solution for an animal husbandry farmer. He's hooked on natural forces, and letting Nature, not Rosey, Have Her Way. Flora thinks Jeff will like it, even if Rosey doesn't.

'You should get one of them things, Miss Penfold,' Ron had advised her when she'd told him she was off in search of a fax machine. 'I could set it up for you.' He licked his lips at the thought.

This has reminded Flora of the fate of her Bosendorfer, the last favour Ron had been doing her. 'I need the piano first, Ron,' she insisted.

'On its way, Miss P, on its way.'

'Well, I hope *you're* not moving it this time, Ron.'

He stared at her, and the nearest thing to anger she'd ever seen on the broad slopes of his face painted his skin pink. 'That weren't me, Miss P, that weren't. That were that Miss Olley-fant. She's an old piggy tart, she is, and a rotten driver with it. Oops.' He covered his mouth with one of his huge hands, the back streaked with a greenish-black substance, probably oil. 'Shouldn't say that, should I, Miss P?'

'Don't worry, Ron. Just get on with the plumbing. And let's get the piano in place before I see about a fax machine. I haven't got any money, anyway.'

She's worrying about the bills, now. Pete Wates catches her at it in the evenings, squatting on her heels on the floor, trying to make income and expenditure balance with some left over. 'What am I going to do, Pete, if I run out of money?'

'Well, you can't live off me, my love. The farm's okay, but my share goes back into the *European Labour Monthly* in the cause of the world liberation of the rural working classes. You ought to be sympathetic, you with your Russian background. But you don't strike me as very proletarian.'

'I am, I am. I'm worried about money. What would you do if you had dependants to support, Pete?'

'I don't, so that's all right. What would *you* do? Sex equality, Flora.'

'I'm less interested in that than you are.'

'So I've noticed.'

She spreads the pieces of paper out. Phone bill £76, poll tax £380, gas £201, electricity £55, Percy Grisewood £8643.20. 'It'll go on and on,' she says despairingly, lining them up across the carpet. 'I should have married a millionaire.'

She's got a streak of coal dust on her cheek, he notices. The firelight turns her brown hair copper. She's taken her jersey off, and her white cotton shirt, tucked lightly into the waist of her jeans, makes her look young – schoolgirlish almost. Only the lines round her eyes suggest something different.

It's 17 January, the day the Allied forces start bombing Iraq. Pete and Flora had watched the news earlier. 'Turn it off, Pete,' Flora commanded. 'That's decided me: I've got to join Meltshire CND.'

Pete laughed.

'Why are you laughing?'

'You know who runs that? Well, he did – I think he may have handed it over to someone else now. Roger Fanshawe, father of Mort on the Honda. I admire your resolve. But I fear that CND doesn't tackle the root problem.' Pete laughed again.

'What?'

'Roger Fanshawe's got carrot fly in his root crops.'

'I don't think you take life seriously enough.'

'Perhaps you take it too seriously.'

Watching her now doing sums in the firelight, Pete realizes that he finds Flora Penfold's seriousness endearing. It's one of her many endearing qualities. In fact, he's altogether endeared to her. 'I love you,' he says suddenly from the red print sofa by the fireplace. 'Yes, I love you.' He leans forward and looks into her face.

Flora takes her eyes from Percy Grisewood's enormous bill. 'Do you? Do you, Pete? Really?' She senses Rural Rosey hanging round the back of her head waiting to say something like Come on now, don't fall for what I fell for, it won't get you anywhere – what good is the love of a good man, if all it delivers is little wellingtons?

'Yes, I think so,' says Pete.

'What does that mean, you think so?'

'It means what it says. I say what I mean. What about you, Flora, do you love me?'

'Before I tell you, tell me what difference it'd make if I did.'

'You're a hard woman, Flora Penfold.'

'And you're a hard man.'

'I hope so. Sometimes. But when I look at you I feel soft, Flora. Like butter.'

'Butter couldn't melt in your mouth, Pete. Sometimes.'

'But margarine could. Does, Flora. Stop distracting me, I'm trying to talk to you about my feelings. Don't you understand how hard it is for a man to do that? And don't tell me you don't read about sexual politics. You're hiding something. Or running away from something. I don't know which.'

Flora gets up from her pile of bills. She crosses the room and tweaks the curtains together to close a slight gap through which starlight might fall into the room. Then she sits down on a chair opposite Pete. She smiles at him: at his earnestness, his boyishly ruffled hair, his Dirk Bogarde eyes, this unexpected admission of his position regarding her. 'What was it we said that first night?'

He waits for her to answer her own question.

'That we weren't either of us looking for a serious relationship.'

'I don't think that was quite it,' he ventures. 'And in any case, time changes people's feelings, doesn't it? It's certainly changed mine. At the beginning, I simply found you very attractive. You were new lifeblood in this place of tradition and – well, I suppose, though I shouldn't say it, decay. You were new growth, change, the future. I was responding to that. But then you stopped being a symbol and became yourself. It's the self that I love, Flora. I don't know what it means. It certainly doesn't mean that you've got to declare any feelings for me that you don't have. That's the last thing I'd want. But I suppose what I'm saying is that I've reached a point where I want to talk about us.' He pauses, looks at her. The seriousness breaks into a sideways smile. 'There you are, that was quite a speech, wasn't it?'

'You're an odd man, Pete. I've said that before. I don't understand you – I don't *know* you, come to that. You don't give the impression of wanting a serious long-term relationship.'

'Of the sort you had with thingy, seen in the Old Sun Inn the other night? I could say the same about you, you know. What do *you* want, Flora? If you're just dabbling in rural fantasy and I'm one of your games, you'd better bloody well say so!'

'Ah, jealousy!'

'I didn't say that. Who was he, Flora?'

'My old lover, Barnaby Gunn. He turned up here one evening, quite unexpectedly. We went for a drink. But the relationship's over. I left Barney to come and live here – I told you.'

'I believe you, thousands wouldn't.'

'I think there *are* some things we need to discuss,' she says quickly. 'But you can forget the games. I'm not playing any. Though I do feel this place is, with me. As a matter of fact, I've been surprised at the strength of my feelings for you. But I've been trying to keep – to keep the lid on them. I suppose one reason is you, the other is me. I've not been all that successful with men. My vision of my life here is of living on my own: I don't want – at least I think I don't want – as we said to each other that first night, a live-in relationship again.' Flora pauses, listening to what she's said and wondering if it's true.

'What about the me bit of it?'

'Well, who are you really, Pete Wates? Here today and gone tomorrow. A farmer, and editor of a Marxist newspaper. A stripper of furniture, to boot. A traveller abroad: the only son of devoted parents at home. I don't know whether you set out to create an aura of mystery, but that's certainly what you succeed in doing.'

'I don't want anyone else to own my life except me.'

'Which means being secretive about it? Knowledge isn't the same thing as possession. If you tell me what you're doing, that doesn't mean I own it – or you.'

'Doesn't it?' A cloud passes over Pete's face. 'We all bring our histories with us into new relationships, Flora. Our wounds, and the resolutions born of them.'

'Your views of women and mine of men.'

'Including those.'

'I'm not sure it's safe to love you,' she admits finally.

'I am.'

'In that case, I love you. But I don't know what it means.'

'That'll do for now.' Pete gets up, draws Flora to her feet and wraps his brown corduroy arms round her. He smells of the country, of this new life of hers. As she rests her copper hair on his shoulder, she feels herself grounded in the earth, in the soil, where green shoots grow and sheep graze for food, where life begins and ends, where shadows pass, and the sun nourishes.

'Tell me about organic farming, Pete,' demands Flora suddenly, her voice muffled by the pressure of his shoulder.

'Changing the subject are you?' he jests.

'No. I think it's the *same* subject.'

'What do you want to know? *Why* do you want to know?'

'I just want to learn about farming, Pete.'

He holds her away from him. 'So you want to be a farmer's wife, do you, Miss Penfold?'

'Now who's changing the subject?'

'That's certainly the same subject. Come on, let's go down to the Old Sun Inn and celebrate the frank exchange of views we've just had.'

In the Old Sun Inn, Fanny's eating a packet of roast beef crisps and Ted's doing the crossword. At the table by the fire, Martin and Bridget Crowhurst are deep in conversation. Across the room Armand and Petula Nevere are having an argument. Jane Rivers, in dark glasses, is drinking Guinness as black as her shades, and with a head on it the same texture as Petula Nevere's curls.

Pete and Flora sit at the bar. 'Pity you don't have champagne on draught,' comments Pete to Ted.

'Got something to celebrate, have you?' asks Fanny sharply, keen not to miss a trick.

'This and that.'

'I can do you half a bottle of bubbly,' offers Ted, without looking up from his crossword.

'Make that a whole one.'

'Where were you, then,' Petula Nevere's voice cuts across the top of Armand's Campari and soda, vivid like the carpet in front of the fire, 'where were you that night when I was in agony all on my own?'

'I told you, Pet, I had a meeting with Schreiber from Amsterdam.'

'I don't believe you.'

'You're overwrought.'

'So would you be in my position.'

'Shush.' Armand looks around furtively, like a bald mouse, his baby-pink skin shining with a light coating of sweat. Petula cries noisily. 'You're making an exhibition of yourself.'

'It's my fault, then, is it!' she shrieks. 'Why is everything my fault? I could tell the world a few things about you, Armand Nevere . . .'

'Shush,' he says again, getting up and hauling her out of her chair. 'I think we should finish this at home.'

Sobbing on her high heels, Petula allows herself to be shepherded out of the pub, while Armand mutters a few good evenings and throws a few apologetic glances over his shoulder.

'I wonder what that was about,' Flora says to Pete.

'Babies.'

'How do you know?'

'Ramsay the vet.'

'The vet?'

'Mervyn Simpson, the local doctor, is his cousin.'

'Isn't that rather unprofessional?'

'What, to have a vet as a cousin?'

'To reveal confidences, you idiot. Tell me, then, what's the Neveres' problem?'

'She keeps dropping them.'

'Dropping them?'

'Babies. Miscarriages.'

'How awful.'

'While Bridget Crowhurst', says Pete, nodding across the room to where the Crowhursts sit, 'is marginally worse off, as she's never yet got as far as a conception.'

'Yes,' says Flora, 'she told me. But then, as she's separated from her husband, she's hardly making it any easier for herself, is she? What is it, Pete? Why are babies such a problem round here?'

'Must be something in the air. Could be coincidence, of course.'

The Crowhursts' voices by the fire are getting louder. Bridget's face is flushed above her white Aran jersey. 'What's a bit of dust?' Martin is saying. 'What's wrong with a bit of dust, I want to know!'

'Filth!' screams Bridget. 'Filth! You're filthy, Martin, like all men!'

'Please yourself.' He scrapes his chair back harshly on the tiled floor and goes to the bar. 'Give me a refill, Ted. And a vodka or two for Bridget.'

'You can stuff your bloody vodka back up where it came from!' shouts Bridget, getting up, yanking her bag from the floor, and making a florid exit.

'Up yours, too,' comments Martin quietly.

'Well, well,' says Fanny, 'quite a night, isn't it?' She smiles happily. Behind her the phone rings.

'That'll be Patsy,' groans Ted. 'I just know it'll be Patsy!'

He disappears to answer the phone. 'I'd better have a stiff drink waiting for him,' confides Fanny to Martin. 'Bridget's vodkas will do. It's maintenance she's after. His wife, you know. It's either money or sex, isn't it?'

'Yes, isn't it,' says Martin wearily, rearranging himself on the tall stool. 'As you say, either money or sex or both. Why do we bother, Fanny?'

'Well, I don't,' she admits. 'I'm fancy-free. Footloose and fancy-free. How are you sleeping these days, Martin?'

'And not only footloose,' says Pete to Flora under his breath.

'She's young, Pete, give her a chance. What's she doing here? That's what I want to know. It's no life for young people, is it, round here? It's okay for us oldies, but then we're not after excitement, are we?'

'Speak for yourself. About age, I mean.'

'Oh yes, you're my toy boy, aren't you?'

'I hate to say this, Flora, but I think I need to. Babies.'

'What about them?'

'Well, we don't want any of them, do we?'

'I'll talk to you about that another time,' she says severely. 'Come on, toy boy, let's go home.'

By now Ted and Fanny are at it behind the bar. 'If you give her that, I'm off,' says Fanny, with an impressive air of calmness. 'That's absurd, that is. I want to go to the Algarve in June. She's playing on your guilt. Can't you see that, you stupid man?'

It's dark in Pudding Bag Lane and even darker in Cabbage Lane, as the light on the corner is faulty and reduced to a thin flickering redness. Navy clouds block the natural light of the moon and stars. Flora nearly falls over a hole in the path. 'Careful, it's the frost. All the roads round here are cracking up.' Pete takes her hand. As they stumble up the dark lane, their attention is drawn to the lighted windows of Wisteria Cottage, and to voices within, and to sounds of breaking glass and solid objects thudding into things. Then Annabel Lancing screams, a high-pitched, hysterical note, and a door slams, shaking the fabric of the house and even, so Pete and Flora fancy, adding to the structural problems of the road outside.

'My God, the Lancings too!' whispers Flora. 'Is no one safe?'

The following morning, when the Meltshire electricity van comes to fix the faulty street light, and Pete Wates is long since gone back to his sheep, Annabel Lancing appears at Flora's window with a magenta eye.

'I need your help,' she says, in a horribly subdued voice. 'I don't know where to turn, what to do. You've got to help me, Flora!' Flora's attending to Rural Rosey, who promptly says: Here you are, Flora, now's your chance to be the lady with the lamp, now's your chance to redeem yourself, and all your sins.

What sins?

Shush. Concentrate on the matter at hand.

'How can I help, Annabel?'

'Look at my face. It's Jasper. He hits me. He always has done. You wouldn't think it, would you, to look at him. A nice middle-class husband and father, good job, pillar of the local community. But he's nothing more than a wild beast, really.'

'Why does he hit you?'

'He just lashes out. I don't think he knows himself. He says I irritate him. I try to be a good wife, Flora. It's not as though I'm a Women's Lib person – I'm not at all. I make a good home for him and the children. Of course he blames Bronny's problems on me. But he's her father, isn't he? I said that to him last night. It was like a red rag to a bull. She won't go to school now. She's been in bed for five days. She just lies there sulking and reading these smutty paperbacks. It's Marguerite Duras, *The Lover*, at the moment. Do you know it?'

Flora shakes her head.

'It's about a fifteen-year-old in Cambodia who has an affair with a hairless Chinese man. I did a degree in English once, you know. A long time ago. It's rather a powerful book – I can see why Bronny likes it. It reminds me of Elizabeth Smart's *By Grand Central Station I Sat Down and Wept*. You've read that, haven't you?' Annabel sighs and spreads her hands on her lap. 'Jasper doesn't like the thought of me having a life of my own. That's part of the problem.'

'Have you talked to Mrs Kahn?' asks Flora.

'No. Why, should I have done?'

'She's a very wise woman. She's a psychoanalyst, you know.'

'Jasper hates shrinks,' says Annabel.

'This isn't about what Jasper likes and doesn't like. It's about you, isn't it?'

'You're right.'

'I think we should bathe that eye.'

Very good, Flora, says Rosey.

Annabel starts crying again. 'You know what I feel I want – my mother. I want to be looked after!'

Don't we all? reprimands Rosey. I think I'm pregnant again, Flora.

'Well, perhaps you should go away for a few days and see her,' offers Flora helpfully.

But this isn't the right thing to say at all. 'Mummy's dead,' wails Annabel. 'She died in the Harrods bombing. She only went to Harrods for their vitamin pills. She liked the labels, you see.'

'I'll make you a cup of tea,' says Flora.

That's right, make your exit, admires Rosey; this whole scene is getting out of hand. I could do with some vitamins myself. Aren't you going to respond to me in my hour of need?

I don't know anything about violence against women, says Flora to herself in the kitchen waiting for the kettle to boil. Pablo scratches at the door. I must get a cat flap fitted. Where *is* Percy? says Flora, opening it. The cat ambles in, fluffy tail like a flagpost. I expect you know a bit, my friend, don't you, there's nothing gentle about you, is there? But we humans are supposed to be civilized.

Olga Kahn is rereading Karen Horney's *Self-Analysis* when Flora phones. 'Local emergency,' says Flora. 'Your expert opinion is needed again.'

'We live in troubled times,' comments Olga when she comes round, 'internationally *and* domestically. The spectre of war abroad causes two opposite reactions: one of social bonding, the other of armed antagonism. I can see which one we have here.'

'Oh, Mrs Kahn!' Annabel starts weeping again.

Flora pours the tea. 'You'll have to excuse me,' she says, 'I've got an appointment with my bank manager.'

'Er-hum. That's all right, my dear,' says Olga Kahn knowingly. 'You go and sort out your finances – they're so much easier than psyches.'

Flora puts on her boots and opens the door. In her haste to escape, she fails to notice that Cabbage Lane is a sheet of ice, on which she is consequently soon sitting. Bruised, she retrieves herself and advances towards her car, ice-scraper in hand. As she de-ices the rear nearside window, she sees something odd on the back seat. Scraping a little frenetically to clear a big enough space in the middle of the window to see through, she deciphers something black and white, about the size of a lamb, she thinks, spread out across the tweed interior of the car. She can't remember putting anything like that there – or, indeed, owning anything like that. Before opening the door to take a closer look, she swallows hard and takes a few deep breaths. And then she looks. It *is* a lamb, a dead, newborn lamb, its little soft white body and black face and paws stiffened with *rigor mortis animalis* and last night's frost.

That'll teach you to lock your car, warns Rosey.

Is that all you've got to say? What am I to do now? I can't drive off to my non-appointment with the bank manager in a car with a dead lamb in the back, can I?

This is rural life, says Rosey sagely. Plenty of people drive round the country with dead lambs in their vehicles.

'Morning, Miss Penfold!' Percy Grisewood pulls up alongside in his van with ladders and Ron sticking out of the back.

'Hallo, Percy.'

As Percy parks the van, Ron unfolds himself. 'We've come to sort out your facilities, Miss P,' says Ron gaily, 'at last, as you would say. And I've good news of the Bosendorfer as well – you should have it in a few days.'

Flora is silent. 'Anything wrong, Miss Penfold?' Percy stands beside her, tightening the braces of his blue dungarees before starting to ping them. Flora looks rather pale, he decides.

'There's something dreadful in my car.'

'Is there now?' Percy takes a look. 'Well, not dreadful so much as matter out of place, you could say.'

'Well I never, Miss P!' Ron peers in, just averting a collision between his head and the door as he withdraws it. 'Whoever put that there, then?'

'Be careful, lad, you've only just got over the piano!'

'That's odd, that is.' Ron scratches the platform of his head.

'You go inside, lad, I'll be up shortly.'

'Oh,' Flora recovers herself sufficiently to remember Olga Kahn and Annabel Lancing with her magenta eye in the sitting-room. 'Go in the back, will you, there are some . . . some guests in the sitting-room.'

'Right you are.' Ron disappears with a clanking of tools.

Percy looks at Flora. 'It is indeed odd, isn't it, Miss Penfold? You must admit it's odd. Brings to mind the meadow pipit, doesn't it, dare I say it, slain in the prime of life right outside your back door.'

'I suppose it does.' Flora feels weak. And the postage stamps on Eve, but Percy doesn't know about those.

'And the little statue in the garden decorated with pictorial representations of a certain Royal person.'

'How do you know about that?'

'We have our ways, Miss Penfold.'

'Please move it for me, Percy. Just move it. I don't want to think about it any more.'

Without further ado Percy leans into the back of the car and lifts the stiff little lamb with his bare hands and carries it out and lays it in the back of his own van, amid the sacks of cement mix, the pieces of wood and copper pipe, and the emulsion paints. 'I'll take it home to Olive,' he says confidently. 'Olive will know what to do with it.'

Flora gets in the car. She thinks she can smell dead lamb, but perhaps it's only a fancy. She drives off down Pudding Bag Lane in the direction of Oakingham. But where, really, is she going?

13

News from the Past

THE LAMB in Flora Penfold's car was born ahead of its time, in a hurry, too young. But lambing time proper is advancing now, and just before it comes Meltshire disappears, as Doris Wates predicted it would, in a second fall of snow. This time the snow creeps up on the countryside stealthily by night, so that the grey-brown colours of winter have all been whitewashed again when people wake and pull back their window coverings in the morning. In Cabbage Lane Flora Penfold, after a night of disturbed sleep littered with real and metaphorical corpses; Pete Wates in his pink-washed cottage, designing a feature on the philosophy of animal liberation for the *European Labour Monthly* and laying plans for a sprint to see his friends in warmer climes; Annabel Lancing, with her sore eye now changing from magenta to a deep purplish-black, rising hastily to prepare breakfast for those of her children who are still willing to get up in the morning; Jasper Lancing, banished after a fearsome intervention by Olga Kahn and therefore fumbling for his clothes in the unaccustomed layout of the Lancings' Liberty-print-sprigged spare room; Fanny in the Old Sun Inn in a baby-doll nightie and Ted in striped pyjamas fighting hard to stay asleep while Fanny fiddles with their openings; Armand Nevere, already dressed and on his way in his Alfa Romeo to Wardour Street, leaving brassy Petula with her coarsely dripping Teasmaid; Brian Redfern, the modest property developer in the house with the yellow door, uneasily contemplating the planning application he's lodged for six executive homes with *en suite* bathrooms on Long Rotton Field; the Crowhursts from one end of the village to another preparing for the daily routines of schoolteaching; Jane Rivers, waking in her black nightgown to a black clock radio playing the slowly plodding funeral march from Beethoven's 'Eroica' symphony; in the Post Office Jack Roebuck sorting the mail and Joan on the phone to her auntie in Melton; and Olga Kahn, glasses resting on Freud's

Interpretation of Dreams, still locked soundly into one of her own. Outside the village the Wates, the Pringles and the Fanshawes (especially the Fanshawes) start their farming day cursing and swearing at the snow, while Abraham Varley, unaffected by the weather, casts an eye or two over the fish in Jacob's Water, and Ron, plumber of many talents, stumbles from his shack in the woods to the building yard, stopping to watch a weasel drag a rabbit carcase under a wire fence in the sparkling whiteness, striping it with dark-red blood – all these dead things, mutters Ron, along with others in the Gwater Valley, scratching his head in discomfort. Olive, who dealt, as Percy said she would, with Flora's dead lamb, is packing Percy's white lunchbox with sandwiches – cold kipper and cucumber, one of his favourites – and up at Overton Hall Lord Oliphant's not there to see the fairy-tale transformation of the landscape as he's up at Westminster, and Cornelia's not there because Dr Mervyn Simpson's had her deported to a private hospital to be treated for her depression and her obesity; so Pleasance Oliphant wakes alone in the huge house and takes her eye-mask off to face the day, which is pouring with unusual viciousness through the linen blinds and the white lace curtains, repeating, it seems, as she struggles up to look, the very pattern of the icy snowflakes in the centrally heated warmth and cushioned luxury of the master bedroom, with its carved wooden four-poster bed and usual montage of pale-faced blue-eyed family portraits on the walls.

The windows of the room face Great Glaston's main street, which is a ribbon of whiteness with two grey tracks in the middle. A Victorian mansion opposite is prefaced with snow-hung fir trees; Pleasance hates the shape of those trees and likes them no more with snow on them than without. She lurches out of bed, pours herself a gin, and gets back in. Her head hurts already with the glare of the snow. The gin softens it, adding an opposing inward liquid glow. Pleasance isn't a happy woman, though there are few whom she'd be prepared to let in on the secret. Certainly not her husband, the leonine Bream, and as she has no family to speak of, there are no candidates there. A friend, the Honourable Caroline Mundie, has been treated to a few lamentations over the years in the restaurant of Peter Jones in Sloane Square, but is now, as anyone in their right mind would be, in the Caribbean, soaking up the sun. 'Why can't *we* go abroad?' Pleasance has been known to say to Bream, but knowing full well his answer: 'An Englishman's home is his castle. Castles abroad are for foreigners and deserters. Besides, I don't like the sun. Mervyn says it's bad for my moles.' Daughter Cornelia was Pleasance's confidante, but this is one of the many things that have proved too much for her.

Apart from Cornelia, there is only Cook. Cook, alias Nicolette Manson, a woman of uncertain age, is now pounding dough for bread in the pine-lined kitchen of Overton Hall, while the keen young staff of TV-A.M. eye her from the corner. 'It's like ice out there.' Cook nods in the direction of the snowy back lawn as Pleasance comes into the kitchen.

'Why don't you have a drink to warm you, Cook?' Pleasance pulls the gin out of her dressing-gown pocket.

'Bad as that, is it?' Cook eyes her sternly, then lets her face relax into dough-like smiles. 'Well, I won't say no. My old bones need all the strength they can get in this weather.'

Pleasance Oliphant, further fortified, goes to visit daughter Cornelia in St Agnes's private hospital in Melton. The car slips and slithers all over the place, and she can't find anywhere to park when she does get there. In the foyer of the hospital, which is lit with soft pink lights and tiger lilies, she flings the keys of the Volvo at the uniformed man behind the desk. 'Park it for me, will you?' she barks. 'I'm in rather a hurry.'

Cornelia has shrunk a little since last time. Grapes and chocolates do not adorn her bedside table, and there aren't any women's magazines either, because of their propensity to contain pictures of food. Cornelia is watching 'Kilroy', which is about shoplifting. A woman admits to stealing Mars bars; Cornelia, unhappy Cornelia, reaches for the remote control and turns her off at the mention of those illicit words. When she sees her mother coming she'd like to turn her off, too, but instead she turns her back to the door and closes her eyes. 'I'm asleep, go away.'

'Corney, please!'

'I'm so hungry. And it's all your fault. The doctor says it's all your fault. You're my mother, you should never have allowed me to get fat. It's your fault Robbie wouldn't marry me. I hate you.'

Pleasance stands at Cornelia's back for a few minutes, then turns round and walks out again. She goes to a phone box and calls Bream in Westminster. 'Can't stop,' he booms, 'going to hear Major on Desert Storm. Bonner's waiting for me at the club.'

'I've had it!' says Pleasance.

'Speak up, old girl, I can't hear.'

'I'VE HAD IT!'

'Have you?' Bream hasn't the slightest idea what she's talking about. 'Good. I'll phone you tonight. Must dash.'

Pleasance slams the phone down. She takes the gin out of her handbag and swallows some more. Outside her car is still where she left it, and the keys are on the desk, which is unattended. The phone rings behind the desk. Pleasance leans over the counter and picks it up. 'Hallo? Yes. Well, I wouldn't say it's really a *hospital*, it's more a kind of *madhouse*. No, I wouldn't if I were you. Try the NHS.' She slams the phone down again and looks around her. 'Ah, Mervyn.' Dr Mervyn Simpson has the misfortune to walk past. 'Just the man I wanted to see. I'm taking Cornelia home today. I'll send a car for her later. You're poisoning her against me. I can't have that. I'm sure you understand.'

Mervyn Simpson, being sensitized to these things, picks up the scent of alcohol on Pleasance's breath. But although he protests about her not being in a fit state to drive, it has absolutely no effect. Pleasance meanders, shakily, back down the B1961. She goes past the Great Glaston turn and continues into Little Tickencote, careering down Baker's Hill right into Main Street and then down Barleythorpe Road. Pleasance's Lancôme make-up is puddled with tears. She's angry with St Agnes's for allowing Cornelia to say these things about her – such things which, in nice families, are simply *not* said. Cornelia has had everything – money, a good private education, her teeth straightened, trips abroad, horses, and an expensive secretarial course when it seemed as though she might not be destined for anything more taxing. She'd even had a young man lined up, too, which had seemed unlikely, given her bulk. Though the vacuity of Robbie Belton's mind impressed itself on everyone he met, he had a clean, reasonably sympathetic manner, came from the right sort of background, would probably have made as good a father as Bream Oliphant – which is not saying a lot – and was not known for cruelty to women or animals. All of which made his last-minute repudiation of Cornelia all the more surprising. Ah well! Pleasance sighs. No one in their right mind, knowing this history, could possibly say that Cornelia didn't have everything to be grateful to her parents – and especially her mother – for.

She begins to feel a little calmer. In the car park fronting the west side of Jacob's Water, there are only two or three cars besides her own. She gets out, and walks across the virgin snow in her expensive Swedish boots. Something has made her come here, to this place that contains her own childhood and young womanhood, though she rarely does, being, unlike Abraham Varley, not given to nostalgia and raking through the past like a mound of dead leaves looking for a buried coin or two. Pleasance prides herself on her common sense. When she sobers up, and if she remembers it, she won't be pleased with her emotional performance today. A flock of birds pass overhead like a clump of grits in the snow-laden sky. The edge of the water has fragments of ice floating on it. Pleasance takes the path and walks round it a little. The sheep that usually deck these fields have been retrieved by Frank Wates and his son Pete and enclosed for warmth in the sheltered fields by the farmhouse. The landscape is barren, like a desert. White snow, icy water, grainy, intemperate sky. Despite the Meltshire District Council's programme of reforestation round Jacob's Water, there are few trees in evidence here, where Pleasance walks; indeed, that's one of the ways in which it's obvious that this lake is no natural occurrence. The few trees that are there carry the snow stoically, turning up flashes of brown, sometimes green, petticoats. By the church Pleasance stops, looking out to the centre of the water. It was thereabouts that the Ruddle house stood, all twenty-five rooms of it, with its outhouses and stables and floribunda roses and scented lilac bushes; there where she and Odile had played as children, as picture-book children, and Mary and Lawrence Ruddle had watched them fondly from the upper windows giving views across and down the hen-speckled drives to Eglethorpe and Lessendine; it was from there that Mary and Lawrence Ruddle set out on their Iberian Airways journey to Ibiza, which landed them on a mountain instead. It was there that Pleasance returned from Florence, and Odile from Athens, to mourn their parents and wonder what on earth to do next; from there Odile launched herself on those appalling adventures of hers, requiring to be rescued time and again by the far more sagacious, but unappreciated (then and now) Pleasance.

Pleasance sees Odile once a year, but it's many years since Odile even recognized her. Pleasance goes to see her sister out of duty, which motivates most of what she does in life. Odile is in a nursing home in Yorkshire, run by nuns, who are most circumspect about the rights of people like Pleasance Oliphant to consign their loved and unloved ones to the care of others.

It is Odile who was indirectly responsible for the flooding of Bisbrooke Hundred and Eglethorpe, for the immersion of Abraham Varley's farm, and for the desecration of Barrow Grange. It was her outrageously selfish pursuit of pleasure that led to the return of this land to the living waters of the flood. That's why she's come to a bad end, that's why she's locked up. Not because she is mad, but because she is bad. Pleasance purses her lips. A large bird lands in front of her with a noise like a bassoon. For some reason it reminds her of Bream. Impenitently brash; making its mark on the landscape, whether the landscape is hospitable or not. And it reminds her not only of Bream, but of his brothers Liam and Emile as well, both of whom Odile had courted in her efforts to find a substitute for Bream. Odile had been vague about these encounters, knowing her sister would disapprove. Emile, a chinless throwback to earlier generations of Oliphants, had spent quite a sizeable chunk of what he didn't have in the casino at Montreux; on, in other words, Odile. In other circles, what Emile had done in emptying the family firm's bank accounts would have been actionable fraud. But the Oliphants pulled their lines of power and extricated Emile from the tangle in which the flighty Odile had trapped him, and set him up in a trout-fishing business with strictly limited funds. These days Emile sits in an office in London's Holland Park running a mail-order business in flies and waders and trout bags and fishing gear, including a special line in the new American graphite trout fly rods. He's given up women, and consorts instead in a mild way with younger fishers at his club (a different one from Bream's) in the Strand.

Though Pleasance is married to him, she has never been able to understand Odile's long-lived and deeply consequential passion for Bream. Bream is handsome and well connected, and he treats women well – that is, with a carefully judged emotional distance. Nothing ruffles him; into that smoothly flowing river of Bream's emotional life no sudden rushes of water escape from dammed underground streams; there are no punishing torrents casting around for a victim. What Pleasance cannot see, of course, is that this emotional immobility was precisely the secret of Odile's attraction to him in the first place: in his refusal to be perturbed lay her challenge. By the edge of the water that laps the very spot where Odile Ruddle offered her body on a carpet of cowslips to Bream Oliphant in spring 1946, and where he, confronted with the despoiling of his view of women as spiritual creatures, found his own unable to comply, a bunch of coots squabble in the sharp shoots of snow-bound grass. Pleasance smiles slightly and turns away from Jacob's Water and the past. It was all a long time ago.

From his superior vantage point, Abraham Varley sees a new black Fiat Panda cutting its way through the snow by Windy Bottom like a polished beetle. Inside the car is Callum Dreifus, BBC TV film producer, and minor character from Flora Penfold's urban past with the aforesaid, abandoned Barnaby Gunn. Cal's listening to a tape of the music for *The Panda Man*; the synthetically histrionic rise and fall of a full-blooded blues singer, actually one anaemically white Sarah Smith from Salford, swoops and soars with the black dots of birds over the ivory countryside. Cal studies the map folded on the wheel: the turn to Little Tickencote should be soon. He's not a country man himself, the bare fields and uninhabited skylines leave him cold. His skin hates the dank clammy feel of country air – give him the steamy littered noise of London any day.

Up Barleythorpe Road he comes, out on to Main Street, missing the turn to Cabbage Lane. Coming towards the centre of the village he spies Alun Lancing with Gwenny, feeding stale bread to the mallards in the iced-up duck pond. 'Excuse me,' he calls, 'can you tell me where Cabbage Lane is?' Alun explains and points.

Cal rings Flora Penfold's doorbell. She doesn't hear, as she's up in the attic with Percy Grisewood trying to nail him down to a reasonable timetable of work while he nails down floorboards. Cal goes round the back and comes into the house through the kitchen, shouting. 'Man down there,' says Percy. 'Rang; you didn't hear, probably.'

'Hallo, Flora. I came round the back, I hope you don't mind.'

'What are you doing here, Cal?' Her voice, surprised, is not unfriendly, though it's not the most welcoming voice he's ever heard.

'I've come on a mission,' he says. 'Cup of tea going, is there? I'd rather have whisky, but I'm driving, and the roads are hellish.'

'You didn't come all the way from London, I hope?'

'Why do you hope? I might have come just to see you. No, okay,' he sees his media charm pulling her like a load of horse manure. 'I had to do a Pebble Mill in Birmingham. I'm on my way back. I've come to relay a piece of rather unfortunate news to you, actually.'

Something inside Flora freezes. 'Barney's nothing to do with me any more, you know.'

'Barney's fine, so far as I know. It's not about Barney. Not directly, that is.'

'Who is it about, then?'

'You remember Barney's friend, Judy Nightingale?'

'How could I not?'

'I know Barney should be telling you this himself, but I fear he's not renowned for his courage. As I was passing, in a manner of speaking, I thought I should, in case he doesn't get round to it. Judy's got AIDS. She's quite ill, actually. Barney's shit-scared. You know Barney – as I said, he's not the most courageous of men.'

Flora thinks – not about Barney, and certainly not about Judy Nightingale, but about herself, as Cal intended her to. Perhaps she has AIDS, too? And Pete Wates?

'How did she get it?'

'Your guess is as good as mine. Could be drugs, though that's unlikely. She was fooling around with them a bit when we were on location in Mexico. Other than that, who knows? Except that it's unlikely to have been the proverbial lavatory seat.' He lights a cigarette.

'You mean you came to tell me this for my own good?'

'Naturally. Don't be so surprised! A Good Samaritan, that's me. Where's the cup of tea?'

'Bitch!' says Flora.

'Judy, I take it? Well, I can understand why you don't like her, but that might be going a bit far. On the other hand, I'm not sure.' Cal pauses, blowing the smoke away from the front of his face. 'I don't know anyone Judy hasn't screwed. Except me, of course. You should have an AIDS test,' he adds casually.

Flora sits tautly, blue-jeaned legs together, hands folded like clamps round her thighs. 'Jesus Christ. I certainly didn't expect this.'

'I'm sorry, Flo.'

'Don't call me Flo!' she says sharply, as she always does.

'I was only trying to be friendly.'

'Who needs friends with enemies like that?'

'It could happen to any one of us, Flora. None of us is immune from such epidemics and moral testing grounds. I take it there's a current man who might be involved in this?'

Flora says nothing.

Cal blows smoke at her. 'From your silence, I assume there is. An agricultural labourer, or somesuch? Sorry! I didn't mean that.' Cal's eyes flicker to the window, where darkness is falling and large flakes of snow are fixing themselves to the window, making a point of some kind. 'You see, if there wasn't one, I might proposition you. You always were the better half of Barney. I'm fond of Barney, so that was a compliment. Thanks for the tea, which I never got. You don't need to thank me for coming, I didn't come expecting thanks.'

'No,' she says, giving him a snowy look, 'you came out of duty, didn't you?'

'That's right. Duty. Let me know if I can do anything.'

When Cal has gone, Percy Grisewood comes bumbling downstairs, empty sandwich box in hand. 'That's it for today. Olive'll have supper on the table in forty minutes and I'll have to dig the van out to get home. You all right, Miss Penfold?' He peers at her in the narrow hall.

'You're always saying that, aren't you, Percy? Yes, I'm fine.'

There's no way I'm confessing my sexual past to a builder, she says to Rosey.

Pour yourself a drink, old girl, you feel as though you need one. I'll have two, though they'll make me throw up. What are you doing about my pregnancy?

Flora looks at her watch. It's too late for the library in Oakingham.

What do you want the library for?

To look up AIDS. But maybe it's not too late for the surgery. I think they're open in the evenings. If I go there now, I might just catch them.

June Pringle, Dr Simpson's receptionist, has had a hard day, and is watching the snow anxiously, as she's going to a dinner dance in Melton. 'Yes, can I help you?'

'I'd like to see Dr Simpson, please.' Flora remembers Annabel Lancing mentioning the name.

'Who are you?' asks June suspiciously. 'You're not a patient, are you?' She prides herself on her excellent memory for faces. She's not so good on names, and is often giving the doctors the wrong notes. But Mervyn Simpson's not the kind to sack June – she's a Pringle from the farming family, and in the rural class system generations of working the land count for a lot. Besides which, Dr Simpson's garden backs on to one of the Pringles' fields, and Diana Simpson wants to buy a bit of it for a neo-Georgian conservatory.

'I'm Flora Penfold. I live in Little Tickencote. No, I'm not a patient yet. I'd like to register, please. But I need to see a doctor urgently.'

'Fill this in.' June pushes a form towards Flora. 'Is it infectious?'

'If I knew the answer to that, I wouldn't need to see a doctor.'

June glares. She's not fond of patients who answer back. 'I'll see if Dr Simpson's still here.'

He's sitting at his desk on the phone to Dr Waterman at St Agnes's re Cornelia Oliphant. 'The mother sent a car, you know,' bellows Waterman, a dyspeptic red-faced psychiatrist, 'but of course the girl won't go. She doesn't like her mother very much at the moment. Neither do I.'

Mervyn feels uneasy. The upper classes are all right as patients – as a matter of fact rather good, as they're not ill very much – but when they get out of hand they really get out of hand. Mervyn phones Bream in Westminster and tells him to come home. 'Do I have to, Mervyn?'

'You have to,' says Mervyn authoritatively. 'Your wife needs you.'

'If you say so.' Bream Oliphant's not a man to shirk his duty, and it's simpler when it comes in the form of easily grasped instructions.

'Excuse me,' says June Pringle in the doorway, 'there's a Miss Penfold out here wants to see a doctor urgently. She won't say why, and she doesn't know if it's catching. A new patient. And can I go now, Dr Simpson, I've got to get my hair done, it's snowing something horrid and Joan-at-the-Post-Office is waiting.'

'Come in, Miss Penfold.' Mervyn looks at his watch. He'll have to get through this one fast – he promised Diana he'd be home by 7.30. She's going to her photography evening class in Oakingham. Though in this weather . . .

'What can I do you for, Miss Penfold? New to the district, are you?'

Flora explains that she moved to Little Tickencote six months ago, that's she's not registered with a doctor before because she doesn't normally need doctors. But that her faith in her own health has just been rudely shaken by the news that her erstwhile lover's girlfriend has contracted AIDS.

'What about him? And has she got AIDS, or is she just HIV positive?'

'What's the difference?'

Mervyn sighs. And to think the HEA spent all that money on the AIDS publicity campaign for nothing! He explains.

'AIDS, definitely. She's in hospital.'

Mervyn stares at her. 'Well, that's very sad for her, and for him, too, I would imagine, but how do you come in to it?'

'They – they were together before he and I broke up.'

'Ah. That's unfortunate. So you want a blood test? Well, I suppose I'll have to put some gloves on. If you think you've got AIDS, there's no need for you to make a present of it to me, is there?' He rummages around in the drawer. 'June!' he shouts. 'What happened to the glove order? Damn, the woman's gone. Ah, here's a packet, passed its sell-by date no doubt, but sufficient for the job, I dare say. I expect you realize there's not much AIDS in Meltshire, Miss . . . er . . .

'Penfold.'

'Ah, as in pinfold.'

'Yes, yes,' she says irritably, 'and Flora as in margarine.'

'Ah, that reminds me – the man from the Look-After-Your-Heart campaign is coming next week. I must phone Domak and get them to lay on a nice lunch. We could do with cheering up at this time of year, don't you think, Miss . . . er . . . ?'

'Penfold.'

'Quite. Here we are, then.' He approaches her with a syringe. 'Look the other way and think of England. They'll fetch it for the hospital lab tomorrow morning. Weather permitting. Result in a week. Hope it's negative, I haven't done my AIDS counselling course yet.' He laughs snortingly, like one of Pete Wates's pigs. 'It's not the end of the road, though. The virus could still show up, up to four years later. But you're probably okay. Did you say this man of yours practised birth control?'

'I didn't. I had a cap.'

'That helps. What type of jelly did you use?'

Flora frowns. 'Why is that relevant?'

'Nonoxynol nine. Kills the AIDS virus. *In vitro*, anyway.'

'It was called Orthogynol.'

'You're all right, then. Almost certainly. If only women realized that the old-fashioned methods are so much better for their bodies than all this invisible stuff – hormones from Californian mares *et al.* sneaking their way round the bloodstream when nobody's looking.'

'Thank you very much, Dr Simpson,' says Flora, as he removes her blood. She feels considerably cheered by the information he's imparted to her, though less so by his manner.

He sits up behind his desk and looks over his half-moon glasses at her. 'I'm a good doctor, you know, though my manner does leave something to be desired. I can't handle the communication aspects of doctoring. I expect that's because my father sent me to public school. Any physical illness, women's plumbing, you'll be all right with me. But if you're going to be neurotic or psychotic, you'd be better off with Waterman in Melton.'

Flora remembers Olga Kahn: 'Are you mentally healthy, Miss Penfold?'

'I'll be all right if I don't have AIDS,' she says.

'Quite so. Well, come and see me next Tuesday. That's the day the Look-After-Your-Heart man is coming, so I should be nicely tiddly by the time afternoon surgery starts. Make it two o'clock or later. Tell June – oh, you can't.' He opens the door and sees the vacant reception area. 'The damn woman's gone again. You'd better phone her in the morning – that is if she decides to grace us with her presence, she didn't last time it snowed, remarkable how many people use the snow as an excuse. That reminds me, I told Diana – my wife, you know – I'd fetch the black-and-whites she took of Life Hill in the snow.'

Flora decides not to tell Pete Wates her – or rather, Judy Nightingale's – news until the result of the blood test is back. The village has other gossip to occupy it, in any case. On the Saturday night after the snow fell, Petula and Armand Nevere came home from a meal at the Falcon in Oakingham to find their back door open and a trail of snowy footsteps through the house. Most oddly, they found nothing missing: the microwave, the video, the new flat-screen remote-control television, the electric hedge-cutter, were all intact. Armand refused to phone the police to report a burglary with nothing missing. It didn't even count as a break-in, as Armand had forgotten to lock the back door. Petula thought he should report it, particularly since it was his fault the back door was left open. He was still trying to calm her down when she opened the wardrobe in their bedroom to hang up her mink-edged frock, and saw that the burglar *had* taken something after all: her shoes were gone, her row of twenty-five pairs of stiletto heels completely and utterly vanished.

Petula fainted. She was fond of her shoes. But there was also something horribly odd about a burglar who took stiletto-heeled shoes. Even Armand admitted that. And he did phone the police station now there was something to report, though he considered his credibility only marginally higher than it would have been had nothing been taken: 'Yes, constable, that's what I said – twenty-five pairs of my wife's shoes!'

And that isn't the end of it, either. The Old Sun Inn, the focal point of sociability for the whole village, shuts its doors late one other Saturday night. By the time they've cleared up, Fanny and Ted are exhausted – though Ted more than Fanny, who still has the energy for a bath; as Ted's libido is as flat as a pancake these days, she's taking to water therapy. But Fanny, closing the bathroom door in anticipation of the apricot foam in which she will shortly lie, looks in the direction of the bathtub and sees that it is already occupied by a heap of dead fish, who all lie there looking at her with their dead, glassy eyes. Like Petula Nevere before her, she shrieks, and Ted, whose head has just met the pillow on his side of the damask-covered Silent Night bed, is forced up in an imitation of manfulness to see what has afflicted her.

'You should have locked the back door,' she complains, again not unlike Petula Nevere. 'Whoever it was must have come up the back stairs while we were busy in the bar.'

'What do you mean, whoever?' interrogates Ted, half-asleep.

'Well, I didn't put them there, and I don't suppose you did either. And they didn't come up the plughole, did they?'

The village of Little Tickencote is definitely having a difficult time. Dead fish, dead lamb, dead bird, crashed piano, stolen stilettos and stamped nipples: though the meadow pipit's demise could have been chance, the others scarcely could. But who in Little Tickencote knows about all these happenings, and therefore knows also that there is some collective mystery to puzzle about? Percy Grisewood, apprised of the two incidents that have befallen Flora Penfold, has speculated to Jack-at-the-Post-Office about her apparent ability to attract ill omens. It is Jack, of course, who knows about Eve's stamps from Ketton's, who deliver the gas; and Jack also to whom Petula Nevere confides the flight of her stilettos, and to whom Ted-behind-the-bar, fetching his weekly supply of girlie magazines, worries about Fanny's growing restlessness and unwillingness to put up with some of the ways of Little Tickencote, including dead fish in the bath. 'I'm afraid I'm going to lose her, Jack,' whines Ted, his moustache drooping. 'It's no place for a bright young girl on the brink of life.'

'You should have kept Pat,' advises Jack. 'Better the devil you know . . .'

Ted takes his magazines and flicks through them. 'What is life for, Jack?'

'Don't ask him,' says Joan, emerging from the back of the shop carrying a crate of tinned tomatoes. 'He doesn't know the meaning of the word life. By the way, is Fanny coming for her perm and lighten tonight? I've got it all set up and waiting.'

Not for the first time Ted notices how alike Jack and Joan are. The same frizzy camel-coloured hair – in Jack's case considerably less of it than there once was – identical pointed noses, and a ruddiness to the cheeks that doesn't come from the country air.

'What do you think, Joan?' asks Jack when the jangling door has closed after Ted.

'Male menopause,' declares Joan confidently.

'I didn't mean that! I meant these happenings!'

'It's like on the telly, isn't it? We need a Miss Marple!'

'Haven't we got one?'

'Miss Rivers, you mean? She doesn't solve crimes, she only creates them.'

Jane Rivers sits at her desk in Stonecrop Cottage the other side of Baker's Hill from the Post Office. She sits in the front window, because from there she can see everyone coming and going. The table is polished with beeswax, and her pens are arranged in a mug that says 'You're a mug' on the side. A log fire burns in the grate. Jane is in a black tracksuit, and deep in thought. Georgia Kelly has just got married, but neither she nor Jane is at all sure that was the right thing to do. Her husband is a one-legged Professor of Psychology. Georgia is attracted to what she thinks of as his intellect and the help it might give her in her detective work. All of which is untypically short-sighted of her, as the man will soon turn out to be a pretentious bore; even the missing limb is due to nothing more glamorous than amputation by an overhasty Number Twenty-four bus. But Georgia, presently enamoured, drinks champagne at her wedding reception in the Sherlock Holmes Hotel, and Professor Steven Malling, looking at her red champagne-wetted lips and bodily curves in the scarlet satin wedding suit – like haemorrhaged tissue against the slushy snow-stacked London streets – congratulates himself like a trout fisherman on landing such a catch.

As Georgia and Steven smile disgustingly at each other and Jane realizes how difficult this is going to be to sort out, she sees Flora Penfold coming up the street, shopping basket in hand. The church clock chimes eleven. Jane opens the front door. 'Fancy a coffee? I've got stuck.' She hasn't seen Flora for a while. People lead secretly busy lives in Little Tickencote.

'Thanks. But I'd better just go and get a few things from the Post Office first.'

'That's right,' says Jack comfortingly, 'you go and have coffee with Miss Rivers. You look a bit peaky. Percy told me about the lamb.'

'Nasty business,' echoes Joan, decanting permanent-wave lotion.

'Since you're the detective-story writer,' says Flora a few minutes later in Jane Rivers's sitting-room, 'perhaps you can tell me who's got it in for me, and why?' She explains about the dead lamb, and the other incidents.

'Maybe it was just a prank,' suggests Jane.

'Some prank!'

'You *are* a newcomer, but then so was I, and Olga too. But on the other hand . . . Thank you, Flora, you've helped me. I think I can get on with Georgia now. But I haven't helped you, have I? I'll need to think about what you've said. And maybe talk to Olga about it.'

Flora can see that Jane Rivers is mentally back in her writing mode. In any case, she's got to get back to The Cottage. Ron's brought the Bosendorfer, and he's coming back to tune it. A plumber tuning the piano? Trust Ron, say both Ron himself and Percy Grisewood. Hidden talents, and all that. And he's cheap!

While Ron's playing 'Limelight' to warm himself up, Pete Wates phones. 'I'm off to the Pig Fair, Flora. I did mention it, but I don't think you were listening at the time. I want to find out about this all-outdoor pig-rearing system. Apparently it's been very successful in Northumberland. We're going to have to take pig farming more seriously now the Germans have reunified. The East Germans are great pork-eaters – seventy-seven point nine kilos per head per year.'

'Well, have a nice time at the Pig Fair.'

'You all right, Flora?'

'As well as can be expected,' replies Flora, with images of Charlie Chaplin in the background, and worrying about the results of Dr Simpson's blood test.

'The Pig Fair's over on Monday, but I may drop into the Mastitis Conference on the way back. I'll phone you on Tuesday. I love you, Flora.'

On Tuesday, having slept only a few uneasy hours that night, Flora is up with the birds, which seem to be making one hell of a noise now the snow has nearly gone. A particularly loud one, which sounds like an electric saw, is swinging on a branch of the apple tree insouciantly looking at her with little Percy Grisewood eyes when she opens the curtains. A mist hangs over Owlston Wood. The sky holds a promise of brightness to match the sparkle of spring in the bird's eyes.

Mervyn Simpson isn't feeling quite so bright. Pleasance Oliphant was on to him again last night, and then Bream phoned this morning. 'She won't let up, Mervyn. And I must say I have some sympathy with her. I've got to get back to London today – another sitting for the portrait, you know. Can't you do anything? Is Corney any thinner? How about a rest cure in Switzerland?'

'Have you been to see her, Bream?'

'Well, apparently she won't talk to her mother, so why should she talk to me?'

'She's angry with her mother; it's probably a good thing.'

'Tell that to Pleasance!' Bream guffaws.

Mervyn despairs of conveying even the most elementary psychological home truths to Bream. 'You go and see Cornelia, Bream, and I'll see if I can fix for her to go abroad. I suppose that way Pleasance might be protected from the worst of Cornelia's anger until she's got it out of her system.'

Mervyn sighs. He's sixty-one and would like to retire soon. The trouble is that his partner, Edwin Passmore, combines doctoring with other pastimes. When Edwin first came to join the practice ten years ago, he seemed just right – white Anglo-Saxon Protestant, suitably receding corn-coloured hairline, wife called Barbara, and two infants with names Mervyn's never been able to remember. Edwin, for his part, had been seduced by the roses over the surgery door, and by the entrée into private practice the situation offered. The whole thing had fallen apart when Barbara Passmore left, taking the two nameless children, revealing the nature of one of Edwin's main extracurricular activities – womanizing, including women patients. Once or twice Mervyn had even caught him *in flagrante delicto* with one. 'You can do what you like outside the practice,' he stormed, 'but I'm not having the GMC involved.' He could just see the headlines in the *Meltshire Echo*.

Askham Hollis, the Look-After-Your-Heart man, is full of patter and soon of Vinho Verde too, courtesy of Domak Pharmaceuticals, who have a local plant and office up the hill. 'Dry wine, good for the heart,' says the rep. 'Remember Archie Cochrane, the man who did the original research on alcohol and CHD? He was very pleased to discover that statistics showed a lower incidence of heart disease in wine-drinking countries.'

Hollis has come to find out what Drs Simpson and Passmore are doing to educate their patients about how to have a healthy lifestyle. He doesn't get the kind of response he's looking for. 'What's the point?' wails Mervyn. 'My patients don't listen to me. It's the other way round – I have to listen to them these days.' He shrugs his shoulders and takes another glass of wine.

'The heart is the seat of the emotions,' declares Edwin Passmore, sipping mineral water (alcohol, he is fond of saying, is inimical to one of his favourite activities).

'What's that got to do with it?' interpolates Askham Hollis, remembering his mission, though not his manners.

'Look after the emotions; the heart will take care of itself!'

'You don't really believe that?' Askham's frog-like eyes protrude with incredulity.

'Suppose I did, what could mere doctors do about people's emotions?'

'That's why the man writes poetry,' supplies Mervyn. Poetry-writing is Edwin Passmore's other lifeline. 'But the patients don't read that any more than they listen to us.'

Edwin's off in pursuit of a busty sales rep. Mervyn can hear him asking leading questions about hormone therapy. He sighs again. 'Difficult job, is it,' inquires Askham Hollis, sympathetically, 'being a country doctor? Not quite like the romantic image, is it?'

'The what?'

'Never mind.'

Back in the practice, Mervyn finds the result of Flora Penfold's blood test on his desk. He opens the door and calls her in. She looks like a firework about to go off, he thinks. 'Sit down, do sit down. I expect you want to know the answer. Well, you're all right, Mrs Penfold. This time. Whatever your husband's got, you haven't.'

'Thank God for that!' Flora lets out her breath, as though she's been holding it for a year or two. Then she smiles. A pretty smile, thinks Mervyn. 'But it's *Miss* Penfold,' she reminds him, 'and he wasn't my husband. And he isn't the one who has it.'

Mervyn looks puzzled. 'Well, in that case good riddance to bad rubbish, I'd say,' he mumbles obscurely. 'But do go on using the nonoxynol nine. You did say you used it, didn't you? Or was that someone else? Yes, I thought so. Lay in a good supply. Tubes and tubes of it!' He laughs and takes his glasses off. 'My God, that was dreadful stuff, that wine. How old did you say you are?'

'I didn't. Thirty-nine.'

'What about babies?'

'What about them?'

'If you haven't had any, you ought to. It's denying a woman's nature not to. On second thoughts, throw the Orthogynol away. Find yourself a nice fertile virgin. Easier said than done round here. I don't know,' he moves his chair away from the desk and leans back, tipping it dangerously close to a yellowing rubber plant, 'it was so much easier in my day. No AIDS, no Pill. If you did it, you knew you might hear the patter of tiny feet. The whole thing's complicated enough, isn't it, without any of these new diseases and inventions? It's a wonder any of us can cope with it at all, really.' He pauses. 'Well, I don't suppose you want to listen to my moralizing.' Giving his chair an extra shove away from the desk, he falls over into the rubber plant. As he picks himself up, dusting the earth off his drug-company-luncheon suit, he says, 'It's fortunate that you're in the clear and I don't need my non-existent AIDS counselling. But I ought to warn you, Mrs Penfold, that you're not theoretically off the hook until four years after your last exposure to whatsername's . . . well . . . body fluids. My receptionist's got a leaflet. If she hasn't gone home early again.'

A lemon sun is high in the sky as Flora comes out of the surgery door. The gentle light it casts on the earth of Meltshire is like the soothing calm of Dr Simpson's 'Well, you're all right this time, Mrs Penfold.' Her step is light. The leaves and the hedgerows are vivid and welcoming. There are no traces of the snow left now. Flora takes a short cut back through Owlston Wood. Coming down the edge of the hill, she stops and stares at the most marvellous sight: a carpeting of tiny mauve crocuses, misty like the gauze of a *Swan Lake* ballet set, round the roots of an oak tree. It's not yet spring, and the tree's budless, but the crocuses poke their pert little stems up, and hold their tiny violet blooms shut still, waiting. A little distance off, over by the hedge, clumps of snowdrops bend their milky campuline heads. The sun weaves its way down through the black-limbed trees and falls into a pool of water. This spectre of nature going quietly about its business, the rhythm of the seasons – as Jim Hoskins had put it on the day of the flasher in the cathedral – fills Flora with a gladness to be alive, with a knowledge of her good fortune, and with a resolve to be kinder herself in future to this world and its inhabitants who nourish her.

And her mother. Since Irina won't visit her here, Flora decides she should go to London and see her. It's only an hour and a half on the train, after all. She can combine it with seeing the *Daily Record* man, and with buying some French crockery she wants for The Cottage which she can't get locally.

Having disposed successfully of the last two missions, Flora takes a bus to Bloomsbury. Through the grimy windows she watches the streets and the people hurrying past, heads bent against the rain that's now drizzling down. Inside the bus it's steamy with the smell of wet umbrellas and soaked wood. People's faces wear expressions of resignation.

Irina opens the door in her dressing-gown. 'Aren't you well, Mother?'

'I didn't expect you, darling. Of course I'm well. Never better. I'm just in bed working. Much the nicest place in this weather. Are you coming for long? It's just that I'm on the last chapter, and I don't want to lose the thread.'

'The last chapter of the book about Galia Molokhovina?'

Her mother nods.

'Good God, after all these years!'

'Well, you couldn't expect me to get it finished with all that other business going on, could you?'

'What other business?'

'All that family business. Samuel, and you and Jonathan.'

'Well, I'm sorry we got in the way,' says Flora in a hurt voice.

'Don't be silly, it wasn't your fault. Come, I'll make you a cup of coffee, then you can be on your way and I can get back to Galia.'

If Flora had cherished any guilty thoughts of her mother feeling alone and neglected by her, she need cherish them no more. Irina's eyes are bright. The flat's a dusty mess, but there's lots of food in the fridge, and a glimpse into her mother's room reveals the big double bed laden with books and papers and a large convector fire burning. Before she leaves, Flora brings out a bunch of snapshots of The Cottage, Little Tickencote and Meltshire. Irina peers at them politely. 'Very nice, darling. Did you take them yourself?' Her tone of voice is historical; Flora hears Irina responding in exactly this way to the trophies she brought home from school as a child.

By the time she gets back to Little Tickencote, it's late. Her car is only one of two in Melton Station car park; the other is a Land Rover. A tall aristocratic-looking man with crinkly yellow hair – it reminds Flora of a 1960s advertisement for permanent wave – follows her off the train and goes towards the Land Rover. He turns to her in the darkness. 'You're Miss Penfold, aren't you? I recognize the car from my wife's description.' His booming voice echoes round the empty car park. He holds out his hand. 'Bream Oliphant from Overton Hall. Pleased to meet you. Been to London for the day, have you? Much easier than driving, isn't it, though that damned wait in Clipsham for the connection can get on your nerves.'

Flora remembers the wedding photograph on the mantelpiece of Overton Hall: Bream Oliphant with his hangover, Pleasance Oliphant with flowers in her hair. She remembers Cornelia Oliphant and her unfortunate non-marriage resulting in the damage to her – Flora's – Bosendorfer. 'How's your daughter, Lord Oliphant?' she inquires politely. 'I hope she's fully recovered from her . . . her disappointment?'

'Will be, will be,' thunders Bream. 'No thanks to the damned doctors, of course. It's Pleasance I'm worried about now. Quite unhinged her, it has!'

It's an odd conversation to be having in an unlit station car park shortly before midnight. After a few moments, Flora takes her leave and gets into her car with a feeling of relief. But the engine doesn't start. She yanks the choke out and tries again. Nothing. 'Shit!' The lights won't work either. The battery must be dead.

What are you going to do about this pickle, then? asks Rosey's voice in her head. Watch out, your knight on a white horse is approaching! Remind me to ask you for one of those.

Lord Oliphant in his Land Rover, having completed one circuit of the car park in order to point his vehicle in the right direction, has noticed Flora's stationary condition, and come back to offer his help. Flora is horribly grateful, and accepts a ride home.

'I won't offer to look at the car for you; other men are much better than I am at that sort of thing. Get Ron down in the morning, that's my advice. You do know Ron, don't you?'

'Perhaps I should get a horse,' reflects Flora. 'Horses don't have batteries that die, do they?'

'*Do* you ride, Miss Penfold?'

'I've never been on a horse in my life.'

'Well, it's never too late to start.' Bream Oliphant is feeling quite pleased with himself – indeed, quite rejuvenated – as a result of a sitting with Mary Widdowson. Such a pleasant, cultured woman! After the sitting he'd taken her out to dinner in a little fish restaurant in Chelsea. The lemon sole had glistened fleshily in the discreet candlelight. 'I'm sorry – what did you say?' He'd got lost in his own thoughts.

'I said,' repeats Flora, 'that I'd never ridden a horse in my life.'

'You could try a bicycle. Good bicycle shop by Jacob's Water,' he offers. 'That's where they rent them out, you know, for day trippers. Lots of people don't approve of it, but I don't mind myself. Think the water's a good thing. Brings trade to Meltshire. Need it at a time like this. Recession and all that.'

'I've got one,' she says.

'You have?' He swerves round the corner out of Melton and changes gear to go up the hill crested by Snelston cement works which, brightly lit and squarely modern, anchor the sleepy countryside in the modern economically recessing industrial age.

'I forget,' says Flora – she doesn't, but it'll do as an opener – 'did you lose land when the reservoir was flooded, Lord Oliphant?'

In the light from the cement works she can see the expression on his face change. Its skin draws in on itself, composing a definitely guarded look. 'Not directly. But my wife's family were badly affected.'

'What was the compensation like?'

'Why, what have you heard?' His question is veritably barked at her.

'I haven't heard anything,' she reassures him quickly, though why he should be upset she doesn't know. 'I was just wondering what it was like for the farmers – whether they got decent compensation or not.'

'The money wasn't bad,' is all he says.

But Flora, having started, is persistent. 'It must have been a dreadful feeling, having the land where one grew up and where one's family lived for hundreds of years just disappearing underwater like that.'

'Indeed.' Like many round here, Bream Oliphant remembers the day the water started to trickle into the valley. It had been the driest summer for thirty years. The water trickled and flowed, but it took five years to fill the reservoir completely. Some famous personage had cut a red ribbon. But the celebrants were thin on the ground. He went, it was his civic duty. Pleasance didn't. It was her home, after all, that was being drowned. Though Jacob's Water had been the Ruddle sisters' salvation; if the reservoir hadn't come along, God knows what they would have done for money. No ordinary sale would have produced such a yield. As for his own part in it – well, he'd only been an enabler, whatever anyone had said.

'That old man Abraham Varley, he was one of the farmers who lost out,' says Flora Penfold, still questioning beside him, 'wasn't he?'

'There's no love lost between myself and Varley,' observes Bream Oliphant, 'as you may have noticed that night of the fiasco in the pub. But he's not a man to tangle with, Varley. He was odd before the water came, and he's been even odder since. They put him in charge of the fish, you know. Anyone else would have taken the money and run. But not Varley. Not only is he responsible for the fish, but he spends all his time there, morning and evening, winter and summer, staring down into the water. What's he looking for? God only knows. Pictures of ruins. Floating ornaments. But of course there aren't any. They bulldozed the land before they let the water in. Razed it to the ground; only rubble left. Here we are.' Bream brings the Land Rover to a halt at the junction of Pudding Bag Lane and Cabbage Lane. 'I won't take the beast down your lane, if you don't mind; might wake the neighbours.'

14

The Ides of March

FLORA WALKS OUT into her garden on the first day of March as the bell of All Saints' chimes eight. The sky is a brilliant Mediterranean blue stretched like a silk canopy over a countryside stirring from the frosts of winter. From the top of the apple tree a bird shouts like Lord Oliphant in his Land Rover last night; but this is a persistent erh-*erh*, erh-*erh* sound, like a squeaky door swinging on its hinge. Cradling her mug of coffee in her hands to warm them, Flora, in dressing-gown and slippers, stands under the apple tree looking up, trying to find the bird. But in the bare-veined branches of the tree, nothing makes itself visible. She reaches out and touches the tips of one of the lowest branches – so low it nearly touches the grass. The branch bears the beginnings of buds, soft furry protuberances that yield milkily to the touch. She lets go of the branch, and it swings back again. Her eyes travel up and across the top of the tree to the chimneys of the Lancings' cottage and to the tall fir trees in their garden, swaying decorously like corseted spinsters. Every branch of every tree is painted with a line of light, and beyond the dry-stone wall glows the green grass of the fields in front of Owlston Wood. In Flora's own garden the grass, shimmering with the same light of spring about to come, harbours huge mushrooms, their caps turned at angles to the straightness of the blades of grass amongst which, like uninvited cuckoos, they nest themselves. Clumps of green shoots by the roots of the apple tree announce the imminent blooming of golden daffodils. Everything is budding, springing into life.

Beyond Little Tickencote, the Gulf War is over and the world begins to take stock of what it has meant. Not far from the spot where Flora stands, a family prepares to take back the body of a young man, twenty-one when his life was terminated by mistake in the Kuwaiti desert. They're proud of what their son achieved but at a loss, deep in themselves, to understand how this countryside, so beautifully advancing into spring, could sensibly harbour such an ending.

In his pink cottage on Life Hill Pete Wates breakfasts on a free-range egg and a plate of Weetabix. He was up at six to a toxaemic sheep, found trembling and with rolling eyes in a corner of the lambing pen by his father the night before. He'd called Mike Ramsay, who'd done what he could, but the condition would very probably be fatal. 'You should reckon on one or two cases in a flock this size,' Ramsay had advised, 'but if it's more than that, you want to look at what you're feeding them.' Pete had taken the opportunity to discuss with Mike the details of the new outdoor method of raising pigs he'd found out about at the annual Pig Fair. But Mike had been more interested in the Mastitis Conference. 'We can handle the florid sort with a jab of penicillin in the teat – though, mind you, there are bugs developing that penicillin can't touch – but it's the subclinical form that's bothering us these days. It can affect milk production by as much as 10 per cent. And it can spread, too. What did the experts at your conference have to say about that?'

'Not much,' Pete had to admit.

'There's experts for you. What about homeopathic remedies – was there a session on that?' As a practising vet, Mike attaches a good deal more importance to his and other vets' own first-hand knowledge of animals than to what he calls book-learning, and this includes a few recent and successful trials of homeopathic treatments, particularly one for foot rot. He's a good vet, a bit like Mervyn Simpson is with humans in a way, good at diagnosing problems and settling the physical ones. Fortunately, animals don't suffer from mental diseases – Mervyn Simpson should have been a vet, really.

After dealing with the toxaemic sheep and one or two other problems that had developed in his absence, Pete Wates sat down in front of his Apple Mac to bring out the next edition of the *European Labour Monthly*. Horst in Berlin and Luigi in Florence had sent faxes with their contributions. He had an interesting piece about the labour implications of the new Dutch laws for slurry-handling. The consequences of the legal requirement that slurry be directly injected into sandy-soil-based grasslands were quite mind-boggling.

While his egg was boiling, Michelle Lapin phoned from Arès about her article on the effects of the economic recession on the labour organization of French oyster farmers. '*Je suis désolée*, Pete,' says Michelle, 'my aunt 'as been ill and I 'ave 'ad ze most frightful *mal de tête*! I zink you will 'ave to 'old it over till ze next edition!'

'Ah, Michelle, zat is indeed a pity! What am I going to do with your space? No one writes like you! We need the oyster farmers – I've got far too much about pigs this time round.'

Michelle promised to try, and to fax him later in the day. She told him that spring had already come to Arès: the water in the Bassin was warming up, the pines in the forest were greenly odoriferous, and the pink azaleas and blue-purple rhododendrons were out. Pete tasted the salty oysters as she spoke, and the cool dry white wine and the crispy cottonwool bread. 'Maybe I'll pay you a visit soon, Michelle,' he said, 'when lambing's finished.' He knew this would spur her on to write her piece, even if he didn't mean it – which, as it happens, he did.

Breakfast finished, he has to interview two contenders for a post on the Wates farm advertised in *Farmers Weekly*: 'Lambing assistant required, March 22 for 4 months. 600 Ewes. Nights. Accommodation provided.'

Valerie Rumpstead is nervous, twisting her white hands this way and that against the skirt of her quite inappropriately urban grey-striped suit. Her feet, in dark-red pumps, sit at awkward angles to each other on the rough cement floor of the farm office, where she has her interview with Frank and Pete Wates. The skin on her face is rough, like the floor. 'Would you like a cup of tea, Miss Rumpstead?' Doris is always sorry for the women; Frank's manner takes no account of other people's feelings, and Pete's not much better. Valerie's eczematous face, partly hidden by a pair of uplifted Dame Edna glasses, smiles crumblingly in gratitude. She interviews badly because of the nervousness, but her references are good. She likes sheep. 'I wanted to be a nurse,' she tells them, 'but I'm shy with people.'

The other contender for the post, Alastair Horn, is a smooth talker in designer jeans. He has aspirations to be a farmer, but dreadful references. 'This young man has a mind of his own. My wife got quite fed up with all the remarks he made about her cooking.' And: 'Alastair reminds me of a garage mechanic. He thinks the insides of sheep are the same as cars.'

Pete and Frank give the job to Valerie Rumpstead. The breadth of her smile litters the lapels of her suit with flakes of dry skin. 'That's wonderful! I'm so pleased! When can I move in?' It transpires that she is homeless – her entire worldly belongings are in a suitcase in the Left Luggage office at Melton Station. The Wates decide to employ her there and then as an additional hand around the farm in the lead-up to lambing time. Doris is called to get the room ready. She takes Valerie under her wing like a mother sheep.

'Beware the Ides of March!' says Pete, striding in on Flora that afternoon as she crouches over the middle bed in her garden, weeding round the Christmas rose. 'This plant has been a great disappointment to me,' she says sternly. 'It's not flowered once. Why is it called a Christmas rose if it doesn't produce roses and has nothing to do with Christmas? Did you have a great time at the Mastitis Conference?'

'Udders,' says Pete. 'Pictures and pictures of Udders. Diagrams of Udders. Videos of Udders. Descriptions of Udders. Udders for breakfast, lunch and tea. Quite turned me on, it did. Come here, Flora, I want to kiss your Udders.'

Later on, watching a few silver clouds blow across the blue March sky, Flora says to Pete, 'I think we should go out to celebrate.'

'Celebrate what? I mean it's a nice idea, but did you have anything in mind particularly?'

'Well this – and us. Four whole months of us. And the fact that despite the peculiar things that happen to me from time to time, nothing really bad has. Survival.' She turns towards him in the bed and runs her finger down his chest to his navel and beyond. 'You know what you said that afternoon a few months ago?'

'Sort of.'

'Well, I love you, too. And I want to talk to you about us, but not now. Now I don't want to be serious.' She holds the softness of his penis in her hand and, burrowing down under the bedclothes, licks it gently, like an ice cream.

'There's a special offer at the Lessendine Hall Hotel – you know, that pricey place in the middle of Jacob's Water,' reflects Pete up above. 'How about it? You could wear your ball gown again. What d'you say, Flora? What? I can't hear.'

Her head appears above the duvet. 'I say yes. Yes, Pete – yes to you, yes to the Lessendine Hall Hotel special offer, yes to Little Tickencote, yes to everything!'

Pete doesn't understand the reason for Flora's good mood. The only thing he can think of is the weather. Spring has a peculiar effect on people. But his own head is too occupied with the next edition of the *European Labour Monthly*, and with the condition of his sheep, and now with the breaking in of Valerie Rumpstead.

When he gets back to his cottage at four, there's a fax from Michelle in Arès. It isn't an article, though, it's a poem in French about her male co-farmers who work the oyster beds. Pete's French isn't all that good, but it's good enough for him to work out that the poem is quite Rabelaisian. It makes Pete think of Michelle's hard white body, of the flame-coloured hair on her head and elsewhere. But I can't print this, says Pete, holding Michelle's poem in his hand and looking at the unfilled space on his Apple Mac screen. Suddenly he has an idea. 'Flora,' he says on the phone – she's in the bath newly and finally out of its cardboard and connected courtesy of Percy Grisewood or, rather, Olive, who did finally have some sympathy with a woman's need for water – 'Flora, can you do me a Marxist version of Rural Rosey for the paper, do you think? Quickly. Like now?'

Hang on a minute, says Rosey, I'm not a Marxist.

'I don't see why not,' says Flora, anxious, in her bright springlike mood, to oblige. 'What kind of thing did you have in mind?'

'Something about milking?'

'You've got udders on the brain.'

'Fortunately not. What about the influx of cheap calves from Eastern Europe? Or the labour implications of once-a-day milking?'

I don't know about you, grumbles Rosey, but I'm not inspired. And milking is incredibly unedifying. I should know, I've done enough of it recently.

'I'll have a go. But I have got some other things to do this evening.'

'What could be more important than this?'

Your own life, hisses Rosey. You don't want to get sucked into doing things for a *man* again! That's what you came here to avoid, remember?

While Flora's drying herself, she remembers the pile of early goes at Rosey, one of which was a skit on the sexism of farmers towards their wives. She gets it out – it'll have to do. Rosey is quite right. Much as she thinks she may love Pete Wates, it'd be wrong to give him the impression that she's willing to be at his beck and call.

In front of the fire Pablo and Dolly sit like china cats, tails neatly curled round paws. Flora eats a cheese sandwich and carries a glass of whisky into the sitting-room. She's going to have another session with Samuel's papers. The cats move out of the way, alarmed, as she heaves a great box of papers into the centre of the room. She digs out the manuscript about Woodcock-by-Water, with the map of carefully drawn cottages and lawns and ducks and cedar trees, and starts reading.

It's clearly the first part of a book which is intended to be a sociological study of rural community life. Chapter 1 locates the village which is the object of study in its economic context: how the people make a living, how many on what kind of farms, availability of local light industry. The next chapter analyses the class structure. Pete would find this interesting, though Flora doesn't. Between pages ten and eleven of the third chapter, which is about The Family, there's a letter on thin blue paper, its position suggesting that it isn't meant to be there. At first Flora assumes it's from Julian Peacock, her father's colleague and literary executor, since there are numerous notes of his attached to or interleaved with the papers – some written at the time, some since. The writing on the blue paper looks like his too. But it's signed 'Julia'. There's very definitely no 'n' on the name. Before the word 'Julia' come the words 'Your beloved'. I'm not sure I want to know about this, says Flora tensely, out loud, and feeling slightly sick. You should have dumped the whole lot in the library, then, says a voice – gender uncertain, it could be either Rosey's or Samuel's – in her head. Flora turns the letter over.

> Dearest Samuel, I think your chapter 3 is quite brilliant. I hope none of my neighbours know any sociologists! Have you got a contract for it yet? My bit is well on the way, but I think we'll need to meet soon. Why don't you come down for the May fair in Bisbrooke, we could have some fun at the same time?
>
> My classes are going well. Arthur Baycock's starting his new option next week. He *is* a dreadfully arrogant young man, but with luck he won't stay long. Indeed, he told me last week he's going to go after the first job in London that comes up – I hope for your sake it's not one of yours!
>
> Sorry to hear about Flora's glandular fever. One of the things I love you for is that you're such a good father.
>
> Hope to send you my first chapter next week. And do come down so we can go to the fair together. Your beloved Julia.

Well I never! Flora puts down the letter and takes a swig of whisky. Despite Pete's remark, it had never occurred to her to think of her father being unfaithful to her mother. She'd always taken his reasons for being away at face value. So, she supposed, had her mother. But had her mother known? Flora rejects an urge to phone Irina: who was this Julia person that father was having it off with in 1960, Mother?

1960 was the year Flora had had glandular fever. She'd really been quite ill for several months. Irina had hated nursing her, as it took her away from Galia Molokhovina. Flora scrabbles through the pages, but there aren't any other stray letters. Of course there might be something else elsewhere in the papers – the other boxes are up in the attic.

Who was Julia, and where did she live? It sounded like the Schubert song Flora had been made to sing at school. What was the name of the place mentioned in the letter? Bisbrooke. She'd heard that name before somewhere. Flora looks for a map. She takes her car keys and goes out to get the Atlas of Britain, but she remembers where the car is – in Melton Station car park. Damn! She phones Pete. 'Do you know a place called Bisbrooke, by any chance?'

'What about your cartoon – have you finished it?'

'Answer my question first!'

'Bisbrooke, did you say? No, there's nowhere called that that I know of. Well, not round here, at any rate. Not any longer.'

'What do you mean – not any longer?'

'The cartoon, Flora!'

'Oh, yes. I've put together a little something you can use.'

'I'm on my way.'

'Pete . . .'

'Got to get this thing to bed,' he says breathlessly a few minutes later.

'By "thing" I take it you don't mean me?'

'No, the newspaper. Quick, where is it?' She gives it to him. 'Not bad – yes, that'll do nicely. Just about the right size. Might have to lose one frame. No, probably not; I can squash it in. Right – thanks, Flora, thanks a lot.' He looks up at her. 'I've got to dash. Said I'd take Valerie round the ewes before she goes to bed. Is something the matter?'

'My father was having an affair with someone in Meltshire thirty years ago. Who's Valerie?'

'Well, so what? Our new lambing assistant. Is it the Meltshire bit that surprises you? How do you know, anyway?'

Flora tells him. 'It changes my whole image of him,' she protests.

'From upright citizen and good family man to lonely adulterer all in the space of however long it took you to read that letter!'

'Yes,' she says miserably.

'Don't be daft, Flora, he's still the same man he was.'

'I want to find Bisbrooke,' she says.

'You can't. It's under the water. It's one of the villages that drowned when the reservoir was built.'

'You're joking!'

'Indeed I am not. But I must dash, Valerie's waiting!' Seeing her sitting there on her heels in a characteristic Flora pose, but looking like a little girl whose world's just come to an end, he feels he shouldn't leave her. 'Do you want me to come back later, love?'

'No, I'll be all right.'

'Put the papers away, and watch telly instead. Stop digging around in the past, and think about the future.'

She sniffs. 'You're right. It doesn't make any difference anyway.'

Of course it does, though. Knowing that her father and this person Julia had a – a thing together in a village whose contours now lie beneath the coloured sails of boats and the calls of birds, under the shimmering surface that first made her think of living here – now that is a very peculiar thought. A thought with a certain emotional intensity to it. It sets up a permanent shudder along Flora's spine. It means her father knew Meltshire. It means the place had significance in his life, as it has now, in hers. It means he may have known some of the very people she knows now – Abraham Varley, the Oliphants, others connected with the drowned valley. It means – well, what it means in terms of Samuel's own psychology she can't say, and isn't sure she wants to.

Over the next few weeks, Little Tickencote, Great Glaston, Jacob's Water, Oakingham, Melton and the rest of Meltshire grow greener by the day. The daffodils and the tulips and the bluebells follow the impertinent misty mauve crocuses and the snowdrops with their fragile bent heads like shy virgins at a wedding. The chilly north-east wind drops, and the warming of the soil is matched by a rise in the air temperature. Bridget Crowhurst meets Flora by the gate to Sheepdyke Field one Thursday morning. 'No school today?' asks Flora brightly.

Bridget shakes her head. 'I had to stay at home, there's something wrong with my plumbing.'

'Oh dear, I'm sorry to hear that.'

'When I woke up this morning, the kitchen was flooded. I had to call the plumber – you know, the one with the great flat head. He said the connection under the sink was loose. Looks like someone's tampered with it, he said.' Bridget shakes her head again. 'I don't know – it seems to be one disaster after another. The water had seeped into the dining-room; my Persian-style Wilton rug is soaked. Martin's coming up after school to help me clear up.'

'It sounds awful.' Flora doesn't know whether to draw Bridget's attention to the most interesting part of this recitative – Ron's diagnosis that someone tampered with the plumbing.

'Did you hear about Petula Nevere's stilettos?' asks Bridget, as though she's reading Flora's thoughts.

'Yes.'

'Do you think this is the same kind of thing?' She looks anxious. 'I mean, if it is, what on earth's going to happen next? Perhaps we should tell the police – what do you think, Flora?'

'I think it would sound a little odd. I'm not sure the police would take it seriously.'

The two women turn their heads as a metallic jangle announces Trevor the vicar coming round the corner on his bike. 'Good morning, ladies! Nice day, isn't it!' He jangles off again.

'He keeps coming round to convert me,' grumbles Bridget. 'It'd be a lot more help if he'd give a hand with the mess. Has he been to see you?'

'He did come once, shortly after I moved in. I told him I wasn't a believer, and he said God was the same thing as nature.'

'I hate nature,' says Bridget miserably, 'don't you? All this *blooming*, and . . . well . . . *greenery*! Do you want to come and have a cup of coffee with me, Flora?' Bridget's voice is abrupt; she lacks any of the usual social graces. Many people interpret this as rudeness, which it isn't.

'Not just now, thanks.' Seeing Bridget's crestfallen face, Flora quickly adds: 'Maybe tomorrow?'

'I think we need to think about the police,' reiterates Bridget. 'There's something funny going on in this village.'

'My sentiments exactly,' says Olga Kahn, to whom Flora confides the substance of her meeting with Bridget Crowhurst. 'Let's make a list:

Bridget Crowhurst – loose connection.

Flora Penfold – dead lamb.

Petula Nevere – stolen stilettos.

Fanny what's-her-name – dead fish in the bath.'

'Don't forget the postage stamps. I suppose the dead bird could have been an accident. Oh – and I have had a few odd phone calls. What about Annabel Lancing?'

'Male violence doesn't come in the same category,' says Olga firmly. 'Endemic, not accidental. But you could have a point. Maybe Annabel's straits are dire enough to protect her from any of these other events.'

'Bridget thinks we ought to tell the police.'

'Not a case for the police, I would say. More in the nature of a psychological investigation.'

'So do you think you could crack it, Olga?'

'Not on my own. But maybe with the help of our resident crime writer.'

'I'd forgotten her. Good.' Flora rubs her hands together. 'This could be quite *fun*, couldn't it?'

That afternoon, Olga Kahn telephones Jane Rivers and they go for a long walk round Jacob's Water. Starting by Eglethorpe Church, they take the path to the stone causeway which dammed the river, causing the countryside to the east to lose the historical benefit of its peregrinations. The earth on the path is the deep moist red of Meltshire, and so are the ploughed fields rising on the right to the skyline. As everywhere else, the earth is broken with bright-green shoots. A little further on there's a field with fat grazing ewes, their flanks about to burst with lambs. Between the path and the water, the still-naked branches of red-brown trees match the earth, and newly planted young ones peek nervously out of their wire cages. The water swishes and laps the red shore, gently. No one else walks the path except black-clothed Jane Rivers and Olga Kahn in her scarlet-lined batwinged cloak.

Olga tells Jane of her conversation with Flora Penfold. 'She's not a hysterical young woman,' says Olga when she's finished. 'Indeed, far from it. She strikes me as quite sane and sensible. Though I, as a psychoanalyst, should of course avoid the use of such imprecise lay terms.'

'Why don't you, then?' Jane looks down, her black boots scuffing the red earth.

'Er-hum. The older I get, the more faith I have in the common sense of the community and the less in the pretensions of experts. It's the basis of the experts' knowledge that must be called into question. Do you know that story, Jane – no, of course you don't – of Freud's disciple Groddeck – not a man I would otherwise admire – who stood up at a congress of non-medically trained analysts who were all busily discussing the anal complex, and shouted out "How many of you have actually *seen* one!"'

'I don't see what that's got to do with events in Little Tickencote, Olga.'

'Come, come, Jane, don't be so disagreeable! I was only illustrating the point. So what do you think?'

Jane is silent for a minute. Then: 'Well, I don't think it's coincidence,' she says. 'Let's consider to whom these things are happening. First of all, they're only happening to the *women*. Secondly, they're happening to relatively *young* women, aren't they? Relatively.'

'In my younger days I would have entertained a diagnosis of collective hysteria,' observes Olga. 'I remember Karen Horney talking about that in her piece on . . . Where was I? Oh yes, the pent-up frustrations of non-motherhood, you know. Like this dam, preventing the river from taking its natural course down the valley.'

'You're right,' says Jane. 'Oh, not about the hysteria, but about the fact that none of them are mothers.'

'Er-hum,' says Olga. 'But neither are we.'

'No, but we've passed our sell-by date, haven't we?' Jane Rivers remembers her own mother, the warped dependency of her early and later years growing in Jane herself a determination not to repeat the pattern. Beside her, Olga Kahn thinks back to the days when she and Raphael lived in Vienna and were in love – days when she would gladly have had a baby or two, but Raphael said no, he couldn't share her with anyone else, and besides, there was his work and hers. 'Pity,' says Olga now. 'I would have been a damn sight better mother than some I've known!'

'I've no doubt,' comments Jane. 'But where does that get us?'

'Someone has got it in for the childbearing women of Little Tickencote.'

'Seems like it. But if it's hard enough in this case to identify the crime, it's not going to be easy to find the perpetrator, is it?'

'You're the crime writer, not I.'

'And you're the specialist in human behaviour.'

'No specialist – just think of me as a woman with experience.'

'Look, woman with experience – look at that!'

They've reached the causeway and, turning back towards the length and breadth of Jacob's Water, the direction from which they came, find themselves looking straight into the fiery coppery face of the setting sun. Its orange-red globe is hung there just above the rim of the earth and water – perhaps it will fall instead of slip over the edge of the earth, or perhaps it will break into a field, streaking it with filaments of gold. The sky, which had earlier been spattered with marrow clouds, is clear now – an absolutely bright duck-egg blue, a backdrop for the henna sun.

'Yes,' assents Olga Kahn. 'Yes, indeed. Every sunset is a first and a last.'

Jane shoots a sideways glance at her; there was a ring of pain in Olga's voice. 'You're no more mortal than I am,' she comments sharply.

'Mortality isn't a matter of degree. The dead don't know they're dead, but the dying sometimes do.' A slight pause – Jane begins to say something. Olga interrupts her: 'I don't want to talk about it, Jane. Not now. Not ever. I must ask you to respect that.'

'I will.' Jane's voice is quiet. The sun's globe sinks lower, so that only the top crescent can be seen, like a bright hair-clip. 'Come on, we'd better go back; it'll get very cold very quickly.'

They walk fast. 'About this other business,' continues Olga. 'I think we'd better do our own detective work. Getting the police involved would be no good for the collective morale of the village. Suspicion breeds suspicion. We must keep our eyes skinned.'

The sky is empty now, but the sun's left a spreading pink glow. Baby clouds, pink-tipped, play over the blushing mirrored surface of the water. A flock of geese rise. 'What *do* they sound like?'

'Frightened women.'

The geese's high-strung cries rise into the sky over the fields as the birds arrange themselves into a neat V-shaped formation.

'I wonder where they're going?'

'They're only out for their evening stroll, like us.'

After a bit, the birds change their flying pattern and come back in towards Jacob's Water in a long flowing line.

15

Lambing Time

THOUGH THE DATE scheduled for the birth of the Wates's lambs, 1 April, one hundred and forty-six days from insemination, hasn't yet quite come, sheep, like women, choose their own timing. The first is born mid-March, when the temperature is still dropping below freezing at night. Pete is worried. 'Hypothermia's the biggest killer of lambs,' he says to Flora, 'apart from foxes.'

'All your animal talk,' she replies. 'I can see I'm going to have to compete. I've made my mind up now the builders have finished: I'm going to keep chickens. What do you think of that, Pete?'

'I think it's a daft idea. You're a town lass.'

'Not any more. I've bought a book called *The Complete Book of Raising Poultry and Livestock*. And I've got you to help me.'

'I'm better at sheep than chickens. Ours have got bumblefoot. But that's Mum's province.'

'"A hard abscess on the back of the foot",' quotes Flora, '"probably the result of having a perch too high, so that the bird lands awkwardly on the hard floor."'

'Very good. So what are you going to buy, Mrs Farmer's wife?'

'Light Sussex or Rhode Island Reds.'

'I wouldn't get too many of them; you'll be overpowered by cholesterol. What about Pablo and Dolly?'

'Ron's coming to build me a hen run. I'm only going to get half a dozen.'

'Ask Mum for the name of our poulterer. He doesn't usually deal in small numbers, but I'm sure he'll let you have a few. I take it you're after point-of-lay pullets?'

'Correct.'

Flora isn't at all sure about the hen-keeping idea, but the spring, and the very fact of having survived her first few months in Little

Tickencote, are making her want to do something to mark her established status as a rural lady.

She shows Ron the diagram in *The Complete Book of Raising Poultry and Livestock*. He holds it in his hand like Pleasance Oliphant's washing-machine instructions. 'Well, I don't rightly know,' he says, scratching his head. 'That's book-learning, that is.' Flora remembers that he can't read, and explains: the idea is that in a small garden like this you can move the henhouse from one side of the garden to the other. So you have vegetables on one side one year, then you give it over to the chickens the next. 'It's quite simple, really.'

She leaves him to it while she goes off to investigate poulterers. Doris Wates is in, sorting eggs. She's pleased to see Flora, as she's beginning to get used to the idea of her relationship with Pete, and she feels it's time they had a woman-to-woman talk.

The farm kitchen is ubiquitously brown – brown-patterned lino, brown units, brown cooker. Doris is wearing a brown jumper and brown check shirt, with a wraparound apron on top. The kitchen smells of stale odours, though everything in it looks shiningly clean. She makes Flora a cup of coffee – it's Camp, out of a brown bottle. 'Pete's out with the new assistant,' she's at pains to explain. 'He won't be in for his dinner till half-past one.'

'I know, he told me.' Flora sits down at the brown-oilcloth-covered kitchen table. What is Pete Wates doing, being fed by his mother still?

Flora's wearing a colourful red and blue sweater from Benetton, her London days. The blue in it brings out the blue of her eyes. Doris, who is interested in grandmotherhood, tries to assess the size of Flora's hips under the table. She lowers her somewhat larger ones into the seat opposite. 'Well now,' she says, 'this is nice. Are you settled now, my dear? In the village, I mean. I hope you've found Little Tickencote to be a welcoming kind of place.'

Flora assures her that she has, and she is.

'It's not what you're used to, is it? You're a professional woman, I hear.'

'I was, Doris. Not any more.'

'Mind you, my Pete's got a head on him. Frank always says it was a mistake he went off to that university. Filled his head with all these airy-fairy political ideas. Doesn't help you get up in the night to an ailing cow or a pig with cramp. I'm not so sure meself. There's nothing like eddication, is there? I suppose you had more than enough of it yourself?'

Doris is trying – not too subtly – to probe into Flora's background. Flora drinks her Camp, trying not to grimace. 'Well, you must admit it makes Pete an unusual kind of farmer, Doris.'

'That it does.' Doris thinks uneasily of Pete's trips abroad. She doesn't know what he gets up to on them, but she imagines that in today's jargon, he has something of a ball. That mayn't go down too well with Flora. She feels almost apologetic on behalf of her son. Flora looks like a clean young woman. Though, on the other hand, coming from London . . . 'Are you planning to stay in Meltshire, dearie?'

'Oh yes. I want to put down roots. London's no place for that. I want to learn about the countryside, about its ways. I've got so much to learn, Doris – about the animals, about the birds and the flowers and the trees . . .'

'But not the birds and the bees, eh?'

'Not at my age, no.'

'And what is that, may I ask?'

'Thirty-nine.'

Doris is surprised. 'You don't look it. I suppose a lot of people say that, do they?' She draws on her brown mug of coffee. 'Not much time left, then, is there?'

'For what?'

Doris flushes slightly, but having started, and being a farmer's wife, she continues. 'You're not thinking of having a family, then?'

'From what I can gather,' parries Flora deftly, 'women round here don't have an awful lot of luck with that.'

'We only had the one,' says Doris reflectively, 'and we didn't give up trying till I was fifty. Pete was a sickly baby, eight months born. Doctor found a fibroid in my womb twice the size of his head. Perhaps that were it, I don't know.' She remembers the vision she used to have of a little girl tripping round the farmhouse, picking bunches of wild flowers from the edges of Flat Acre Field, running in and out of the dappled summer light in Owlston Wood, getting on the tractor with her dad, being tucked up in bed with a Beatrix Potter lampshade filtering light on the uneven cream walls. She turns her mind back to Flora. There's no knowing – maybe the little girl Frank and she never had would have grown up like this; if so, she would've been proud. Yes, she can imagine feeling like a mother to Flora. 'Would you stay to dinner, dear?' she asks tentatively. 'It's only sausages – or veggie-burgers – and Yorkshire. But there's an apple pie after, and a thick jug of fresh cream – from our own cows, you know.'

Flora, who only came by to get the name of Doris's poulterer, accepts her invitation in view of her current feelings for Pete Wates, and her hopes, though unadmitted, for the longevity of their liaison.

You do remember you came to the country to escape from a man, don't you? It's not Rural Rosey's voice but Miranda's.

I'm not going to *live* with Pete Wates, Flora defends herself. Anyway, this relationship is quite different.

Is it? I'm not so sure. You've just got an odd taste in men, Flora.

Pete, Barney, Lars: and the others in between, going back to Bruce's deflowering in Mecklenburgh Square. Pete, Barney and Lars, but the great passion was Lars. Faith, hope and charity, but the greatest of these is charity. Lars wasn't charitable – indeed, far from it. He'd dealt Flora a series of hard-hitting blows to her self-esteem, and had ultimately left her, though it could be said he'd never been with her, as there'd always been his wife, the patient, waiting Elisiv, to whom he returned as a ship, knocked about and despoiled by storms, sails perpetually back into harbour.

Lars and Flora had met when she was only twenty-one. She'd been on a student trip round Scandinavia. It was June, and she and her friends had just seen the midnight sun in Kiruna. They were on a train back to Stockholm. They had to stand with their rucksacks. Lars had given them his seat. While Flora and Dale both perched on it, and as the train sped efficiently through the orderly landscape, Lars and Flora, who'd been sitting on the outer edge of the seat, had got into conversation. He was a writer. Of fiction. He'd been up teaching a summer school in a place called Boden, and was returning home; he and his wife, who had green eyes and linen hair long enough to sit on, lived in a wood-framed house round the coast north of Copenhagen. They had a little baby, a boy, Per-Erik. Lars was handsome in a careless antiseptic Scandinavian way. He wore a green-and-blue-checked shirt the day Flora met him, and had a gold locket round his neck which he never, throughout their entire relationship, opened.

When the train stopped in Stockholm Station, Lars asked Flora to meet him for a drink the next evening. Dale was very disapproving, and so were the others. 'You don't know anything about him, who he is, or where he's been. If you're not back by the ticket office at eleven o'clock, we'll call the police.'

'Nonsense!' Flora tossed back her long hair and laughed the carefree laugh of the unlined face and short experience of the young. 'I can take care of myself.'

At nine o'clock Lars took her to a little hotel by the harbour, and into a white lace-dressed bed. The hotel was done up in nineteenth-century style, with lights like gas lamps and candles, and fireplaces with dark chairs in front of them. Many years later, when Flora saw the film of *The French Lieutenant's Woman*, she recognized the scene. But it had been summer when she and Lars met on the Swedish train in 1973, and there'd been no need of any artificial light – the sun had come at a discreet angle through the lace curtains on to the bed, and on to them. What was it about her relationship with Lars and his with her? Flora had never really understood. But she had felt at one with him, as though the difference between man and woman had, though essential to the union, been dissolved in it. When she and Lars made love that first time and all the other times since, wherever they could meet – in the sands of Jutland, one summer in a pine forest, many times, though not as many as Flora would like, in London – whenever they made love, Flora lost her consciousness of self and gained a sense of wholeness with humankind, and with the natural world, of which at those moments human beings seemed merely atoms, grains of sand in the measureless, timeless acreage of life. She'd never felt like that before or since. With every other man, the feeling of being separate remained. She was in control, knew what was going on; she knew where one body ended and the other began, understood the difference of spirit and character. But with Lars it was another meaning of sexuality altogether. Life itself; the life force. It almost seemed as though her decision to live in the country had been a direct result of falling in love with Lars – a kind of delayed, long-term effect of their relationship. She knew it couldn't be so, rationally: but on the elemental level – the one farmers and psychoanalysts deal with – this was the truth of the matter.

Flora and Lars met for ten years, whenever he could get away, and later on, when she'd settled in to a job, whenever she could. But the arbiter of their meetings was never really her, it was Elisiv. Per-Erik grew up, but Elisiv did not – or Lars's feelings for Elisiv could not liberate themselves from the rock of guilt in which they were anchored. He lied to Elisiv, of course, but then one day she looked in his passport and saw 'Passport Office London, Heathrow' stamped in it three or four times when he'd told her he was merely in Umea, or Uppsala, or Oslo. Lars went out to ring Flora from a phone box and came back to find his clothes on the front lawn with his passport, and Elisiv standing there with a lighted match. At every moment (and there were others like this) when it seemed as though his marriage was over, he dragged it back from the brink like a suit of second-hand clothes from a pawnshop, and the one time when it seemed he couldn't, he asked Flora to join him at a day's notice and she couldn't, and he never forgave her, taking this as evidence that she didn't care enough for him after all. Though Flora reserved her body for him for a decade, Lars was more profligate with his, joining it regularly with the green-eyed Elisiv's and even producing a little playmate for Per-Erik in the dark winter of 1976, when Flora also found herself pregnant. Twenty-four, in love with a married man who lives in another country and screws his wife twice a week and goes shopping with her and cuts short his weekends away because of meetings with architects about the construction of carports, twenty-four and desperately in love and alone and pregnant. In the end, Flora had an abortion. Everyone told her there was nothing else she could do. For a while after that she didn't see Lars. And then he resurfaced, and they went for a brief holiday together in the Canary Islands, and he promised to leave his wife . . . and he didn't. Flora got rid of him eventually, but it wasn't easy, and then, after a while, she met Barney, and began slowly to feel healed.

And now Pete Wates. He comes in through the farmhouse door, scraping the mud of the yard off his boots. 'I think we've got a lamb for you, Mother,' he says. 'The old lady with toxaemia – she's pegging out. Dad's bringing the lamb over.'

Doris turns round from her labours with the sausages and veggie-burgers. 'That's grand, that is; I like to keep my hand in! Your young lady's here, Pete.'

Behind Pete comes Frank, a bundle wrapped in rough soiled cloth in his arms. 'Here you are, Mother!'

Doris wipes her hands on her apron, takes the bundle, and walks with it to the fireplace. She sits down on the big wooden chair and unfolds the cloth. 'There you are, poor mite, you'll be all right with Doris. He'll need some Premix, Dad,' she says. 'This one's too weak to start on milk right away.'

Flora watches curiously as Doris dries the little lamb, and in the warmth it begins to make feeble *baa*-ing noises. She puts it by the fire, in a cardboard box lined with newspapers and old cloth, and prepares a bottle for it. 'Colostrum substitute,' she explains to Flora. 'It does for hedgehogs as well, the manufacturers say.'

'What's colostrum?'

'My, you *are* a townie! It's what comes out of the ewe's udders in the first few days after lambing. Women, too, come to that.'

'Don't mind Mum,' says Pete. 'She's never been outside Little Tickencote in her life.'

Doris laughs. 'That I have!'

Pete's reading *Farmers Weekly*. Frank stands in the doorway. 'When's dinner ready, Mum?'

'Just as soon as I've fed the little one. It's no use asking him to help,' she says to Flora, 'he's all hands and no brain in the kitchen. Men are all the same, aren't they?'

'Yes, aren't they?' agrees Flora, smiling across the brown kitchen at Pete.

After lunch, which is good and very filling, Flora drives off to Doris's poulterer, George Arden, where she purchases four Rhode Island Reds and two Marans, the breed favoured by George for its suntan-coloured eggs and good winter egg-laying performance. 'They're not quantity layers,' advises George, 'and you'll need to look after them, as they're very shy at first. But you'll get quality out of them.'

Flora confines Pablo and Dolly to the house and empties the hens into the hen run constructed by Ron. George gave her a sack of blood and bone meal and one of grain, and advised a plentiful supply of water and a box of grit.

The two Marans are crouched in the corner of the run, their little heads and small bright eyes darting in every direction, looking quite unnerved. The four Rhode Island Reds, on the other hand, their orange-red plumage brightening up the end-of-winter garden considerably, are strutting about like the owners of a stately home.

'Maybe I should have got chicks.' Flora pokes a rhubarb leaf from the compost heap through the wire in the direction of the Marans, but they just get up and move anxiously away.

She's out there again early in the morning – a wet, silver-grey morning – to see if the hens have got any goodies for her. When she opens the wire gate and goes in, two of the Rhode Island Reds shriek at her and ruffle their feathers in what she assumes is a correctly proprietorial manner, but the Marans continue to sit there, a disconsolate grey slag heap in the corner. 'Oh dear, what are we going to do with you?' Flora feels around in the straw, and after a bit of fumbling her hand closes in on one warm egg. Victory! She withdraws it, studies it – its faintly speckled light-brown oval is as perfect as a jewel – and decides to have it for her breakfast. As she turns round she sees, too late, that she left the wire gate open. Pablo has joined her, and is hissing and arching everything he has at the poor grey Marans. They cower; he advances. She grabs him, but he's all poised to fight, which reduces his manoeuvrability; struggling to keep hold of him, she drops the egg and then treads on it, so that its lovely golden yellow dissipates itself in clumps on the grainy soil.

After a couple of days the Marans are still sulking in the corner of the hen run. Flora goes to seek Doris's advice. The little lamb is busy sucking, and another has joined him. 'Don't you find it's too much, Doris, feeding lambs as well as men?'

Doris giggles. 'Well, Valerie and I take it in turns.' Flora met Valerie at lunch over the Yorkshire and sausages. She's relaxed a little now she's out of her suit.

'Did you check the vent? Mind you, George ought to have done that.'

'I hate to say this,' admits Flora, 'but what's a vent? I don't seem to have got very far in the chapter on chickens in my *The Complete Book of Raising Poultry and Livestock*.'

'It's where the egg comes out of. The vent of a layer should let two to three fingers in.'

'Ugh!' says Flora.

'Are you sure you're cut out for this, dearie?'

'No, but I'm giving it a try.'

'Marans are moody. You could give them a nestbox of their own with a couple of china eggs in it.'

'What about a cock? Would that help?'

'It might help the cock, but it won't do a thing for your egg-laying! And it'll make you lose your beauty sleep. Haven't you heard the cockerel on Pringle's Farm? Crows like the devil. Old Pringle keeps him just for annoyance. Could be they're broody. But not likely, as they're so young. No, I'd give them their own quarters and wait for a bit.'

'Thanks, Doris.'

'She doesn't know what she's up to, that girl,' confides Doris to Frank Wates later. 'And don't say women are all the same, biting off more than they can chew, because you know they're not. That Valerie, for example – now don't tell me she isn't a good find!'

'I think I'm going to have one of my turns,' confides Frank back to Doris. 'I can feel it coming on, I'm all light-headed like.'

'Well, it's not a very convenient time, is it? I only hope Pete and

Valerie can cope. I can't be going out at all hours with William and Mary to look after.' She points at the lambs either side of the fireplace.

'I'll just go and lie down, Mum. D'you think you could bring me some Ovaltine later?'

'Wants waiting on as well,' grumbles Doris as she makes up William and Mary's next bottles and cuts up a nice piece of liver to put in a casserole for the evening meal.

'Mrs Wates!' cries Valerie's voice down the kitchen path. 'Is Mr Wates there?'

'Which one would that be?'

'I think we've got a hind presentation, she's been straining for a while, and it'll need the two of us.'

'Mr Wates senior is having one of his turns, and Mr Wates junior is off somewhere. I dare say you'll find him in front of his wretched machine. You'd better phone him.'

Roused from his wretched machine, Pete goes with Valerie to the lambing pen in Quarry Field. 'You should put your glasses on for lambing, you know, Valerie. These are the hind legs of two different lambs.'

'Gosh, are they?'

'You'll have to help me push these two back in and then go and call the vet. Gloves on – where's the jelly? Lay her on her back, Valerie.'

'I wish we had a mobile phone.'

'Can't have everything, Valerie.'

It takes a couple of hours to disentangle the lambs and get them out alive. Mike Ramsay's got his arm up one of Pringle's cows with a transverse lie, so Pete and Valerie have no option but to cope on their own.

'On the farm in Yorkshire where I was,' says Valerie, looking at the two newborn lambs, which happen to be male, 'we castrated right away. Do you want me to do it, Mr Wates, or will you?'

Pete looks somewhat sorrowfully, and not without empathy, at the lambs' little woolly testicles. It almost sounds as though Valerie enjoys it. 'No, Valerie. On this farm we wait a bit. Let them get over the shock of being born first.'

'Like circumcision,' says Valerie happily.

'Well, sort of.'

As he clears up, Pete reflects that if Flora was upset at the agricultural details of lambs' conception, she'd find even less acceptable the ins and outs – and particularly the outs – of their birth. He himself is inclined to side with Doris in viewing the way Flora's throwing herself into country living as somewhat foolhardy. He knows what will happen with the hens – either they'll be a total disaster, or they'll lay far too many eggs, and Flora won't know what to do with them. Why doesn't she stick to her cartoon-writing and her flute lessons? Both of these seem to be paying reasonably well. The *Daily Record* has accepted Rural Rosey, and Flora does half a page once a week, for which she is paid £150. This compares well with the remuneration from flute lessons – it's hard graft getting notes out of some of Meltshire's young, and even the most ambitious mother pays only £7.50 an hour.

'I think one of my Marans is egg-bound,' Flora says to Miranda, who's just come back from a holiday in Crete.

'Sounds horrible. What's a Maran? No, don't tell me. I think I'll tell you about my holiday instead.'

'There won't be any more holidays for me,' says Flora, when Miranda's finished reciting her adventures with a Cretan restaurateur. 'I've got to be on hand to look after my hens.'

'Okay, tell me about your wretched hens, then.'

The description in *The Complete Book* of what to do with an egg-bound hen sounds tricky: liquid paraffin one end and Vaseline the other. If these fail – which they have – then the hen has to be held over hot water. Flora boils a kettle and puts newspapers and a bowl on the floor. Making sure the cats really are somewhere else this time, she plods out to the garden and scoops the Maran out of the hen run and carries it squawking into the house. With the hen under one arm, she pours boiling water into the bowl with the other, then takes the hen firmly in both hands and lowers it over the water. It's difficult to get the egg-laying bit in position without getting the hen's feet wet. When she's in the middle of this, Olga Kahn taps at the window. Flora shouts at her to come in. 'What *are* you doing, my dear? It looks like some strange rite.'

'It is. It won't lay, you see.'

'Er-hum. Well, I'd be surprised if it'd do anything after what you're putting it through. Are you sure this is right?'

'Come and help me, Olga, I can't get the angle right.'

'My God, what is this?' says Bridget Crowhurst, who is passing The Cottage for the same reason as Olga Kahn, it being the night of the village council meeting. The Maran is showing more spirit than it has shown since Flora bought it, fluffing up its feathers and trying to make a getaway. Grey feathers are flying through the air like dingy snowflakes. Olga Kahn, squatting on the floor, is showing the tops of her stockings, and Flora's jeans are soaked through with the water intended for the hen's vent. After waiting for a bit, Bridget says, 'Olive oil is supposed to work better than water.'

'How would you know?'

'I've just done reproduction in the fowl with the fourth-years.'

Wearily, Flora bundles the Maran into a towel and delivers it back to the henhouse. 'It's all book-learning, anyway, isn't it? That's what our dear friend Ron said when I asked him to build the henhouse.'

'Come on, Flora, you've got to get out of those clothes and come to the council meeting. Brian Redfern wants to build six executive homes on Long Rotton Field. We must fight it with everything we've got.'

Brian Redfern defends himself rather badly. The rest of the meeting is occupied with dog-fouling on footpaths, the appointment of a new co-ordinator for the Neighbourhood Watch scheme, and the renovation of the village hall, beginning with the Gents' cloakroom and ending with much discussion on the subject of curtain fabric.

'It's such a nice evening,' says Flora, coming out of the hall after the meeting and sniffing the aromatic night air, hung with the odours of opening daffodil and hyacinth and tulip blooms, laced with the heady vivid greenness of the hedgerows, and the trees and the grasses and even the new season's plantains pushing their tobacco-like leaves up in the middle of velvet lawns to annoy proud Meltshire gardeners. 'In fact it's like wine, the air, can't you feel it? I'm going for a walk – does anyone want to come?'

'Anyone can see *you* haven't been in the country long,' comments Bridget. 'No, thank you, as you know, I can't stand it. And I've got a pile of English tests to mark.'

'If you don't mind, my dear,' says Olga Kahn on the other side, 'I am feeling rather tired. I think I'll just have a cup of tea and go to bed.'

Flora's quite glad to be on her own. The village hall is in Manor Farm Lane, at right angles to the church. She walks up the lane a little and crosses over, vaulting the stile into Sheepdyke Field with a lightness reflecting her spring-intoxicated mood. A few metres into the field, she pauses. In the navy darkness trees rustle, enjoying the feel of leaves returning to their branches. Flora thinks it's a sound we don't hear in the wintertime, yet we don't miss it because we don't ever *think* about hearing it: it's a sound that's so much a taken-for-granted part of our world that we can't even speak of it to ourselves. The bushes edging the field are alive with scurries and scampers. Flora walks on. Approaching the river, Little Tickencote's very own tiny river, she sees sheep lying in the grass – clotted white shapes, inanimate almost, in the light of a half-moon – and under the big cedar tree. Most of them are asleep, but a few wander on their matchstick legs, rooting in the darkness. Ahead of her on the path around the field one of them blocks the way, standing diagonally across the path. As Flora advances, she expects it to move out of the way, as sheep usually do, but this one doesn't. The reason for its stationary posture becomes evident as Flora comes up behind it, for out of what she has learnt would be called a vent in the hen is hanging this plastic-looking bag of water, ripe and full and glistening in the half-moon light. As she watches, the bag bursts like a balloon, and out of it comes a volume of clear liquid, and the legs and nose of a lamb. She has to resist an impulse to move forward and pull on the lamb's legs, helping the mother with what must be, at the very least, an uncomfortable situation. The ewe's woolly sides inflate and deflate like a pair of lungs, and a minute or two later the whole lamb falls out on to the path. It lies absolutely still; Flora thinks it must be dead. Something smaller, some other material of birth, follows the lamb. Then the sheep turns and noses the heap of flesh gently, then starts to lick the lamb, which responds with quivering movements. The ewe seems to be drawing something off it and eating it, and as she does so the lamb begins to struggle to get up. But instead of helping, its mother hinders its efforts, because her licking is so vigorous that it knocks the tiny lamb sideways again and again. Flora wants to set the lamb steadily on its feet so that it will have a chance of making its own way in the world. She stands there ten, twenty, thirty minutes, and still the little thing's not been allowed to make it, and then finally it does, going straight with its newborn nose for the dirty knotted wool of its mother's underbelly and what Flora now knows, from the conversation in the Wates's kitchen, is called colostrum. Its little black legs splayed at all angles, the lamb sucks at last. And the ewe is momentarily still, giving up her empty bulk to the service of new life in the calm darkness of Sheepdyke Field at midnight as across the lane the bell of All Saints' chimes the hour.

Ewe and lamb are part of the old, the natural order, which so much of 'civilization' has eroded, ridiculed, destroyed. There is no interference; all the two need is each other and this ordinary field under the ordinary moon, with the trees moving ever so slightly with their new leaves' cloth and the stubble of cut hedges bursting into bud, and the rains of winter swelling the stream as it trickles under Pooh Sticks Bridge. All they need is the darkness, and the comfort of other sheep nearby: the ones with lambs still in their bellies, and the ones with lambs curled up next to them asleep and dreaming of the frolics of spring. The picture of Abraham Varley buggering the sheep flashes through Flora's mind, and suddenly seems not quite so sinister. The desire to enter one's separateness into another is natural; but the urge to harm, with which Varley had followed his taking of the sheep, is not. The union of flesh with flesh must be benign. In its benignity is life; anything else is death.

She looks again at the sheep and its new lamb. The lamb is being licked again – this time it's holding its little face up as though it's enjoying it. Now Flora feels something different. When Lars had made her abort his child, fifteen years ago now, she had minded the loss of a certain kind of relationship with him – she had cried out against the meaning of his act for his valuation of *her*. It wasn't motherhood she mourned. Not the opportunity to push the big strong head of a baby out into the light, not the obligation to give suck, to cherish, to watch over – like this ewe here, like Annabel Lancing and her errant Bronny, like Doris and her grown-up son who still comes home for his dinner, though he wanders the globe and God knows what else in between times.

Doris had said: It's getting a bit late, isn't it? And Dr Simpson . . . She'd thought it herself from time to time, but only really as one thinks one may eat a box of chocolates or fly to Naples and see Vesuvius before it's too late. Now Flora knows what it is she wants to do. She wants to have a baby with Pete Wates. 'Thanks, Mum,' she whispers at the surprised ewe, whose concentration on the act of reproduction is now beginning to wane, and who's noticed Flora watching these most private of acts uninvited in moonlit Sheepdyke Field.

It's not in Flora's nature to waste time, so the next day she makes herself an appointment to go back and see Dr Simpson. In the surgery, she finds herself sitting next to Olive Grisewood. Olive is reading *Plain and Purl*. 'Hallo, Mrs Grisewood.'

Olive holds the magazine down a fraction. 'Good afternoon, Miss Penfold,' and then repositions it directly in front of her face.

Olive is here for some advice concerning Percy's haemorrhoids, which have been troubling him recently. They've tried Preparation H and witch hazel, but they've reached such a state that they're putting him off his food now. He won't come himself. It's not manly to visit the doctor. So Olive comes instead as messenger, describer of symptoms, harbinger of diagnosis. She leaves Dr Simpson's surgery with a prescription for something considerably more powerful. 'And remember to take the paper off first,' cautions Dr Simpson after her, remembering old Mrs Pringle, who didn't, and got into quite an uncomfortable pickle as a result.

'Ah,' says Mervyn Simpson expansively, looking at Flora's notes. 'Miss Flora Penfold. The Cottage, Little Tickencote. What can I do you for, Miss Penfold?'

'You said that last time,' she points out.

'Did I? Doctors have a habit of repeating themselves. Has something to do with the fact that there are no new illnesses, no new pains under the sun. Whatever it is, you can be sure we've seen it all before.'

He turns the pages of Flora's file. 'Ah yes, AIDS scare. Receded now, has it? Keep up with the nonoxynol, mind, tubes and tubes of it. Stick it up everywhere!'

'Yes, yes,' says Flora hastily. 'But actually I'm thinking of giving it up.'

'Probably a good idea,' says Mervyn, somewhat gloomily, 'sex never did anyone much good anyway. At worst it gives you something nasty, at best a yukky stain on the sheets and a pain in the heart.'

'I didn't mean sex, I meant the nonoxynol. Contraception.'

'How old are you?'

'We've been through that one as well.'

'My apologies.' He flicks through the notes: '1952. Well, unless you're suffering from ovarian hypotrophy, I'd say it was definitely too soon to throw precautions to the wind or anywhere else.'

'I want to have a baby, Dr Simpson!'

'Do you, now!' He peers at her over his half-moon spectacles, which remind her of the half-moon in Sheepdyke Field last night. 'Tell me more.'

'What is there to say? I'm thirty-nine, I want to have a baby before it's too late. It will be too late soon, as you yourself pointed out last time I saw you.'

'Did I say that? And is that why you've decided to launch yourself on the career of motherhood? My God, what power we doctors have!'

'No, not because of what you said.' She can't bear the thought of telling Dr Simpson about the ewe and the lamb – he'd be bound to get hold of the wrong end of the stick. In any case, the scene, and its imparted knowledge, feel too private. 'I've been thinking about it, that's all. I've just decided it's what I want to do.'

'Well done. I like a woman who knows her own mind. But why are you telling *me* about it?'

'I thought you might give me a check-up. Tell me if it's okay to go ahead – that sort of thing.'

He's studying her notes again. 'Minor problem – doesn't say here you've got a husband. Mind you, it could be June; she's appalling at taking histories. Sometimes I think she makes them up.'

'I'm not married, but I am in a relationship.'

'Always sounds like a bath or something, don't you think? "In a relationship." What else do they call it, stable union? Even worse, makes you think of manure. Yes, I know, I'm old-fashioned. Well, that's all right then. I take it this In-A-Relationship chap wants a baby too?'

'I haven't asked him yet.'

'Oh.'

'Dr Simpson, please could you get on and do the medical bit? That's what I've come for, really.'

Mervyn takes this as a slight reprimand, but gets on with the job. He doesn't really mind taking instructions from the patient, it saves a lot of trouble if the patient thinks he or she is getting what they want. Even if it isn't what they need.

'Two ovaries, normal uterus – what more do you want? Have you ever been pregnant before?'

She tells him about the abortion. He's impressively noncommittal. 'Any trouble after? Infection? Fever?'

'No, nothing.' His gloved hand inside her makes her think of the ewe's water bag, and of the poor Maran's vent.

'You're a normal woman. That is, anatomically speaking. I can't vouch for the rest of you.'

Flora, putting her clothes on behind the 1930s green screen, says, 'There's only one other problem, Dr Simpson. I've heard that women in the Gwater Valley can't conceive.'

Dr Simpson finishes scribbling in Flora's file, closes it, and sits back in his chair, tilting it into its customary position proximate to the dusty rubber plant.

'Who told you that?'

'A number of people in the village. I don't know what to think.

Except that it does seem to be true. There *are* very few children round here, and those there are weren't born here.'

'I don't know what to think either,' admits Mervyn. 'They say it's something in the water, you know. They say it started to happen two or three years after the filling of the reservoir. I agree with you, the birth rate does seem to be a bit on the low side in Little Tickencote and Great Glaston, but then it is generally lower in the countryside these days. It's the women – they don't want to be stuck at home with children in the villages any more. Women's Liberation gone wrong. That's my view; no doubt you don't share it.' He thinks about Diana and the rearing of their own four children, now thankfully out in the world, though with a horrible habit of coming back. The eldest, David, is back now, thirty-four, divorced. 'He's even borrowing my socks again,' says Mervyn sorrowfully, out loud. 'That takes the cake, that does!'

'What?'

'Never mind me. It's statistics, you know – lies, damned lies and statistics. Or whatever that saying is. Of course there *was* witchcraft around here once. Amelia Woodcock – she lived in Eglethorpe, one of the villages that was drowned. She had several daughters, as I remember. One of them was a witch, too.'

'But you don't believe in witchcraft, do you, Dr Simpson?'

'Might do,' says Mervyn grudgingly, 'on my bad days. Or my good ones. There isn't a rational explanation for everything, you see. Take doctoring. Half the drugs we use are a waste of money. Placebos – sugar pills – work just as well. Probably more than half, come to think of it,' he muses. 'And if that's not witchcraft, then what is?'

'Well, if you're suggesting that there are still witches around who are making women infertile, there's presumably not a lot I can do about it, is there?'

Mervyn stares at her thoughtfully for a bit. 'You know what I'd do if I were you?' he says eventually. 'Go away. Take Mr In-A-Relationship chappie – assuming he agrees to the whole plan – take him off somewhere, preferably somewhere nice and warm, with good food and wine, and have a nice little holiday. In the middle of your cycle, remember. Works like a charm!' He laughs. 'Against witchcraft, that is! That was how David was conceived, a good two years before he was supposed to be. Kos, in the Aegean. Donkeys and whitewashed houses, and blue, blue sea.' Mervyn screws up his eyes with the pain of remembering it.

'Thank you, Dr Simpson.'

Flora's neat figure is about to make an exit. 'Do me a favour on your way out – ask June to make me a cup of tea, will you? She'll need to open some new milk. Yesterday's was off.'

16

Relieving Tensions

FLORA PENFOLD and Pete Wates stand in the bar at the July dinner dance in the Lessendine Hall Hotel, drinking cocktails. Flora wears her blue velvet-bodiced dress, twinning her spring-blue eyes. Its thin straps lie on her creamy shoulders, reminding Pete of summer lobelia trailing light stone walls; for the countryside has moved into summer again now, with long days and other colours and blooms replacing the pastel silks of cowslips and daffodils. Outside the hotel hang great baskets of spilling crimson fuchsias, looking as if they're about to drop their blood on the pavement beneath.

Pete Wates is stiff and trim in a dinner jacket and starched white shirt and tie, but his luminous eyes still glow with their earthy moist agricultural warmth. 'You do look funny,' observes Flora, glass in hand. 'I'm surprised this sort of thing isn't against your politics!'

'Play-acting,' remarks Pete. 'All the world's a stage – that sort of thing. Can't be serious all the time, Flora.'

'No, but I want to be serious for a few minutes tonight.' I must choose my time carefully, thinks Flora, not knowing how Pete Wates, vegetarian Marxist organic farmer, is likely to respond to the unexpectedly procreative wish of newly converted rural woman. He should, however, understand, as Mervyn Simpson might not have done, how the sight of the struggling lamb had been the triggering factor.

Sitting at their table by the raised dais of the dance floor, Flora sees the doctor and his wife across the room. At least, she supposes the woman he's with is his wife. Mervyn is parcelled, like Pete, in black and white, and he's tugging at his tie.

'Leave it alone, Mervyn,' says Diana crossly, 'you ought to lose some weight.'

'That's what the Look-After-Your-Heart chap said,' observes Mervyn gloomily. 'What am I going to do about Edwin, Diana?'

Diana lifts her salt-and-pepper hair from the green-bowed menu. It occurs to Mervyn that the menu resembles a will. No doubt he should make one. 'I think I'll have the cucumber soup and the salmon.' She takes off her Varilux glasses, and rests them on her hair. 'You'd better have the same. Edwin's over there.'

Mervyn turns round and looks behind him. 'That's what I mean. Who's he with now, for God's sake?'

'Leave the poor man alone. It's none of your business who he's with. He's divorced now.'

Mervyn takes another – not very surreptitious – look. Edwin waves. 'It's that woman from the village – you know, the schoolteacher.'

'I don't know, and I don't want to.'

'Don't be horrible, Diana.'

'You're not supposed to talk to me about your patients.'

'Well, who else am I going to talk to about then? June couldn't care. She can't even get their names right. Besides, there's the business of your conservatory. I can't run the risk of rubbing her up the wrong way. Mike listens, but to him they're animals. And Edwin's always off womanizing. Or writing poetry. I don't know which is worse. Did you read the review of the new one in the *Meltshire Echo*? What's it called . . . ?'

'*Evergreen*,' fills in Diana.

'That's it. And over there is the young woman who thought she had AIDS.'

'Shut up, Mervyn!'

'I went to see Dr Simpson on Wednesday,' says Flora light-heartedly as the band strikes up 'I Could Have Danced All Night'. 'Look, he's at the table over there, with his wife, I suppose.'

'He's a bit morbid for a doctor, don't you find? Last time I saw him he told me I had terminal acne. I was fifteen.'

Flora's having a hard time saying what she wants to say. A bald man with a snowy fringe round his shiny head steps over to their table. 'Excuse me. Miss Penfold? I'm Henry Gosling. Of Gosling, Perry and White, solicitors, in Oakingham. We spoke on the telephone, if you remember, some time ago. About Miss Greetham's cottage.'

'Oh yes.' Flora looks up at him and begins to get to her feet.

'No, please don't get up. I just wanted to say hallo. I take it the move was successfully accomplished? How do you find Meltshire?'

'I'm very happy here,' says Flora, lamely.

'Well, I expect we'll meet again. Don't let me keep you from your meal.' Henry Gosling makes his dapper way between the tables back to his own.

'He interrupted me,' complains Flora. 'And how did he know I was me, Pete?'

'ESP, I expect. Or witchcraft. Maybe someone told him.'

Flora tries again. 'I want to have a baby, Pete.'

Pete Wates's spoon, laden with unripe avocado and oversharp vinaigrette, stops in mid-air. 'Do you, now? Whatever gave you that idea?'

Flora tells him all about her witnessing of the ovine birth, about the magic of the moonlight and the lamb's entrance to the earth in the waters of the flood. Pete watches her face carefully. 'Well, I suppose it is dangerous stuff. Country life, I mean. Farming is actually the second most dangerous industry in Britain, I was reading an article in *Smallholder* about it. Causes one death a week; machines are involved in 34 per cent of them.'

'Pete, please!'

'Sorry. But rural life is also dangerous in the sense of being seductive – that's what you meant, isn't it? I mean look at the two of us, sitting here like stuffed peacocks. I'll think about your scheme for peababies. In due course. What did Mervyn Simpson say about it?'

'He said I was a normal woman physiologically speaking; he didn't know about the rest of me.'

'Neither do I. Is this anything to do with finding out about your old man's floozy?' asks Pete suspiciously.

'Is what? No, of course it isn't. Anyway, I don't know if he had one, do I? I'm going to invite Julian Peacock down – he may be able to throw some light on it.' She pauses. 'Julian and Julia – it's funny, isn't it? It's got nothing to do with my wanting a baby,' she insists.

'I'm just making psychic connections.'

'Well, don't. Leave that to the experts. It's biology – time's running out for me, Pete.'

'I obviously don't have the same sense of that as you do.'

'You're a man.'

'True enough. The band's playing our tune, shall we dance?'

'I want to go to France,' whispers Flora, creamy shoulder against stiff black worsted. 'You know, the part of France you've been telling me about, where there's a slip of land caught between a river and the ocean? The way Lessendine sticks out in Jacob's Water. Where they farm oysters the way you do sheep. Take me to France, Pete, and give me a baby.'

'Not now,' says Pete, 'there's too much to do on the farm, what with the harvest and everything. We're taking delivery of a new muck-spreader next week, with a wind-up jack and a crossfeed conveyor. Valerie can't be expected to cope on her own.' He remembers with a shudder Valerie's unpropitious eagerness to get her hands on the new-born lamb's tiny furry testicles. 'Anyway, I haven't decided yet. About the baby, I mean. You'll have to be patient, Flora.'

On the other side of the dance floor, Dr Edwin Passmore tries to dance cheek to cheek with Bridget Crowhurst. Bridget's two-toned hair has been trimmed and set by Joan-at-the-Post-Office, and she wears a white print frock in which she reminds Edwin of an upside-down aconite. His preferred date, a young friend of Fanny Watkins, let him down, and he asked Bridget on the spur of the moment, seeing her walking with that jerky step of hers past the surgery window. Despite – and behind – her tribulations, Bridget Crowhurst is – or could be – an attractive woman. The drawing-out of this person from her understated aconite frame presents something of a challenge to Edwin Passmore.

But Bridget wants to talk about her infertility. 'You have children, don't you, Dr Passmore?'

'Edwin, please. Yes, two.' He'd rather not think about them, off with Barbara and her new bloke, a solicitor or some such.

'Were they born here?'

He looks around him at the little raised dance floor and the flora and fauna of the Lessendine Hall Hotel.

'I mean in the Gwater Valley.'

'Oh no. They were born in Wembley. Why?'

Bridget tells him the local theory about women's infertility.

'Just old wives' tales,' he says firmly. 'Don't you believe it. But I don't do the gynaecology,' he adds, equally firmly. 'Mervyn takes care of that.' He is aware that his own attractiveness to women is increased by their thinking of all that familiarity he must have with their insides; it is none the less true that too much medical proximity to their odours and effluences decreases his own libido. Sex is a tricky business.

Later, when the band has moved into a sloppy mood, and Mervyn Simpson has been borne off home by a disgruntled Diana, and Flora and Pete are off in his bumbling Austin back down the hedgerows to Little Tickencote, Bridget Crowhurst surprises Edwin Passmore by asking him if he will consider fucking her for a change, and for the sake of her much-thwarted desire for motherhood. What amazes

Edwin most about this request is Bridget's use of the word 'fuck'. 'I'm not a prude,' she says, noticing his reaction. 'I think you'll find me quite down to earth. And if it's an old wives' tale, then the medical touch should be able to do it, shouldn't it? Your place or mine?'

A full summer moon hangs over the Gwater Valley, and over the curly croissant of Jacob's Water separated from it by the B1961 linking Melton and Oakingham in a black tarmac ribbon. Beyond Five Arches Viaduct to the north, and Owlston Wood to the south, where the land rises from the shallow of Little Tickencote, fields of chrome-yellow rape shine in the moonlight, yoking their sickly-sweet smell to others: of opening honeysuckle and early roses, of flowering thyme and wild lemon mint; of pig and cow and sheep excreta stickily coating grass and concrete, of Bidlington rubbish tip, where old bedsprings roast in the compost of rotting apple cores and potato peelings and the tough lime trunks of broccoli. But though the moon burns with a tranquil light, the countryside is far from quiet. Glow-worms wiggle, the chemicals on the females' tips shining in the hedge by the River Welland's eastern opening into Jacob's Water; white-tailed rabbits scamper in Dead Bunny Lane. Owls call and bats fly, and the hides of the Nature Reserve at the north end of Jacob's Water are a hive of activity, in memory of some bees that fried in one nearby during the recent heat wave. A colony of feral cats in a deserted barn in Hamble Woods carries out its mating ritual: the males yowling and calling, the female singing and displaying, till at last the big orange one grabs and mounts her, holding her still by the skin round her neck in the selfsame grip as she will later use for shifting her tiny kittens out of danger. As the tom cat's marmalade flanks contract in the nettled moonlight of the old barn, Edwin Passmore and Bridget Crowhurst get down to it in her white candlewick-covered bed. But Edwin finds the mattress too soft, unconducive to successful humping. Perhaps a contributing factor to Bridget's barren state? 'I can't feel you properly,' he complains, reaching for the interior of Bridget's pelvis in the sprung interior beneath him. He falls and slides out of her and in again; she is wet like a lake. Edwin fights against the realization that this was not a good idea. Bridget awaits, he feels, only the physical act of his casting seed into her – she's really not interested in anything else. He has a sense, unusual for him, of being used.

Others in Little Tickencote mimic the efforts of Edwin Passmore and Bridget Crowhurst, and construct their own. Across two streets in Cabbage Lane, Flora Penfold and Pete Wates will copulate confidently without thought of conception, as Flora believes the old wives' tales Edwin Passmore can't believe. But Pete, in the midst of their foreplay, when Flora is touching his tight little balls and he, with a finger in her cunt and another teasing one of her nipples, is delighting in the concentration on her face, is heard to say, 'All right, Flora, I'll make a baby with you one day,' and she, responding, comes in delicate waves over his slightly dirty finger, with fibres from the new organic pig feed lodged under his hard-ridged farmer's nail.

This is not all, nor should it be on such a hot lusty night. Peeking into Armand and Petula Nevere's bedroom, with the blue-green branches of the cedar brushing past it, the moon is witness to another feral ritual. Armand, dressed in black lace bra, suspender belt and stockings, with his ginger head in a turban of some sort, is masturbating on to the prostrate form of Petula, fully clothed in a man's grey suit and tightly necked tie on the bed. She could be asleep, except that she's smoking a large cigar. The thrusts of Armand's slimy penis poking out between the triangles of the nylon suspender belt are all in the direction of the rings of cigar smoke round Petula's head. Harder and harder he rubs. But a night owl calls, and a slate moves on the kitchen extension, disturbing his concentration.

In her smoky sitting-room at Number Eight Church Lane, Olga Kahn sits reading Karen Horney's *Neurosis and Human Growth*. She is occupied with a passage in which Horney discusses the difference between her ideal of the real self and Freud's notion of ego – the one a restrictive functionary concept, the other an expansive view of people's humanity as residing in a 'spring of emotional forces'. Olga is struck by the aquatic metaphor. She passes to the next chapter, 'General Measures to Relieve Tension', which is concerned with strategies for preserving a semblance of inner peace: denying the real self, blanking out inner experiences, ignoring connections.

At length Olga puts the book down and empties her sherry glass. She clicks off the light and goes into the kitchen, which is awash with dirty plates and half-drunk cups of tea, but, in the angle formed by the garden window with the back wall, presided over by a vase of perfumed yellow roses. 'Lovely,' says Olga, 'lovely.' The roses make her think, not of friendships and emotions of the past, but of those abiding now. She reaches for the green push-button phone and dials. 'Hallo, Jane. It's a wonderful night, isn't it? Are you coming over?'

Out of the village towards Great Glaston Percy Grisewood lies on his back, snoring lightly, with two of the new suppositories Olive got for him safely up his bum. Olive is cuddled up comfortably against him, dreaming of the children they never had: a boy with Percy's assured air and his own infant lunchbox, and a curly-haired girl in pressed gingham frocks.

Ron the plumber and man of many parts, in his shed in Woodcook Spinney, listens in his own innocent sleep to tunes and rhythms of which the world, in its civilized cruelty, has deprived him: Chopin preludes, especially Number Fifteen; Schubert's 'Rosamunde' overture, recently popularized in an advertisement for furniture polish; and the crashing and banging of Tchaikovsky's '1812', performed annually by the Meltshire Symphony Orchestra in Melton Town Hall. Ron always gets a ticket for the front row, where his platformed head obscures a whole series of other people's views.

Another half a mile away, Lord Bream Oliphant sits at his grand leather-covered Victorian desk sipping brandy, and tracking his stocks and shares in the rosy pages of the *Financial Times*, which is all he's good for this time of night, and most others. His wife, Pleasance, is redecorating Cornelia's room, though why now and why her (and why at all) Bream can't imagine. Stripped to her Harrods undies, Pleasance is majestic on the stepladder with a lambswool (New Zealand, not Meltshire) roller soaked with Dulux one-coat emulsion. A radio catches blobs of paint and emits Mantovani. All Cornelia's furniture is piled into the middle of the room, all her possessions: the size 18 and size 20 dresses, the size 42 and size 44 bras, the extra-large pants; the records and tapes of Heavy Metal, Primal Scream, *et al.*; the books about horses, the fat, romantic, dog-eared paperbacks, the letters from Robbie Belton, and the lists of wedding gifts requested and received in happier days. Pleasance rubs the wall with her roller almost as hard as Armand Nevere rubbed his penis. The covering of the erstwhile primrose-flowered room with this staunch single colour is not at Corney's own behest, for what *could* she behest, bundled up and delivered to the unsafe keeping of the François Garnier sanatorium on a ledge above Lausanne? Pleasance, who covers up her emotions both out of inbred upper-class habit and in order to keep on top of them, likes to think that in Corney's conscious moments, she will find resemblances between Lake Geneva, over which her present bedroom looks, and Jacob's Water, over which this one does. Kept from visiting her daughter by Dr Riemann, the small, neat psychoanalyst who runs the clinic ('No, Lady Oliphant, I must insist, we must give the transference time to work'), what else can a mother do but resort to painting walls?

'Let her get on with it,' Mervyn Simpson had advised, when Bream Oliphant had called him to check out this latest turn of events. 'It's probably just as therapeutic as what Dr Thingummy is doing, and a good deal cheaper.'

A cloud masking the intruding rays of the moon passes unnoticed by Pleasance Oliphant, who has the main light on. But the momentary disappearance of the natural light interferes with the coupling of Bronny Lancing, lying on straw in an old barn at the edge of Owlston Woods with Mortimer Fanshawe's best friend, Calvin. Calvin's trying to fit a coral Tight Fit Durex on his penis when the moonlight goes. It droops like a catkin. 'You haven't done this before, have you, Calvin?' accuses Bronny. 'Why didn't you say? Let me do it.' She takes his cock and licks it into shape so that as the moon slips out from behind its cloud, Calvin's first girl-induced seminal fluid milks out into her mouth.

'Ah!' Calvin puts his head back and makes an animal noise. 'Can't we do it without that thing?'

'No, we can't,' says Bronny firmly, slipping it on. But its latex enclosure so resembles the fantasized vaginas of Calvin's adolescent dreams that he ejaculates there and then instead of inside Bronny. 'Oh well,' says Bronny philosophically, 'never mind; I expect you'll be able to do it again in a bit.'

Her parents lie next to each other under the Jacquard duvet in the master bedroom of Wisteria Cottage. 'But it's at least six weeks since we had sex,' moans Jasper.

'I'm worried about Bronny.' Annabel's eyes are wide open, imagining things.

'You're always worried about Bronny.'

'She's always doing things I have to worry about. And you're a rotten father, Jasper.'

'Don't say that, Annabel, it's not fair. I love you.'

'You only say that when you want my body.'

'Don't you want me to want your body?'

'No.' Annabel turns over. Fortunately, at this point Jasper hears a bell ring which he suspects isn't in his head, and gets up to look out of the window. Martin Crowhurst, complete with cerise crash helmet, is cycling through the village: the ringing of the bell was to shift the two mallards that sleep in the middle of Pudding Bag Lane. Martin's troubled by his insomnia again, and this time he's tackling it with exercise. Up he goes, up and out of Little Tickencote, his heart pumping away and his lungs swimming with the cooling night air, and the muscles in his legs going like bits of elastic, pinging back and forth like nobody's business.

Martin crosses the B1961 and takes the cycle path down to Jacob's Water. Eglethorpe Church gleams. He dismounts and stands by the old Norman door of the church for a few moments looking at the still plains of the water and the white-gold grasses edging it, tipped with moonlight. He's not thinking about what lies beneath; for Martin Crowhurst, it's only the surface of things that matters. But it's eerie here by the old church, even for such a matter-of-fact man as Martin.

Across the causeway something moves – a man, who also stands and watches, though Martin himself can only surmise this. He gets back on his bicycle and sets off in an easterly direction, bumping the black mountain tyres over the crumbly red Meltshire earth. Grasses make way for him, nettles spring back alarmed, the bell of All Saints', Little Tickencote chimes once, down in the valley. And then another noise: Fanny Watkins in Ted Rippington's Vauxhall, coming back from a visit to her friend Debbie in Oakingham. They'd had a takeaway from the Meltshire Chinese, and fetched a video from Dean's in Station Road – Debbie's housebound now, with baby Paula, smelling of Johnson's talc in her appliquéd-duck-lined cot. Fanny wants a breath of air before tackling Ted – asleep, no doubt, back in the Old Sun Inn. She parks the Vauxhall on the brow of the road and walks down towards the causeway, where Jane Rivers and Olga Kahn had seen such a vivid sunset streaking the Meltshire sky not long before. It's lonely on the causeway, but Fanny's not afraid. She's not afraid of anything – not of men or children, not of wild animals or tame, not of the night or the heat of the day. Fanny Watkins knows that fear obstructs living. Having seen the lives of others ruined by it – her mother and father; Ted in the Old Sun Inn, hiding behind his cheap fake mahogany-covered bar, eating his microwave meals, taking short change from ex-wife Patsy and consorting perspiringly with Fanny from time to time – there's not a thing she won't do because of fear. Fanny won't stay with Ted for long, but for now it suits her to have her bed and board with him. Now, if that actor friend of Miss Penfold's had come up trumps . . . Fanny is a young woman with aspirations. Not for her the dull routines of ordinary life. The star-spangled glamour of the media world awaits her, just as surely as over the causeway the chilled depths of Jacob's Water await the kisses of the morning sun, and the fields of rapeseed wait to gather more of the sky's yellow into their own.

Visions of the future accompany Fanny as she walks. An otter by the nature hides whistles back, and a weasel swims nimbly in the brown water. She pauses, watching the movement. As she watches, a water snake slips from side to side, tangling in the weeds. Suddenly there's a wind over the countryside – nothing gentle, but a quick brash wind, stirring everything green into movement: all the trees with their curly catkins and their Chinese-painted blossoms, all the ivy in the hedgerows and the grasses in the fields of the Wates, Pringle and Fanshawe farms, and the cereal crops awaiting their ripening. Fanny moves out of the open, where the wind is lifting her red skirt, and stands by a pussy willow tree, her hand touching its cracked bark. The tree is one of a group, positioned there by the rural landscaper hired by the Jacob's Water reforestation committee back in 1974. The trees are beginning to seem part of the landscape now, with moss and lichen spreading in primal patches up their stems. They form a company, like a troupe of ballet dancers chatting and adopting positions among themselves. It's one of these Fanny imagines moves behind her, and at first her fearless nature only marks it as odd – hasn't she the same feeling as everyone in Little Tickencote and the valley of the Gwater: that there's something pre-modern, anti-rational, savage and magical both, about these hills and dips of Meltshire? Why should a tree not move? Fanny shrugs her shoulders and wraps her red skirt round her thighs against the pull of the wind.

It happens again, and it's not a tree. It's a man in cycling gear, a crash helmet and dark glasses, and a costume of cerise and lime-green stripes. 'Who are you?' asks Fanny impertinently. When he says nothing, she adds in a friendly tone of voice, 'It's windy here, isn't it?'

Martin Crowhurst, driven mad by his insomnia and by other things, doesn't answer. Instead he unzips his cerise and lime-green cycling shorts and takes out the last penis of the Gwater Valley night, purple-toned in the windy moonshine, and hung with the sickening smell of the nearby rape fields.

Fanny stares at the offering for a moment. Then, 'You'll catch a chill like that, you will,' she says, and walks briskly off, admitting only quietly to herself the odd pang of fear clutching her stomach along with the remnants of the Meltshire Chinese.

17

An Unfortunate Episode

'JULIAN, it's Flora Penfold.'

'Oh, hallo, Flora. How are you?' Professor Julian Peacock, sitting at his desk in Queen's College, is dealing with his mail before flying off to Madrid for the biennial European Sociological Association conference, which this year is on Theories of Revolution and Social Realism: Conflict or Consensus? When the phone rings, Julian's staring at an irritating request for study leave from Vanessa Perring, who joined the Department a few years ago from Cambridge with glowing reports and a PhD in Peace Studies. 'She'll be wanting a Readership next,' mutters Julian, scribbling 'Refused' along the bottom of Dr Perring's neatly word-processed page. No doubt she'll challenge his decision (she ought to; he would in her place), but at least that'll be after the summer.

Flora Penfold puts *her* request to Julian Peacock: that he might like to come down one evening and have dinner with her in Little Tickencote, as there's something relating to her father's papers she'd like to discuss with him. Julian peers into his diary. He doesn't want to go to Little Tickencote or anywhere else to have dinner with Flora Penfold and discuss anything, but he does feel a strong sense of moral obligation to Samuel Penfold still. 'There's not much time left before I go off for the rest of the summer, I'm afraid, Flora. It'll either have to be Wednesday or Thursday of this week or we'll have to leave it till October.'

Flora can't wait, so it's Thursday.

I wonder what she wants? Julian puzzles over this for a moment before cancelling the two appointments with students made by his secretary, Miss Witherspoon, who fends their endless, reasonable requests to see him. The students will have to wait, unlike Flora. Professor Peacock wants to get his hair cut and call in at his travel agent.

'Julian Peacock is coming to dinner with me on Thursday,' announces Flora to Pete. 'You could come as well if you like, but you might be bored.'

'With a peacock? Noisy things. How are your hens, by the way? Mum asked.'

'Four eggs a day – I'll have to start selling them. Rural Rosey won't be pleased.'

'So you think this peacock might be able to throw some light on his *alter ego*, Julia?'

'I do.'

'I won't come, if you don't mind, Flora. It's a busy time of year for us farmers, as you know. Now lambing's over and the rape's in, we've got the rest of the harvest to see to. Timing is all, you know. But I think it might be soon. Have you heard about Fanny from the Old Sun Inn? She didn't come home the other night after visiting a friend in Oakingham. Ted's furious. Thinks she's scarpered. Well, to be truthful, he alternates between fury and panic. Dad found the car by the causeway over Jacob's Water on his way to pick up a new Digital Grainmaster – ours has bust.'

On *her* way to the Post Office to buy some washing-up liquid, Flora calls on Olga Kahn. 'Have you heard the latest mystery, Olga?'

'About young Fanny Watkins? Yes, dear.' A gramophone record turns in the corner of the room, making disconnected sounds. 'Come and sit down, I've just made a pot of tea.' Olga hauls a pile of books and papers off the chair by the open window. She sits down on the other one, nursing her mole and jiggling to the jerky rhythm from the corner. 'That's the cuckoo, dear. You're a flautist, aren't you? "*Ging heut' morgens übers Feld.*" "Over the fields I went at morn", you know. It's his first nature symphony.'

'What do you think happened to Fanny, Olga?'

'Er-hum. Haven't a clue. But time will tell, it always does. Mahler became a vegetarian, you know. He thought it would curb his sex drive.'

'Did it?'

'I think it was fairly curbed already. Of course Freud said he had a mother fixation. He was only five foot four. Quite a tiny man, really.' Olga gets up and turns the gramophone off. 'I'll play you the third one day. He used to compose his symphonies in the summer at Steinbach in the Attersee. In a hut. His friends had to bribe the local children to keep quiet. A view of water was important to him, you see. You might like the third. Sun, flowers, animals, man, angels, love.'

'Sorry?'

'The six movements. But you haven't come to hear a lecture about Mahler, have you? What have you come for? Don't tell me, I should know.' Olga squints across the room at Flora. 'I must be losing my touch. Perhaps if I say er-hum enough, you'll tell me, eh dear?'

'I don't know what it is, Olga, I'm just beginning to feel very uneasy.'

'Don't blame it entirely on Little Tickencote. It's probably existential. Have you got enough to do, dear? I'm a great believer in work. Cures most things. That and time. "*Meine Zeit wird kommen*," he said, and it did. So will yours and mine. Mine first, I dare say. Have some more Typhoo?'

On the doorstep, Olga Kahn says, 'You can't expect us shrinks to be perceptive all the time. Sometimes it's a necessary defensive reaction. Our knowledge of the human soul can be too much to bear at times. Then we have to close ourselves off from it. I'm writing a passage about that now. Come back in a day or two when I've finished it, and we'll go for a walk over to Long Rotton Field. It's your first summer in Meltshire, and there are many sights to see!'

As Flora walks down Church Lane and across the field to Pudding Bag Lane, she hears Mahler resuming through Olga's open window. Instead of going down Cabbage Lane home, she walks up Manor Farm Lane to Pat Titmarsh's house. Not to get eggs, but to offer some. It's always the same: the faded chintzy kitchen with the scent of sausage grease; Pat, standing there smiling with her awful teeth stained yellowish green sticking out all over the place, and with that dreadful gap in the middle.

By the duck pond Pablo is consorting with one of the mallards. Duck and cat are about the same size. From a safe vantage point on the cassock of grass holding the telephone box (looking for all the world as though it's about to take off, as in 'Dr Who'), Dolly's eyes glint, narrow slits, in the sun.

Flora goes through Samuel's papers in preparation for Julian Peacock's visit. No, there can't be any mistake. There's the village, the map, meticulously drawn, and here's the letter: 'Your beloved Julia'. Although she searches for other bits of evidence – notes about local characters, descriptions of the scenery – there's only the map and the letter, and the sociological treatise which wraps its real character as fiction or non-fiction safely in dry academic language.

Flora feeds the chickens and does a few minutes' weeding between the lettuces by the golden rod and the still-unflowering Christmas rose. What was that the vicar had said about St John's wort? She goes inside and looks it up in her wild-flower book: 'Common St John's wort, Hypericum perforatum. Sepals pointed, untoothed; herb of St John the Baptist, gathered on the eve of St John's Day and hung in windows as protection from demons.' On impulse, Flora drags a handful of the yellow flowers and hairy stems from the ground, ties them into a bunch, and hangs them over the kitchen window.

It's difficult to settle to anything. She should tidy the house, send out bills for flute lessons, work on the life and times of Rural Rosey. She should prepare tonight's supper, ring her mother. It is remiss of her not to do these things. But she is affected by the season, by the bustle of the big harvesting machines, by the sense of time moving and waiting for no man – or woman. By the feeling of immanence, of something beyond humankind nestling in the garden and in the flowers and trees of the fields and lanes, in the grasses bounding the little lapping waves of Jacob's Water. Perhaps she is disturbed by her own suspended mission to become a mother. Certainly, as she's confessed to Olga Kahn, events in Little Tickencote, with their own peculiar momentum, are no solace, but a drama of their own.

She takes her bicycle out of the shed and goes off down Cabbage Lane and Barleythorpe Road towards Windy Bottom and the B1961. The sun is high in the sky now. The noise of combine harvesters chugging their way through corn and wheat and barley seeps over the trees from beyond Owlston Wood and Sheepdyke and Long Rotton fields. The air hums with machinery and with butterflies, red and white, and with bees in the lavender bushes, and with general whirrings of wings in the bright sky.

Flora cycles slowly in the sunshine, breathing air which is musty with the dust raised by the harvesters. Out of the village and on to the open road. A woman walking her dog says good afternoon. Children on miniature pink cycles quieten and eye her as she passes. Up from Windy Bottom the road rises, shining in a light heat haze. Flora changes gear, lowers her head and sticks her elbows in the air like a turkey. She makes it to the top without dismounting, triumphant, stands there looking down, and feeling herself to be a figure of some stature. Below her the countryside is heaped with light, and in the distance the blue-layered hills and copses call. Creamy sheep laze in a field; trees are ranged on the rising crest of a cornfield; chestnut cows and suckling calves graze in long grass; golden church spires rise to heaven; and a meadow of bright-crimson poppies stretches like a loud garment on a washing line. Nearer to her, by the side of the road, are sheaves of milky cow parsley, and shiny ivy and purple vinca, and tall, lanky buttercups mingled with wild pansy and the starry blue flowers of borage and field speedwell. Musk thistles point their busty heads away from flowering nettles in some sort of vain competition. Flora can see dusty red clover, and the nervous pink arms of yellow-budded stonecrop reaching at precisely paralleled angles out of the walls. Her heart, racing after the climb, settles into a more even rhythm. She cycles again now, down, with the air rushing past her, and the exhilarating whizz of the wheels on the smooth road taking her over Weston Way and into the fringe of landscape round Jacob's Water. On a plateau of raised ground she stops again, this time laying the bicycle down. The grass has recently been cut here, and swathes of dry nestle among the green and growing. Flora sits down, crosses her legs and looks at the water, flat and silver but chased with odd swirls and motions, as though submarine creatures dance and move where their fancy takes them; or as though buried habitations and human lives continue to pull the water in directions it doesn't want to go. There's a scent of pine trees here, their essence fetched by the breeze and laid gently over other odours: of cowpats, dead rabbits, mangled birds, ebony crows bent on desecration, butterflies in their last hours and the decaying blooms of white convolvulus and fiery opium poppies. The August sun paints the water with a band of gold, against which the masts of sailing boats form a crisscross pattern, and fishermen in rowing boats stand contoured black against the blinding light. Water, sun, air, trees, flowers: what was it Olga Kahn had said? A symphony is like the world. *This* world, here and now: truly a Garden of Eden, says Flora Penfold out loud, to the elements, to the pine trees behind and the waters below, to the clover and the daisies interrupting the growing grass, and the bluebottles nourishing themselves off cowpats; yes, this is truly a Garden of Eden!

Flora is suffused with joy. A punch-drunk feeling akin to being in love. A delight in being alive, existential, as Olga Kahn would say. A sense of solidarity with the natural world. This is what I chose, says Flora Penfold – to herself this time; this is what I chose when I decided to live in the country. And I was right!

Though she'd like to stay and watch the sunset, Flora must go back to Little Tickencote. Julian Peacock is expected, and he is prompt, drawing up outside The Cottage at 8 P.M in his pale-blue Triumph sports car, then reversing round the corner into Pudding Bag Lane, where there's more room to park. He's driven all the way from London with the hood down, so he slips a comb through his disorganized grey hair before lifting the knocker on Flora's front door. A tall man with a slight stoop, suntanned from skiing and generally emanating an air of easy privilege, he bends now like a sunflower trying to see into Flora's sitting-room window while he waits for her to answer the door.

Flora has laid the table in the garden. There's cold tomato soup and a fresh green salad with a baked aubergine and mozzarella dish. Julian has brought wine: a Chablis, from the College cellars. He pours it, golden as the light over Jacob's Water, and they drink it, feeling it going down like the milky fluid of the opium poppies in Long Rotton Field.

Julian – who's never liked Flora very much, but has always disguised this feeling, along with most others he's ever had as a man – looks at her critically in the hazy butterfly-filled garden. She looks different – wilder, he thinks. Her skin's browner, but also coarser. Her bright copper hair has been streaked by the outdoor light – it looks as if it's been professionally tinted. Her white sleeveless dress allows him to see that she no longer shaves under her arms. Tufts of soft brown silk pick up the light. Moreover, the topography of her breasts is also unpleasantly visible to him – the bras presumably went as well. All the accoutrements of civilization disposed of on the rubbish tip of nature! Julian swallows another few mouthfuls of the golden liquid, and feels himself sweating slightly. He loosens his tie.

'Take it off – why don't you?' invites Flora absently, stroking Dolly, who is wrapping herself round her ankles asking for her dinner.

Having loosened his tie and rolled up his sleeves, Julian feels slightly better. But then he begins to itch. At first he just scratches and forgets it, but then, when new itches keep appearing, he looks down at his skin to see what's afflicting him.

'Storm flies,' she says. 'It's the harvest, apparently. You can't do anything about them. You'll get used to them; I have.'

Julian rolls his sleeves down again. They eat their soup. House martins quarrel in the apple tree, and tiny hard apples fall.

'It's beautiful here, don't you think?' inquires Flora. 'Do you know, Julian, I think I could go for the rest of my life quite happily without ever seeing London again.'

Julian thinks of his delicately furnished little house in Chelsea with the pale carpets, the Chippendale furniture, all kept bright and shiningly clean by Rupert and the cleaning lady. The cooling domestic images make him want to get on with this – whatever it is. 'What did you want to see me about, Flora? Something to do with Samuel's papers, did you say?'

'Did my father like the country, Julian?'

'Why do you ask?'

'You know those boxes of papers he left me? I've been going through them recently. I've found some stuff – it looks like the manuscript of a book on rural sociology. Can I show it to you?'

Flora gets up to fetch it. Julian amuses himself in her absence by killing storm flies. Amazing little buggers. You can hardly see them, and they certainly don't look as though they've got wings, but they do a kind of backwards flipflop and off they go. He squashes them with the middle finger of his right hand, then dips his napkin in the Chablis and cleans his skin with the golden fluid. Idly he wonders what Flora has dug up for him. He'd always meant to check the contents of those boxes before she got at them, but she'd beaten him to it.

Flora comes out of the kitchen door, bearing a pile of yellowed papers. 'Sorry, I forgot where I'd put them. See, this is it.' She pulls out the chapters bound in ribbon and the map, duck pond and all.

Julian peers at it over his aubergine. His grey-blue eyes behind the steel-framed half-moon glasses register something – a flicker of recognition, perhaps. 'Very well drawn, isn't it?' he says noncommittally.

'It's not Samuel's hand, though, is it?' interrogates Flora relentlessly. 'He could never have managed anything as fine as that.'

Both of them think in their different ways back to the living persona of Samuel Penfold, immense and bear-like, overweening and gentle, bumbling and courteous, thoughtful and inept. Of course it's not Samuel's hand, thinks Julian, I remember very well drawing that map. Why the hell didn't I sort through this stuff before she got to it? That wretched village – what was it called? Frightfully wet summer. No chance of these damn little flies then. He frowns and studies the lower branches of the apple tree, wondering what to say next, unaccustomed to being at a loss for words. 'Why is it important, anyway?'

'It's important to me. I want to know.' Julian shifts in his chair. 'I can't *bear* mysteries. Don't you want to know about your past, Julian?' Even as Flora says this, she realizes she's talking not only about whatever Samuel Penfold was up to all those years ago, but whatever's happening in Little Tickencote now. How can she take control of her own life without the benefit of understanding? And how can she understand if people keep the truth from her?

Julian Peacock's relationship with the past is different from Flora Penfold's. There's the past he owns and the one he's reluctant to own: Samuel Penfold, unfortunately for Flora, belongs to both. Flora finds Julian's silence sinister. 'You know something, don't you, Julian? Of course you do. You were closer to him than anyone.' Flora has a sudden image of herself at about the age when the beloved Julia letter was written, or a little later – of herself breaking into bud all over, and Julian coming to dinner in the Bloomsbury flat. Irina had still been fussing around getting dressed, and Samuel wasn't back, and Jonathan was away on a school trip. Flora had let Julian in and taken him into the sitting-room, and poured him a drink and imagined herself a grown woman, or a courtesan, entertaining him all on her own. Yes, she'd been in love with Julian Peacock, in that way young girls have of trying out their first affections on the safely untouchable. She hadn't, of course, understood then that Julian was gay. Such things were not discussed in Bloomsbury: indeed, they were not of much interest in a household dominated by historical research and sociological theories.

But the frustrations, unacknowledged at the time, are coming out now. 'Tell me, Julian, please, whatever it is you know!'

'Some things are better left alone, Flora.' He pours himself some more wine.

'I'm a grown woman,' persists Flora, thinking of that earlier self. 'Whatever it is, I can handle it. But I'd much rather know. Don't you see, it's the things you don't know that you have the worst fantasies about!'

'Look here,' says Julian Peacock, his silence turning into impatience and words coming to his aid once more, 'aren't you getting all this rather out of perspective? All you've found are some chapters of an unpublished book. They tell you about a bit of your father's life you didn't know existed, but that's no big deal, is it? It's hardly surprising, in view of his interest in Sorokim. Pitrim Sorokim, the sociologist, you know.' He sits back in his seat. There, that's it, it's settled.

'But that's not all.' Flora is persistent. 'I found this too.' She pushes the thin blue letter across the table, between the oily plates and the storm flies. 'I thought it was a letter from you at first,' she continues with a veneer of chattiness, 'but there's definitely no "n" on the name.' Abruptly she moves her plate away and stands up, as though, having asked for it, she doesn't want the answer. 'I'm going to the loo.'

Julian picks the letter up. Bisbrooke, that was the village. How could he have forgotten? It couldn't be far from here. He turns it over: 'Your beloved Julia'. Well, it had been true at the time. A long time ago. An unfortunate episode in many ways. He'd always supposed Irina had known all about it. A sharp bird, Irina. Like Flora. Whom he's definitely not going to confide in, he decides that now. For Samuel's sake – to protect his memory. Too much damage could result from the story coming out. Not only about people's private lives, but about the College. About, for instance, how senior appointments are made. His own, for example. No, far better to let sleeping dogs lie.

Julian is drawn from his reverie by a sound to his right in the darkening garden – the sun must have set at least an hour ago. 'Oh, I'm sorry!' A woman sidles out from behind the staked peony bush, its magnificent vanilla heads shrivelled to papery tassels, but concealing the pert pink and green buds of a second, later, flowering. The woman is dressed in black – black trousers, black blouse, black socks and sandals, black glasses, black hair, like the devil. 'I'm sorry, I didn't realize Flora had guests. I did try the front door, but you can't hear it from the garden.'

Julian stands up, his fly-encrusted napkin falling to the ground. 'She's just gone inside for a moment. I'm Julian Peacock, a – a friend of hers.' The hesitation before the word 'friend' is noticed by both of them. He extends his hand.

'Jane Rivers.'

'Pleased to meet you. I'm only up from London for the evening,' he says conversationally, though Jane Rivers doesn't look at all interested. Fortunately, just then Flora emerges from the kitchen.

'Jane! Come and sit down, I was just going to make some coffee. This is Julian Peacock, a friend of my father's from London.'

'Yes, we've introduced ourselves. But no, I won't stay, thank you, Flora. I just came over to tell you the news.'

'What news?'

'It's bad news, I'm afraid. About Fanny Watkins. From the Old Sun Inn. Her body's been found. It was washed up on the shore of the sailing club at the southern end of Jacob's Water. She's been dead a few days, they think.'

'Jesus Christ!' Flora's face pales. She sits down, clasping the edge of the table for an anchor. Dead birds, stolen shoes, decorated statues, lifeless newborn lambs recumbent in the back of cars, disconnected plumbing, and now young Fanny, the recipient herself – she'd told them all once – of the nasty trick of a bath full of dead fish. Fanny, washed up in front of an array of pleasure boats, cold and waterlogged and finished. Why? And who would want to?

Julian is relieved that the spotlight has passed from his transsexual peccadilloes with Samuel Penfold in the Meltshire village of Bisbrooke Hundred twenty-three years ago. It had all been far less revealing of him than of Samuel, in any case. Of course, Flora reveres her father: to her Samuel is pure and noble in life and in death. But most people's purity and nobility are only a cover for more human sins. Samuel Penfold had always been larger than life – ordinary life wasn't able to contain all the things he wanted to do with it. That stuffy sparrow of a wife, always off in the BM, couldn't see how constraining it all was, and the gloomy Bloomsbury flat, and Flora and her pert brother Jonathan providing the misleading template of a cosy nuclear family didn't help. It was no wonder Samuel kept parts of his life separate. It was wrong for history to join what Samuel had chosen to keep apart. Though in Flora Penfold's persistence to uncover the mystery of the map and the letter on the thin blue paper lay that very same spirit of her father's – Samuel's quest for the answers to difficult questions, his refusal to take no for an answer.

Julian looks up at the two women: Jane Rivers, the darkly clothed messenger of doom, by the peony bush, and Flora Penfold the other side of the table, head in hands with the shock of learning about death. Flora is a woman, but she is also her father. Samuel incarnate. The image releases a voice, Samuel's, in Julian's head. 'Tell her, Julia. Tell her the truth – she deserves it. I'm willing to take the risk, and so should you.' Julian shudders; but the shock of being made to remember softens him. He owes it to Samuel – Samuel would say he owes it to himself. Julian has the feeling of being a wire through which emotional currents are merely passing. The feeling is associated for him with Meltshire – he'd been occupied by it that summer in Bisbrooke, when the rain had kept wildlife at bay. Emotionality, empathy, disclosure – it's a side of his nature which he's kept buried since. Meltshire brings it out in him once more.

But Julian Peacock's own shock is caught between that of the two women, Jane and Flora, learning about death. 'Why don't you come and sit down, Miss Rivers?' says Julian gently. 'You've had a shock, too. I'll go and make you both some coffee.' If Jane notices the odd 'too' in this offer, she says nothing.

While Julian is poking around in the kitchen looking for the coffee, Flora leaves Jane in the garden for a moment and joins him. 'It's very nice of you to do this, Julian,' she ventures formally, but meaning it.

He lifts a packet of Melton Co-op's finest from the shelf. 'I'm not *all* bad, you know.' He looks around for something to open the packet, but it's only a distraction. 'You weren't meant to find those papers – I don't know why Samuel left them to you.' He speaks very quickly now, anxious to get the words out of the way. 'It was a peculiar episode in many ways. But I did love Samuel, and I like to think that redeems it. Not only physically, but intellectually. We had – we had a fine passion for one another.' He stands there, incongruously, awkwardly, with the packet of coffee in one hand, his eyes unsure whether it is safe to look directly at her or not.

Flora tries to take this in, while in the darkening garden black-clothed Jane Rivers sits, watching rooks circling overhead, making their throaty bedtime noises. 'So you were Julia?' she asks, for confirmation.

'Yes, I was Julia.'

Flora can feel only relief. The pieces fit; it's out in the open. Did she know already, in some part of the murky semi-consciousness that flourishes so well in the Meltshire soil, that Julian was Julia – that her father, that solid, respected, patriarchal bear of a man, had once loved another who wasn't one really, but a woman in disguise?

Julian's face in the darkening kitchen looks old and drawn and sad. It could be any gender. Flora realizes suddenly that death and love are both genderless. The division between man and woman makes no difference when lives are fused or at an end. She dwells, momentarily, on the idea of fusion. Of physical love between Julian Peacock and her father. Like the sheep and Abraham Varley. But she can't reconcile the image with the thin, tired-looking person in her kitchen. Samuel is dead, and so is Fanny Watkins. Responding to these thoughts, Flora suddenly, lightly, touches the crisp sleeve of Julian's shirt, which is dotted with the remains of storm flies. 'I'm glad you told me, Julian. And I understand about the love. I loved him too.'

'Of course you did. By the way, I always regretted that the book wasn't published – it should have been. Perhaps you can do something about that one day?' Julian Peacock brings their moment of intimacy to an abrupt end. 'Is it too cold to take the coffee into the garden, do you think?'

He drinks his own quickly, before making his way back to London to pack for the Madrid conference, leaving Jane Rivers and Flora Penfold to discuss the latest of Little Tickencote's afflictions.

The inquest, which is held a few days later, finds no obvious cause for young Fanny Watkins's death. Fanny's parents take the body of their errant daughter back to the dull hamlet of Lower Lessendine, by the western shore of Jacob's Water, whence Fanny had originally sprung like a leaping Jack-in-the-box to mistress Ted Rippington and the Old Sun Inn. Ted sits in his kitchen, moping. Discarded wife Patsy in Streatham hears the news and voices the view – hardly surprising – that she herself is not surprised That Tart met a bad end. The village of Little Tickencote is stunned. It's used to mysterious happenings, but on a minor scale. The local police carry out a few desultory investigations, in the course of which Jasper Lancing comments on his sighting of Martin Crowhurst crash-helmeted and cycling through Little Tickencote in the early hours of the night the pathologist now deems to have been probably that of Fanny's death. But Martin Crowhurst, questioned in turn, seems a benign enough chap, and recalls seeing nothing unusual on his trip round the countryside – though, as he points out, it is probably the case that chronic insomnia, the reason for his being out and about at all hours, affected his normal powers of observation. 'Dr Simpson told me to try exercise,' he tells Constable Medlar. 'I can't teach with Temezepam in my bloodstream.'

Mervyn Simpson confirms this – the advice, not the curricular impact of Temezepam. 'Crowhurst is chronically depressed, I'd say, but no one's interested in my opinions these days. It was my wife who suggested the bicycle.' Diana, practical Diana – in Mervyn's own chronic depression, he sometimes feels he should hand the entire practice over to her. 'And in answer to your next question, Constable, I didn't have any relevant contact, professional or otherwise, with the poor young victim.'

Fanny had only ever come to see him for the Pill and a septic ear, due to sticking too many unsterilized needles in it. Mervyn had never been able to understand why women went in for self-mutilation. He'd tried to talk to Diana about it once on holiday in the Dordogne. She'd been shaving her legs with his razor at the time. He'd worked out his own theory eventually. They carved themselves up, or they ate themselves silly like Cornelia Oliphant, or they took to the bottle like her mother, or they lived their own lives like Flora Penfold. He blamed Women's Liberation, as he'd said to Flora and quite a few other women over the years, though he fancied they weren't as taken with his theory as he was. His own son David, back at home at the age of thirty-four, is the only one who now listens to Mervyn's theories about women, needing, as he does, to find an explanation for the recent dissolution of his own marriage to a hotelier in Eastbourne. Malevolently, Mervyn thinks he should direct the police to Edwin Passmore, whom he'd seen more than once in the company of bubbly Fanny (walking by a rape field on a spring Sunday morning as black crows swooped over their heads, and in the Italian in Oakingham when Meltshire had been subjected to its second fall of snow, and Edwin had been introducing Fanny to the delights of a dish of squid squirming in garlic butter).

Mervyn doesn't tell the police this, but he does ask Edwin about Fanny after morning surgery. 'She was registered here, Edwin,' he points out. 'You really shouldn't have been messing around with her. When will it ever stop? I take it it wasn't you who tipped her into the reservoir?'

'I may be a lecher, but I'm not a murderer, Mervyn. The two motives are quite distinct, as any undergraduate psychology student will tell you. Anyway, I was with another patient that night. Unsuccessfully, as it happens.' Just thinking about Bridget Crowhurst's sprung interior makes Edwin sweat. 'Can you do this weekend for me, Mervyn? I've got to go and see the children. Barbara says Justin is suffering from the lack of a father.'

'Biology isn't all, you see, Edwin,' declares Mervyn, 'you have to put some effort into it from time to time. And you've got a nerve asking me to do next weekend – it's the Melton Flower Show.'

Jane Rivers is there early in the day, and Olga Kahn, after a more relaxed start, cranks up her old Beetle and lurches up Baker's Hill, past British Gas's rural gasification programme, which is rapidly advancing on Little Tickencote. The Flower Show is always a sight for sore eyes. Speaking of which, the Lancings are there, too, as Annabel has dragged Jasper to look at some new agriframes which she thinks could be used to create a fine gazebo in the garden of Wisteria Cottage.

'What do you think, Jane?' asks Olga, looking at a display of Himalayan blue poppies nestled among a selection of blue and purple foliage plants.

'Too blue,' observes Jane. 'Now, if you crossed the red with the blue, you might get something approaching an inky hybrid.'

'I wasn't talking about the poppies, my dear. I meant the death. I didn't expect anything like this, did you?'

'Did you ever finish my *Problems in Paradise*?'

'Er-hum. No.'

'Page two hundred and twenty-one. I anticipated it.'

'Let's sit down.' Olga sweats a little – not with the heat, but with the pain. 'What was it, then?' she says, settled on a fancy white cast-iron bench. 'Was it the water? H_2O and the stuff of dreams?'

'You and I come at this from opposite ends,' says Jane slowly. 'You have theories, I work with empirical observation. That's why we make a good team. But yes, I have observed that water is a common theme in many of these untoward events. Rain, the waters of birth, other fluids. Animals that live in water. And it all started when Jacob's Water itself was created. This led me to predict – on the basis of observation, you understand, not theory – that sooner or later someone would drown there.'

'It is theoretically possible that her fall could have been accidental,' comments Olga drily.

'Oh no, someone pushed her.'

'So why is it being treated as misadventure?'

'Bureaucracies avoid truth, and that includes the police. Most of the structures of the modern state are designed to prevent people understanding who they are and what they're capable of.' Jane speaks from experience – her long years in the probate office. 'We know, the village knows, that the answer lies amongst us. One of us is to blame, but that's not even the point, really. History loads the individual with responsibility, drives him or her to a particular course of action. But that person is only the carrier for a deeper cultural drama.'

'Er-hum. You call that empirical observation?'

'I work backwards. From observation – fact – to explanation. For you it's the other way round. But whichever way round it is, we reach the same point in the end, don't we, Olga?'

As the two women sit there, a bronze sculpture of a scantily clothed woman kneeling in a pile of silver undergrowth starts dribbling water from her hands. The dribble builds into a pool, and then to a jet projecting itself across the plants.

'Do you know Jung's *Modern Man in Search of a Soul*?' asks Olga.

'I know many who are, but not that particular one.' Jane's humour is always delivered with an absolutely straight face. In any case, Olga is already mentally launched on her passage from Jung.

'"I might, perhaps, content myself by referring to Columbus, who, by using subjective assumptions, a false hypothesis, and a route abandoned by modern navigation, nevertheless discovered America. Whatever we look at, and however we look at it, we see only through our own eyes."'

'I admire your facility for quoting verbatim. How do you manage it, Olga?'

'My mother taught me. Who else?'

'I agree with the sentiment.'

'Shall we move on? I'm anxious to see the wild-flower garden.'

Mervyn Simpson's feet are already planted in front of the feathery mini-meadow. He knows both Olga Kahn and Jane Rivers. Women like that are Diana incarnate. But he has had occasion recently to change his view of Olga's invulnerability. She'd come to see him to tell him about her terminal condition. 'I don't want anything done, Mervyn,' she'd said firmly. 'This is my illness, not yours. I'm only telling you because I may need your help.' Seeing his face, she'd added quickly, 'Oh no, nothing like that. I'm not planning a premature exit, I intend to take my time. I shall do it at my leisure, if you like. But morphine *et al.* may come in handy. I merely wanted to apprise you of the situation!'

'Good morning, ladies!' Mervyn would have tipped his hat to them if he'd been wearing one. 'Rather artificial, don't you think?' He gesticulates at the crescent-shaped arrangements of red campion and yellow ragwort, white wood anemones and blue flax.

As Jane starts to say something, he notes Annabel Lancing approaching – a lady he's keen to avoid, in case she quizzes him about the contraceptive state of her daughter Bronwen, for whom he's just prescribed the Pill. Bronwen had been frank with him about the premature ejaculatory habits of the Meltshire youth, trapped by Durex in Owlston and other woods. 'Excuse me, I must go. The daily round calls, you know.' With a second metaphorical tipping of the hat, Mervyn disappears round the gazebo Annabel Lancing had been admiring earlier.

Bronwen's GCSE results come by the morning post. She's failed all of them, except for art. Annabel rants and rails. Jasper locks himself in the garage to build a bookshelf for his speakers. Bronwen gets the afternoon bus to Oakingham, screaming over her shoulder at her mother that this is the last she may ever see of her. Again! says the child Alun, taking his Desmond Morris video of farmyard animals and his flute round to Flora for his weekly lesson.

'It's a good thing you brought that, Alun,' says Flora, referring to the video. 'I'm having trouble with my hens again.'

That's the thing about living in the country, it keeps returning you to all these practical considerations which keep your feet firmly in the present rather than in visions and fancies of the past. Flora thinks a good deal about her father and Julia(n) Peacock. She tells Pete, who whistles through his teeth and pretends to be amazed, but isn't. 'We all have shadows in our past,' he remarks, challengingly.

Flora's egg-bound Maran is no longer egg-bound – in fact, quite the opposite. Now she's taken to eating them. Doris has told Flora to add crushed oyster shell (available in sacks from George), but the Maran's destructive conduct continues. Though it gets over the problem of excess supply, it really is a most revolting thing to happen, and Flora is especially disturbed by it, as she herself is thinking of motherhood.

Flora tells Olga about the egg-eating problem before the memorial service held the next day in All Saints' for poor young Fanny Watkins. Trevor Tilley had suggested the service, with his usual keenness to grasp any opportunity for soldering together the few filaments of religion, or need for transitional rituals of one kind or another, still remaining in Little Tickencote and the other villages in his parish.

Trevor reads from the New English Bible – in part, no doubt, because he thinks its language more appropriate to the character and lifestyle of Fanny Watkins. He chooses a passage from the First Letter of John: 'Our theme is the word of life. This life was made visible; we have seen it and bear our testimony; we here declare to you the eternal life which dwelt with the Father and was made visible to us . . .

'Here is the message we heard from him and pass on to you: that God is light, and in him there is no darkness at all . . .'

The rest of the passage is about sin, and lying, and the remedy being Jesus Christ. They sing 'Abide with Me'. Flora is surprised at the mellowness of Pete Wates's voice beside her. Fanny's parents aren't there because Ted is – Ted is the great defiler in their eyes. Ted doesn't sing, he just looks mournful.

Coming out into the light of the churchyard afterwards, Flora realizes her own eyes are moist. Not that she had really known Fanny, but there for the grace of Jesus Christ, and so forth . . . 'I think I've got the answer,' says Olga.

Flora turns. 'You know who did it?'

'No, child, not that. I mean to your egg-eating problem. It came to me in the middle of the vicar's reading. It was the word "light" that did it. You need to darken your henhouse. Too much light makes them see what they've done. I'm sure that's it.'

Olga's solution works, though in the ensuing weeks Flora's hens have to contend with the incommodious interruption of Little Tickencote's sinful life by British Gas. A gang of jeaned men, their chests and backs painted burnt sienna by the natural energy of the sun, take drills to Main Street and Barleythorpe Road, and Manor Farm, Pudding Bag, Sawpit and Cabbage lanes. Rural Rosey suffers, though in the creative interludes that do occur Flora gets her back on the trying muscular sexism of British Gas.

Once the trough starts appearing in Cabbage Lane, flute lessons have to be held in the evenings. 'I think it's time to go away, Pete,' Flora cajoles, both in order to escape the noise and in order to advance to the next stage of her life. 'The harvest's in now, and Valerie's agreed to stay, hasn't she, because of your father's bad turns?'

All of which is true. Valerie Rumpstead likes Ladywood Farm – there's a strong incentive for her to do so, as she has no other home. Doris likes another woman to talk to, if you can call Valerie that. And Frank's turns are multiplying, as they always do at the onset of winter – it's the thought of all that cloud and rain and cold and gloom descending on Meltshire with the leaf mould the trees force on you, and the ugly naked plants, the sheep to be shepherded out of craggy frozen places, and the problems with the heating in the pigsty – Pete didn't think about that, did he, when he went on about the new method of outdoor pig-rearing? British Gas is the final straw this year. Doris tells him they'll have to have a new boiler, as the old one won't convert – 'Two thousand pounds or thereabouts,' she says comfortably. 'Ron can do it.' 'We haven't got the money, Mother,' says Frank. 'We have got the money, Mother,' says Pete. 'You'll get it done in time, don't you worry. The rape harvest was swinging this year. I'm glad we thought of planting that new high-yielding variety – it's the low glucosinolate levels that do the trick. By the way, Dad, I've been hearing from a colleague in Holland about the trials of night sowing. They reduce weed cover by 78 per cent. I think we ought to try it.'

Frank stomps off to bed, muttering about new-fangled ideas. Doris says, 'I'm not worried, son. Let His Majesty work his way round to it. We'll manage with Ketton's till spring; by then he'll have changed his mind. There are few advantages to living with a man as long as I have, but being able to predict his behaviour is one of them. Speaking of which, when are you and your not-so-young lady getting together, which I take it you are, as neither of you are giving any signs to the contrary?'

'Now you mention it, Mum, Flora and I did think we might take a little holiday.'

Doris approves. 'How about Devon? That can be nice at this time of year, and in my opinion your Flora needs fattening up. There's the Titmarshes' caravan, lodged in the Peak District – I've heard that's very nice.'

'I'm taking Flora to France, Mum.'

'Oh? One of your business trips?' Doris looks quizzically at him.

'Well, I do have a little business there, it's true.'

Flora herself finds it surprisingly hard to get away, despite the fact that the trip was her idea (courtesy of Mervyn Simpson). She's a woman of the country now: who will feed the chickens, collect the eggs, nourish the pussies, and pick the falling apples from the ground? Young Alun Lancing can be depended on to take care of the hens – in fact he'll enjoy having a chance to sit in Flora's garden in his duffel coat watching them, now the atmosphere in Wisteria Cottage has reverted to slanging matches.

Flora calls on Olga to suggest that she might like to help herself to some of the apples. Though it's nearly lunch time, Olga's still in her nightdress, a large flower-sprigged linen affair. 'Are you all right, Olga?' The old lady's – this is the first time Flora's thought of her as an old lady – cheeks look thinner than before, and there's a gaunt look around her grey-blue eyes.

'Just a tummy upset, my dear,' says Olga briskly, 'nothing to worry about.'

Flora's about to suggest calling the doctor, when Mervyn Simpson appears behind her. 'Ah Miss . . . er . . . Mrs . . .'

'Penfold,' supplies Olga. 'She just came to see me about . . . Why did you come, Flora?'

'About the apples. I'm going away for a week; I wondered if you could go and clear the lawn of some of them. They'll be wasted otherwise.'

'Ah,' says Mervyn, though not about the apples.

'You can count on me,' says Olga from within her flower-sprigged nightdress, in which she reminds Mervyn of one of those fearsome ladies constructed as prows of ships.

Pete Wates and Flora Penfold fly to Bordeaux in October, rent a car and drive out to the Bassin d'Arcachon, whose still, flat waters remind them of the reservoir in Meltshire. They stay in a small hotel on one of the wide roads leading from the centre of Arès to the shore. Hydrangeas, faded to less souciant colours now, still bloom, though Arès is about to be struck by a sudden early winter frost.

Pete takes coffee with Michelle Lapin in the Café des Artistes by the church. A few metres from their table a local farmer is carried to his last ritual in a coffin decked with plastic orange gladioli. All these deaths, thinks Pete. 'There is a message in these reminders of mortality,' says Michelle, in French. 'We're none of us getting any younger, are we, Pierre, and how is the cause of the revolution being advanced, now that the environmental movement is sucking our energies away from the powerful injustices of labour relations in the rural capitalist economy?' She draws on her Gitane and orders more coffee.

While Pete and Michelle contend the merits and demerits of the environmental movement in a mixture of French and English, Flora walks round the oyster beds and the neighbouring pine forest, which is now hung with the diamanté sparkle of frost. Silver coats the pine trees, the branches of bushes, twigs and overturned brown leaves on the ground; everything crackles and shines with a purifying light. In huts by the bay the oyster farmers sort their catches warmed by butane gas and by the thought of all the money to be made from slipping oysters down people's throats at Christmas time. But Arès, though sparkling, doesn't hold the same challenge as Little Tickencote, which awaits Flora, an Arcadian repository of mixed metaphors and mysteries, the other side of the Channel. Stumbling over the frosty ground of the Arès forest, she even believes it might all be a dream.

'Write about it,' urges Pete Wates, in response to the voicing of Michelle's political concerns in the café by the church, as the plastic gladioli return from their sad duties. 'Write me a piece for the *European Labour Monthly*: radical politics – an environmental threat.'

'You did not like my poem, then, Pierre?'

'Most unusual,' he deems, 'but I have to admit, Michelle, I do see the paper more as a vehicle for – as it were – rather more overtly *political* tracts.' He doesn't want to upset her, particularly as he hasn't told her about Flora, and he fears, if past years are anything to go by, she may already have prepared her lacy bower above the Uniprix.

'Okay.'

'Okay?'

'I will write you a piece. And now I must go. I 'ave to meet my friend, Alice, in ze oyster 'ut. We are partners, you understand, Pierre. Ze recession, 'e eez killing ze leetle man. *Et femme!*'

Michelle and Alice see Pete and his friend Flora later on from the lacy bower. The English couple stand at the edge of the bay's receding tide, looking at the unsailed boats and thinking of Fanny. Afterwards, Flora conceives in the hotel with the faded, frost-bitten hydrangeas.

A few weeks later she goes to meet Mervyn Simpson again.

'That was quick,' he observes. 'How are your apples? And why are you coming to see me if you know you're pregnant?'

'I thought you could confirm it.' Flora sits, hands crossed on her lap, as demure as any young wife in the early reaches of motherhood.

'Waste of time. If you are, you'll have a baby. If you aren't, you won't.'

'I could go and see your partner.'

This, as it was intended, strikes Mervyn as a threat. He doesn't like the thought of Edwin's multicontaminated hands investigating Flora Penfold's gynaecology. 'Oh, all right,' he says, crossly, 'pee into a bottle and June'll take it to the Melton General on her way home. If she remembers.'

'You know that young woman with the bright-blue eyes,' he tries to confide to Diana later, 'the one who went to the Lessendine Hall Hotel dinner dance in that fetching blue frock?'

Diana is outlining her lips with coral lipstick, prior to her evening class.

'Well, she's pregnant!' Mervyn must admit to taking a degree of personal responsibility for this accomplishment.

'Poor sod!' says Diana unsympathetically.

Mervyn looks at her in the hall. 'Didn't you like having our children, then?' he asks sadly. 'Was it all a mistake?'

'More like a nightmare. There's a lasagne in the microwave. I won't be back till late. It's creatures of the night this week; I'm hoping to catch an owl. Don't wait up.'

Flora is torn between a desire to keep the knowledge of her pregnancy to herself, and the contrary impulse to shout it from the rapidly baring treetops of Meltshire. She doesn't want to tell anyone in case something goes wrong, or it's a mistake, like Diana Simpson's. There's also the embarrassment of the local infertility. Why should she, an infiltrator of local mores, a mere newcomer, succeed, where others have failed, but not because they feared to tread? Bridget Crowhurst, wan, lying about her age, and flooded with plumbing difficulties.

Petula Nevere, affected by the gravity of her stilettos, and dropping babies like little curled-up fieldmice. Olive Grisewood, the knitting builder's wife replacing as a focus of maternal concern her own babies with Percy's haemorrhoids. And others, maybe, as well: Joan Roebuck, hairdresser and Postmaster's wife; Ted's Patsy, now fled to Streatham; Pleasance Oliphant, who, with the material resources and well-fed ovaries of the upper classes, ought to have had more than one obese, unhappy daughter. Or, indeed, the grandparents of Flora's future offspring, Doris and Frank Wates, trying for a second Pete in the farmhouse beyond Owlston Wood till Doris's body had passed its half-century mark.

Flora, musing on – and worried by – these reproductive misadventures, and under the influence of maternalist environmental thoughts, goes to Boots in Oakingham to buy a water filter. While she's there, she visits the bookshop and buys an armful of books about how to have perfect babies. Dipping into these as she waits to pay merely increases her anxiety, and she goes back to Boots to buy vitamin and mineral pills, additive-free cosmetics, and a large bottle of baby oil to protect her stomach and thighs from the natural ravages of stretch marks.

When Pete Wates goes to the Post Office for his paper the next day, Jack Roebuck's eyes glint. He whistles. 'Well then, the Dutch jaunt worked wonders, did it?'

'French,' says Pete. 'What do you mean, anyway?'

'Joan. Never misses a trick. Saw your lady in Oakingham buying baby books. Wasted on Little Tickencote is Joan; a woman of her intelligence should have been Prime Minister.' Jack turns his attention to defrosting the chilled foods cabinet for the first time in five years. 'You should look after her,' he calls out after Pete, chipping the ice away from the sides with a fish slice.

Pete calls on Flora, who is sitting contentedly by the fire reading Penelope Leach's *Baby and Child*, and drinking diet Cola, with Dolly on her lap. As Pete looms in the doorway looking at her, he is seized by an emotion which is new to him. 'What about the woodsmoke?' he demands. 'And the canned drink?'

'What about them?'

'Well, you've got Our Baby to think about now!'

'I *am* thinking about Our Baby, that's why I'm reading this book.'

'Carcinogens,' says Pete. 'The fire and the chemical additives.'

'Phooey.'

'It's my baby as well as yours.'

'How do you know I'm pregnant, anyway?'

'Jack-at-the-Post-Office told me.'

'I won't bother to ask how he knows. I think it's time we told a few people ourselves, Pete. Not too many, in case I lose it – more than 90 per cent of human conceptions fall by the wayside, you know.'

'You shouldn't read those books.'

'But Dr Simpson said I should be all right. This is an out-of-county conception.'

'Are you happy, my love?'

'Disgustingly. And you?'

'Fairly disgustingly. We've got a lot to talk about, though, Flora. For instance, are we going to go on living in different houses? How will you manage with the baby? Do you think we should get married? What about your flute lessons? What does all that breathing and blowing do to Our Baby?'

Flora puts out a pregnant hand and strokes Pete Wates's arm. 'It doesn't surprise me that you want to have this baby organically. It's just the details we'll need to discuss.'

'I've been talking to Mike Ramsay about mastitis. There's a farm in Wales where they *never* use antibiotics. Just a high-pressure hose. Mike says the secret of their success is that the milking is always done by members of the family.'

'Well, that's what we're going to do, isn't it?' says Flora happily.

18

Looking Back

THE YEAR has come full circle: soon it will be tupping time for the ewes again, and Flora Penfold, successfully tupped herself, has been in Little Tickencote for twelve months now, learning the quaint ways of the countryside – about the muck behind the rural idyll, the bogs into which sheep and other animals fall, the difficulty of telling weeds from flowers, the raucous noises of birds and rape-cutters, slicing plates of butter off green sickly-scented fields; and something it's hard to put words around, though many in Little Tickencote try: the manner in which all of this undoubtedly depends on some other allegory, some set of fables as yet unfathomed, about the meaning of life on our dicey old-fashioned earth.

In Cabbage Lane it is the winter of Flora Penfold's content. By and large, that is. She is anxious about money still, but her income from cartoon-drawing and flute-teaching is now about £800 a month. Interest accrues in the bank, and in the vegetable garden new little carrots, parsnips and white Lisbon onions push their way down in the nicely wormed earth, recently vacated by rows of perpetual spinach which had perpetually bolted, shooting horribly bobbled stems up to heaven. The Marans and the Rhode Island Reds lay; and Flora hands over the surplus to Pat Titmarsh, who sells them for her, taking a cut of the proceeds. Though Rural Rosey disapproves of this arrangement, deeming it ideologically unsound, Flora must get rid of the eggs somehow, and she can't just throw them away or foist all of them on the gullible – for the time being irredeemably parasitical – Our Baby.

About whose existence everyone else is pleased, surprised, envious, upset, disapproving, or a mixture of two or more of these. Take the prospective grandparents first, as Flora and Pete had done: 'At last!' cried Doris Wates in her brown kitchen, thinking of the real human William or Mary she'd be feeding next winter by the fire. The news brought no more than a wry smile to the face of husband Frank: 'A grandfather, eh?' Doris mentions marriage, but is told not to mention it again. In London, Irina Penfold reads through her biography of Galia Molokhovina, making amendments and corrections, and remembering her own childbirths and how very uncivilized they'd seemed. She expresses concern that Flora will be all right – meaning this in a number of different senses. 'Don't worry, Mother; I'm not.'

Even ex-lover Barnaby rings up one day to congratulate Flora on the happy news. Barney himself is not very happy about it. 'We should have had babies, Flora,' he moans. 'Why didn't we?'

'You didn't want them,' she points out reasonably. 'And you were enough of a baby, or rather too much of one, for me.'

'Still doing the Clever Miss Analytical trip, are we?'

'Only when necessary. How are you, Barney?'

'Not well, Flora, not well.'

'What does that mean?' Conscious of Judy Nightingale's predicament, Flora is bound to wonder about Barney's. But he comes right out with it. 'Cal told me he told you about Judy. Interfering slug. You're all right, Flora – you must be, or you wouldn't be preggers. Me, I have the beastly thing somewhere in my bloodstream. I'm not ill, it's just lurking somewhere.'

'I'm dreadfully sorry, Barney.'

'So, you see you were right not to succumb to my charms the last time we met.'

'Oh, Barney!'

'I do love you, Flora. Especially when you say "Oh, Barney" like that.'

Flora cries for Barney, and goes to see Mervyn Simpson about the baby and herself. Mervyn Simpson had raised the matter of her age, which will be forty in the lambing season, and then dismissed it on the grounds of the healthy sparkle in Flora's cornflower-blue eyes, and it being far too late to do anything; no point in locking the stable door after the horse has bolted, but what about your stable union, Miss Penfold?

'I think you should call me Flora,' she says, 'as you and I will be meeting fairly often in the coming months. I can't worry about my age, and my stable union is – well, stable.'

Mervyn anticipates with pleasure the addition of a gravid Little Tickencote woman to the clientele of the surgery antenatal clinic, whose comings and goings he regards largely as a ritual, carried out not for the fetuses' but for other people's sakes – his own in part, though God knows what the White Paper will do to his income from this source; he certainly hasn't got time to read it, and Edwin's preoccupied with the publication of his new book of poems, which is about to be celebrated in F.K. Taylor's bookshop in Oakingham with a crate of pink champagne.

'Don't tell me, Miss Penfold . . . Flora . . . you want a home birth, I suppose. Well, I suppose we could just about manage that. It won't be me that manages most of it, though, it'll be your good self and our staunch lady midwife, Miss Constantine Barker. You'll find her bark is about the same as her bite.' He chortles to himself in the proximity of the rubber plant, which shines with a new lease of life. 'Have you met Miss Barker? No? Well, you will. She's not too up-to-date, but I've never considered that matters much myself, as babies have been on the scene ever since Adam and Eve, haven't they?'

Flora has a little more difficulty with Miranda than with Dr Simpson. Miranda considers her perfectly insane to be saddling herself with a baby as well as the rural idyll/nightmare. But after the initial incredulous reaction has passed, she does express a little envy. 'My images of motherhood are largely drawn from fiction,' she confesses, 'which is probably as good a place as any to draw them from. Do you remember that book – I think it was the sequel to Lynne Reid Banks's *The L-Shaped Room* – where a mother and nursing child sit under an apple tree and everything is sort of lush and green and happy?'

'That's exactly what I'm aiming for,' admits Flora, 'though I'm not sure about the apple tree.'

Flora doesn't actually tell Bridget Crowhurst or the Neveres or the other women in Little Tickencote with whose involuntary barrenness her own fertility may be jealously compared. Jack-at-the-Post-Office will spread the news. Although he and Joan never had any children of their own either, Joan has made it clear that children had not been one of their life goals. While she said this, Jack, uncharacteristically, remained silent, occupying himself with the oiling of the cash register.

To Olga Kahn, struggling to get dressed and keep bland meals down, and generally maintain some fabric of ordinary life, Flora's baby is not only a very good sign indeed that Little Tickencote may be returning to health; she also feels rather grandmotherly towards it, and says so to Flora a little shamefacedly, but Flora doesn't mind. 'This baby needs as many parents and grandparents as it can get, don't you think, Olga?'

'Not too many,' advises Olga. 'Think of the poor child's psychodynamic structure, let alone its need to be good at arithmetic. You're not much of a counter yourself, are you, Flora?' Olga tries to be cheerful to cover up the pain.

'I made a discovery before I went to France,' confides Flora, 'about my father. He lived with another man once, a man who was pretending to be a woman.'

'That doesn't strike me as particularly odd,' acknowledges Olga.

'It doesn't?'

'From what you've told me, your father was unlikely to be contained by convention. Like you. And experiments in sexuality are more rife than most people care to think.'

'The strange thing is, Olga, they lived here. Here in Meltshire. In Bisbrooke, before it was flooded with the reservoir.'

'Well I never! Well, that probably does give you an odd feeling.'

'It does? I mean, why does it?'

'All that submerged emotion,' pronounces Olga. 'The horror is symbolic, you see.'

'My father wrote a book about it. Well, not about the submerged emotion, but about Meltshire. There are maps too. Would you like to see them?'

'Bring them round sometime. Jane and I are trying to crack the mystery of Little Tickencote's nasty happenings. You never know, they might help.'

Annabel Lancing is pleased about Flora's pregnancy too. She has visions of being able to impart to Flora some of her own painfully collected knowledge about motherhood – tips about pregnancy sickness ('My God, I remember it with Gwenny especially, they always say it's worse with girls'), about cramp ('I used to drive Jasper mad waking up in the night with it – calcium tablets work wonders'), about breathing exercises ('Forget them, I had epidurals with all of mine, there's no escaping the plain fact, Flora, that childbirth *hurts*'), about wind in babies ('Mine always slept with dummies, it was the only thing that helped'), toilet training ('Alun was simply dreadful, he went behind the dustbin for *ages*') and so on, right up to adolescence, about which even Annabel realizes it would be hard for her to claim much in the way of expertise as yet. Little Gwenny and Alun Lancing's eyes are drawn to Flora's abdomen, as their acquaintance with gestation, due to living in these parts, has been limited to the habits of sheep and cows and dogs and rabbits (not a good example, as fertility practically equals mortality). They ask questions, which Flora answers.

Bronwen Lancing, back at home on the Pill minus most of her GCSEs, stops talking about midwifery with Flora's all-too-real example next door, and switches to art instead. She comes round one day when her mother is out, with an armful of drawings to show Flora. The drawings are good – Bronwen has an unusual facility of suggesting the ambience of a scene with one or two sweeping lines. And listening to Bronny talk about her life and her aspirations, Flora understands how what is liberating for her – this countryside, this community (albeit not organic in quite the way she at first thought) – can, for someone of Bronny's age, present itself as enclosure. It's not clear whether Bronny hates the country or her parents the most. Although she calls Little Tickencote boring, objecting to the sense of nothing ever happening, it's not an experience of peace she principally speaks about, but of violence. For Bronny, Little Tickencote and Wisteria Cottage have been irremediably violent, with the lashing of her mother's body by her father's hands only echoing the lacerations of her mother's bitter tongue and the deep morbidity of the surrounding landscape, given over to disease and pests and dying animals, and plumbing problems and generally disgusting happenings. 'I have to get away from here, Flora,' pleads Bronny. 'Please help me.'

Go on, then, says Rural Rosey, it'll make a good theme for the *Daily Record*. Besides which, the child deserves your help. She's cut herself off from all other sources of aid – teachers, her parents, Mortimer Fanshawe. I won't embarrass you by calling it ideologically unsound. You know enough about the country now to realize it doesn't suit everyone. I'm even thinking about leaving it myself now you've stopped my husband from getting himself fixed.

Flora takes Bronny up to London to see Miranda. It's December, and raining; the sky crosses over from the crisp clarity of Little Tickencote to the muddied ceiling of London about halfway through the train journey. They have lunch with Miranda in an Indian vegetarian restaurant in Euston. Bronny's eyes shine at the vision Miranda sketches for her – both in words and on the paper tablecloth – of Art College and the wide, wide world beyond (though, unfortunately, with a few more GCSEs). After lunch, Miranda kindly bears Bronny off to collect brochures, and Flora goes to see her mother.

Bronny's delight in London isn't shared by Flora, traipsing in her unwaterproof boots through the litter-covered streets of Bloomsbury. Irina is sitting at her kitchen table with ink on her face, two pencils behind her ear and another in her hand, and with the pages of her life of Galia Molokhovina spread out in front of her between the cherry povidlo and the bubliki. 'Come in, darling,' she says, opening the door on Flora as though she expected her, which she didn't – Flora hadn't rung first to say she was coming – 'how do you spell "promissory" – is it one "s" or two?'

Flora goes through Irina's list of editorial queries with her mother. But she refrains from actually reading any of the manuscript, in case it isn't any good after all these years.

'Oh, it *was* wonderful of you to come and help me with this!' exclaims Irina, poking another pencil behind her ear. 'Did you bring my botva as well? I think I shall write a cookery book next.'

They clear the table and have a pot of Russian tea. Rain pours down outside. 'Do you ever go out these days, Mother?' asks Flora.

'Well, I did go out about a month ago, but the square was locked and I couldn't find my key. I get the groceries delivered – there's a marvellous little Cypriot shop round the corner that will do that for you. Books I get by mail order. It's remarkable how many things you can get by mail order these days. Look at this.' Irina gets up and pulls a box of goodies out of a cupboard. 'See, darling, this is called a Whisper Two Thousand, you can hear whispers a hundred feet away with it, isn't it sweet! And this is what they call a space pen, it writes upside down, and under water, and everywhere! And this' – Irina produces yet another strange-looking piece of equipment from the box – 'this is an instrument for removing hairs from noses! Terribly ingenious, don't you think! These I got for your baby.' She brings out a set of gaudy Russian dolls. 'Aren't they pretty? You had a set when you were a child, but I can't find them – in fact, I can't seem to find very much these days.'

The flat is even more littered with boxes and piles of things – papers, clothes, packets of food, newspapers, mail-order catalogues – than before. They sit in the kitchen because it's the only space left for sitting in. Were this not the winter of Flora's content, she might worry about what will happen when the chaos of Irina's life finally drowns order: who but Flora, who is miles away in Little Tickencote, will look after her mother then? Certainly not brother Jonathan, and she wouldn't wish brother Jonathan's wife Janet on anyone. But it is not a time for uncongenial thoughts of this kind. 'Do you ever see Julian Peacock these days, Mother?' Flora asks.

'He telephones me every Sunday at eleven, regular as clockwork. Ever since his own mother died. I think it's important to him. Your father asked Julian to look after me, you know, Flora. As though I needed looking after! It was Samuel who needed that.'

'What do you and Julian talk about, Mother?'

'The weather mostly. Or the price of stocks and shares. My health – but that doesn't take us long, I've only got a touch of arthritis. We're a long-lived family, Flora. The women, anyway. Galia Molokhovina lived to ninety-two. She attributed her longevity to the tisane she drank every morning – rose petals and wild mint and camomile. You could try that, now you're living in the country, couldn't you?'

Her mother, Flora realizes, speaks like Olga Kahn. Both of them are tuned to past events. Perhaps the present is simply less interesting than the past.

'What else, Mother? What else does Julian Peacock talk about when he rings you?'

'Why do you want to know?'

'I'm just curious.'

'No, you're not. No one's ever just curious. Especially not you. All right then, Julian talks about Rupert. The man he lives with. An accountant. Or something like that.' Irina looks vague. 'Now, why did you want to know? Is that what you wanted to know? Why this sudden interest in Julian Peacock?'

Flora starts to tell her mother about her discovery among the papers Samuel bequeathed to her of a manuscript about rural life. Irina doesn't seem at all surprised. 'That Russian sociologist your father admired – what was his name? Sorokim, that's it – *he* wrote about the country, didn't he? That's why, I'm sure. Samuel was always scribbling something. I never thought it fair, you know – I can say it now, it's not really done to speak ill of the dead – I was fond of Samuel, you know that, but sometimes I used to lie awake at night wondering why God let Samuel write all those books when he only gave me the time to write one.'

'Mother,' interrupts Flora, 'were you and Samuel happy?'

'Is it any concern of yours? I don't think it is. What one's parents do in their private lives is better not thought about.' Irina wrinkles her nose, thinking about her own, dear, migratory parents. 'On the other hand, I don't know – at least you're still interested in me, which is more than can be said of that brother of yours!'

'Were you, Mother?'

'Most of the time, most of the time.' Irina turns her eyes to the window and stares out of it, as though considering whether or not to say something. 'Next you're going to ask me about your father and Julian Peacock, aren't you? All right, I'll tell you. I'll tell you, since I know you're not going to stop asking until you get the answer. It was the same when you were a little girl. Jonathan could be fobbed off with half-truths, but not you. "But *why*, Mummy? What does *that* mean?" I can hear your little shrieking voice following me round these four walls even now!'

Irina pours herself some more tea. Outside, the rain sloshes down. Flora thinks comfortably of her carrots and onions being soaked, and of how sweet the countryside smells after rain. 'When your father first got to know him, Julian was a postgraduate student at the College, one of the brightest of his generation, Samuel used to say. But that didn't help him with – what do you call it? – his gender identity. That is what they call it these days, isn't it? Julian Peacock isn't a real man. I'm not sure what he is, really. Are you sure you want me to go on, Flora? Yes? All right. Well, as I remember it, Julian went off to somewhere in the country to try living as a woman. He was going to have a sex-change operation, you see. But the doctor thought he should try living as a woman first, to see how he liked it. He got some kind of job in a local college and went to live in a village in the middle of nowhere to see if he liked being a woman.'

'And did he?'

'I never asked him. It wasn't my business. Why am I telling you this?'

'Because I asked about Father's interest in rural life.'

'Whatever Julian and Samuel did together, it was not my business. I never allowed myself to think of it very much, in any case. He was not going to leave me and you and your brother to live with Julian, or anything like that. He was not that mad. I don't know what they had together, but I know they did have a fine intellectual relationship, and that was a good thing for me. I didn't want to listen to Samuel developing his sociological theories all the time, did I? I wanted to think about Galia. Are you shocked, Flora? You shouldn't be.'

This is *not* the substance of one of my cartoons, thank you very much, says Rural Rosey on the train on the way home. My mores are more conventional than yours. Besides, this newly acquired knowledge of yours is of no interest to anyone but yourself. It's not even remotely relevant to the world of funny happenings in Little Tickencote. In fact, it's a red herring really.

I don't know about that, Flora muses, watching the passing countryside, and Bronny Lancing opposite, happily absorbed in dreams and brochures. Why, after all, had Julian Peacock tried out his life as Julia in the country? And in that particular bit of the country? She imagines Julia(n) in Bisbrooke, a village she's now read about in an old book, with an old wishing well, and an orchard of cherry trees; she tries to see Julia Peacock striding out into the dewy morning with a frock on, its loose feminine folds hiding dangly biological secrets. But it's a caricature she sees walking there. None the less, Julia(n) Peacock had gone to the country in order to find him/herself. That was worth thinking about.

'It's part of our fantasy about rural life, isn't it?' Flora confides to Pete Wates that evening, as they sit in front of the fire. 'The idea that we can find our true selves in it?'

'Not for those of us who were born here or spent most of our lives here,' he answers. 'Take Bronny Lancing, for instance, as you did today to London. Or myself.'

'But you stayed,' she points out. 'You decided to stay in the country and be a farmer. You didn't have to do that, you could have left.'

'I could have left,' he repeats, 'but instead I've got irons in other fires. Politics, and the European connection. It's important for me to feel part of a wider scene. And I'll tell you what's especially important, Flora – it's the idea that fancies of the sort you had – or have – about the country are *not* about the past. They're not simply harking back to an archaic golden age when country folk walked around in smocks and every village had an idiot, and everyone knew their place and was happy in it. An era before machines and artificial insemination and the Cottage Garden Society.'

'You shouldn't mock the Cottage Garden Society,' Flora reproaches him. 'I've just joined it.'

'Don't interrupt me, dearest. I was trying to be serious for once.'

As winter settles in, there is the usual crop of damaged animals and minor disasters in the Gwater Valley, though it's milder than last year, and scarcely a snowflake drops on Little Tickencote, or, indeed, on Great Glaston, to which Cornelia Oliphant returns from her Swiss rest cure thinner but not cured, while her mother Pleasance takes her place by being carted off to a home for alcoholics. 'I never realized', says Bream innocently to Cook, 'how much she drank.'

'Didn't you, Sir?' Cook always calls Bream 'Sir'; it amuses her and reflects the distance she feels from this man, who is hardly at home and when he is doesn't notice what's going on anyway. 'So it'll be just you and Cornelia for Christmas, then, will it? Or will Mr Emile and Mr Liam be coming?'

Bream feels the need for the solidarity of the male clan around him at this time of family crisis, so he invites both his younger brothers for Christmas. Emile, now sixty, brings his new PVC waders in the hope of trying them out in Jacob's Water. Liam – fifty-seven, and still employed in some vague capacity on the editorial board of a dictionary – brings his notebook, in which he writes down anything that might be useful linguistically. Over the Christmas period, Cornelia comes up trumps in the new role of mistress of the household foisted on her by her mother's illness, which she regards as mere moral weakness (whereas her own had been real, and not her own fault at all). Cornelia and Cook organize a splendid Christmas lunch, with a free-range goose from Ladywood Farm, prefaced by oysters from somewhere in France, flown in specially. Being responsible for producing the food somehow reduces Cornelia's own appetite for it. But after two glasses of wine, she starts to cry. 'Come on, Corney.' Uncle Emile slaps her on the back. '*Gaudeamus igitur!*'

'I didn't do Latin, Uncle Emile,' sniffs Corney.

'Neither did I,' admits Emile. 'Did I, Bream?' They enjoy a private laugh about some of the goings-on that went on instead. 'What I meant was, you should be enjoying yourself, shouldn't she, Lee? You've got your whole life ahead of you. Which is more than we have.'.

'But I've wasted it,' sobs Cornelia. 'I've thrown it away! I couldn't be a wife, and now I've driven Mummy to drink!' Dr Riemann's efforts to locate Cornelia's wrongdoings in the Oedipal drama have clearly not quite taken root.

'Never mind, never mind.' The three men utter jovial platitudes. Cook comes in and bears Cornelia away. 'You're coming to my sitting-room,' she says firmly, 'and we're going to watch a nice panto on my video. After that, we'll have mince pies and call your mother. I dare say you three gentlemen' – she casts a suspicious eye round the table – 'can find a way of amusing yourselves.'

And that's how it comes about that Bream, Emile and Liam Oliphant descend in Bream's Land Rover to the shores of Jacob's Water on the afternoon of Christmas Day, so that Emile can try out his new PVC waders, and Bream and he can talk about the past, and Liam can stand there with his shoulders hunched in his Harris tweed overcoat and his hand on the little book in his pocket in case any new words occur to him.

The light is already beginning to fade by the time they get there. It chases the fish, fattening for the next season, under the water. It falls between the outlines of trees on the opposite shore, and meets a mist uprising from the Christmas fields. The Oliphant brothers, more bibulous than usual – though Bream, mindful of dear Pleasance's fate, the least of all – recall the time when dear Pleasance and dear Odile, both now differently institutionalized, peopled the long-since-drowned architectural folly of Barrow Grange. 'Where would it have been, then, Bream?' asks Emile, up to his thighs in water.

'It's not a river,' observes Liam, as he would correct a spelling. 'It's a reservoir. The word can mean either a natural or an artificial lake. From the French *réserver*, to reserve . . .'

'Over there,' waves Bream, 'past the church, before the causeway. I remember the hill, it was quite a climb from Cedarton. You could see Barrow Grange from the top of the hill, but when you went down the other side it disappeared round a bend in the road.'

'What happened to the old girl, Bream?' It's Emile's voice again above the waders. 'Is she a gonner yet?'

Bream tells him.

'Poor old girl. She was pretty, wasn't she, Odile. Not like your Pleasance. Such a beautiful girl!' Emile sighs.

Liam, behind him, shifts from one foot to the other. 'Why the English language couldn't come up with a perfectly good Anglo-Saxon word for a source of water for towns, I'm sure I don't know.'

'Shut up, Lee!' Emile turns on him. 'You loved her too! We all loved Odile.' He stares into the muddy waters that circle his legs, not a fish in sight.

'Are there any holes, then, Em?'

'Not in these, Lee. There are a few in your head.'

They remind Bream of nursery squabbles. Indeed, in many ways his brothers seem to him never to have grown up. For all three of them, puberty had forced itself on them with an outrageous and premature flow of androgens, but life hadn't equipped them to turn pharmacological into social adulthood. Then or now. Bream himself is the nearest approximation.

'Don't you know the chappie who does the fish round here, Bream?' asks Emile. 'We've got these new reservoir lures in from Saskatchewan. The waggletails and the Flashabous are particularly jolly.' 'How did you do it, Bream?' he goes straight on to ask, as though the two thoughts were connected. 'I mean, how did you sort out that awful mess Odile and I landed in at Montreux?' He recalls that particular summer with a clarity that only increases with age. He was happy then. He and Odile, amid the flowers and the casino of Montreux, watching the pleasure boats coming and going, fucking throughout the long afternoons. His penis salutes the memory like a large fishing maggot. He pulls the elastic of his anorak tighter.

'There was only one way. This.' Bream nods at Jacob's Water. 'It wouldn't have happened otherwise. There was a lot of local resistance. But I pushed the bill through, for the compensation, which was generous. Without it Pleasance and Odile would have been bankrupted.'

'So it's all Odile's fault, eh? Crikey.'

'And yours.' And mine, thinks Bream. Men can take rejection, but it drives women mad. His eyes travel to a point in the lake south of where Barrow Grange would have been, to the woods where cowslips had once traced the outline of Odile Ruddle's undoubtedly delicious body. There is another part to this story, one which concerns Odile, but it's all so long ago, he doesn't want to embark on it with his brothers now.

'If it weren't for sex,' says Emile slowly – this will be quite the most profound thing he's said for a long time – 'we'd all be saved. Sex is our downfall.'

'But without sex,' says Liam unexpectedly behind them, 'we wouldn't be here at all!'

Bream and Emile turn to look at him, as a rowing boat passes in front of them and across the middle of the water. Abraham Varley has to row hard against the wind. It takes him forty-five minutes to cross the water, by which time the Oliphant brothers have taken their memories home for a bottle of Bream's claret and some of Cook's mince pies – if there are any left after Cornelia, nourished by the video of *Cinderella*, has recovered her appetite.

It's also dark in the little cove by the Meltshire Water Authority outlet, where Abraham moors his boat and gets out in a pair of waders Emile would have scorned – but they've served Abraham well for ten years now. On the shore, Abraham takes the path up to the road by Hamble Woods, where the lights round the Water Treatment Works give it the appearance of a square-tiered wedding cake against the starless sky.

19

The Black Dog and the Rainbow

OLGA KAHN lies in bed listening to Mahler's *Das Lied von der Erde*. From her high oak bed with its starchy horsehair mattress, she can see out of the window; without moving at all, she can see the spire of All Saints' Church and the fields with sheep in them and beyond that Barratt's Coppice, which is always such a delight to walk in at springtime and as the summer blooms and ripens. Just now the dead twigs will crackle and snap when you walk on them, but soon the pale mauve crocuses, and then the bluebells and the bright daffodils, will all be there again, and the dog violets and the wood anemones, and, where the lattice of the trees parts at the edge, a crowd of impudent butter-hearted daisies. Olga Kahn sees what she sees, and imagines what she has seen, and has no time any longer for sights that may never pass her eyes. Mahler wrote *Das Lied* – a song cycle accepting life's evanescence, redeemable only through the glories of nature, but culminating ultimately in loss – after his little daughter died, and when he knew he himself had heart disease and not long to live. *Das Lied* is not about the conscious life; every note in it calls up the shadowy images, symbols, and half-remembrances of the unconscious. The brown metallic tape in Olga's cassette player relays the words of the final movement, 'Der Abschied', which, being about leavetaking and going home, even though the dear earth will blossom into spring again, exactly parallels her own calmly morbid mood: '*Wohin ich geh'? . . . /Ich wandle nach der Heimat, meiner Stätte./ . . . Still ist mein Herz und harret seiner Stunde!/Die liebe Erde allüberall/Blüht auf im Lenz und grünt aufs neu!/Allüberall und ewig blauen licht die Fernen!/ Ewig . . . Ewig . . . /*'

The music relieves her pain, because it enables her to feel in the company of others who have known they're going to die and have managed to live through such a time, not only accepting it, but using it to dwell constructively on what life has given them. Olga sighs.

Mahler never heard *Das Lied* performed. Perhaps he wasn't quite as accepting as one liked to think he was, as he resolutely called it his ninth symphony, thus making his ninth his tenth and his eleventh the one he died without completing – what composer could not be affected by such premonitions when Schubert, Beethoven, Bruckner and Dvořák had all died after composing nine symphonies? Be thankful you haven't written nine symphonies, Olga admonishes herself. But you have finished your memoirs. The last ribbon on the Corona is worn thin; the typed sheets lie next to it in a brown envelope with a note enclosed in case her days are more limited than she thinks they are. 'To whom it may concern: please give this manuscript to my dear friend Jane Rivers, to whom I entrust the task of publishing it. I give her full permission to edit the manuscript in any way she thinks fit.'

Olga changes the cassette to the ninth symphony. Music is her main nourishment, now that eating has become difficult. She still gets up and dressed every day, though only for a short while in the afternoon. Jane does her shopping and comes to see her every day, and Pat Titmarsh brings her little delicacies – thin chicken soup, grapes, water biscuits. Bridget Crowhurst fetches her books to read, but doesn't stay long, as illness is not her forte. Even that queer Petula Nevere calls with flowers from her garden. Not much at this time of year, but she manages to find some. Joan Roebuck does her hair *in situ* and Olive Grisewood has taken to coming 'to tidy the place up a bit', as she puts it. Olga's not one for tidiness herself, but she does appreciate the fragrantly laundered pure cotton sheets Olive brings, laying them on her old horsehair mattress with the same care and consideration Percy uses for his building work. Yes, the women of Little Tickencote and Great Glaston are rallying around. Including, of course, the young – not-so-young – Flora Penfold, Olga's newly acquired substitute daughter. And then there's Dr Simpson's nurse, and Dr Simpson himself.

The nurse and the doctor come regularly; Olga can almost tell the time by them – by their visits, and the church clock. All the time she needs to tell, anyway. The others appear by her bed in odd sequences which, of course, only she knows about. They come when they want to, to suit their own needs, as well as their understanding of hers. Apart from Jane, Flora comes most often; she's like a breath of fresh air in Olga's sickroom, bright-eyed and with a blush on her skin given by the baby, even if she is approaching forty.

'Why did you tell me it was only a stomach upset, Olga?' Flora had demanded angrily.

'It is, dear. People don't like to hear the word "cancer". What difference would it have made, anyway?'

'You should have told me the truth.'

Olga had fixed her with one of her looks. 'Er-hum. Your pursuit of the truth is unusually vigorous. Not everyone likes it as much as you do.'

'How can you be so calm, Olga?'

'Because I know the truth! All right, child, I'm quite fond of it myself. Now tell me about the baby, and what you've been doing. I need to feel in touch.'

Olga leaves the back door open for this endless procession of people who pass through her cottage. When she dozes off, as she's about to do now, she tends to mix up the good-hearted neighbours of the present with various others from the past: patients, supplicants, ghosts, lovers, farmers: unkempt, unholy walkers through the collective unconscious of the Western world, every one of them.

The music becomes a dream sequence. Olga has shed forty years and is in America, in Pennsylvania, where she went with Raphael so that he could study haemoglobin and she psychoanalysis. Near where they lived was an artificial lake set in the middle of a small town on the advice of a rather avant-garde architect who had himself been through a protracted analysis, organized around his somewhat fancifully reconstructed fetal experiences as a sufferer from excess *liquor amni*, and who came out of it (the liquor and the analysis) considering that people generally did better if they had water to look at. The lake he designed was an elegant one. It had been decorated with large pale water lilies and a brood of ducks, even some slinky gold and silver fish, and fringed with young willows, which trusted their fronds to its artificially monitored chemistry. Children played by the lake, and mothers clutched at the children playing by it in case they fell in, at the same time exchanging stories and secrets and what is now disparagingly known as gossip. An awful lot of the town's important business was transacted in the environs of that lake.

Olga and Raphael had walked and sat and talked by it. For all his faults – and no one was more conscious of these than he – Raphael's mind had been worth talking to; since his death, it's that Olga has missed the most. Now, sleeping in the high oak bed in Little Tickencote, Olga imagines she is sitting again with Raphael, a skinny, amber-coloured man, listening to him expound on the genetics of fruit flies, while the miniature cherry trees round the Pennsylvania lake cast their dancing clouds of pink-white blossom down to become the lake's own captured inverse fancies. Raphael had been a good man. His goodness flows over Olga now like honey – kindness, that's what one needs. She had walked and sat by the lake alone, too, considering the monstrous erosion of orthodox Freudian theory caused by Karen Horney's teaching and writing; the primacy of little girls' knowledge of their vaginas, the cultural basis of penis envy; womanhood as a positive state; the oppressiveness of the monogamous ideal.

But as the end of life approaches, one spends more mental time at the beginning. And here Olga is a tightly ruled child again in post-First World War Vienna, in the apartment on Grubestrasse dominated by the aunts and cousins and grandparents of her mother's clan, all talking rapid domestic German and drinking cream-topped coffee in the sitting-room with the long windows and dull-green velvet sofas. Arnold Kahn flits in and out; here today and gone tomorrow. Where was he off to all the time? In the child Olga's fantasies her father went perpetually to fairyland, the land she read about in her picture books, full of gauze frocks and silver wands and hobgoblins and meadows with high bells tinkling across them, whence he returned with the delightful bounty of sweets, sickly cakes and toys and, for her mother, bunches of stiff damask roses tied with silky ribbons Olga would later claim for her hair – her long brown hair, tied like a mare's tail. Olga moves uneasily in the horsehair bed. Tails and tales, in relation to the unravelling of which there's still mental work to be done. Olga's not quite finished yet, either with her own life or with that of Little Tickencote.

Present time invades her dusty, redolent unconsciousness like a stuttering alarm clock. She opens her eyes suddenly, wondering what it is that has woken her up. Then a step on the stairs and a voice calling: Dr Simpson.

Olga sits up. The March sun has moved to the centre of the window; it is afternoon. 'I must have dozed off,' she says, as Mervyn lifts the latch on her bedroom door. 'I'm a lazy old woman, aren't I, Mervyn? I should have been up by now.'

Mervyn Simpson sits down on the chair by the bed. The room carries the unmistakable scent of sickness: the stale, clammy odours of bedclothes and people sweating their childhood dreams into them, the fragrance of human flatulence trapped in air pockets. 'I shouldn't worry, Olga,' he consoles, 'sleep's a good analgesic.'

'I know that,' she says, 'but I think I'm worried I might not wake up at all one of these days.'

'You won't one day, old girl.' Mervyn has learnt to respect the dignity of death and the dying, and especially the position each dying person adopts towards it: some want to know, some don't; some to talk, others not; though on an unconscious level Mervyn is convinced that everyone must be aware when their living days are numbered. Olga's attitude has been straightforward from the beginning: this is what's happening, and you and I must let it take its course.

'How is the pain, Olga?' Mervyn asks, conscious of his particular medical role in this ending of Olga Kahn's life on earth.

'Pretty bad. It doesn't make much difference whether I eat or not.'

'But if you eat, you bring it up?' Olga nods. 'Time for morphine, don't you think?'

'Perhaps. But there are still things I have to do, Mervyn, it's too soon to die. I need a few more weeks.'

'Do you want to go into hospital? We could put you on an intravenous drip there.'

'Good Lord no. What a dreadful notion!'

'I thought you'd say that, but I had to suggest it. I'd be failing in my duty if I didn't.'

'I know, I know.' She pats his arm consolingly.

'I'll get Ruth to bring you in some Allvit, it's a drink, very easy to digest. Should keep you going for a bit. And I'll write out a prescription for morphine and give it to her. Just a low dose; we can increase it later, if needs be. Can I do anything else for you, Olga?'

'No, I don't think so. Oh yes, would you mind awfully making me some tea? Jane's not coming in till later today, and I'm terribly thirsty. I find lemon mint is best. The mint's in the stone sink by the back door. Just six or seven leaves. If it's not too much trouble.'

Mervyn Simpson stands in Olga Kahn's kitchen waiting for the kettle to boil, and reflecting, as he often does, on the nature of doctoring. Why is it that in the long, painful course of his medical training no one told him that sometimes the most healing thing a doctor can do is to make a cup of lemon mint tea for someone?

When he takes it upstairs, Olga has dropped off again. He puts the cup down gently. She wakes up. 'There was something else, Mervyn. I've just remembered. Young Flora Penfold and her pregnancy – I've been worrying about her. Tell me, is she going to be all right?'

Mervyn's amused by Olga's use of the word 'young'. 'I don't see why not,' he says, in answer to her question. 'She's fit, she wants it, she conceived outside this damn valley. I haven't seen her myself recently, a healthy woman's got no need for a doctor at these times. Connie's doing it, and she certainly hasn't mentioned anything amiss.'

'Good. I'd hate anything to go wrong. Flora is so *innocent*, don't you think, Mervyn? So *trusting*.'

Mervyn nods. 'You know her In-A-Relationship chappie?'

'Her what?'

'The father of the aforementioned fetus. The stable union, as it's called. Pete Wates from Ladywood Farm – him of the stripping business and the radical politics. Is *he* to be trusted, do you think, Olga?'

'Oh yes, yes. You think because he's not a conventional farmer he'll let her down?'

'I'm not an expert on people, Olga.'

Olga reaches for her mint tea. 'You may say that, Mervyn, but if you and I can't understand people, what chance do ordinary mortals have?' She sips the tea. 'That's the point, really. No one is ordinary. Pete Wates is just extraordinary in visible ways. God knows what the rest of them are up to. And you would know more about that than I, I expect.'

Mervyn Simpson nods again, thinking of diverse encounters in his consulting room over the years which he'd given up reciting to Diana because she never believed him and was out taking photographs anyway. Olive Grisewood as narrator of the waxing and waning lifestyle of Percy's haemorrhoids. He used to insist on Percy coming himself, but Olive had been adamant. He'd only ever seen Percy when he came to tackle various jobs around the house. For all he knew, they weren't his haemorrhoids at all. 'Comes of walking on two legs,' he'd said once to Olive. 'What do you expect us to do?' she'd responded tartly. His cousin Mike, the vet, had been able to throw almost as much light on the afflictions from which Mervyn's patients suffered as his own medical training. Take sexual disorders, for instance, which Mervyn found it hard to. According to Mike, these were rife among sheep: in the old days a good 20 per cent of ewes failed to be knocked up because the rams preferred each other. What it was that Petula Nevere's husband suffered from precisely Mervyn found it hard to say. Dressing up in ladies' underwear – Petula had wept when she'd described it the other side of his rubber plant – taken with a general failure of body hair did suggest a hormonal component. But on the other hand, if that was the case, where did Petula get all her miscarriages from?

None of my business, he'd decided, with regard to that one. Some people's problems are easier to tackle than others. Not that Jane Rivers had liked his suggestion about how to cure the rampant psoriasis on her head.

'Are you going to go on sitting there all day, Mervyn?'

Mervyn shakes himself. 'Sorry, got lost in my own thoughts.'

'You like coming to see me, don't you?' observes Olga. 'No, don't say anything. I'd like to go back to sleep now, if you don't mind.'

As Mervyn Simpson steers his way through it in his battered Honda, the relative peace of Little Tickencote is rent by a builder's lorry and a removal van. The Neveres are finally having their dormer window built, and Bridget Crowhurst is finally leaving the village. The last straw for her was the burglary one night of her school bag, bulging with the third years' essays on pollination, from its resting place in the hall. The school had been reasonably understanding, and the third years delighted, as most of them knew a good deal more about pollination than Bridget, but were considerably less capable of writing anything sensible about it. Bridget could have lived it down so far as Melton Comprehensive was concerned, but the incident had totally tipped her over the edge with respect to rural living, always an abomination anyway – the smells steaming off the roads and fields, the noise of birds cooing and whirring in the sky, the wretched lambs bleating all the time, and their equally awful mothers calling for them. The sequence of macabre events in Little Tickencote put the lid on it. Why, she'd only just got the compensation from the insurance company for the ruining of her Persian-style Wilton rug by the loosened plumbing connection.

At one end of the village Bridget supervises the loading of her belongings into a van bound for the urban climes of Glasgow, where a school friend of hers lives alone with a cat and two spare rooms Bridget will rent while sorting herself out. There's no shortage of teaching posts in Glasgow. Bridget should have left Little Tickencote at least two years ago, when she and Martin split. That's what Martin thinks, too. Perhaps in Glasgow Bridget will find a nice man whose scrotum, sufficiently cooled by the wearing of a kilt, will be able to yield her a baby. This had been Flora Penfold's advice – to get away. The news of Flora's pregnancy hasn't made it any easier for Bridget. Flora is a good deal older than Bridget, and has been considering motherhood for a good deal less long. Bridget wonders why Flora isn't worried about losing the baby, why she doesn't leave the place for ever.

Misadventures do cross Flora's mind, but Little Tickencote is where she's settled and where Pete Wates lives, so how could it be otherwise? Pete wants her to live with him, but the cottage on Life Hill isn't big enough for two, and though The Cottage on Cabbage Lane is, Flora doesn't want to relinquish her independence. 'One day,' says Doris, 'you'll have the farm, but Dad and I'll be here for a few years yet.' Doris wants Flora to consider it for lambing – for if Flora were upstairs in Pete's old room with the yellow-goosed wallpaper, Doris will be on hand to fetch and carry for her grandchild. Flora is stubborn, Doris gets cross, and Pete has to arbitrate. 'She means well, Flora. She doesn't understand why we don't set up house together and do it all properly.'

The most Flora will agree to is that Pete should move in before the birth so that he's on hand to help during and after. 'With you, and Connie and Dr Simpson, I'll be quite all right. From what I've read it's basically the same in humans as it is in animals. But that doesn't mean you can bring Valerie to this one.'

On the day in March when Olga Kahn dreams of the apartment on the Grubestrasse and lakes in Pennsylvania and elsewhere, Flora's concentration on Rural Rosey's own parallel (final) pregnancy is broken by the Neveres' building works. I never wanted to have this baby, grumbles Rural Rosey; it was your idea. One would have done me. I would have made him have the vasectomy. Then in two years, when little wellingtons are all at school, I could have done something interesting, like move back to London and become a computer programmer.

There's no future in that, explains Flora. It's not what this cartoon is about. You love the country really.

I do?

I think I'll put you away for today and go for a bicycle ride. Are you sure that's wise, pregnant lady? Be quiet, Rosey, think about yourself for a change.

Flora cycles north out of Little Tickencote towards Melton, and then down one of her favourite routes, a grass-covered track marked 'Unsuitable for motor vehicles' which cuts through the fields for a couple of miles before coming out on the hill peering down over the causeway of Jacob's Water. The March air is sharp, but Flora wears a tracksuit covered with an oiled wool jumper, a purple woolly hat, and gloves. The exertion warms her. The baby's movements, which felt at first like an army of tadpoles in a jam jar, have settled down to recognizable kicks and prods: the movement of the bicycle seems to soothe it.

On Flora's left, in the distance, the sky is a dark grey-blue, and faint bangs of thunder thud across the fields. Where the track comes out on to the road, she turns right away from the storm and up a not-too-irksome hill, where she rarely goes; usually she takes the more familiar route towards Jacob's Water, or the one down Life Hill, to where Pete Wates sits now in his pink-washed cottage in front of his Apple Mac, composing the next edition of the *European Labour Monthly*.

The angle of the road was deceptive, and just as Flora thinks the incline's over, it rises again. She's already in first gear, and her legs and lungs won't make it. She gets off. Ahead the road, an old Roman one, stretches straight as a die up and down over the gentle hills. A few more metres, and she'll be able to go soaring down it. It's very quiet up here, as she stands recovering her breath and looking around. It's then she notices to her left a building partially shielded from the road by a fence of pine trees. A board says 'Domak Pharmaceuticals UK', and the gates are open. Curious, Flora wheels her bicycle down the path and sees a long flat modern building with two big chimneys set in a white concrete drive, with weeds poking up here and there through cracks in the concrete. There's only one car parked there, and no obvious sign of life. Except that as Flora stands there watching, the figures of two men step into her line of vision, walking round the side of the building. One wears a brown zipped windcheater and a checked cap. The other's bald head, fringed with a dusting of white hair, looks remarkably like Henry Gosling's.

Flora feels suddenly uneasy, though there's no clear reason why she should. She stands on public land, and who could be more innocent than a woman out for a bicycle ride preparing her pelvic muscles for the feat of birth? She feels so uneasy that she decides not to make her presence known to the two men. But why would Abraham Varley and Henry Gosling be visiting Domak Pharmaceuticals? Come to that, how and why do they know each other?

She pushes her cycle to the top of the hill, gets on and makes her escape. Down the bottom, she's uncertain which way to go, as there's no signpost and she's lost without one. There are three choices. The road ahead is a continuation of the one beyond, lancing its rule-edged greyness through a landscape overhung by the metallic texture of the storm. Of the other two roads, one leads enticingly between fields of infant wheat, while the other would take her over a red-brick bridge and round a blind corner. To add to her predicament, it now begins to rain – large, light drops from the epicentre of the storm. Flora curses her lack of foresight in bringing no map and no rain cape. She decides to take the road over the bridge, as its general direction is downward, and you never know what may be round the corner.

She can see a signpost ahead, which is a relief. Just after the signpost, and coming towards her, is a man in a hooded anorak, also on a bicycle and accompanied by a large padding black dog. Flora thinks nothing of this, and is preparing to say good afternoon, as people in the country do, when the black dog suddenly breaks away from the cycle and rushes and lunges at her. The man calls him fiercely several times and the dog goes back, but not before Flora is seized with fright, and almost loses her balance. 'I'm sorry,' says the man from beneath his hood, passing her, 'I can't think what got into him.'

'It's all right,' she says weakly. When the man and the dog have gone, she gets off and stands there in the menacing countryside. She puts her hand to her stomach, but the baby moves like a football team. The black dog was only a dog. After a few minutes she rides again, comforted by the regular motion of the wheels. The rain has stopped here where she cycles, but not in the distance where the colour of the sky indicates that it must be falling in veritable torrents. The signpost tells her which way to go; she's not so far from home, after all. The peace is local, but it prevails. Now Flora cycles on an even road lined with oak trees on one side and open to a pale cornfield on the other. The cornfield lies like a piece of light golden lint over the cold earth and under the storm-crossed sky. The line where it meets the sky is pure and clear, accentuated by the sky's thundery colour. And now a rainbow falls in a flowing arch from heaven to cornfield: outrageous in its colours, red, yellow, violet, indigo, blue, joining earth to sky, like the jewels on the floor of the cathedral on the day that changed her life, but, like them, willing to hold its splendour only for a moment, only as long as you watch, so that if you turn away from it and back, it's gone, and nothing but the wide, vacant, angry sky remains.

The church clock is chiming five when she gets home and wheels her bicycle through the back garden, which is washed with the fresh smell of rain. Adam and Eve look at her blandly. Pablo crouches by the Christmas rose, which guards what, according to him, is an interesting tunnel by the stone wall. Under the apple tree the host of white-gold daffodils bend their faces – except that they don't any more. Someone has cut the lot, and laid the result across the step of the kitchen door. The daffodils' stems are crushed, their innocent heads no longer rampant but dismally recumbent, and mixed with clods of earth.

Flora sits down on the garden seat, conscious once more of a rapidly, audibly beating heart. What *is* this thing that is going on?

'Excuse me!' There's a knock at the garden gate – Petula Nevere in crimson stilettos and yellow trousers, the colour of the murdered daffodil hearts. 'I was upstairs just now – you know, with the builders, who are fitting our dormer window – and I looked out and saw what had happened. I'm ever so sorry. I just want to say that. We haven't talked much, but I know we're both victims of this – this thing, whatever it is.'

Flora nods. 'Thank you. I suppose you didn't see who did it?'

'No such luck. They were taking a risk in broad daylight, weren't they?'

'Come in and have a cup of tea,' invites Flora. 'Get away from the building noise for a bit. I want to close the door on those daffodils.'

'You must be very happy about the baby, then?' says Petula, over comforting tea and toast. 'It must be ever so nice to feel a baby in there, moving and growing. Mine never get further than ten weeks.' Now it's Flora's turn to say she's sorry. 'I've had the stitch, but that didn't help. It's not gravity, they just die. Armand says it's my past. I think it's his hormones, or this place. What do you think? That's why we're going for the dormer window. You have to have something to look forward to in life, don't you?'

20

Cook's Way

LAMBING IS WELL UNDER WAY when the first cuckoo in the Gwater Valley is heard on 21 April on the road from Manor Farm to Windy Bottom. Pete Wates hears it *en route* to Ladywood Farm, where Valerie Rumpstead is grappling womanfully with a breech presentation in a Blue-Faced Leicester. 'Yes, I have called Ramsay,' hisses Valerie, panting with the effort of pushing the lamb back in. 'It'd be easier with a mobile phone, as I keep saying. But now you've come, you can help me by shoving the old lady on her back. And pass me the jelly.'

Pete does what Valerie commands, reflecting on the enormous distance she's come in expertise and self-confidence, but particularly self-confidence, since she first arrived at Ladywood Farm in her grey-striped suit last spring. Even her eczema seems to have got better. Valerie's proving her worth not only on the farm, but to farmer's wife and farmer's mother Doris, as well, for whom she's provided company in the damp winter evenings, and a soul mate with whom Doris can discuss matters such as converting the house to natural gas, and the kitchen from its outmoded brown appearance to something a little more encouraging. Together Doris and Valerie have been perusing magazines rampant with flashy descriptions of ostentatious culinary furnishings, and thumbing through samples of wallpaper and catalogues of kitchen units and wall and floor tiles. Valerie fancies a nice Dutch blue, with some Mexican wall tiles depicting corn, but Doris is all for yellow – a soft pale yellow like cowslips or perhaps a brighter one, resembling tulips, though certainly not the chrome yellow of rape, which she can't abide – not just for its colour, but for the festering sugary odour the plant casts over the countryside. Doris sprays her house, and even the garden, with Johnson's Spring Flower air freshener to get rid of the smell of the rape. The spray gets into Frank's lungs, and is likely to give him turns. It's a good 'break' crop, is rape, and it brings them money.

The colour of the Ladywood Farm kitchen will continue to be debated for some time. Meanwhile, Valerie Rumpstead helps with lambing and asks for a pay rise. She's been reading the *European Labour Monthly*, and has discovered that the Wates's employment policies aren't quite consistent with Pete's politics. 'I don't even have the traditional perks of a farm labourer,' declares Valerie self-righteously, 'a tied cottage, and a little garden, help in times of sickness. What about BUPA? This is naked exploitation.'

Pete wonders about the word 'naked', as Valerie's heavily clothed in mohair jumpers at the time. 'What about the poor sheep?' he asks, deflected by viewing the mohairs. 'What about *their* exploitation?'

'Don't change the subject. I want a pay rise!'

'You're becoming a strong woman, Valerie,' says Pete. 'I admire that. But let me give you some advice: don't exhibit it too much in front of Father; it has the opposite effect on him.'

This year Valerie is allowed to help with the lambs' castration, though only after a decent interval has elapsed since the trauma of birth. As Pete had predicted, Flora is horrified at this ritual, but then much of country life continues to horrify Flora. Last year, walking with Pete round the fields of Ladywood Farm, and others, she'd noted how consistently the lambs' fate appeared to have befallen young cows as well. 'Makes better meat,' Pete had explained, 'cows or sheep – it's the same principle.'

'But how can you defend such a barbaric practice? Particularly being a vegetarian?'

'I can't. But it's another matter to convince the local farmers to abandon these practices. We will, on Ladywood Farm, in time. But not many revolutions happen overnight, Flora.'

For Frank Wates, the neutering of livestock is a purely economic proposition – as, indeed, is the whole of farming. 'If you had your way, lad,' grumbles Frank often enough, 'we'd all be sitting here starving surrounded by fat happy animals and pretty flowers that don't feed no one.' You see, says Pete to himself and to Flora, I have to bide my time. For now it's only small changes.

As small changes are made to the lambs, the full flush of spring comes to the Gwater Valley. Lathery hawthorn blossom decorates the hedges like scraps of paper in a writer's wastepaper basket; spring flowers colour the greening grass; the horse chestnuts on Lyndon

Road hold up their pearly blossoms like alabaster candles against a wall of green; and cowslips hang their little pouchy heads by the edges of fields sprinkled with castrated and uncastrated lambs feeding greedily from their mothers, their black tails wagging with joy. Only the daffodils under Flora's apple tree fail to rejuvenate, though they will, given another season. Flora tried to be philosophical about it when she told Pete and Olga, to pass it off as a trivial event – guess what's happened now, someone's chopped my flowers! Pete's response was to say he ought to stay with her every night, to protect her. Olga said, 'Of course, it's the baby. Don't be surprised if there aren't one or two more untoward happenings.'

Talking of these, says Flora to the lambs, as she passes them on her pelvic-floor-strengthening cycle rides, if only you knew what fate awaits even those of you who haven't been tampered with! She remembers from last year the awful days when the fields are rent with the cries of sheep and lambs trying to find one another in the new *mélange* of body smells that is consequent on shearing: the ungainly posture of the skinny, chilly-looking mother sheep and quivering noses and still tails of the lambs; and after that the even more awful time when the quivering noses are much reduced in number, and the countryside is full of the unassuaged pain of ewes calling for the lambs that have gone to be sold and made into Sunday and other dinners.

Flora pats her stomach protectively. Don't worry, little one, I shan't abandon you. On the contrary, she's already taking mighty steps to protect him or her, what with the reading of the advice manuals, the imbibing of vitamins, the regular trips to Connie Barker's antenatal clinic, and the procuring of Percy and Ron to kit out bedroom number two in The Cottage as a nursery, with built-in cupboards finished in old pine, and a mellow sanded and varnished floor which will carry a warm, cheerful rug when she's had the time to find one, and a little flowered washbasin in the corner of the room to cater for what the books refer to as Baby's Needs.

Trevor the vicar comes one day when Percy is banging away and Ron, singing Tchaikovsky's 'Romeo and Juliet' overture, is making gendered plumbing connections. It's late May by now, and Flora's own lambing is a mere eight weeks away. The vicar notices the dried bunch of St John's wort above the kitchen door: 'You've decided to trust in herbs, have you, Miss Penfold, rather than in God?'

'It was you who told me about the St John's wort,' points out Flora, who is making a cup of tea, wishing to be hospitable to Little

Tickencote's vicar, though not to the extent of adopting religion for him.

'So it was. And are you keeping well, Miss Penfold?' Trevor Tilley looks meaningfully at Flora's stomach.

'I am.'

'Not worried overmuch about the curse of Little Tickencote?'

'I seem to have avoided it so far. Well, not entirely; there have been a few minor incidents.'

'Have you heard my water? I meant to mention it when I came before. The sound of the river by the altar in the church.'

'I'll come and listen sometime,' says Flora, entertaining the somehow parallel image of Connie Barker listening with trumpet pressed to her stomach for the rush of water round the baby.

'Ted Rippington's still sorrowing,' says the vicar, conversationally.

What an odd word, sorrowing!

'The death of a person of ripe old age is one thing, but that of one so young quite another, don't you think, Miss Penfold? Fanny Watkins's murder is a blight on the village!'

'The police never found anything conclusive, did they?'

'The police may not have done, but whoever it is is known by God, you can be sure of that. Whoever it is, God is watching him; he walks in the light of God's knowledge, but not in forgiveness.' Trevor takes his tea into the garden.

'I thought God was all-forgiving.'

The vicar seems a little taken aback by this. 'In time, in time.'

'You must have a really difficult job, Vicar,' observes Flora, trying to be sympathetic, 'what with all this crime, all these illicit unions' – she glances down at the result of her own – 'and all these generally sinful things occurring.'

'The Church must move with the times. Which reminds me, Miss Penfold, are we going to see you in it now your time is approaching?'

'I told you, Vicar,' says Flora, 'I'm not a believer. I might make the harvest festival, though; I rather fancy watching those lines of little children holding all manner of fruits and vegetables and tins of baked beans, and thanking God for the Common Market and the services of cow-castrators.'

The vicar looks shocked.

'Sorry, I didn't mean to be outrageous.'

'What about a christening?' Trevor Tilley lives in hope – he has to. The font in All Saints' hasn't been used for ten years now. He likes christenings. He likes holding babies and making them cry and everyone smiling – the proud mother, and the proud father . . . 'Marriage?' he inquires hopefully.

'I don't think so. I'm sorry to disappoint you, Vicar.'

Trevor sighs. 'It's all right, Miss Penfold, I'm used to it. As I said, times have changed. It's just not quite what I thought the ministry was all about when I decided to take it up.'

'I can see that. Perhaps it's a bit like the difference between images of country life and the real thing.'

'Have you been disappointed, then, Miss Penfold, coming to live amongst us here?'

'Not disappointed. Surprised, perhaps. Before I came, I saw the country as a pleasant, essentially *good* place. You know, where people are nice to each other and considerate and nothing bad happens because – well – nothing much happens of any kind at all. But it's not really like that.'

Trevor sighs again. 'No, indeed not. I don't know what's going on round here, Miss Penfold, but I don't like it. It's almost a case for exorcism, I feel. I'm not terribly surprised you're hanging up herbs against the devil. If I weren't a vicar, I'd be doing the same myself.'

The advancing spring also brings Pleasance Oliphant back from the nursing home where Mervyn Simpson sent her to dry out. She is sober and ready for her reunion with daughter Cornelia, who has grown in self-confidence by the same kind of amount as Valerie Rumpstead, but for different reasons. Due to the temporary freedom from her overweening mother (it's not Pleasance's fault she's overweening – think back to her own circumstances and need to mother the needy Odile), Cornelia has been able to see her father – and, indeed, her entire background – a good deal more clearly. It seems to her, with all the wisdom she can muster from this new vantage point, that her role has been fundamentally misconceived. For all the material luxury heaped on her, she has lacked what Pete Wates writes about *ad nauseam* in his *European Labour Monthly*: the right to unalienated labour. Or, in fact, the right to labour of any kind at all. Fripperies and time-wasting suit some people, but not Cornelia Oliphant. She ate because she had nothing else to do. She ate and fattened herself up for Robbie Belton, who rejected her, because she knew that as Mrs Belton she would also have nothing to do. Cornelia confides her new-found insight to Cook, from whom she feels she may have derived it in the first place. Watching Cook's days mould themselves more or less happily round the requirements of her job, the household, round the regular production of food, Cornelia has come firmly to the conclusion that Cook's way is better than hers.

Cook looks as though she knew this already. But 'You try telling that to Sir,' is all she says.

When Cornelia does, the result is incomprehension. 'But what do you mean, *work*, Corney? Do you mean in Tesco's or something? I can see that might be amusing for a while, but . . . why do you want to *work*? I shall go on giving you an allowance until Mr Right comes along, you know.'

'He's been and gone,' says Cornelia, with a passing pang of fondness for Robbie Belton.

'Plenty of fish in the pond,' says Bream kindly, thinking of Jacob's Water.

'Life isn't just a fishing expedition,' retorts Cornelia.

'No? What is it, then?' Bream's own lifestyle ill fits him to understand what his daughter is on about. It's always seemed to him quite sufficient, having Overton Hall and the estate and the conditions of one's stocks and shares to look after, peppered by occasional visits to the House of Lords and Mary Widdowson. Especially Mary Widdowson, who has become his great solace in times of trouble. Unfortunately, the portrait is nearly finished now, with the exception of a square of landscape detail on the right edge.

Cornelia, not to be deterred, puts a plan to her mother when Pleasance comes home. Cornelia and Pleasance are to start a business together, she announces. This will provide an answer to both sets of problems – her eating disorder and her mother's drinking one. 'But what will it be, darling?' cries Pleasance, delighted with the idea.

'I don't know yet, Mother,' admits Cornelia. 'Perhaps an antique shop? Or something more rural. What about herbs?'

And that's how it comes about that a new shop-front springs up in Melton: 'The Green Herb Company'. 'A bit pretentious, don't you think?' comments Bream, completely mystified. 'And what about non-green herbs? There must be some of those.'

Cornelia, who's consulted a PR company, insists that the name must have 'Green' in it. Pete Wates, with whom she's also discussed this idea, and his lady, a very sentient artistic type, agree with her.

'I don't know what to do, Mervyn,' confesses Bream to Mervyn Simpson – not for the first time, or the last. 'Women mystify me.'

'You know my theories on the subject, old chap. Don't look to me for any further enlightenment. I should just give up and let them get on with it, if I were you. They'll probably make a mess of it and come running to you in tears in six months' time.'

'But they're even asking me for money, Mervyn!'

'Well, what's unusual about that?'

'I mean *capital* for the business. They want twenty thousand pounds of my money!'

While Bream Oliphant prevaricates about the wisdom of lending his wife and daughter this sum, they go to the NatWest in Oakingham and borrow it from there. It's remarkably simple. 'Why didn't we do this before, darling?' enthuses Pleasance on the way home. 'Isn't it *fun*!'

'It's not supposed to be *fun*, Mother, it's supposed to be *work*. We're going to pay ourselves salaries and turn ourselves into independent women.'

'Good Lord, are we? What fun!'

While the Oliphants (or two of them) sort themselves out in Meltshire, an apparently disconnected scene takes place in a private mental hospital run by nuns in Yorkshire. Our Lady of All Souls, where Odile Ruddle has been incarcerated for nineteen years, sees few visitors. The woman who draws up in her car on a Saturday in the middle of June is certainly a stranger to Our Lady. She is a formidable figure, stepping out of her black Mini, dressed in matching garb. Inside the hall she has to take her dark glasses off to see at all in the dusky interior. 'Good afternoon. I've come to visit Miss Odile Ruddle. I did ring. Jane Rivers is the name.'

The young novice looks at her curiously. The only person who comes to see Miss Ruddle is her sister. She comes once a year, bringing two potted hydrangeas and a box of crystallized fruits, and stays half an hour. The bills are paid regularly by Lord Bream Oliphant, the old lady's brother-in-law. 'I'll just go and fetch the doctor,' she says.

While Jane waits, she looks around. It's not a prepossessing place, though an attempt has been made to make the reception area homely, with floral chair covers and watery landscapes. A disinfectant smell hangs over the place, as invasive as the scent of rapeseed is in Meltshire.

The doctor is at pains to ensure that Jane Rivers knows the condition of the old lady she's come to see. 'Of course she's not that old – only seventy. She came to us with a diagnosis of premature Alzheimer's in

1973. In such patients, the body tends to age prematurely, too. We keep her mildly sedated; it's kinder to her, and it does make things easier for the nuns.'

He leads Jane to a medium-sized room on the second floor, with a pleasant enough view over the front lawn, and further away the green-golden blur of a real summer landscape. There are several pieces of fine furniture – a velvet chesterfield, a mahogany chest, and an ornate mirror with angels on it. In a bed against the right-hand wall is a shrivelled doll-like figure, wrapped in a shawl, with hands lying aimlessly on top of the pink cover. Odile's straight silver-grey hair has kept its fine silky texture. Her pale-blue eyes are open, but vacant, looking at and seeing nothing.

'She doesn't recognize anyone,' says Dr Stark. 'On her good days, she gives us all names – from the past, presumably. She can be quite amusing then. She calls Sister Josephine Pleasance. I believe that was her sister's name.'

'Is,' corrects Jane.

'Miss Ruddle.' Dr Stark bends low, puts his face right in front of Odile's and seems almost to bellow. 'Miss Ruddle! You've got a visitor. Aren't you lucky? You've got a visitor!'

'Thank you, Dr Stark,' says Jane, firmly but politely. 'You can leave us alone now.'

'Are you sure you'll be all right?' He seems nervous. 'Ring the bell if you want anything.'

Jane waits until Dr Stark has closed the door, then she draws up a chair and sits by the bed. 'Does he think you're going to attack me or something?' She picks up one of the listless hands and holds it, looking at it – at the blue veins crossing it, and the creased milky skin, and the pearly, surprisingly unmarked, nails. 'I don't think that's very likely, do you?' She strokes the hand for a few minutes without saying anything.

The silky head turns and looks at her. 'Hallo,' says Odile Ruddle, suddenly, like a bird. 'Hallo!' She nods her head disapprovingly. 'It's not warm today, is it? Not a nice day. Did you bring my money, then, as I asked you to?' The look in her misty blue eyes is a little agitated.

'Shush,' says Jane. 'No I didn't, but it'll be all right.'

'Will it? That's what they all say. I told Pleasance the stables needed clearing out, but she brought all these babies home instead. The place was full of babies; I didn't know whose they were!'

When Jane says nothing, Odile looks at her almost as though she were living in the present, after all. 'Why are you crying?' she asks sharply. 'I didn't tell you to cry, did I?'

Jane says in a low voice, not expecting the old lady to hear, 'No, indeed you didn't. I wanted to come to see you. I just wanted to see you. That's all. Please forgive me if I've upset you. It's not what I intended. I hope you're all right here, that they're kind to you. Some of us do lead lives that haven't turned out quite right, but it's not our fault. No, it's not our fault.'

She sits in silence for a while, watching Odile sleep. Then she bends and kisses the crenellated forehead, and slips away.

Jane Rivers, detective-story writer, is also detective of her own life, and of Meltshire's. Not for nothing had she learnt in the probate office how to track people through the rituals of birth and death, of inheritance and disinheritance, of burial and disposition, of recovery and birth. But Jane Rivers, clever detective though she is, is having problems with her writing which the visit to Our Lady isn't designed to unblock. The problems centre on the plight Georgia Kelly's got herself into with the one-legged Professor of Psychology in the sequel to *Problems in Paradise*. Realizing that the Marriage was a Mistake, Georgia finds her various escape routes dogged by Professor Malling's own agendas, which constitute the main plot of what, for the time being, is called *A Desperate Remedy*. Malling has to get his own back on a crowd of rumbustious n'er-do-wells in the Glasgow slum where he was raised, for mocking his physique during an unhappy adolescence. His training in psychology has unfortunately given him no insight into his own.

At such times of writer's block, no amount of sitting at her desk and staring contemplatively at the paper and out of the window will do the trick. Walking helps; the physical action of moving one's limbs can sometimes free the mind in sympathy. And so, after the trip to Yorkshire, and as the Meltshire summer waxes, Jane Rivers is often to be seen on its byways and fields, meditating her own, Georgia Kelly's, and other people's fates. One afternoon in mid July, she takes the road to Lyndon and sees two blackbirds unpleasantly dragging a dead pheasant across the road, leaving feathers and bloody entrails on the crusty newly tarmacked surface. Although it's high summer, the countryside seems to be full of decay. Stinking rabbits lay flattened on Dead Bunny Lane as Jane passed it just now, and there was a dead crow in the entrance to a cornfield. Jane's perceptions have something to do with the curse that hangs over the villages of the Gwater: the countryside is full of omens. In Owlston Wood she stoops and picks wild flowers for Olga: yellow, violet, red. The wood won't miss them: the earth will replenish and regenerate. But Olga Kahn won't. More useful than walking as an antidote to writer's block is talking, and particularly, for Jane, talking to Olga Kahn. Now Olga is ill, now Olga is dying, Jane won't have that – her – any more. Over the past seven years, she's become dependent on Olga as a sounding board for ideas and problems; and on Olga's ability to identify and sort out where the real confusions lie.

Now, in her last illness, Olga can still talk to Jane about Georgia Kelly and her scrapes – and, indeed, does so – but there's a shift in Olga's perspective which is making her less patient than she would otherwise be with Georgia's mistakes, and with the procrastinations and weaknesses of other fictional and real-life characters as well. Jane feels that Olga is impatient, too, for the first time, of Jane's own commitment to the genre of detective-story writing. It's hardly a noble pastime. But it *is* writing. In its core of creative work, Jane feels she is making more of her life than simply living it. To survive is not the point. To move on a step; to react to or against one's given role and status, so as to change them – to transcend survival, *that* is the point.

A *modus vivendi*, that's all Jane would call it. From trapped beginnings, she's made a life for herself. Not a perfect life, nothing grand or visionary – she couldn't cope with that. But something intelligible, and manageable – in which, however, there are few friends, few confidantes. Except for Olga Kahn. Now Olga is dying, Jane spends a lot of time in her cottage, and has recently taken to sleeping there at night as well. Olga won't have a nurse in, or any other help, and it's something that Jane does well, looking after a sick person, for didn't she have the long apprenticeship of tending to her own crabby mother, which was, however, an altogether different experience from helping the courageous and selfless Olga Kahn to die? Jane knows from practice all about pain, and about how it's the little things – the pillows propped at certain angles, the cup of liquid warm but not too hot – that make the difference.

Olga is grateful for her attentions. Who else would do these things for her, were it not for Jane? Young Flora Penfold might have done, had she not gone in for motherhood. Olga's got no family left – only nephew Daniel, who helped her to settle here, and who is currently in South America. Daniel will be sad to know she died, and he will get half her house and money – such as it is. Jane will get the other half. She's left a simple will, and a note requesting cremation. The will says that if people want to remember her, they should plant flowers on the common land of Little Tickencote – flowers for everyone to see.

That afternoon, coming back from her walk to Olga's cottage, Jane goes to pick up a few things from her own on the way – from her Cottage on Baker's Hill opposite the Post Office where the comings and goings of Little Tickencote can be observed – stamp-buying, money-collecting, provisioning, gossiping – and from where Jane can see Jack Roebuck behind the counter and Joan on her darting trips between the shop and the back room where her washing basin, two hairdryers and baskets of brightly coloured curlers and chemicals await the chance to decorate or damage the heads of Little Tickencote ladies. Jack Roebuck knows Jane Rivers can see him, and he can see Jane Rivers, too. Sometimes Jack fancies that Jane is writing about him. He said this to Jane once; she replied staunchly that she never writes about anyone in the village; that would be much too dangerous.

But why does Jack think Jane is writing about him? Perhaps it's not only fear, but a hidden desire to be reborn in print that lies behind his concern. When people say they don't want to be written about, they very often mean that they do. Not that Jack would want his story told in such a manner that it could be attributed to him; but there is a story to be told, and it has been quite an effort for Jack and Joan Roebuck to keep a lid on it all these years.

'Incest,' psychoanalyst detective Olga had said, when Jane had talked to her about it recently, 'is, as we now know, far more common than was once thought. Freud realized that, just as he knew that women's stories of being sexually abused by their fathers and others weren't fanciful accounts but real happenings.'

'So you knew all the time, Olga, about the Roebucks?'

'Er-hum. "Knew?" "Know?" What is knowledge? I put two and two together like anybody else, and made four. Not many people would take the same trouble as you, Jane, to check out the birth certificate, and the absence of any other sort. It doesn't get you anywhere, except that you do feel you "know" in a way I don't. I merely surmise. You have proof. But in the end it comes to the same.'

Jack and Joan Roebuck watch Jane, as she comes back to Stonecrop Cottage to fetch some things for Olga. They know what she's doing. 'It won't be long,' says Jack to his sister. 'The nurse is giving her morphine now. Go and see her, Joan, even if she doesn't need her hair doing. This is a time for women to help each other. Take some Kleenex, and some Cussons' Imperial Leather soap. Perhaps a box of those thin mint crisps, behind the birthday cards. Maybe she could get one or two of those down her.'

Olga is sitting up, watching the sun dappling the fields and the dark-green tops of the trees in Barratt's Coppice, when Jane comes back. 'I've made you some tea,' says Jane, laying the tray on the table by the bed, 'and I've brought you some nice fresh goat's yoghurt from Ladywood Farm. And I've picked you a few flowers.'

Olga looks at the offerings on the tray distractedly. 'Thank you, dear. I'll have the tea in a minute. I'm waiting for the injection to work. The nurse has just been.'

'Does it hurt a lot, Olga?'

Olga shrugs. 'Pain is relative. It's the worst pain I've ever had, but what does that mean? Sit down, Jane, stay with me a while. I've been thinking. About Little Tickencote and its happenings. I feel an urge to get it all straight before I die. I found that place in *Problems in Paradise* you mentioned yesterday, and I think I've cracked some of it. But you'll have to help me with the rest.'

Olga bends over, and picks up the cup of tea. She puts the saucer on the window ledge, which is on a level with the white pillows, and holds the cup carefully. It's as though every action requires thinking about, if it is not to cause her pain – or perhaps because it does.

'Do you know Heine's poem about the Lorelei, Jane? The sirens who lured sailors to their deaths. In the symbolism of the unconscious, water represents woman, the primal element. Among the Venezuelan Indians, the dead turn to water, and then they return to earth as women: women were made from water. Or if not, then in our own cultural origin myth, from Adam's rib.' Olga stops, and looks at Jane. 'Am I rambling on?'

'Yes, but I know what you're talking about. You're talking about Jacob's Water, and about the links between that and the queer things that have been going on.'

'They date from when the reservoir was created, you said once, I think.'

'I believe so.'

'That's consistent with my theory.'

'And with mine.'

'That someone who didn't want the reservoir is causing these adverse events to happen.'

'Precisely.'

'At first I thought it was the Oliphants, but they lack imagination. Most of the other people who were directly affected have left the area. With one well-known exception: Abraham Varley. It's no secret that Abraham is drawn to that water. He both hates and loves it. I don't know why they gave him the fish to look after, that always seemed to me a very dangerous idea. But Abraham could have done all those things, couldn't he, Jane?'

'He could, yes.'

'Including causing poor Fanny's death?'

'Yes, it's possible. But what's the motive, Olga?'

'Er-hum. Spoken like a true detective-story writer! Yes, the motive. Well, this has taken me a while, and I've not got very far. This is where I need your help.' Olga takes a deep breath. 'We have to go back a bit, to start with. Eve eats of the Tree of Knowledge, which lands both her and Adam in trouble, but particularly her. Because she tempts Adam to eat, to know, she is seen as temptress *par excellence*. Because women are seen in carnal terms, Eve is Adam's downfall sexually. Men fear women because of sex, because of what women know – which is more or less everything.'

Olga lies back on the pillow. Beads of sweat sparkle on her forehead. 'Open the window, Jane, would you?' she goes on. 'Abraham Varley was married to a witch's daughter, Zillah Woodcock. What happened to her, Jane, do you know?'

'She disappeared in 1974, when the valley was drowned.'

'Ah! I thought as much. It's obvious that Abraham Varley has more than the usual complex attitudes to women, and the usual ones are complicated enough, God knows. You only have to look round this place to see that. Think of Jasper Lancing beating up poor defenceless Annabel, or Jack Roebuck living with his sister, or Mr Nevere in Tiptree Cottage, or . . .'

'Yes, yes,' says Jane, impatiently. 'So Little Tickencote is full of all the normal human destructiveness and mess – what do you expect?'

'Some people expect something different in the countryside,' observes Olga. 'Flora Penfold, for instance. By the way, Jane, Dr Simpson's nurse told me Flora should be having her baby soon. Should be tonight or tomorrow, Ruth thinks. Isn't that exciting, Jane!'

'It is,' says Jane, 'but get back to where you were, Olga, before you forget it.'

'Yes, where was I?'

'With men and women.'

'Well, that's not original, is it? Ah yes, Abraham Varley. He blames women for the drowning of the valley and his farm. That we can ascertain by working backwards from events to their causes, as it were. But beyond the fact that he was intimately acquainted with the daughter of the witch, and that she was probably the first woman he punished for the flooding of his farm – beyond that I cannot see. My knowledge of the human condition – if you can call it that – won't get me any further. It's empirical facts I need. Though young Flora's father's papers have helped. I told you about those, didn't I, Jane? A most fascinating manuscript about the community flooded by Jacob's Water – not just about the social networks, but the cultural *set* of the place, which is what we need to know. The rest of it *you* know, don't you, Jane? What do you say, Jane?'

'How do you know?'

'Well, I know you. To a certain extent. This – this friendship we've built up over the years has given me some insight into your character, though you do clothe it in black and generally behave like a dark horse. Knowing you, I can surmise that there are things you know that I don't. So I have to rely on you for the rest of the picture. Why has Abraham Varley got it in for women, Jane? And what does that have to do with the drowning of the valley?'

The late-afternoon sun flashes in and out of the trees, and a light wind lifts the curtains at Olga Kahn's window, relieving the scent of sickness in the room. A crowd of swallows lifts itself into the sky. 'They're like the birds you see over Jacob's Water, aren't they, Jane? I'll never go there again, now. So many places I'll never see again, so many people . . . But I'm not complaining. I've had a good life, and an interesting one. My mind has been engaged, I've never been bored. That's the most important thing, Jane. Who are you, really, Jane? It's quite safe to tell me now.'

Jane Rivers waits a minute, thinking, while the wind wanders the room and Olga watches her from the high bed. 'I'm Abraham Varley's daughter,' she says quietly, then. 'I am his daughter.'

'Ah!'

'So now do you understand?'

'I'm beginning to. Abraham and Odile had a liaison . . .'

'Before Abraham married Zillah Woodcock,' interrupts Jane.

'Whatever, whatever.' Olga waves a dismissive hand. 'That's really of no account now. Zillah the witch figures in the Penfold manuscript,' she interpolates, thoughtfully. 'You might like to read that bit. Ask Flora, I've given the papers back. So you were adopted, were you, Jane?'

'A few days after birth. It was arranged by a local doctor. Not Dr Simpson, another. In Cedarton, I think.'

'Is that what brought you to live here?'

'I wanted to come back to my origins. To the landscape which arranged my birth. The country, not the individuals. That's how I think of it.'

'I understand that. But to go back to the puzzle – although you were adopted, it was a scandal, was it not, all the same, an out-of-wedlock child in such a well-connected family? The child – you – was kept a secret. But perhaps someone found out, there was blackmail . . . and that, on top of Odile's misbehaviour with money at the casino, wherever it was, produced a strong economic motive for the Ruddles to sell out. Yes, that's it. Those are the missing pieces, Jane.'

'It's as we said, Olga – you and I approach things from different directions, but we reach the same place. I wasn't chasing the puzzle of Little Tickencote, but my own origins. When I found out I was adopted it was a shock, but I didn't do anything about it for a long time. Then, when I came here, after a bit, I decided to try and trace my mother. That wasn't too difficult, though it took a while. But of course the birth certificate didn't have any information about my father. I got that from Pleasance Oliphant, after a struggle. She didn't want to tell me. She's my aunt, Olga – imagine that!'

'Er-hum. We don't choose our parents, Jane. If we did, we shrinks would be out of business.'

'I find it hard to feel any sympathy for her.'

Olga nods.

'Now my mother, that's different. She's still alive, I've seen her. She's a little crazy old woman. They abandoned her – Pleasance and Bream Oliphant. She had a raw deal. But I suspect she gave as good as she got, in her time.'

'So Pleasance did tell you that Abraham was your father?'

'I told her I had a right to know. She said no one but her knew. Abraham doesn't know – he was never told.'

'And have *you* told him?'

'No, I'm afraid to.'

'Why, if he's your father?'

'What is biology, Olga, except for conveying odd insignia, such as streaks of white hair?'

'What?'

Jane puts her hands up to her hair, and lifts it. 'There, Olga, now do you see?' At the front of her hair is a brilliant streak of white, standing out amidst the ordinary brown. 'It's like Abraham's. A recessive gene. If I didn't wear a wig, everyone would know.'

'Er-hum. Put the wig on again, dear,' instructs Olga. 'I've got used to thinking of you with black hair. That's a detail, too. But why don't you want people to know?'

'What kind of person is Abraham Varley? We know, don't we? We've just worked it out. I'm not sure I want to own him. In fact, it gives me a very odd feeling. Except that I can tell you this, Olga – it's better knowing who your father is, even if he's a man like Abraham Varley, than not knowing at all.'

'Origin myths,' mutters Olga. 'The rule of the father. All right, Jane, we're nearly there. Let's finish it before the pain comes back. We have one mystery left, don't we? Why the spell against children in the Gwater Valley, which our neighbour, Flora Penfold, is at this very moment defying?'

'Witchcraft,' says Jane. 'What else could it be? But how, and why?'

'Adam and Eve again. "The goddess Kali dances on the corpses of slain men. Samson, whom no man could conquer, is robbed of his strength by Delilah . . . Witches are burnt because male priests fear the work of the Devil in them." Karen Horney, "Observations on a Specific Difference in the Dread Felt by Men and Women Respectively for the Opposite Sex".' Olga closes her eyes and continues her recitation. '"The series of such instances is infinite; always, everywhere, the man strives to rid himself of his dread of women by objectifying it. 'It is not', he says, 'that I dread her; it is that she herself is malignant, capable of any crime, a beast of prey, a vampire, a witch, insatiable in her desires. She is the very personification of what is sinister.'"'

'I don't doubt you're right.' Jane Rivers leans back, folds her arms, relaxes somewhat.

'Not me. Karen Horney. By the way, I've left my own manuscript for you to tidy up.'

'As if I didn't have enough untidy manuscripts of my own!'

'It's good for you, Jane, you know that. Work. You read her, Horney. The conflict between dreading something and wanting it. Work is the only solution. Count yourself lucky, my friend.'

'So what about witchcraft?' persists Jane.

'The witchcraft theme is pretty strong. I didn't know how strong until young Flora produced those papers. We can only surmise. But working backwards from events to causes, it'll do as an explanation. Though there probably is another, better one somewhere.'

'Well, at least I'm not the daughter of a witch myself,' says Jane gratefully.

'No, you aren't. Remember that party last year in the Old Sun Inn, Jane? You were the black witch and I was the white.'

'It's true, isn't it, Olga? I'm the bad one.'

'You're no blacker than I am. Except for your disguise. Don't blame yourself for anything, Jane, it's a very destructive emotion. You must certainly not blame yourself for Abraham Varley. He is not your responsibility, just as you were never his.'

While Jane ponders on this, the sound of Olga's breathing changes, and she sleeps. Getting up to close the window, Jane sees how terribly thin she is now – almost as thin as her own mother, lying with the nuns in a pool of jumbled memories. The yoghurt lies uneaten on the table, the teaspoon of thick honey in the middle catching the falling sun as it glints through the window, and over Olga's bed to rest in a bright puddle on the old wooden floor.

As Jane Rivers stands there, she sees the very pregnant Flora Penfold make her way to the church. It's a double vision for Jane: at the same time as she sees Flora, she also sees Odile Ruddle, with a straightened back and a youthful sparkle in her eyes, carrying her and Abraham Varley's unborn baby, beneath a flower-sprigged maternity dress, through the meadows between Bisbrooke and Eglethorpe in the days when the cows Sally, Rainbow and Curly nuzzled the hedges of Varley's farm, and the lilacs on the wide path fronting Barrow Grange were home to a thousand butterflies. Oh yes, she'd researched it all; much of it, in fact, appears, slightly veiled, in *Problems in Paradise*.

Jane watches as Flora unhooks the red-painted iron door covering the church porch, and goes inside. Flora has come to find the spot where you can hear the disappeared Gwater River rushing and chortling in underground channels beneath the earth. It's late in her pregnancy: everything is difficult and nothing is satisfying – only the birth will be that. Marilyn Hoskins had rung up this afternoon from California; she'd just heard about the baby from a mutual friend, and had called to enthuse: 'Jim and I are *so* happy for you! You did mean it, didn't you, Flora, about getting back to nature! We're planning another of our trips in the fall; we'd adore to come and stay with you for a few days!' And no sooner had Flora put the phone down on Marilyn than there was her mother on the line: 'I'm sending you a package from Bettergoods,' said Irina, 'subtitled "The best in homecare . . . for all your home needs". A net laundry bag, a knitwear-drying platform, a fun bin – that's for the baby – and something called a Bug Katcha – very ingenious, it has a little plastic shutter which plops down and catches the fly or beetle or whatever so you don't even have to touch it! Now don't you think that's clever, darling!'

It's hot in The Cottage, and the geese that wander Pudding Bag Lane from Pat Titmarsh's garden are crouching in the shadow of the wall for shade when Flora walks over to the church. Inside, it's cooler. She walks up the central aisle to the place to the left of the altar where Trevor Tilley said the sound could be heard. She stands there on the cold stone inhaling the faintly incensed air, the scent of waxed wood and white summer roses stacked in brass vases by Mrs Pringle, Dr Simpson's receptionist's mother, whose turn it is to do the church flowers this week. The air settles round Flora, and the profane noise of the countryside retreats beyond the oasis of silence that pretends to be God's holy place. Now Flora is stationary, the baby moves inside her, but flesh double-glazes the sound of fetal limbs splashing. Is there any other splashing to be heard? Flora strains her ears. But instead of the muffled rushing Gwater, there are men's voices coming out of the room at the back of the church, under the bell tower. After a moment or two, Bream Oliphant pushes the blue curtain aside over his broad shoulders; after him comes Brian Redfern, with his typically round-shouldered gait. Bream's lordly voice rises above the piles of navy hymn books: 'Thanks for the hospitality, Tilley. We'll see what we can do about you-know-who. Right will win, left will lose.' Bream guffaws, and slaps Brian Redfern on his rounded back. 'And don't worry about the planning meeting, Redfern, the Chairman's a friend of mine. Twenty Scandinavian homes, did you say?' Brian Redfern says something then that Flora, who is shielded from view by the oak pulpit, can't hear. 'The sailing club's doing well, isn't it?' It's Bream's voice again. 'I'm glad we got that one through. All this stuff about preserving the environment's all very well, but England's a commercial country. I think the boats add colour, anyway. What? Don't mention it. Glad to help, old chap. By the way, have you had the plans for the leisure complex drawn up yet?'

With much clanging of the big wooden door, the men leave All

Saints' to Flora, who still stands by the altar where the underground river ought to be heard. And when the air has disposed of the unsettling conversations about subjects unsuitable for a church, she does hear it, or fancies she does: a deep, just-audible roar that brings to mind black fern-laden waters speeding with volcanic power through the gusty gaseous bowels of Little Tickencote.

21

Adam and Eve

The spire of All Saints' rises up between the cottage in which Olga Kahn is dying and the one in which Flora Penfold is giving birth. In Flora's cottage, it is the midwife Connie Barker who sits beside the bed. Connie is knitting a blue-and-white football jersey for her nephew, Jason, who lives in Taunton. Everything is ready – the sterilized delivery pack, the baby's cot and clothes, the mother. Connie is an old-fashioned midwife – she believes in letting Mother Nature take her course, aided by some iron principles of midwifery: never leave a mother alone, check the baby's heart regularly but between contractions, if in doubt call the doctor, but otherwise don't – doctors have an unfortunate habit of meddling. Connie lets all this new-fangled stuff about water birth and delivery in a squatting position and letting the cord pulsate for hours before cutting it just wash over her. *Her* mothers – not that there are very many of them these days – deliver the old way. Fashions in childbirth come and go. Birth is women's business. The greatest skill is waiting.

Connie's needles click, and on the bed Flora breathes heavily. The sun has set now, and the patch of sky that can be seen through one of the windows is streaked with pink. It'll be a fine day tomorrow. Connie listens to Flora's breathing. 'Not so fast, dear,' she admonishes, 'or you'll feel dizzy.' She puts her knitting down and her hand on Flora's abdomen. 'That's moving down very nicely.' She looks at her watch. 'When did you say Mr Wates would be back?'

'Nine o'clock,' says Flora, gasping.

'That's all right, then. He can make me a cup of tea when he comes. Nothing for you, though, my dear, not till after you've got this babe out into the world. Then you can have as much tea as you like!'

Watching the sunset by the eastern shore of Jacob's Water is Abraham Varley. He looks the same as he has for years – the same clothes, the same dull expression. He stands in the same position, with the causeway to his right and the sailing club to his left. Behind him a fence of young willows shields him from view, and in front is the flat blue-and-silver stretch of water, over which birds swoop and fly, calling to each other, and under which lie his farm, his land, his house, the beloved reaches of Bisbrooke Hundred and Eglethorpe, razed to the ground and gone for ever.

Not in Abraham's head, though. When he looks at the water, he sees it all exactly as it was, even with Zillah sitting by the kitchen range, and the pots boiling on the stove, and the door open letting the sunlight and the fragrant air in. Zillah was a small, dumpy woman with a swarthy skin – she could have been a Spanish gypsy. Thick black hair and moody, flashing eyes. A rare smile, but a quick temper. People had been surprised when Abraham married Zillah, daughter of the witch, Amelia Woodcock, possessor and purveyor of all sorts of satanic secrets. Zillah had, indeed, acted as healer and counsellor to the whole village, and several others. Her powers had been held in high esteem. There were people she'd cured of things that never should have shifted – tumours and fits and malignant fevers and broken hearts. There were things she did she never should have done. Abraham can see her now, mixing the herbs and potions together, stirring them in one of her iron pots, casting spells over man and beast and woman in her own dastardly way. Whatever she'd done and however she'd done it, there was no doubt she'd taken the fire out of him. He'd wanted her at first the way a man does – the way he wanted Odile Ruddle – and he'd had her, but then he'd wanted her and she wouldn't let him have her, and finally he couldn't even if she had. Abraham shivers. A formation of swifts passes overhead. Well, Zillah had got her comeuppance when the bulldozers came. No one could have found her where he'd put her, trussed like a chicken for the Sunday oven. He'd taken her power with him, though. There was no sense leaving that behind – it'd be no use at all at the bottom of the water, for what would the weeds or the fishes do with the mixtures of a witch? No, Abraham needed those, needed them to take vengeance on the women of the Gwater Valley who had taken away his livelihood and his manhood. It had started with Odile and his loving of her, his imagining that her fine white body and artistic, cultured soul could be part of his life, that they might make a life together in the farm by the village of Eglethorpe with Sally, Rainbow and Curly, with the chickens, and the sheep, freely roaming the green fields. But his fancies had been a ridiculous joke in Odile's eyes. She had laughed at him. She had thought he was a fool. She had used him. He'd really believed they would get married and have children together and be happy. When Odile had gone, he'd picked out Zillah – for didn't his father say he had to marry someone? 'Find a good woman . . .' Well, I've news for you, Father: a good woman is impossible to find.

Father had wanted inheritors for the Varley name. Abraham had been cheated of that by Odile's treachery, and by Zillah's enmity. He saw no reason why others should have what he couldn't. It pleased him to frighten the women of the Gwater Valley with his pranks, and Fanny Watkins deserved what she got for being such a teaser. Like Odile. But these were just frills round the edge of Abraham's master plan, which depended on the lore of the Woodcock witches – the mix of henbane, monkshood, and the nine-fingered Helleborus niger – Christmas rose – given to prevent fertility. The formula, handed down for centuries, had been used by knowledgeable women long before the advent of the contraceptive pill. By studying Zillah's books, Abraham had learnt how to make it, and by studying the plans of the reservoir to which he naturally had access because of his role as fish-stocker, it had been quite a simple matter to put the two together. Over the last few years, making the plant extract had become easier with the help of the men at Domak Pharmaceuticals. They had been quite interested when Abraham had told them of the mixture's potential as a 'natural' contraceptive pill. It made Abraham laugh, this use of the word 'natural'. Why, didn't folk know that some of the most natural things were the most cruel? Mother Nature is no angel.

The Domak men had said they'd give him some money when they'd got the formula to the right stage for patenting. But Abraham's not interested in the money. Money can't buy back his farm, can't restore to him the living of the dream he once had. He's tired of it all now. He's tired of thinking about the past, and hating the present; he's tired of the trips across the Water to the Treatment Works; he's tired of the gossip. He's tired of waking up in his gaunt little house on Life Hill, and seeing the awful wonderful water there: complacent in the sunshine, or holding rain and clouds of grey, looking back at him as if to say Sorry old chap, but I've got it, it's mine now. He's almost come to think of the water as a woman: vain, self-proud, teasing. Clothed in elegance, but a vampire beneath. The poisonous blue-green algae that fringe the waters are no surprise to Abraham – for him they're merely one outward manifestation of a deep, ineradicable horror.

As the water and the sky lose their vivid colours and settle into the shadowy blues of a summer night, the moorhens stop their squabbling, and a nightjar calls its churring song. The lights round the vanity of Eglethorpe Church are lit for the tourists, and a smell seeps up from somewhere, a smell of putrefaction – dying fish and water fowl, the fermentation of silage and manure gone wrong. The smell assails Abraham's senses, but instead of understanding it as an odour of the earth, he thinks it comes from within himself – he feels it as welling up inside him, as oozing out of every sticky pore. He is a bad man; he's let the Varleys down. Through all these years of meddling with the psyches and bodies of Gwater Valley women, Abraham's known that, but pushed the thought away. Circumstances make some people act bad. It doesn't mean they *are* bad. But in the end what you do contaminates: you become what you do. The smell is unbearable now, and there is only one way to cure it. Water, that abominable she-devil, which cleanses even as it poisons – which, in the very act of annihilation, purifies.

As Abraham Varley walks into Jacob's Water to rid himself of the awful smell of decay, bell-ringers practise in Lessendine Church across the Water. The cadences of the Lessendine bells, wafting over the pink-silver water and the tops of trees, enter Abraham's head as the sounds he used to hear in Spring Farm long ago – the bells of Eglethorpe Church before it was deconsecrated, the chiming of the hours and the seasons, the calling to prayer on Sundays and at other times – Christmas, Easter, harvest time – marking God's time and nature's time, greater than the times of man and beast, though so intertwined that they are also one and the same. Echoes and resonances and scenes and images and dreams and fancies draw Abraham into the water, his pain and his salvation; they draw him on and on. As the sun-tipped shallows start to lap his head, the smell, that pungent reminder of badness and decay, leaves him and he is cleansed, and at that moment his farm rises out of the water ahead of him, just as it used to be, untouched and whole, with Sally and Rainbow and Curly nuzzling the hedgerows of Buttercup Field, and waiting to be milked, and all the fields of oats and wheat and barley lying there open to the warming sun, with the red poppies and the lilac cornflowers and the blue Jacob's Ladder at their silky edges. Abraham holds out his arms in greeting, to embrace it all: he is home at last.

Flora, labouring in The Cottage in Little Tickencote, can just hear the Lessendine bell-ringers, too. Pete Wates is back now, and is downstairs making himself and Connie Barker a cup of tea. He opens Flora's back door and studies her little garden in the growing dark. What will it be? A boy? A girl? When will it be? Will Flora be able to cope with the hard iron fist of nature forcing new life out of old? Her cries from the bedroom upstairs mix with the bells in the air above the lavender and the catmint, where Pablo and Dolly sit side by side as though in solidary awareness of the solemnity of the occasion. Or because they're hungry. Pete gives them a tin of Whiskas, and takes the tea upstairs. 'Not long now, dearie,' Connie Barker is saying. 'I can feel the head.'

Mervyn Simpson, calling in at Olga's house, as he now does regularly twice a day, decides to check up on Flora Penfold at the same time. He knows this will annoy Connie, but he can't help that. Flora's on her side when he gets there, and Connie's undoing the delivery pack.

'Ah!' he says expansively, rubbing his hands. 'Time, is it?'

Connie frowns at him. 'Well, it's not your doing, Dr Simpson; there's no need to take the credit for it. Could you fetch a chair for the doctor, please, Mr Wates?'

So he's to be a viewer, a bystander, is he? Well, that'll suit him fine. He sits down and watches Flora and Connie. They seem to have evolved a working partnership. Connie tells Flora what to do, and she does it. If only Edwin would behave like that! Mervyn sighs and mops his head. 'Too hot in here, is it?' barks Connie sharply. 'I'm afraid you'll just have to tolerate that, Dr Simpson. We can't have a chill in here for the little one!'

Half an hour later, after a certain amount of controlled commotion, another person joins them in the room. A little girl! Pete looks, and exclaims. Connie Barker looks, and wipes. Mervyn Simpson just looks. Flora cries, and says, 'Let me look!' As they give her the baby to hold, and the child's periwinkle eyes open into her mother's face for the first time, Flora says, 'There's something else happening down there; I can feel something else happening!'

'Shush, dear, it's only the afterbirth,' says Connie, but it isn't, it's another baby. A good deal smaller than his sister, almost by way of being an afterthought, a little boy slides out, unaided and complaining with a powerful cry, on to the bed.

'Good Lord!' says Mervyn. 'Undiagnosed twins! That's one for the book, isn't it!'

'Where did you come from?' Connie scoops him up and checks him over. 'Must have been lying behind your sister. Hiding, were you?'

Pete laughs, a great belly laugh, and Flora's still crying. 'Two! But I only wanted one!'

'You don't always get what you ask for on this earth,' says Mervyn gloomily, thinking of Edwin Passmore and various other things.

The second baby is settled in the crook of Flora's arms. She looks, bemused, from one little screwed-up face to the other.

'It must have been the French air,' says Pete.

'What am I going to do, Pete? I don't know how to look after one baby, let alone two!'

'You'll learn. Nature is a great teacher.' Pete thinks of the sheep and the cows and the pigs, and how motherhood is more than an instinct, though it is that as well. 'And you'll have me to help you.'

'And me,' says Connie Barker. 'At least at first. I shall come and show you what to do!'

'And me,' says Mervyn Simpson, not to be outdone. 'I dare say I've a role to play in this.'

'Dr Simpson,' Flora turns to look at him, 'I must thank you for your advice. If you hadn't believed the old wives' tales these – these two wouldn't be here now.'

'A good man – and that includes a good doctor – knows his place in the world. Isn't that right, Dr Simpson?'

'It is, Connie. But I'll just have a quick look at the babies now I'm here, if you don't mind.'

A few minutes later he hands them back to Flora. 'There's nothing wrong with these two that I can find. The boy's a bit small, but I expect he'll grow. It's time to pack up, Connie, and leave these two to – to these two.'

'I was doing that anyway,' she says crossly.

'Of course you were.'

'How is Olga, Dr Simpson?' asks Flora.

In the midst of life is death. 'On her last legs, I'm afraid.'

'I'd like to show her the babies.'

'She'd enjoy that. But go soon.'

Mervyn calls in on Olga again before he goes home. 'She's asleep,' says Jane. 'We had a long talk, and she was rather tired.' But Olga stirs when she feels Mervyn in the room. 'Young Flora's had her baby,' he whispers. 'Thought you'd like to know. It was twins. Boy and girl.'

A smile crosses Olga's face like the moon flashing out from behind a chubby cloud. 'That's good, that's very good.'

'They'll be coming to see you just as soon as Flora can get out of bed, so be sure to wake up in the morning, old girl!' She's asleep again; he doesn't know if she's heard.

As the clock beside Olga's cottage strikes twelve the next day, Pete and Flora carry their babies from The Cottage in Cabbage Lane to Olga's bedroom. There was a shower of rain in the night, and drops of water catch and play with the sun. A sweet smell rises from the earth: the sky is a placid blue. Down the track which leads from Pudding Bag Lane to Church Lane, Flora stops, and turns to look over the gate into the fields. She holds her son, the tiny baby who came out as an afterthought. Pete, next to her, has the girl. Both babies sleep, as the sun touches their dewy faces for the very first time, and the grasses and trees of Little Tickencote move around them, gently rustling, and the fragrances of the hedgerows rise and linger round their tiny nostrils, and seep into their rosy infant lungs.

Flora does feel weak, as Connie Barker had predicted, as though her legs are made of cotton wool, and as though she has to learn to walk again now the football team has gone from her front. She is light-headed, floating almost, wrapped in a keen appreciation of her good fortune in the face of the world's evil and pain and punishment and death – and Olga Kahn's own dying, which cannot be far away. None of this is what Flora expected her move to the country to give her, but the country has its own logic, which has to be followed, and this place most of all. It was an accident that she landed here – the result of the Hoskins' visit, and her own response to tales told of Meltshire and its magic. Magic isn't the word she would use now. But it is strange that her father had known this area. And stranger still that he left that particular collection of papers for her. In her light-headed mood, Flora even fancies that Samuel might have known what was going to happen to her, and wanted her to know that he was with her – in place, if not in time – albeit in the guise of his affection for a person who is neither man nor woman.

At this thought, Flora turns to her newborn son, and to his sister, lying in Pete Wates's arms. There's nothing unclear about these two. These two are her faith in the future, her reason for being alive. These two recall for her, even in their newborn insouciance, that feeling of union that riddles her past, with Lars Lyngby over all those years of tears and trouble and pain and joy. Now she has that feeling again, is reunited with nature, with herself.

The little boy opens his tiny coral mouth and yawns. His ivory fists rise from the soft snowy padding in which she carries him, and stretch out and up to the sun, like a flower. Flora thinks with pain of those who do not have this gift of life. Of all the women in Little Tickencote deprived of it. Of all the men in the world whose sex discriminates against them. Of Barnaby Gunn, with the AIDS virus in his bloodstream. Of all lovers past and present and to come who are part of her, whose secrets are her secrets, and on whom the golden yolk of the country sun would shine if only they would let it, if only they would give themselves up to its rejuvenating, though complex warmth.

The father of Flora's children stands close to her, and his eyes meet hers. 'I can't believe it, Flora. Aren't we clever?'

'Aren't we lucky!' she replies, holding the child close and gazing out over the matching fertile countryside.

'You know what,' says Pete, 'we ought to call them Adam and Eve.'

Flora laughs helplessly. 'Don't make me laugh, it makes my bottom hurt. I don't think they'd thank us if we did that.'

'I'm not sure children do that anyway. Thank their parents, I mean.'

Just then the vicarage gate opens, emitting Trevor Tilley without his bicycle.

'Ah! Pete, Miss Penfold. What have we here? Two for the price of one? Two new souls – what a blessing!'

Flora is firm. 'Remember what we agreed, Vicar; it's not two christenings. Or even one.' She wishes she could fix him with an eye he would recognize as one that had witnessed the unsavoury property dealings (and God knows what else) in the church. But she is in a charitable mood. In any case she has learnt, now, what the country delivers: scenes of beauty, presents of life, undercurrents of roaring rivers and corruption. Crooked souls, and wise ones; mangled loves, and straight ones. Essential mysteries – those of human life itself – which can be only partially unravelled by efforts in the here and now.

'Never mind, never mind, it's God's blessing all the same. It's God's blessing on Little Tickencote, and about time, too!' Trevor touches the little girl's forehead lightly with his finger. 'How beautiful,' he murmurs.

'We were just going to call on Olga Kahn.'

'So was I.'

When Olga opens her eyes, they're all there: the vicar, Dr Simpson, Jane, Flora, Pete, and Adam and Eve.

'Help me sit up,' she commands. 'I want to hold them.' Dr Simpson and Jane organize her pillows, so that the frail body is in a position to cradle two others. Olga looks at the babies, arranged on her deathbed. 'How wonderful, Flora!' she says, in the same tone of voice the vicar had used. 'Mervyn told me last night. You see, Little Tickencote can't be such a bad place after all. The birth of these children will cancel it all out; the bad spell is over now.'

'"Death is not an unhappy thing when you learn how to conquer it . . . By another thing, called birth,"' recites Trevor Tilley, unexpectedly. 'George Bernard Shaw, *Back to Methuselah*. I don't only read the Bible, you know. The Meltshire Amateur Dramatic Society did it a few years ago.'

Jane sits on the bed. She speaks quietly, but with some urgency. 'Abraham Varley was found this morning, drowned, Olga.'

'I'm sorry for you, my dear. But Abraham's time, like mine, had come. I had a feeling it would soon. Remember: it doesn't matter now what he did, or how he did it. Whatever it is will stop.' A soft smile plays on Olga's dry lips. She looks from the babies to Jane, and back again. 'An end and a beginning. New life for old.' If the others in the room think this exchange odd, they let it go. It's no odder, after all, than many things in Meltshire. And the presence of death often gives everything a different, unexceptional appearance, anyway.

'It's as I said,' repeats the vicar. 'Birth conquers the unhappiness of death.'

'I'm not quite dead yet,' retorts Olga, with some of her old spirit, though faintly. 'But you'd better take your babies back, Flora. My old arms are getting tired.'

'Oh Olga,' pleads Flora, 'don't die! I don't want you to die! Stay with us and help me look after them. Think of all the guidance I'm going to need!'

'There's plenty of that around here,' says Olga firmly. 'The place is full of people who'll fill your head with useless advice. You won't need an old shrink to confuse you further.'

'Oh Olga!' Flora, weeping, scoops her newborn children out of Olga's arms.

'Shush, child. It's your hormones. No, it isn't: it's only natural that you should be upset. Nature is like that. Nature gives and nature takes away. That's the Garden of Eden for you. Full of death and sin and nonsense, but with good things too: life and love and babies and flowers.' She lifts her head and looks out of the window to the blue, blue sky and the cornfields. 'And flowers,' she repeats. 'Now go home and be a good mother to your babies, so they can develop fantasies and origin myths of their very own.'

Later that evening, as Flora suckles her babies and the pathologist in Melton examines Abraham Varley's waterlogged body, Jane Rivers sits with Olga Kahn. Olga's cassette player reproduces the final Adagio of Mahler's ninth symphony. The diatonic steps of the first, hymn-like theme, leading chromatically to the second, intemperately sad one, mingle with dancing, sparkling particles of dust in the bilious air. A puffball floats through the window and leaps lightly about, banging into walls and dropping milky filaments on to Olga's bed. Olga's sleep is tranquil, and the rhythm of her breathing is light, like the puffball. Jane, dry-eyed and wigless, is motionless, watching, until and past the moment when the light breathing in the bed simply ceases. Eventually she gets up and turns the music off, and then stands, touching the bed and Olga, taking one of the still-warm hands in hers, and looking from Olga's peaceful resting face out of the window where a full harvest moon, blood-orange, hangs in the dark-blue sky of the Little Tickencote night.